Also by Chris Babu

The Initiation
The Expedition

WITHDRAWN

THE INSURRECTION

CHRIS BABU

PERMUTED
PRESS

A PERMUTED PRESS BOOK

The Insurrection
© 2020 by Chris Babu
All Rights Reserved

ISBN: 978-1-68261-883-7
ISBN (eBook): 978-1-68261-882-0

Cover art by Ryan Truso
Cover photo by Greg Berg
Interior design and composition, Greg Johnson, Textbook Perfect

PERMUTED
PRESS

Permuted Press, LLC
New York • Nashville
permutedpress.com

Published in the United States of America

For Mom and Dad

Although I did not become an astronomer,
I'll never forget how you taught me to see magic in the stars
and brightness in the dark.
Sorry about the seventy-five-pound telescope
still sitting in your shed.

New America

Meadow

Gate to Meadow

59th St. Bridge

Dorms

Norman Thomas High School

Lily's House

Mr. Kale's Apartment

Madison Square Park

Gate to Lab

Lab

Gate to Precinct

Precinct

Brooklyn Bridge

Bureau Headquarters

Pier 15

Brooklyn Bridge Park

40 Rector Street

75 Wall Street

Palace

Battery Park

CHAPTER 1

Dripping sweat, Drayden adjusted the clunky bulletproof vest the Boston government had insisted he wear, wondering if it would save his life. At the moment, he hated them for it. He, Sidney, Charlie, and Catrice were riding bicycles south on Route 3, lugging camping gear and supplies in backpacks. Periodically consulting a map, Drayden led the way down the heavily overgrown highway.

Despite the brutal expedition, which had ultimately revealed the horrific truth about New America's corruption, Drayden was hopeful. He was eager to complete their current mission and optimistic about toppling the authoritarian Bureau back home. Given the abundance of life he'd seen throughout the expedition, he was even emboldened about finding his mother alive.

Hope was a curious thing—both the remedy to misfortune and the cause of complacency. During the tortuous Initiation, Drayden held onto hope the same way he clutched the rickety plank over the fiery chasm in the final challenge. He wouldn't have survived otherwise. At the end of the expedition, he hoped Kim Craig's insurrection against the Bureau would prevail. Therein lay the negative side of hope. It was passive, because "hoping" was like waiting around for change without actually doing anything to bring it about. For now, Drayden would be as active as possible.

1

The problem was, of course, they were stuck 250 miles away in Boston. What could they do to help vanquish the Bureau besides *hope* someone else handled it? Not a lot, other than make sure they were 100 percent ready for their return trip. In three days, the Boston leadership would send them on a ship down the eastern seaboard, depositing them close to New America. In addition to reuniting with their families, Drayden would have the opportunity to search for his mother before they entered the city.

He quickly refocused on the ride, swerving his mountain bike around a mammoth tree. The condition of the roads in the outside world ranged from severely overgrown to impassable. Bushes, dense grasses, and full-size trees covered Route 3 these days. Having ridden almost forty miles, his legs burned from the exertion. Everyone wore the exhaustion on their faces.

"Dray...Drayden!" Charlie called out. "We gotta stop. Time out."

Drayden rolled to a stop and took a swig of water, swishing it around his dry, cracked mouth and throat. Charlie couldn't ride a bike with gears, so the excursion was especially tiring for him. Fortunately, he rode an adult dirt bike this time rather than a little girl's bike, as he had on the expedition. The memory brought a smile to Drayden's face.

Sidney wheeled her bike under the shade of a tree and collapsed on the cool grass. "I'm going to be so pissed if we don't find a flag," she groaned.

While it sounded trivial, a major obstacle on their return trip would be reentering New America, which was surrounded by guarded walls. They'd departed for the expedition with Bureau flags in their backpacks to wave upon their homecoming, so that the Guardians manning the border would recognize them as Bureau members. Midway through the disastrous journey, their Guardian escorts had launched an assault and stolen the backpacks, most likely for the food, water, and gear. Now without any flags, how would they get in? Those guys showing up first and thwarting their entry was another potential complication.

Prior to their decisive confrontation with the Guardians in the marsh, Drayden and Sidney had noticed they weren't carrying the backpacks. That meant they'd snatched the items they wanted and left the packs behind. It was far from a guarantee any flags remained, but without another plausible way to reenter New America, this jaunt was worth making to hunt for them. Being fifty miles each way, they would need to camp overnight.

The second purpose of the trip was to hit up the windmill farm near the intersection of Route 3 and Route 3a. On the expedition, Catrice had proposed harvesting the deep-cycle batteries, which could provide some pivotal leverage when they returned home. With the expedition having gone off the rails, New America still desperately sought batteries to store power, because the existing ones were failing.

Drayden splashed water on his face. "Besides the windmill farm tomorrow, I was thinking we could stop by Professor Worth's house on the way back. It's just off Route 3 on Route 53. Even if we strike out on the backpacks and batteries, this trip won't have been a total waste."

From the time Drayden had met Professor Worth, a former math professor at MIT, he'd wanted to hang out with him. The old fella was a solitary survivor, an encyclopedia of practical knowledge, plus Drayden simply liked him. It was hard not to after he'd saved their butts, driving them to Boston, granting the head start that allowed them to defeat the Guardians.

"He'd probably want to know what happened to us," Charlie said. "Gotta think he'd want to hear about Eugene's backstabbery too. You could tell he never liked Eugene."

Drayden glanced at Catrice to see if the mention of Eugene's betrayal elicited any reaction, but she remained detached and silent. "Let's get going," he said. "It's only about ten more miles."

The late May afternoon was unusually torrid, the blurry heat rippling over the few patches of remaining pavement. Although they were carrying weapons and had taken Boston's version of the Aeru vaccine, the real world carried myriad risks, as they'd learned on the expedition. Run-ins with predators like bears and wolves were possible. A confrontation with a violent gang, such as the one that had held them hostage in their camp, was a persistent threat.

In a puzzling twist, that particular group had possessed a Bureau flag, which they'd apparently gotten from the Guardians under unknown circumstances. Those four soldiers presented the other serious hazard, because they had slipped away after losing the concluding battle with the teens. Who knew where they were now?

Drayden and company rode in silence and kept a watchful eye out for people or cars ahead. Finally, they reached the intersection of Route 3 and Route 6 in Sagamore, where they'd camped for the night in the woods. Now it was just a matter of unearthing their old campsite, in an inconspicuous clearing they'd randomly selected.

Huffing and puffing, Charlie touched his index finger to his chin. "Sooo...how do we find a campsite we fell into out of desperation?"

"We can roam around for a while," Sidney said. "We'll eventually find it, right?"

Drayden appealed to Catrice, who had isolated herself the past three days. "Any ideas?"

She wrung her hands. "We could recreate our walk. Go down Route 6 and come back this way like we did a week ago. We might remember where we went into the forest."

"Great call," Drayden said.

The crew hiked about a half mile on Route 6 before turning around and slowly retracing their steps.

"How realistic should we make this?" Charlie asked. "My back was killing me and Dray was all whiny about being sick." He leaned forward, holding his back, and made exaggerated frowny faces.

Drayden smacked him on the arm. "I think when I saw Route 3 I said something about finding a place to camp."

"This is a stupid idea," Sidney muttered. "The forest looks exactly the same everywhere."

Catrice crossed her arms but didn't respond.

Despite the unnecessary jab, she was right about the second part, Drayden noted. Nothing stood out; no gap in the brush they would have snuck through. He pointed ahead. "We can see Route 3 pretty clearly now. I think we would have gone in somewhere around here? Let's each enter the woods about fifty feet apart. Yell if you see anything."

Thick with overgrowth and thorns, the shaded forest blocked Drayden's view beyond a few feet and slowed him to a crawl. He whacked the lush bramble away with his rifle, mindful of his bad ankle—courtesy of the Initiation—on the uneven terrain. So far, nothing rang a bell. Doing the quick math in his head, he estimated the search area at roughly a square mile.

"You guys!" Sidney shouted in the distance. "I found it!"

Using her voice as a beacon, Drayden trudged his way over, the four of them reconvening in front of a modest clearing. Scattered dirt, rocks, and shell casings evidenced the fierce battle that had taken place. At the crack of dawn, the Guardians had unleashed a heavy onslaught of bullets, plus a grenade for good measure.

Drayden experienced visceral flashbacks, reliving the terror of the incident. However, the benefit of hindsight colored the event much differently. Eugene had seemed incredibly brave at the time, staying behind to cover them as they made their escape. Now they knew he was never in danger, as he was covertly working with the Guardians.

They tiptoed their way into the clearing as if it were a crime scene, finding, as expected, four backpacks—one for each of the teens. Three had been ransacked, surrounded by empty plastic water bottles, barren food bags, and a discarded pill bottle. The fourth lay ostensibly untouched, on the far side of a makeshift firepit.

"Jackpot." Charlie rubbed his hands together as he went for it. "Please have a flag."

Drayden scratched his neck. The Guardians had ravaged the other three backpacks like a sleuth of bears. Evidently, they'd plundered anything useful. Maybe the three of them looted one pack each, or found too much to carry? But that made no sense. Food was likely their main goal, and each pack only contained a meager amount. They absolutely would have scoured every one.

Drayden's jaw dropped.

This is a trap.

He darted toward Charlie, who was steps from the pristine backpack.

"Charlie, freeze! Don't touch it!"

He dove at Charlie's legs, like he was executing a takedown in jiu-jitsu.

"Why not?" Charlie turned his head, just as he grabbed the backpack with one hand.

Drayden tackled him, causing him to tumble forward and lose his grip on it.

But it shifted slightly.

Drayden saw the flash first, the grenade hidden beneath it detonating instantly with a deafening boom.

His last thoughts were of flying through the air.

His last sensations were heat and pain.

CHAPTER 2

Mom?
Hold on, she was saying. *Hold on, Dray.*

It was like one of those badly dubbed Kung Fu movies the Bureau occasionally played back home. Her face, her lips moving, yet not her voice. Where was she? Paradoxically, she appeared right in front of him and also so far away.

"Mom, I don't understand. Hold onto what?"

Just hold on.

Wind was blowing in Drayden's face, stinging it. He was bumping up and down, bouncing around, which hurt terribly. Why was he in so much pain? He opened his eyes.

"Hold on, Dray!" Sidney shouted.

In darkness, they were moving rapidly. In a car. They launched over rocks and careened over bumps, every movement making his head throb unbearably.

Pain.

His whole body felt broken, particularly his legs. Hyperventilation began.

"Drayden, we're getting you help!" Sidney gently held him around the shoulders, keeping the knit blanket securely in place.

He went to speak but it hurt too much. His head, his face, his lips. "Where...what's...what's going on?" he mumbled. He was so thirsty. His mouth was completely dried out.

Professor Worth turned back briefly from the driver's seat and eyed him.

"There was a grenade, Drayden," Sidney said. "Under the backpack. Do you remember?"

He grimaced. "Yes. My legs. Do I still have them?"

"Of course! You're going to be fine. We're taking you to a hospital. We should be there any second. Just hold on."

"Oh God...water...please."

Sidney touched a bottle to his lips, tilting it slightly, and he tried his best to lap it up. As the liquid dribbled down his chin and over his neck, soaking his wounds, the intense burning shocked him to the core, causing his whole body to shudder.

He groaned in agony, his vision blurring. Upon refocusing, his gaze drifted past Sidney to the next seat.

Her face puffy and pale, Catrice was leaning forward, holding onto something in the front seat.

Drayden's eyes followed her arms to her hands, which were gripping a person around the shoulders. Similarly swaddled in blankets, his hair was matted with crimson blood and his face mangled. He was unconscious.

Drayden drew in a quick breath.

Charlie.

He shut his eyes.

When he opened them, he found himself on a bed in a dim, white room, the window suggesting it was nighttime. Although the full-body pain had diminished, his legs throbbed and his head was pounding.

To his left, Catrice was asleep in a chair, slouched with her chin in hand, her tousled blonde hair obscuring her face. Professor Worth rested in a seat beside her, his arms crossed, legs outstretched, and mouth agape. He was snoring.

The grenade.

Drayden cringed, trying to get a look at his body to see the damage, but he was draped in blankets. An IV was in his right arm, while his left was bandaged.

How could he have been so stupid and naïve, failing to anticipate a booby trap from the Guardians? It was so obvious. The instant he saw the untouched backpack he should have known. There he went, overthinking everything to the point of inaction—as he so often did—costing them dearly in the process. He struggled to shake the image of Charlie, unconscious and gravely wounded, in the front seat of the Jeep.

Please be alive.

They were scheduled to leave in three days for New America. He had to reunite with his father and brother. He needed to search for his mother. God only knew what had gone down inside the city since they'd left.

"How are you feeling?" Professor Worth sat up and removed his glasses, rubbing his eyes.

"I...I've been better." He tried but failed to smile.

"You're very lucky, Drayden. It could have been much worse."

Drayden furrowed his brow. "How...? Professor Worth, thank you for saving me. How did you though? I don't understand what happened."

Professor Worth cleaned his lenses and put his glasses back on. "Catrice stayed with you and Charlie after the accident. Sidney rode her bike to my house. I gathered some supplies to treat you on the scene, then we picked you up in my Jeep and brought you to Boston. I must say, I was quite impressed by the procedures here. They whisked you right in and doctors were tending to you and Charlie immediately. Good thing people don't need to worry about health insurance these days. You wouldn't even understand what I mean, since you were born Post-Confluence."

Drayden's eyes widened. "How is Charlie?"

"He's...okay," he said, nodding. "A little worse off than you are, but he'll be fine. I meant it when I said you were lucky. After discussing the explosion with the girls, we determined that the grenade mostly detonated underneath the backpack, which protected you from much of the shrapnel. Charlie incidentally shielded you as well. You both took damage to your legs and got quite a jolt. He has some injuries to his face; you both have burns and likely concussions. But your vital organs were spared because of the Kevlar vests. No major arteries hit in your legs, either."

Drayden rubbed his temples. "My head is killing me."

"That would be the concussion. The hospital did give you pain-killers and sedatives to help."

Drayden wasn't sure how he felt about being called lucky. Lucky to be alive, sure, but not so lucky to be in an explosion.

Professor Worth folded his hands on his lap. "What you did was very brave, Drayden. You saved Charlie's life. If he'd picked up that backpack, he would be dead."

Drayden processed the professor's words. He didn't feel brave; he'd simply reacted. It wasn't a conscious decision to risk his own life. He'd genuinely wanted to protect his friend—much like his late friend Tim had usually done for him.

"There's something else," Professor Worth added before Drayden had a chance to respond. "While you were asleep, Sidney and Catrice caught me up on what transpired after I dropped you off at the Neponset River Reservation. They told me how you defeated the Guardians and did so without killing them. Bravo, son. That was a brilliant plan, and you displayed a tremendous level of humanity for somebody in that position."

Drayden couldn't fight off a smile this time. As usual, he succumbed to his relentless craving for flattery. He was such a glutton for praise, and hearing it from someone as esteemed as Professor Worth was a big deal. "It almost failed. Captain Lindrick didn't fall into the muddy pit and then Eugene stabbed us in the back. But it worked out in the end."

"It's an incredible story." Professor Worth licked his lips. "You should be proud of yourself. If you could pull that off, I have no doubt you can take on this horrid Bureau of yours."

Drayden shook his head. "Um, no. We beat three exhausted guys, one of whom was badly injured, and had a giant lead to plan it. You're talking about an all-powerful government, with an army on their side. I'm a sixteen-year-old with no authority. The best I can do is hope the insurgents plotting to overthrow the Bureau are successful."

The professor wagged a finger. "Don't be so quick to underestimate yourself. There is power in numbers. There is power in the will of the people. And there is power in intelligence. All three are in your favor."

Something in his words sparked an idea. "Professor Worth, I'm not a leader. I can't plan this. There's no clever plot I can devise to outduel a government. That's way over my head." He paused. "But I bet you could. You have experience in life. You lived before the Confluence, saw revolutions. Can you come with us? Please? You'd be such a huge help. We'll all go together, and then we'd get you home."

Professor Worth erupted in deep, old-man laughter, which gave way to a coughing fit. "No, no. I'm an old dog. I live here. New America is not my home, and I'd be no help. You and the citizens of New America can do this, I have no doubt."

"No, actually, we can't. I can't. I'm serious, Professor. Please?"

He waved Drayden off. "You don't need me. I'd be an old geezer slowing you down. Besides, I have my house and crops to take care of."

Drayden tugged on his left earlobe. "Professor, no offense, but you're like seventy?"

He drew his head back. "Sixty-eight."

"I mean...you live alone, you're kinda old. What else...like—"

"What do I have to live for?" he asked with a smirk, his eyebrows raised. "Ah, the age-old question. What do any of us live for, regardless of age? I live to see the beautiful sunrise every morning. I live to learn, to enjoy the food I cultivate myself. I live to recreate technology which no longer exists, using the limited tools at my disposal. Each day is a new adventure. I live to live."

Drayden deflated. "Fine, good answer. But...please? How about living to change the world? Save thousands of lives? You could be part of something epic, bigger than one life."

"I admire your spirit, Drayden. I do. But I'm sorry, I cannot. I *can* offer you this. When you're feeling better, time permitting, why don't you come visit me?"

Drayden rolled over. "Why?"

"I can teach you a few things."

The following morning, while Drayden's physical pain gradually subsided, his mental anguish flourished. Having failed to protect his friends from a blatantly transparent trap, his negligence now jeopardized their return trip home. He had yet to see Charlie, but he knew his dereliction of duty was also responsible for his buddy's injuries.

The evolution of his bodily pain wasn't exactly a decrease; it was a change, from a smothering blanket of agony to a more localized misery. He could feel each individual laceration, puncture, bruise, and burn. Thankfully, there were no broken bones or internal injuries. He didn't need the doctor or Professor Worth to tell him his legs had borne the brunt of the damage. His legs were letting him know. Unable to walk yet, he required a nurse's assistance to use the bathroom. He could only imagine how awful Charlie was feeling.

Whatever the official verdict on their scheduled boat trip might be, he couldn't foresee any way to physically make the journey. They were expecting an update from a representative of the Boston leadership, and her arrival was imminent.

Drayden thought "her" without knowing the rep's gender. Virtually all the leaders in Boston were women, which was a breath of fresh air compared to the overwhelmingly male Bureau.

Sidney hovered over him, finger brushing his hair, having washed his face with a cloth. "What else do you need?"

He closed his eyes momentarily. "Nothing, Sid, thank you. I'm good."

Catrice was slumped in the chair again, staring out the window, her expression blank.

Drayden appreciated Sidney's devoted attention. He did. He just wasn't sure it was *entirely* authentic, because it was a little over the top. He felt guilty for the thought, but it seemed like she might be rubbing their budding relationship in Catrice's face. If so, judging by Catrice's demeanor, it was working.

Sidney picked up a bottle of water and brought it to his lips. "Here, you need to hydrate." Before he had a chance to object, she dumped it down his throat.

It went straight into the wrong pipe and he started gagging, coughing a good amount of it back into her face.

"Shoot, sorry Dray!" She wiped his neck with a towel and dried herself off.

"*Acckk...cccchhh*...no worries," Drayden squeaked.

An animated woman in a navy suit entered the room as if she were about to lead a conference on motivation and empowerment. She stopped and cupped her hands together, leaning forward slightly. "How is everyone doing today?" she asked, carefully enunciating each word.

Catrice fake smiled.

Sidney sighed. "Okay."

Drayden coughed a few times, each one making his head pound. "Good, good," he croaked, his windpipe clogged with water.

"Great!" She pulled up a chair and sat. "Excellent. Alright then. Why don't you all gather around?"

Catrice slid her chair over beside Drayden's bed. Sidney plunked down on the bed and held his hand.

"My name is Annie Hill. I'm with the Department of the Interior and the mayor has asked me to take over arrangements for you, now that it looks like you'll be here a bit longer." She frowned. "I'm sorry! I know, not what you wanted to hear. Word got around to us through the hospital about your accident, and we consulted with your doctors. Drayden and Charlie are clearly in no condition to make a dangerous journey, so, on the doctors' orders, they will not be released in time to catch our boat down the East Coast."

Since Drayden had assumed this to be the case, her announcement was largely a formality. Still, having it confirmed took the wind out of his sails a tad.

Sidney teared up, her cheeks reddening.

Drayden wondered if she was over-tending to him because she hoped to help him recover in time to catch the boat, and it had nothing to do with Catrice at all. Her priority, always, was getting home to her younger sister, Nora, who was under the care of her grandparents.

Catrice, on the other hand, showed no reaction whatsoever.

"But don't worry," Annie continued, "I'm not just the bearer of bad news. We have another ship leaving in two weeks, and—"

"Two weeks?" Sidney yelled.

Annie was taken aback. "Why, yes, and I thought you'd be—"

"I can't wait that long, Ms. Hill. I can't. My little sister needs me right now. There could be a war going on for all we know. You have to send us back sooner."

She drooped in her chair, unclenching. "Please, call me Annie. I understand. I do. I wish we could ship you home right away. Unfortunately, that is when the next boat leaves."

Drayden cleared his throat. "It's all right, Sid, we'll figure something out." He squeezed her hand. "Annie, I'm confused. We've been here a couple days. There're boats coming and going all the time. How can it be that the next one doesn't leave for two weeks?"

"You must be referring to merchant ships coming to our port to trade. Some are from foreign governments, some are private, but yes there are boats coming and going frequently. Those just aren't ours. *Our* next boat leaves in two weeks."

"Could we hitch a ride on one of those merchant ships?" Drayden asked.

She shrugged. "I'm not really sure. We have no control over them. We're trying to keep you safe and offering free transportation. I'm not sure you'd get either from someone else. Almost certainly they'd want to be paid."

Sidney's eyes bulged. "Dray, can we try?"

The numerous logistical problems were compounding in his mind. "Annie, is it cool if we look into it? Obviously, we have no money."

"Absolutely, feel free. If we can help facilitate it at all, let me know. My office is in the Capitol building and my door is always open for you. You're welcome to stay in your current apartments until you depart and your meals will continue to be taken care of."

In spite of the lamentable developments, Drayden forced a smile. "Thank you. We appreciate everything Boston has done for us. We won't forget it. If we're ever able to repay you, we will."

She tilted her head. "It's our pleasure. Whether you're a Boston citizen or not, we're all people, and we should care about each other."

Drayden agreed. New America could learn a lot from Boston.

"That reminds me." She flashed a finger, her tone reverting to businesslike. "This may be nothing, but it may not be. It definitely involves you, so I want to make sure you're aware."

Sidney glanced at Drayden, her expression a mix of befuddlement and concern.

Annie paused, as if debating the best way to proceed. "I was informed of a...*situation* at the border. Two men tried to enter Boston. When they refused to turn over their weapons, which is standard procedure here, they were sent packing. The border police couldn't remember the last time that had happened, so they reported it up the chain. We investigated, and we believe they were your Guardians."

A chill ran down Drayden's spine. "Wait. Did you say *two* men? Are you sure?"

"Yes. We know you said there were four, so we double- and triple-checked. There were only two of them."

"When was this?" Sidney asked.

"Yesterday."

"Do you know which two?" Catrice asked. "Is there video, or did you get descriptions of them?"

She nodded. "Yes, we have surveillance all over the city, especially around the borders. One was an African American male, and the other was dark complected."

"Sergeant Greaney and Lieutenant Duarte," Drayden said. "I wonder where Captain Lindrick and Eugene were."

Sidney gripped Drayden's hand so hard it hurt. "I bet Lindrick died! I shot him in the foot. That would get infected."

Drayden gritted his teeth. "Annie, how could you guys let them leave? We gave descriptions of them as soon as we arrived." Despite piecing together some answers about the expedition, much of it remained speculation. They couldn't know definitively that the Guardians were trying to reestablish a trading partnership with Boston, or were delivering drugs in a locked box, without questioning them. Plus, the Guardians had committed atrocities for which they needed to be held accountable.

"I hear you. I'm sorry." She rested her elbows on her knees. "We had alerts out to the border police, but they made a mistake. The men should never have been allowed to leave." She sat up tall. "If they try a second time, we'll be ready."

Drayden's brain was playing out the hypotheticals around their attempted entry. Maybe Greaney and Duarte had split from Captain Lindrick and Eugene. Or, if they knew capture was a risk, they held two people back to mitigate it. Yet why would they want to enter at all? And why now, after several days?

Annie pursed her lips. "I hope you all know you're safe here. We won't let them get to you. In any case, if there's further news, I'll let you know immediately. Don't worry, you're in good hands with us."

Drayden recalled those same words from Captain Lindrick before they'd left on the expedition. *You're in good hands with us.* He imagined, in a narrator's voice, *"They were not in good hands."* Having been defeated by Drayden and his friends, and shut out of Boston, it was anyone's guess what the Guardians were up to now. Most likely they'd be trying to get back to New America as well. While troublesome, especially if they made it home first, they would have a much more difficult time securing transportation without the resources in Boston.

Annie stood, waited awkwardly for a moment, and left.

Drayden, Sidney, and Catrice remained silent at first. "I don't think we have to be too stressed out about the Guardians," Drayden said, as much to convince himself as the girls. "We should focus on getting home."

Sidney's eyes were wild. "Dray, should I start looking into another boat?"

He considered it for a second. "Yeah, why not? Let's not panic, though. As long as the Bureau thinks we died on the expedition—and it's pretty clear the Guardians were under orders to kill us—our families shouldn't be in any danger. If this overthrow plot starts, everyone in the city will be at risk, so we do need to get back sooner rather than later. How about talking to some people by the docks?"

"I can totally do that," Sidney said.

"I think you should both go. Power in numbers," he said, repeating Professor Worth's words.

Catrice looked directly at him for the first time in days.

"Just, do me a favor," Drayden added. "Beware of creeps." He wasn't sure if they understood what he meant. Two beautiful teenage girls approaching grizzled men for help sounded like a scenario ripe for abuse.

Sidney cocked her head. "We can handle it."

Drayden nodded. "I have no doubt. Oh, one more thing to start working on. We need a way to raise money to pay the boat fare. Anyone have a talent?"

Charlie looked dead. His head was bandaged, his face bruised and battered, and stitches formed a wide crescent under his left eye. For such a normally muscular kid, he appeared to have lost weight. He was sprawled out, asleep with his mouth open. Besides an IV, he was hooked up to all sorts of monitoring equipment, much of it glowing with multicolored lights.

A nurse had left Drayden in a wheelchair next to Charlie's bed in a dim, windowless room. The artificial light of the hospital made day and night blend together like oil and vinegar, fusing into a completely new element until the individual parts could no longer be distinguished. There was just time.

"I'm sorry, Charlie," Drayden whispered. Horrible memories came flooding back of the Initiation challenge in which he had failed to disarm a bomb, and the resulting explosion had killed his best friend Tim. A virtually identical thing had taken place this time. Except, in fairness to himself, he had responded differently. In the Initiation, he'd run from the bomb. With the grenade, even though it was a reaction rather than a conscious choice, he ran toward it. Unlike Tim, Charlie would survive.

His mind had all but blocked Tim's death from memory out of self-preservation. As he thought about it, he wondered what had happened to Tim's body. Had the Bureau returned it to his parents so they could properly bury him? God, had they left it there to rot? He still wasn't ready to think about it.

In another startling parallel, Charlie was now his best friend—a fact he'd never acknowledged before. Sure, his crowd of friends only went three deep, but their friendship wasn't just about convenience or incidental proximity. Charlie was a loyal companion. It was astonishing since he had been Alex's best friend at the start of the Initiation, and Alex was Drayden's archenemy. After Alex and Tim had both perished in the Initiation, two of the most unlikely boys became best buds.

Judging by the evidence and injury history, perhaps Drayden wasn't such a valuable friend to have. Both Tim and Charlie staunchly protected him. When the time came for Drayden to reciprocate, he fell short and they paid the price. It was his job to anticipate the Guardians' trap. Charlie counted on him to be the brains, to be the strategist. He'd hesitated, overthought the situation, and failed. *Again.*

"There he is," Charlie groaned, his eyes closed. He opened them and flashed a smile.

Drayden hooked his thumb at the door. "You good to go?" he cracked. "Everyone's waiting downstairs. We're gonna catch a show in the park."

Charlie nodded slowly. "Yeah. Lemme just take this catheter out."

"Aw, dude." Drayden grimaced. "You have a catheter?"

"Don't you?"

Drayden made a face. "Um, no. The nurse helps me to the bathroom. Didn't that, like, hurt?"

"It hurt more than a grenade to the face. Actually, I don't remember when they put it in. But I do remember that the nurse was a guy, and his name was Rick. Are there no female nurses for Charlie? I had Jeff back home."

"Don't worry, I won't tell Jeff about Rick. I don't want him to get jealous."

Charlie chuckled before closing his eyes. "How are you doing? You don't look so great either."

"Better than you. Legs are busted up. Concussion. I'll live."

"You know what they say. If you always keep your feet on the ground, you'll have trouble putting on your pants."

Drayden scratched his head. "I don't...I don't know what that means."

"I don't either."

Drayden took a deep breath. "Hey, Charlie. I'm really sorry. It was my fault. I should have smelled that trap sooner and never let you get anywhere near the backpack. That's on me. I just want you to know, it won't happen again."

Charlie furrowed his brow. "What? What are you talking about, bro? I'm the dummy who picked up the backpack! You saved me. Saved my life. Thank you, bud."

"You've saved me plenty of times too. I feel like it's my responsibility to watch out for that stuff. If I'd been sharper, both of us would be fine and we'd be getting on a boat home in two days. Which, by the way, is no longer happening."

"Oh no. Damn. When's the next boat?"

Drayden picked at his fingernails. "Two weeks. But Sid and Catrice are working on finding an earlier one."

Charlie lifted his head off the pillow. "Working together?"

"Working...at the same time, in the same place. I can't exactly say they're working together. Another thing that's all my fault. I screwed this up royally."

Charlie tried to wave his hand through the air. "Ah. Shkat happens."

"What do you think I should do? You saw what went down on the expedition. Seemed like Catrice dumped me for Eugene, and Sid and I got kinda close. Whenever I needed something, she was there. It just kind of happened. Then at the end, Catrice was stumped, said she never cared about Eugene. Called me out for ditching her so fast for Sid. Now Sid is fawning all over me in front of Catrice, who's barely spoken in days."

"Who do you like better?"

Drayden hesitated. "I don't know. I have no idea what to do."

"It'll work itself out. They'll be fine. First of all, we're sixteen. Second, you're not that great of a catch."

"Thank you. You make a good point."

"I'm teasing. But if it was me, I'd give Sid a chance. You already know Catrice."

Drayden was silent, thinking about Charlie's advice.

"What else did I miss?" Charlie asked.

"Oh yeah, we found out that Greaney and Duarte tried to enter Boston yesterday, but wouldn't give up their weapons and were turned away. Unfortunately, the police didn't detain them. No clue why it was only those two."

Charlie rolled his eyes. "Flunks. You know, I was thinking. I don't want to be a Guardian anymore."

Drayden couldn't help but notice that Charlie believed they had a future, including jobs, when they went home, as if life would simply return to normal. It was hard not to be touched by his innocence. Given Charlie's condition, Drayden didn't feel the need to spoil the fantasy. "I don't blame you. Screw those guys. What do you want to do instead?"

He bit down on his lower lip. "I don't know. I'm not good at anything else. I'm not smart. I always hoped to be a Guardian one day and never worried about it. I guess I'm kind of lost now."

"Yeah, it's hard to have your dream wrecked. I wanted to be a scientist. I know you; you're a lot smarter than you think. You can do whatever you want."

"Dray," Charlie said softly. "I don't want this to sound weird, but...don't leave me, okay? Like when this is all over, and you go off with Catrice or Sidney, or whatever. I wouldn't know what to do if I didn't have you around."

Drayden teared up instantly. Maybe it was Charlie's brush with death, or the meds, but he'd never heard Charlie speak so earnestly. Drayden rubbed his eyes. "Jeez, man, you're making me cry. I'm not going to leave you. I wouldn't do that. We're buds, right? I'm not going anywhere. You're my best friend."

"Really? I am? You're my best friend too."

Drayden cracked his knuckles in the awkward silence that followed. "I feel like we should hug right now, only neither of us can stand up."

"You want me to buzz Rick? I can have him lift you and drop you on top of me."

They both cracked up.

"Ow, that hurts my brain," Drayden said.

"Dray, do we need to worry about the Guardians?"

In truth, he'd been obsessing about it ever since Annie Hill dropped the bomb about their attempted entry. Even though he dismissed the threat in front of Sidney and Catrice, it was quietly eating away at him from the inside. His baseline anxiety level had skyrocketed as a result.

"I'm sure we're safe here in the city. Once we leave, they become a problem because they're out there somewhere. But the fact that only two of them tried to enter really bothers me. It tells me they're up to something. I wouldn't sweat it too much, except for one thing."

"What?" Charlie asked.

"Eugene."

CHAPTER 3

Finally discharged, Drayden took his first glorious steps outside the hospital five days after the accident. He was sore and a little headachy, but the freedom and the fresh air, tinged with the scent of lilacs, made his remaining ailments tolerable. He felt rejuvenated being outdoors and having something to do. Pulling on his green New York Yankees hat was a minor victory too, having almost lost it in the explosion. Since his mother's exile, he'd rarely taken it off.

Sidney, practically glowing, hooked her arm inside his. "You look fabulous. Good as new." She rested her head on his shoulder.

"Thanks. I feel decent."

Catrice was hovering close on his other side. "You feel up to checking out Faneuil Hall and meeting this sea captain we found?"

"Yeah, definitely. I've been bored out of my mind for a week." Drayden immediately detected the marked difference in Catrice's mood. While she didn't necessarily come across as happy, she was present, as if she'd relented on his and Sidney's nascent relationship.

They were strolling east along Cambridge Street, and though he tried to ignore it, his legs were already a bit fatigued. Not that he was in peak physical form before the accident, but it was amazing how rapidly his body had deteriorated and atrophied with zero exercise. Still, he relished the warm sun on his face and the breeze that smelled like summer.

Although Boston's infrastructure put New America's to shame, this section of Cambridge Street was dilapidated. Buildings were crumbling and the storefronts were long abandoned.

"Can you guys fill me in on this sea captain deal?" he asked.

Sidney peeked across his chest at Catrice, biting back a laugh. "You want to tell him about Johnny?"

Catrice snickered. "What a miniature flunk. No, you'll tell it better."

Drayden just about tripped over himself. Were they joking around? *Together?* What had happened the past few days? Working as a team must have compelled them to sort out their differences.

"Well," Sidney said, chuckling, "we didn't actually get on the docks, because you have to go outside the walls, and then back through immigration. Too difficult. We did find out that the boat people drink in bars and taverns around there. We tried this place called The Black Rose. It was overflowing with sketchy dudes, and as soon as we walked in everyone stared. This scrawny guy—couldn't have been taller than five foot four and looked twelve years old—came right up to us with his chest puffed out. Called himself Johnny." She paused to unleash the giggles. "We told him what we wanted and he claimed he was the captain of a ship called The Hamburger. And yes, it seemed like he thought of it on the spot. I told him he didn't look old enough to be the errand boy, and Catrice asked if his dad was around, which was brilliant."

Catrice was wiping her eyes.

"Then three guys marched over and tossed Johnny aside. Like, threw him, and he fell over a table. More guys came over and surrounded us. I'll admit, I was scared. Everyone was talking at the same time, saying they'd be happy to help us. Catrice and I were going to run out until this huge guy—and I mean enormous—started pushing people away, telling them to stop being creeps and that he'd crack their skulls if they didn't back off. Everybody was terrified of this guy. He was probably the biggest person I've ever seen. Block head, blond buzz cut. Long story short, he was nice, apologized for everyone else, and told us about his fourteen-year-old daughter back home in Virginia. His name was Bud. He feels legit, this guy. We both think so. There's just something about him. He said he'd do it for a hundred dollars a person."

"I don't even know if that's a lot," Drayden said. "What does a hundred dollars buy in Boston?"

"We did some research, walking around Faneuil Hall," Catrice said, "where we're headed right now. There are lots of shops there. A loaf of bread costs two dollars. A package of pasta is five dollars. A sack of oranges is eight dollars. I think those need to be imported."

Drayden deflated. They would have to earn the equivalent of fifty loaves of bread *each* to pay for passage.

"Great job, you guys," he said. "When does Bud's boat leave?"

"Wednesday," Sidney said. "That's a week before the Boston boat. Today's Sunday, so we have three days to come up with the money. He said he's at The Black Rose every day around four o'clock and to come back if we want a ride. We thought you'd want to meet him, and we might as well do that now."

Drayden didn't want to be cynical, and he trusted Catrice and Sidney's judgment, but it was hard not to be skeptical of "Bud." He wondered whether Bud would be willing to give him and Charlie a ride, or just Catrice and Sidney.

The trio followed Cambridge Street as it made a sweeping right turn. Sidney led them off the road onto an expansive brick walkway to cut between the buildings.

"We thought of some ideas to raise the money," Sidney said, "and figured you might have more when you saw Faneuil Hall. It's full of street performers, musicians, vendors, all kinds of stuff.

Basically, Catrice can draw and I'm good at sports. She was going to sell some drawings and has been hard at work, sketching Boston landmarks, like the Capitol building and the Paul Revere statue. They're really good. She also wanted to set up a stand at Faneuil Hall and draw portraits of people. If we took a little of the money she made and bought a basketball, I could do tricks. You know, spin the ball on my finger, head, and try to get tips."

Jeez, Drayden thought. Even if they had a month, they would be lucky to earn a hundred dollars *total.* He cursed himself for being so pessimistic. At least they'd come up with something. Not only was he bereft of ideas, he had no talent, besides offering to tutor kids in math. He couldn't fathom anyone wanting a math tutor for two days, or one without official qualifications.

"Good ideas. Very entrepreneurial. I have no talents. I wish we had stuff to sell, but we've got zippo."

After passing a massive, hideous gray building, they descended a cement staircase that deposited them on Congress Street.

Crowds flocked in front of an exquisite brick building that looked like it dated back to the Revolutionary War. A petite, gold-plated tower capped the three-story structure, which was vaguely shaped like a giant barn.

Lively classical music filled the air, courtesy of a string quartet. Row upon row of booths sold everything under the sun: flowers in a rainbow of colors, paintings, clothing, trinkets, furniture, tools, and food. The savory aroma of frying chicken evoked memories of their first encounter with it on the expedition.

"Holy cow," Drayden said, his mouth hanging open.

"It's magical, isn't it?" Catrice asked.

He flipped his Yankees cap backwards. "I wish we'd found this sooner. And I wish we had some money so we could buy whatever they're cooking. It smells so good."

Sidney hooked his arm again. "Let's go look."

As eager as Drayden was to dive into the festivities, he was just so tired. Perhaps he should have rested today.

Once they pierced the mob, a cacophony of noise ringing in his ears, he was overcome with claustrophobia and sensory overload. A woman in a voluminous hat was haggling with a merchant over the price of a wood carving. Two young boys were blowing bubbles and trying to pop them before they hit the ground. It was so cramped that he, Sidney, and Catrice had to walk single file.

"See!" Sidney shouted. "This is why we thought we had a chance to make enough money here. There're so many people. If Catrice can draw fast, I bet we could even make it in a single day."

Drayden stopped in front of a diminutive mustached man who was roasting nuts and some type of sugar inside a metal pan, the heavenly smell wafting through the air. Drayden stared, his mouth watering, as the girls drifted ahead.

The man offered one in his palm. "Wanna try?"

He took it, and, after the first crunch, nearly cried out in glory. The toasty, sugary coating on the peanut melted in his mouth. It was the greatest thing he'd ever tasted.

The guy dangled a bag of them. "Five dollars."

Catrice grasped Drayden's arm and hauled him along. "C'mon, Dray."

They reached an area with a huge circle of people centered around some boys performing a dance routine. More booths selling goods fanned out past the throng, but they would have to navigate way around it to get there, so they paused and took in the show.

"Aren't they amazing?" Sidney asked.

About ten boys were showcasing a type of dancing Drayden had never seen before, moving along to an old-fashioned radio. The dancers spun on their heads, and balanced on one hand, often using herky-jerky movements like a robot. A skinny boy tagged in and the others stepped back for his solo. Among other mind-blowing acrobatics, he busted out an insane move where his feet appeared to be walking forward but he was sliding backwards.

"Wow!" Drayden exclaimed, joining the fans in applause.

Sidney grinned at him, apparently amused by his enjoyment of the performance.

Something caught Drayden's eye and his smile faded. His heart began pounding, the surge of adrenaline immediate.

It can't be.

The dancers blurred in the foreground as he zeroed in on a man about a hundred yards away at one of the stalls, his back to Drayden. Even covered up in jeans and a long-sleeved white T-shirt, his muscularity was pronounced. The thick neck and crew-cut brown hair were all too familiar.

Eugene.

Drayden's jaw dropped. He couldn't speak. He tried and nothing came out, so he froze in a panic.

Sidney glanced at him and wrinkled her nose. "Dray, what's wrong?"

He just looked at her.

"Drayden?"

He pointed, leaning down with his head near hers so she could follow his line of sight.

"What? I don't see anything."

Catrice noted their activity and took in the booths past the dancers.

"There!" Drayden forcefully whispered. "White T-shirt, long sleeves."

"What about him?" Sidney asked, her palm up.

"It's Eugene!" Drayden blurted. "It's Eugene."

Oh God. He found a way in.

Sidney squinted. "I don't think that's him."

"It might be," Catrice countered.

Drayden took Sidney's hand. "Let's follow him. But keep our distance."

After skirting the fringes of the audience, they made it to the opposite side, twenty-five yards closer. Never once turning around, the guy flipped up a hood on his T-shirt and strode away through the masses, carrying a brown paper bag.

"I know that walk," Drayden said, turning back to the girls. "I'm telling you that's him."

Sidney was shaking her head. "It just looks like any guy, Dray."

The man picked up the pace with the crowd thinning. He turned right at the end of the brick building, disappearing around a corner.

They tried to catch up, hindered by Drayden's fatigued legs, and stopped short at the same corner to peek around it.

No sign of him.

"Dammit," Drayden grunted. "Let's go." He hustled across the brick-covered plaza, which was enclosed by more buildings containing stores.

Clusters of shoppers milled about, casually eating and chatting.

Dizzying himself, Drayden spun around, scanning the area. The guy could have ducked into one of these shops if he sensed he was being followed. Eugene was extremely sharp, and always acutely aware of his surroundings.

"It probably wasn't him," Catrice said.

Sidney gently stroked his arm. "Drayden, I think what Annie Hill said has you a little paranoid. It's understandable. We're all tense. I honestly don't think that was Eugene. How could he have gotten in?"

Drayden punched his fist into his palm. "Damn! He was in casual clothes. If he came to the border alone, dressed down, and fabricated some story, they wouldn't stop him." He didn't mean to yell, but he was amped up. "It's not like we gave them a photo. Sure, yeah, watch out for a jacked white kid with brown hair. They wouldn't even look twice. All he had to do was steal clothes from someone on the outside and come in unarmed."

"Drayden, calm down," Catrice said softly. "I think Sidney's right."

He flopped onto the curb beside the brick building's rear. Maybe he was wrong and it was all in his mind. He'd been nervous about Eugene for days.

He hung his head low. "I want to go home. I'm not feeling well, and I'm really tired. I can come meet Bud tomorrow. We still have a few days."

"I think that's a good idea," Sidney said.

After they snaked through the crowd, crossed Congress Street, and climbed the steps beside the ugly gray building, Drayden touched the brim of his hat. From the Initiation to the expedition, any time he needed guidance or inspiration, he felt the cap his mother had given him all those years ago. It may have been the paranoia, but as he gripped it now, he felt like he was being watched.

Drayden collapsed on the metal folding chair in his tiny kitchen. He was sweating, and, even with the shades drawn, his sweltering apartment was unbearable. After resting, he poured himself a glass of cold water, savoring the sensation of it cascading down his esophagus, cooling everything in its path.

He replayed the "Eugene" incident over and over in his mind, grasping for any clues he may have missed in real time. Of course, his suspicious brain played tricks on him, suggesting that Eugene had turned his head slightly, revealing his unmistakable profile. Only he hadn't. That never happened.

Drayden pressed the chilled, empty glass against his brow. In all likelihood, the girls were right. It hadn't been Eugene. He'd projected his anxiety onto some random dude. It was highly improbable that Eugene would find clothing that fit, attempt to enter, be admitted, and be precisely where they were at the same time—right after Annie Hill had warned them about the Guardians. It would have been too many coincidences in a row. The odds were astronomical.

Even if it *was* Eugene, why was he so scared? He'd gone full panic mode, which made little sense. He'd already fought Eugene and his cronies in the Neponset River Reservation and bested them. The whole expedition he'd been a step ahead of the guy, catching on to his duplicity before anyone else suspected a thing. If it hadn't mattered that Eugene was a strong, tough guy then, why should it matter now? Drayden's mind was superior to Eugene's fist, based on their *one* battle.

That was the crux of the problem. He feared he never really was better than Eugene. He was *lucky*. If Drayden considered it like a scientist—and he fancied himself a student of science—the sample size of their encounters was a single event. In a lone confrontation, he'd defeated Eugene. Hardly proof. It was a coin flip that happened to land his way.

The other problem with the supposed superiority of his brain to Eugene's brawn? Eugene wasn't just strong, and skilled at fighting and weaponry. He was smart. Drayden had witnessed it firsthand on the expedition. He was extremely cunning. Reflecting on their one clash in the swamp, Drayden now knew that Eugene had been juggling multiple balls. He'd had to give the impression that he was on board with crushing the Guardians while simultaneously guaranteeing the ploy failed. He'd needed to worry about rejoining the Guardians. The pressure on him in the battle was immense. It was a tainted victory for Drayden, so there was no reason to assume he could defeat Eugene a second time.

Thankfully, the point was moot. It couldn't have been Eugene. He decided he would try to stop fretting about it and focus on their real problems. First and foremost was securing a ride on Bud's boat, for which the girls' plan to generate money was woefully inadequate. It wasn't as if their issues ended there. Presuming they did get home... what then? How would they enter the city? Where should they go? He speculated they'd be in immediate danger inside the Palace, seeing as the Bureau evidently never expected them to return. That one detail essentially made their arrival strategy impossible to plan. They would have to wing it. Having missed their chance to visit the windmill farm on Route 3, they'd need to stop at one in Long Island and hoof it all the way to New America, somehow lugging heavy batteries. If that failed, they would return to New America without any leverage.

Drayden picked up the white envelope on the table and opened it again, removing the letter from Kim Craig. He craved some of Kim's strength, and boy did she have plenty. It would take a person as tenacious as Kim to topple the Bureau, so for now Drayden hoped she would succeed. He felt guilty for opening the letter. She had made him promise to only open it if he reentered New America and found her dead, since he didn't know anyone else involved in the insurrection and no one knew about him. She had also divulged the name Robert Zane, a Bureau executive they were grooming to take over for Premier Holst. But Drayden couldn't exactly pop in to visit that guy, even under the most ideal circumstances.

After the expedition, and the revelations about New America— the Bureau had lied to its citizens about nearly everything, including the knowledge of outside life, commerce, communication, and New America's place as the drug-producing capital of the new world— the stakes had been too high to keep his friends in the dark or ignore the letter. It had been a huge disappointment though. In fairness, Kim had remarked that the content had to be benign enough to be meaningless in the wrong hands. Except it was nonsensical to him as well. It disclosed two addresses: 40 Rector Street and 300 Albany

Street, 8I. Real helpful! He supposed if she were dead, he would go to the first address on the list.

He tossed the letter on the table. Given his exhaustion and the dimness of his apartment, he figured he should sleep. He made his way through the living room gingerly, since the shin bone seemed to exist solely as a tool for finding furniture in the dark. Thoughts of Kim called to mind another name: Ruth Diamond, Kim's aunt in Boston. In his first meeting with the Boston leadership, he'd asked if they knew of her and they hadn't. That didn't mean she wasn't there. It could be worth asking around, because if she was living in the city, she might help them. What if she were rich and would pay their passage?

Approaching his closed bedroom door, he hung a left to use the bathroom and froze. Nervous heat engulfed his face.

A note was taped to the bathroom mirror. He couldn't read it without light, but the white paper was unmistakable.

Nobody else had access to his apartment. Nobody.

Someone might be inside right now.

He scurried into the kitchen, quietly opened a drawer, and removed a butcher knife. Shaking, he backed up against the front door. Reaching behind, he unlocked it in case he needed to make a run for it. He surveyed every visible inch of the apartment, noting the places he could not see.

The curtains in the living room. The space on the far side of the couch. His bedroom. Behind the shower curtain.

He clenched his jaw and flipped on the lights. Hugging the wall, he shuffled to the hall leading to his bedroom and viewed the living room.

Nothing.

Heart pounding, he tiptoed to his bedroom door, keeping an eye on the bathroom. As silently as he could, he turned the knob and eased the creaking door open before stepping back.

When nothing happened, he flipped on the light.

Just a rumpled bed, and random clothes strewn about.

He faced the bathroom. Tensing his muscles, he switched on the light and charged, kicking in the shower curtain, his knife ready.

It was empty.

Exhaling the breath he hadn't realized he'd been holding, he examined the note.

What the hell?

It was gibberish. No, not gibberish. Another language? No. Jesus, it was coded. The note read:

yawuaeiat omifnyllo uilfdolis rlledubve fysriweee tiwdhsee heeyinrn ettostee noouwou doltavg

Recognizing he'd been distracted, Drayden peered into the mirror, half expecting to see Eugene behind him with a gun.

He was alone.

He snatched the note off the mirror and brought it to the kitchen, taking a seat at the table. He scrutinized the words, his mind racing. How had someone broken into his apartment? Why did they leave this note? Why would they code it? Drayden surmised his questions would be answered if he could decode it, so he fetched a pencil.

Perhaps he just needed to unscramble the letters, like an anagram. He tried the first word: yawuaeiat. It contained the word "await" with "aeyu" leftover. Not much else there. How about backwards? That was "taieauway" which kind of looked like "takeaway," if the code substituted certain letters out. The second word backwards yielded "ollynfimo," and that didn't resemble anything. Hmmm. He needed help.

Drayden left his apartment with the note and knocked on Catrice's door, then Sidney's door. "You guys, it's me!" he called.

Catrice opened up, wearing leggings and a faint smile. "Hi."

"Hold on." He knocked on Sidney's door a second time. "Hey, Sid!"

No answer.

"She might be asleep," Drayden said. "Can I come in? I have to show you something."

Catrice stepped aside. "Yeah, sure."

Sitting side-by-side at her kitchen table, Drayden explained how he found the note and walked her through his attempts to solve it.

Catrice collected a pencil and paper. "Even though we've done a lot of brainteasers, like in the Initiation, I don't think I've ever had to crack a code."

"Me either," Drayden said.

She chewed on the end of her pencil. "How about if, instead of unscrambling the letters, each one represents a different letter? Let's take the first word and replace each letter with the one after it in the alphabet." She wrote *yawuaeiat* followed by *zbxvbfjbu*, transposing each letter by a spot. "Or not. How about the letter before each one?" She scribbled *xzvtzdjzs*.

Drayden felt like he was back in the Initiation, working on a puzzle with Catrice. Sitting close to her now, the smell of her hair so familiar, he recalled their chemistry together. When he refocused on the code, a peculiarity jumped out. "Catrice, the first five words all have nine letters, the next three eight, and the last two have seven. Something's going on there."

"Yeah, you're right, that has to be important. I wish I knew how."

Drayden slammed his pencil on the table, his despair and frustration boiling over. "Who would leave me a note? A coded note, no less. It can only be one person."

"Eugene?"

"Who else could it be? I just happened to believe I saw Eugene today, and a mysterious note turns up in my room? You understand odds. When two highly unlikely events occur almost simultane-ously, the chances of them being unrelated are extremely low. Obviously, this note came from someone intelligent if they knew how to make a code."

She tapped the pencil on the side of her neck. "I don't disagree with you. But if Eugene wanted to contact you and knew where you lived, he could do it in person. If he wanted to leave you a note, there's no reason why he would need to code it. I'll add that I'm pretty sure that wasn't Eugene today. He's taller than the guy we saw."

Despite her logic, Drayden wasn't convinced, because there wasn't anyone else who could have left the note. "Good points, but can you come up with any other possibility?"

She stared into space. "The hotel has a key. Could have been someone here." Her eyes lit up. "Or somebody from the Boston government. People know about us now. I'd assume they've heard we're hoping to overturn the government when we go home. Maybe someone has an interest in stopping us. If New America was about to reintroduce drugs or alcohol to Boston, there may be people who want them to succeed. Or there are drug dealers here who want them to fail. Either way, I think there are lots of candidates who might have a vested interest in our return. Eugene is low on the list actually. As for coding it, I'm not sure. The only thing I can think of is they didn't want you to know what it said until we left the city, like, knowing it would take time to decode."

Drayden tugged on his left earlobe. "Showoff."

Catrice copied down the coded message. "I'm going to keep working on it. As of now, I can't solve this."

Drayden bowed his head. "I can't either. But I know somebody who can."

CHAPTER 4

Wearing a lightweight tracksuit, Drayden stopped in front of Professor Worth's house and eased off his bike, praying the professor would drive him back to Boston later. He doubted his body could handle the ride twice. The bulletproof vest wasn't doing him any favors, but he'd pledged to never complain about it again.

He'd come alone so Catrice and Sidney could get to work on making money. As much as he wanted to help, the coded note felt too pressing to put off. Charlie was close to being released from the hospital, although not there yet. The girls had objected to Drayden going out solo, but ultimately he'd talked them into it. Now that he found himself in front of Professor Worth's home, he wasn't sure what to do.

The residence itself was a simple two-story farmhouse. A full-size barn stood to the left, and fields of crops, smaller outbuildings, and sheds expanded behind it. Everything was meticulously kept, appearing the way it must have existed before the Confluence. It looked innocuous enough, except Professor Worth had mentioned his property was heavily booby-trapped to protect him from gangs and would-be thieves. They'd learned over time—the hard way—not to mess with him.

Drayden shifted uncomfortably on his feet, pondering how Sidney had contacted the professor after the accident. A stone walkway stretched from the street up to his front door, fifty yards away. He took one step and thought better of it.

"Professor Worth!" he shouted. "It's Drayden!" He cautiously advanced, watching the house. "Professor!"

Drayden unholstered his pistol, in case his yelling attracted the wrong kind of attention. No, he couldn't hit someone from five feet away, but they wouldn't know that.

"Professor Worth, it's Drayden!" he repeated, inching forward.

The dark curtains in a ground floor window parted, exposing two barrels of a shotgun. Moments later, the front door flew open.

"Stop, Drayden! Don't move!"

He froze in his tracks.

Professor Worth popped inside for a minute and hurried down the front steps. Taking a wide, elliptical path through the yard, he knelt by Drayden and pointed at the sidewalk.

"See this?"

Drayden didn't see anything. He squatted, finally catching it.

A tripwire.

"Another foot and you would have been in a net." Professor Worth eyed the tree overhead. "If you'd missed this one, I don't want to tell you what the next would have done. Don't worry, though, I turned them off."

Drayden scratched the back of his neck. "Professor, right on the front walkway? What if a person is lost and innocently walks up asking for directions?"

"That doesn't happen out here. If someone's coming to my door, it's for nefarious purposes. Come, follow me." He led Drayden inside, taking the same circuitous path, ostensibly to leave the trip-wires undisturbed.

The house was cozy and tidy, brimming with dark wood and antiques. Unfinished projects lay everywhere. A wristwatch in a million pieces waited to be rebuilt under a microscope. A model airplane, partially finished, sat on a desk. Professor Worth stopped at the modest kitchen and pulled out a chair for Drayden at the table.

He dropped into it like a sack of bricks, wondering if it would be rude to take a nap.

The professor set a cold glass of water and a warm loaf of bread in front of him. "Just baked that."

Drayden gulped the water. "Thank you so much." He wiped his mouth with the back of his hand and tore into the fluffy bread, leaving a mess of crumbs on the table.

Professor Worth sat across from him. "So. I'm glad you decided to visit. Do you know when you're going home?"

Drayden finished chewing before speaking. "We have a ride on a Boston government boat in a week, but we don't want to wait that long. Sidney and Catrice are trying to raise money to pay a private merchant ship to take us. They want a hundred dollars a person. We don't have any money, so Catrice is drawing pictures to sell and Sidney is doing basketball tricks for tips." He shrugged. "I know, it's not the best. We're not sure what else to do." He snagged his backpack off the floor. "I would have visited anyway, but I also need your help."

Professor Worth arched his brows. "What can I help with?"

Drayden stood, hoisting his backpack onto the table. "Do you mind if I take off this Kevlar vest? It's driving me nuts."

"Please."

Drayden unzipped his lightweight black jacket and removed the heavy vest, dumping it on the floor. He sat back down, feeling weightless in a T-shirt, and rifled through the pack for the note. "Before I get to this," he said, holding it up, "I wanted to ask if you could drive me to the windmill farm on Route 3, just south of where Route 3a crosses over it."

Professor Worth placed his hand on his cheek. "What for?"

"The batteries. New America is in desperate need of deep-cycle batteries. They've worn out. Seven of forty-four are toast and the others may crash at any time. There're already some power outages, but if all the batteries die the city can't make clean water or food. Or, well, drugs to pay for food. If we return with batteries, they may provide leverage to keep us alive. If we show up empty handed, we're effectively worthless and there's nothing to stop them from killing us."

"I see." He looked away, rubbing his chin. "Those batteries on Route 3 are long gone. Other people had the same idea many years ago. Batteries are a hot commodity in this Post-Confluence world."

Drayden slouched, disappointed but not surprised. New America wasn't the only place in need of batteries to operate equipment or store power. He prayed the windmill farm he'd identified in Long Island was in an unpopulated area and undiscovered.

"Strike one. Let's hope this note isn't a fail." He slid his chair over. "I know you were a math professor, and I happen to be pretty good at math myself. I was the top student in my school. I had to solve all these brainteasers to pass the Initiation we told you about. But I've never had to crack a code before. I found this on my bathroom mirror and I don't know who left it. I guess if I decode it, I'll find out. Can you help?" Drayden reexamined it himself.

yawuaeiat omifnyllo uilfdolis rlledubve fysriweee tiwdhsee heeyinrn ettostee noouwou doltavg

He eagerly handed it to Professor Worth, who studied it for a minute and passed it back, his expression enigmatic.

"Well?" Drayden asked. "Do you know how?"

"Yes."

Drayden waited a few seconds and said, with a hint of annoyance, "Can you tell me?"

"No. I want you to solve it. What have you tried so far?"

Drayden was getting impatient. Their journey to New America being a non-trivial affair, was this really the right time for a cryptography lesson? "I tried rearranging the letters like it was an anagram. Then Catrice and I tried substituting the letters by shifting the alphabet one spot in both directions."

"That's called a ROT1 cypher," the professor said. "This is not that. Do you notice anything else?"

"Yes. The first five words have nine letters, the next three have eight, and the last two have seven."

"You've basically solved it."

Drayden threw his hands in the air. "Can't you tell me then?"

Professor Worth removed his glasses, placed them on the table, and folded his hands together in front of him. "Drayden, if you're going to wait for people to do things for you, they'll never get done. If you don't believe you can solve problems yourself, you'll always seek help from others. You must believe in yourself. You can do it. Look around you." He waved his hand through the air. "Do you think I had someone telling me how to build a windmill, how to fix a car, how to convert a gasoline engine to ethanol? No, I had to figure it out on my own. I didn't just learn skills. I learned I'm capable of anything as long as I believe in myself. I don't need you to tell me your class rank to know how smart you are. I already know. You need to think about this more, and while you do, you can help me with a project I was in the middle of."

Having been appropriately shamed, Drayden slumped. "Fine." He'd thought about it plenty, though, and struck out.

"Follow me," Professor Worth said. "Very carefully. Walk exactly where I do."

Drayden complied, trailing him down a meandering path into the fields, at one point passing a headstone adorned with vibrant flowers. He recalled Professor Worth mentioning his wife dying of Aeru shortly after the Confluence.

The professor stopped at a rectangular section of fresh soil with string along its borders and rows of little holes inside. Dozens of plants, each around a foot tall, sat in miniature pots around the exterior of the plot.

"You will be helping me plant these tomatoes," Professor Worth said. "Take one of those plants and come here." He proceeded to demonstrate the steps, removing it from the pot, setting it in the soil, and packing the base with dirt. "In this first row, I want you to plant ten tomato plants." He touched the next row of unfilled holes a few feet to the right. "Here, I want you to plant another ten, and so forth, until you get to the sixth row. Then plant nine. After five rows of nine, start planting eight. Get it? Five rows each, decreasing by one as you go on."

Drayden held up a palm. "There's room for more than ten plants in each row. Why not more?"

"Because I want no more than ten," he said, like it was self-explanatory.

"Totally, yeah, ten's a good number, nice and round." Drayden gave him a thumbs-up and got to work. Despite the disturbing note in the back of his mind, he quite enjoyed working on the farm, getting his hands dirty, sweating in the afternoon sun. He felt useful and enjoyed the company of the professor, who occasionally wandered over to review his progress. After an approving nod, he would continue digging holes.

Drayden was on the fourth plant in the first row of eight when it hit him. *Rows of nine, followed by rows of eight.*

He stood, dropping his shovel on the ground, and stared vacantly at Professor Worth.

I got it.

Professor Worth rose to his knees, reading Drayden, and smiled.

Drayden charged back to the house, leaving the professor in the dust. Once inside, he washed his hands and sat at the kitchen table with the note.

He wrote the first word vertically—*yawuaeiat*—nine letters, like a row of plants, going down the page. He wrote the second word—*omifnyllo*—to the right of the first, also vertically. When he was done with the nine-letter words, he started a new section with the eight-letter words.

Professor Worth, his arms crossed, watched in the doorway.

The blood drained from Drayden's face, goosebumps covering him.

Oh my God.

"No!" he screamed. He slammed his fist on the table. "Did you know what it said?" he shrieked at Professor Worth.

"Yes."

"Then why did you make me waste my time doing all that gardening?"

Professor Worth cocked his head. "You weren't wasting your time. You were solving the problem, and you needed to know you could do it all alone, without help. You had to understand that whatever the letter obligates you to do next, you can do as well."

Drayden removed his hat, tugging at his hair while reading the decoded letter one more time:

yawuaeiat omifnyllo uilfdolis rlledubve fysriweee tiwdhsee heeyinrn ettostee noouwou doltavg

y o u r f		t h e		n d
a m i l y		i e t		o o
w i l l s		w e t		o l
u f f e r		d y o		u t
a n d d i		h i s		w a
e y o u w		s n t		o v
i l l b e		e r e		u g
a l i v e		e n e		
t o s e e				

your family will suffer and die you will be alive to see then die
too we told you this wasnt over eugene

Drayden clutched his Yankees hat in his lap so it wouldn't blow off. Sitting beside Professor Worth in the Jeep, they raced up Route 3 toward Boston, mostly in silence. They hadn't spoken much since he'd decoded the note from Eugene.

He couldn't stop thinking about his father and brother. Eugene was going to kill them, and even worse, said they would suffer first. The inherent cruelty of it was terrifying. Eugene's personal vendetta shouldn't involve his family. None of this was their fault. With no way to warn them, his only option was to make it back to New America before the Guardians.

He was still miffed about the professor withholding the content of the note in light of its explosiveness and urgency. Although, if he was being honest, they couldn't leave sooner anyway. It was Monday night and the earliest boat left Wednesday morning. Nevertheless, with the note exposing a direct threat against his family, he felt Professor Worth shouldn't have been so nonchalant about it.

"Where are you staying in Boston?" Professor Worth asked, breaking the silence.

"The XV Beacon Hotel, where the government put us up. It's right next to the Capitol building."

"I'm trying to recall if that was around Pre-Confluence, but I can't remember."

Drayden delicately removed the note from his backpack, finding the conditions too dark and windy to read it. Eugene had handled this very paper. It connected them, much like their personal history was now eternally linked.

"Professor...why would Eugene code this note? Why wouldn't he just make his threat? The coding of it bothers me almost as much as what it says."

"Perhaps to show you how smart he is? Knowing you would need time to decode it could have been a way to make you feel inferior to him. That's rubbish though. It's not hard to devise an extremely complex code that could only be solved with a computer. Making the code is the easy part."

Mission accomplished, Drayden thought. It had made him feel inferior and stupid, especially considering how basic it turned out to be.

"The other possibility," the professor said, "is that he needed to buy time before you understood the note. What would you have done if you'd received that threat directly? Gone to the police or government. They would have started searching for him immediately."

A lightbulb went off in Drayden's head. "I'm going to tell the Boston government about the note, but I bet he was arranging a boat home for him and the Guardians. We saw him near the docks. Maybe he wanted to make sure he was gone by the time I understood what the note said."

"That could be."

It was very smart. Greaney and Duarte must have tried to enter the city to scope out the entry protocol. They purposely kept their weapons to ensure they were banished. Then the Guardians sent in Eugene alone, disguised, to arrange a boat for them. Drayden imagined it would stop outside the city to pick up the other guys. Their scheme only required them to rob people outside the city for Eugene's clothing and the money for the trip. Having murdered nearly twenty villagers in the race to Boston, they wouldn't have any objection to stealing.

While Eugene wouldn't have known how much time it would take Drayden to crack the code, he knew Drayden was smart and it wouldn't take him too long. That implied he and the Guardians had left for New America.

His father and brother were in imminent danger.

"Professor, that means those guys are likely on their way home already."

The corners of Professor Worth's mouth turned down.

"We need to be on this boat Wednesday. Or take an earlier one." Drayden wiped sweat from his brow. "If we don't leave for another week, the Guardians will have too big a lead. They could kill my family. They'll lie to the Bureau about what happened on the trip. God knows what will go down when we get there a week later. Professor, do you have any ideas about how we can make money for our fare?"

He blew out a long breath, puffing his cheeks. "I can't think of much that doesn't take more than a few days. Are you certain you don't have anything valuable to sell?"

Drayden contemplated it. "Just our Bureau pins. I don't think those are worth much to anyone here, plus we may need them in New America."

"You have weapons. You can't sell them in Boston since they're forbidden inside. But you could try to sell a gun outside."

"To who?"

Professor Worth licked his lips. "Gangs. That would involve interacting with them, though. I could arrange a sale for you."

Even taking into account his lousy marksmanship, Drayden hated the idea of parting with his weapons. Kim Craig's rebellion was severely outgunned as it was. They needed every weapon available. "Let me see how the girls did today."

Drayden was feeling overwhelmed. The Guardians, probably on their way back now, sought revenge on him and his family. His friends were counting on him to get them home, but they didn't have the resources. Their hypothetical arrival in New America was fraught with danger. He was no match for Premier Holst, his malevolent chief of staff Harris von Brooks, the sniveling creep Nathan Locke, and an entire zone of Special Forces Guardians. He was just a kid. If the Bureau was waiting to execute them, there was virtually nothing he could do to stop it.

"Professor, I know I already asked, but...can you please come with us? I know you have a life here, and I respect that. I do. Given how many lives are at stake though, I'm appealing to your sense of humanity. There are seventy-five thousand people in the Dorms, my zone, who are in jeopardy. I don't know how to get involved, how to help the insurrection. I'm too young."

Professor Worth regarded him warmly. "Drayden, you speak as if I'm somehow the key in your battle against the Bureau. I'm nothing of the sort. I'm an old man. I was a math professor—not a historian, not a warrior. I wish I could help, but I sincerely believe I'd be a liability. I've lived my life the same way for a quarter century now. Me and my farm. I can't just abandon it to go on a quest with some teenagers. I'm too old, too set in my ways."

"Don't you care about all these innocent folks? The Bureau might kill everyone."

"I do care, but it's not my battle. Those aren't my people. Let me show you something." He reached across Drayden's lap and unlatched a compartment on the dashboard. After rummaging through, Professor Worth handed him a picture frame.

While difficult to see in the darkness, he could tell it was a photograph of a woman with short hair.

"That is my wife. She is my everything. I plan to spend eternity with her. She's buried on the farm and I have every intention of being beside her when I'm gone. I've made arrangements for a friend to ensure I'm buried there. So, you see, I cannot leave." He gazed longingly at the photo, taking his eyes off the road. "My sweet Ruth."

Ruth.

"Not Ruth Diamond," Drayden said with a chuckle.

Professor Worth slammed the brakes.

Drayden flew forward, the seatbelt saving him from plunging through the windshield. "Jesus!" he screamed, his heart beating through his chest.

"What did you say?" Professor Worth asked. "How did you know her name?"

Drayden's eyes widened. "You gotta be kidding me. Your wife is Ruth Diamond?" He was practically shouting. "Do you have a niece named Kimberly Craig?"

The professor stared at the steering wheel as if deep in thought. "Kim Craig...why...yes. My gosh, I haven't heard that name in thirty years. I don't understand, Drayden, how do you know about Kim Craig and my wife?"

Drayden explained Kim's role as lead figure in the resistance, and their relationship, marveling at the curiosity of life. While his mother had often yammered about karma and fate, he'd never believed in it. The incredible coincidence notwithstanding, it would have been better if Ruth Diamond were a wealthy Bostonian who could pay their boat fare. But this might be the next best thing.

"You have to come with us now!" Drayden stated emphatically. "Your niece is my mentor, and, as a senior leader of the insurgency, she's in grave danger too. She asked me to bring back help on my mission to Boston. You *are* the help!"

"I...I mean—"

"Professor, you have to admit. This seems like fate, no? You're a mathematician. I don't need to tell you the odds of us meeting."

"I don't believe in fate. I will admit this is extraordinary, but I simply cannot come with you. I'm too old." He put the Jeep in gear and sped off.

On I-93, as the twinkling Boston skyline came into view, Drayden racked his brain for any argument to persuade the professor to join them, but he came up empty. If his niece wasn't sufficient reason, what more could he say? Professor Worth was being a coward and he didn't have time for cowards.

At the gate, Professor Worth rolled to a stop and shut off the engine. He scooted out to help Drayden lift his bike from the back seat.

Regardless of his disappointment, Drayden didn't want to leave angry. The professor had done so much for him, saving his life before the end of the expedition and after the grenade. Drayden owed a lot to this old man.

"Professor Worth, thank you for everything. I don't know what else to say." He extended his hand.

The professor pulled Drayden into a hug. "Good luck, son. I believe in you. Now you believe in yourself."

As the gate rumbled open, Drayden watched Professor Worth drive away, knowing that this time, he'd never see him again.

CHAPTER 5

Dark circles under their eyes, both girls were despondent. The upbeat and seemingly content version of Catrice had vanished. Sidney held Drayden's hand as they walked east down Court Street, en route to The Black Rose. In contrast with the nearby Faneuil Hall, this area was decrepit, much like large swaths of New America.

"We really tried, I swear," Sidney said. "It may sound lame but I'm proud of the sixty dollars I made. Catrice brought in fifty, ten of which went to pay for the basketball. We busted our butts from sunrise to sunset. If I knew more tricks, or if Catrice drew faster, maybe we could have made a little more."

The ugly, overcast day was fitting. A hundred dollars was a decent sum, no doubt, but far short of what they needed. With Bud's boat leaving tomorrow, their only hope was negotiating with him.

"You guys did awesome," Drayden said. "There's no way you could have made four hundred dollars in one day. A hundred is amazing. Let's pray Bud will be reasonable."

Catrice remained mum, her eyes fixed on the asphalt. Sidney had often chided her for not pulling her weight on the expedition, and even during the Initiation, so the slight about drawing too slow probably stung.

"I still don't get why Eugene didn't just wait till you got home and then kill you," Sidney said.

Drayden swallowed hard, wondering the same thing.

"Too risky," Catrice said. "There's a ton of surveillance here. Plus, based on the note, he thought it was meaner to force you to witness your family's deaths first."

Early that morning, Drayden had sought out Annie Hill to let her know about Eugene and his inflammatory note. She was apologetic and said they'd immediately review the surveillance tapes to search for him. Drayden knew it was futile.

He'd also revealed it to the girls, and they'd been equal parts shocked that Eugene had left it and horrified by its message. Despite the note being delivered to Drayden, it didn't specifically mention him or his family. It could have been interpreted as a threat against them all, except Catrice, who was fortunate to not have any family to distress over.

The Black Rose was a miniscule bar, painted emerald green with a garish red door. A steady buzz of chatter, laughter, and howls inside filtered out to the sidewalk.

"After you introduce me, you guys should take over," Drayden said. "This is your show. He obviously liked you, and this is our last chance. If you think of anything on the fly, go for it."

Neither Catrice nor Sidney appeared optimistic.

The bar was dingy and smoky inside, crammed with boorish men stumbling around, spilling pints of beer on the floor. Two women at the bar were attracting loads of attention. Likewise, Catrice and Sidney drew numerous eyes the second they entered.

Three burly men immediately headed their way.

"Hey, Bud!" Sidney shouted.

At the mere intimation she knew him, those guys hit the brakes and went about their business. Bud, easily identifiable by his size, glanced over from the corner seat at the bar and waved them forward.

Drayden followed Sidney, weaving through the tight space between chairs and patrons who refused to budge. Catrice was clinging to the back of his shirt.

Sidney sat beside Bud on a stool which was suddenly vacant. "Hi, Bud," she said with a smile and flip of her hair.

Catrice popped around Drayden's shoulder. "Hey, Bud."

"Ladies." Bud swigged his beer.

Sidney touched Drayden's arm. "Bud, this is our friend we told you about. Drayden."

Drayden tried to radiate toughness, standing as tall as he could, to no avail. Pushing his shoulders back only highlighted his puny chest.

Bud was massive, well over three-hundred pounds. He looked like a Viking.

"Hi, Bud, nice to meet you." Drayden extended his hand.

Bud shook it, completely engulfing it in his gorilla mitt. "What was your name, kid?"

"Drayden."

He smirked. "Okay. What can I do for you?"

Sidney scooted closer to Bud. "We wanted to thank you again for your offer to give us a ride. It's incredibly generous. See, our families are in danger. There's a group of soldiers trying to beat us home to kill them." She poked Drayden. "Drayden found this note in his room, and it was coded for some reason, but it says this guy is going to kill our families, and us too."

Drayden flashed the note in front of Bud's face.

The guy barely looked at it, swallowing half his glass of beer in one gulp.

Catrice nudged Drayden out of the way, perhaps sensing they were losing the guy. "Bud, we did our best to raise the money to pay your fare, but came up a smidge short. If we don't get on your boat, we can't leave for another week."

Drayden didn't realize how intimidated he'd be by Bud, and was at a loss about how to broach asking for a lower fare.

"We respect your price," Catrice said, "but is there any wiggle room? We're sorry to ask. All we can do is hope you have pity on us."

Bud stared straight ahead, expressionless, and didn't respond for a few seconds. "Listen, kids. Sorry you got problems. We all do, don't we? I got a great ship, she's fast, and I don't got a lot of room. I'm doing you a big favor as it is. You're welcome to try some of these other blokes around here, see how that goes. As I said, you won't find a better price. Or, if you do, it might come with enslavement."

Catrice calmly pulled out a pencil and a rolled-up sheet of paper. "I'm an artist. I could draw a portrait of you to leave with your daughter when you're at sea. Or a picture of your boat? To make up the difference."

Sidney wiped away a tear.

Bud looked at Catrice, then Sidney, and back to Catrice, his face softening a touch. "How much you got?"

"A hundred," Catrice said.

"Pffft," he chuckled. "A hundred? Total? Sorry, kiddo. I tell you what. I haven't a clue if you all are telling the truth or not, but I'm in a good mood since I'm going home tomorrow. I'll do it for seventy-five a person. Best offer. If you're in, be at the dock at nine o'clock tomorrow morning with the cash." He took a gander around the bar. "I suggest you scram as well. The crowd is getting antsy, and I don't want to have to smash anyone on your behalf."

Drayden wasn't sure if they should thank the guy or not, but the girls did before they all hurried out and drifted up State Street in defeat.

"I don't know what to do," Drayden said.

Sidney was teary-eyed. "I want to scream. We have to get home."

Out of time, luck, and ideas, they needed a miracle. Even having Professor Worth arrange a gun sale would take days, between trekking to see him, lining up a buyer, and making the exchange.

"I can't believe I'm saying this," Drayden gulped, "but I'm considering robbing a bank or something. We would leave the city tomorrow morning."

Catrice whacked him on the arm. "We can't rob a bank, Drayden. We can't steal the money."

Sidney's face lit up. "Boston's done a lot for us, right? Why don't we ask Annie Hill if they'll pay the rest of our fare?"

"Can't hurt to ask," Drayden said. "I was just there. Wish I'd thought of it." But Drayden already knew the answer. If Boston was willing to finance their voyage, Annie would have mentioned it. They were stuck in Boston for another week, the Guardians were going to kill their families, and there was nothing they could do about it.

"He's back!" Sidney rushed Charlie and hugged him gently.

"There he is," Drayden said, winking at him.

"Welcome home, Charlie," Catrice said. "How are you feeling?"

"Man, I'm happier than a witch in a broom factory. I missed you guys." He hugged Catrice and Drayden, then painstakingly lowered himself onto the couch in his apartment.

Drayden watched him, recollecting their conversation in the hospital, and the affirmation of their mutual best friend status. While Drayden had noted the similarities between Tim's death in the Initiation and Charlie's near-death by the grenade, he'd somehow failed to notice an eerie connection. Having had the stitches removed, Charlie now sported a half-moon shaped scar under his left eye, like Tim had. The scars weren't oriented the same way, but still. Charlie was physically transforming into his former best friend, if only he would shrink by about eight inches.

Charlie rubbed his hands together. "Tell me you guys have some good news."

The others exchanged a glance. Sidney sat beside him and caught him up on the travel dilemma and Eugene's note.

Charlie took it in stride. "What are we going to do?"

Drayden removed his hat and rounded the brim. "On our way here, we tried asking Annie Hill, our new contact in the government, to help us pay the fare and she said they couldn't. Against government policy. She agreed it was stupid because they're basically paying money for us to stay here, but she said there's a budget for providing services, not for giving out cash. I did tell them about Eugene, and we asked them to transfer our weapons to the gate by the docks, just in case. The offer stands to go on their boat next week." He sighed. "We're out of ideas for leaving any earlier."

Drayden tried to push away a perverse thought that kept flashing through his mind: relief. He hated himself for it, because it was so damn cowardly. Their families were in danger. Yet, as things stood now, having exhausted every option to get home, they were powerless to help. Whatever was set to happen would happen, through no fault of their own. On the other hand, had they scored a ride, the burden would rest on his shoulders to save his family from Eugene. It would mean battling the Guardians, and he already knew he had doubts about his ability to beat them a second time. If he failed, the blame would be all his.

Drayden acknowledged the gutless feeling, so he could face it and deal with the fear behind it: He'd been lucky so far. It was irrelevant since they were stuck in Boston for another week. His father was brilliant, and his brother extremely tough. They would need to fend for themselves. When he did make it to New America, he had to worry about supporting Kim Craig's plot in any conceivable way.

"God, my poor parents," Charlie said. "And your sister, Sidney. And your father and brother, Dray." He side-eyed Catrice before looking away.

"I think Eugene was just trying to scare us," Catrice said. "There's no reason to do anything to your families. I bet he wanted to make sure we knew they were alive, so we'd know they were down but not out. Even though the Bureau is corrupt, we've never heard of Guardians being allowed to murder innocent citizens."

"I hope you're right," Drayden said. "Listen, we need stuff for our trip next week. We don't know how long we'll be outside the walls before we get into the city. It could be a while. We have to bring food and water. We also need to stop at this old windmill farm in Long Beach, Long Island, according to my research. If we find batteries, we'll have to lug them for miles, so we need to buy some kind of bag large enough for two people to carry together. We need tools to extract the batteries. We can grab food right before we leave so it doesn't spoil, but maybe we should use the hundred dollars that Catrice and Sid made and buy the other stuff now."

Sidney put a hand on Charlie's shoulder. "You feel up to coming along?"

He cocked his head. "Is a frog's butt watertight?"

"I...I don't know."

"I'd say he's ready," Drayden said.

They rode the elevator down to the lobby and emerged onto a gloomy Beacon Street. Thinking about the best place to shop, Drayden peered west then east, toward Faneuil Hall.

An old man was loitering there, his back to them.

"Professor?" Drayden said incredulously.

He turned around, looking sheepish, dressed in a ratty brown suit with a boxy leather suitcase in one hand. A rusty, dark green wagon with thick treaded tires sat beside him.

Professor Worth stood at attention, smoothing out the wrinkles in his suit. "Where's our boat?"

Sidney touched his arm. "Professor Worth, what are you doing here?"

He furrowed his brow. "Drayden invited me to come on your journey, and I'm accepting the offer. Am I still invited?"

Grinning ear-to-ear, Drayden swallowed up the professor in a warm embrace. "Thank you," he whispered in his ear. "But you're a tad early. We don't have the money to pay for the boat tomorrow, so we're not leaving for another week."

Professor Worth set his suitcase on the ground. "Ah, yes. I may be able to help with that." From his inside jacket pocket, he pulled out a fat envelope and cracked it, revealing a wad of hundred-dollar bills. "Gather around here." He stepped over to the wagon and removed the cover. "If this journey is to be a success, we need supplies. I believe I've thought of everything."

Despite never having seen deep-cycle batteries before, Drayden recognized them immediately.

"Drayden, I must apologize. I told you the truth when I said the windmill farm had been raided long ago. I just failed to mention it was raided by *me*. I needed the batteries for the same reason your government does. I'm not giving these to you because I care about New America, but because I care about you kids. I understand you must have the bargaining leverage these batteries provide in order to save your lives."

"Thank you so much," Drayden said. "But why bring two? I would keep one for yourself."

"I have another at home, and you need two. One to bring in, to show you have batteries. And a second, to prove you have more. There's no reason for them to know you *only* have two. Yet you must have at least two in case they call your bluff."

Charlie punched Drayden in the shoulder. "That's a smart guy right there." He pointed at a sack behind the batteries. "What's in the bag?"

"An inflatable dinghy, like a rubber rowboat," Professor Worth said. "The ship we're taking might have a way to transport us from the boat to the shore, but it's not as if it will be floating up to a dock, right? This has never been used, so I've no idea if it works or if it has any holes. I figured I'd bring it along." He touched a wooden pole with a white cloth tied to the end. "A white flag I made for your entry into New America. I have loads of weapons. And, of course, I brought this wagon to help us move the batteries, which are quite heavy."

Drayden hadn't even thought about getting to shore from the boat. Professor Worth was already proving his value. "Professor, I don't know what to say. Thank you so much. You've saved us so many times now that we could never repay you. What made you change your mind? You were so set on not coming."

He gazed into Drayden's eyes. "You did. I *am* an old man, and I have nothing else to do here. I'm alone. I could live out my days at my farm and die of sickness or an accident someday, or I could go on one last adventure. I would also like to see my only remaining family member before I pass on. I bet Kimberly will be quite surprised. I have every intention of returning to my farm, mind you. This is not a one-way trip for me. In the meantime, I've made arrangements for my crops to be taken care of."

"Kimberly?" Catrice asked, looking puzzled.

"Ah, right, only Drayden knows. Kim Craig, who I understand runs surveillance in New America and is, sort of, heading up this insurgency against your Bureau, is my niece. Ruth Diamond was my wife. Quite a coincidence."

Sidney hugged him. "Thank you. I need to get home to my sister. Thank you, Professor."

The time had come for Drayden to bury that earlier feeling. If he was to be successful, he needed to quash the shameful relief he'd briefly experienced when he believed they were stuck in Boston. The impromptu mission to stop Eugene and the Guardians from killing his family was back on, and demanded he step up to the plate. Assuming he prevailed, a much bigger task lay in wait: helping Kim Craig's insurrection topple the Bureau. Hopefully, luck would be on his side once again.

CHAPTER 6

The first and only time Drayden had ridden on a boat, it sank in a storm. Standing in the entryway to the dock at 9:00 AM, spying Bud's ship, which the captain had described as "great" and "fast," Drayden reckoned they would meet the same fate.

The thing was a piece of junk. True, he knew little about boats, but the fact that it was taped together set off alarm bells. Did the random piece of wood nailed to the green hull serve a purpose? Because it didn't inspire much confidence. The whole floating monstrosity was paltry for a cargo ship, roughly a hundred feet, with the pilot's tower in the rear and a soot-covered smokestack directly behind it.

Drayden readjusted his green Yankees cap, pulling it snug. Fortunately, the day was calm and clear, unlike their trip to Boston. If the boat went down, it wouldn't be due to the weather.

The teens, for the first time since they'd entered Boston, wore their gray camouflage Guardian uniforms adorned with Bureau pins, and carried their full weaponry—M16A4 rifles, Glock-22 pistols, and hunting knives. Professor Worth's wagon was all but overflowing from their additions: water and food for the trip, extra ammunition, rope, an empty backpack, four flashlights, and the maps.

The Bureau had offered a reward for completing the journey to Boston and threatened a consequence for failing. If they succeeded, their families would theoretically be moved to nicer apartments and receive double food allocations. If they failed, their families would be sent back to the Dorms. The mayor of Boston had penned a letter to Premier Holst as proof they'd made it, plus she'd given them a commemorative coin and sheets of official Boston government letterhead. Even though the entire expedition had been a sham—and the Bureau's "reward" almost certainly was too—they didn't want to take a chance.

Whether intentional or not, considering their value, the government had left the bulletproof vests with their weapons, so they took them out of necessity.

Sidney rested her hands on her hips. "*That's* what we're paying seventy-five dollars a person for?"

Catrice appeared seasick already.

Bud, wearing hip-waders and a T-shirt with the sleeves ripped off, was tearing around the dock, barking orders at his crew as they prepped for travel. He hadn't noticed the group yet, offering a glimpse of the unfiltered version of himself. If any word escaped his lips that wasn't a swear, Drayden didn't hear it. The giant man was sweating profusely and generally looked pissed.

"Dear God." Professor Worth closed his eyes and crossed himself.

"We should let him know we're here," Sidney said, waving. "Hey, Bud!"

He glanced over, before raising his fist at one of his crewmembers, screaming, "What the hell is wrong with you?" After his rhetorical question, he waddled their way.

Professor Worth tightened his tie, stood tall, and struck a serious note. "Let me handle this."

The girls eyed each other, then Sidney crossed her arms and smirked. "Have at it."

"Didn't expect to see you all," Bud said as he shambled up. "If you're here, I assume you have the cash." He lit a cigarette. "I won't ask where you got it." He looked Professor Worth up and down, blowing out a long breath of smoke. "I don't remember saying I'd bring your grandpa."

"He needs to come," Sidney said. "We're sorry we didn't mention him before, but we just found out."

"I said four passengers."

"Mister Bud," the professor said, "I understand you agreed to seventy-five dollars a person for the kids. Not only am I willing to pay a hundred for my own passage, but we'll each pay a hundred dollars, which was your original price. Fair enough?"

Bud chewed on his lip. "Five hundred dollars?"

"Yes, sir," Professor Worth said.

"Don't think I can do it." He puffed on his cigarette.

Catrice moseyed over to the wagon and returned with a sizable sheet of paper, which she carefully unrolled and handed to Bud.

His jaw dropped, first staring at the picture, then at Catrice.

It was a portrait of the hulking captain, made significantly more handsome than the man himself.

"Deal," Bud said quietly, holding out his hand to the professor.

Professor Worth plucked the envelope of cash from his jacket. He slipped out five one hundred-dollar bills and passed the money to Bud, who excitedly counted it and gestured toward the ship. "Come aboard. We'll be leaving in about fifteen minutes. Be careful on the gangway, it's not too sturdy."

The gangway was the most rudimentary ramp imaginable— basically a slick plank of metal, absent any railing, sloping up from the dock to the ship and swaying along with it.

Catrice cradled her stomach. "I think I'm going to be sick."

Charlie leaned into Professor Worth. "Professor," he said loudly and slowly, "we're going to get on the ship now."

Professor Worth gawked at him.

"What are you doing?" Drayden smacked Charlie on the arm. "He's not senile."

Sidney lifted the wagon's handle. "Charlie, can you help me bring this up?"

Both slung their rifles over their shoulders. Sidney pulled it, walking backwards, while Charlie guided it from the rear. He grimaced, rubbing his left leg, clearly not recovered from his injuries. In addition to bobbing with the ship, the gangway wobbled with each step. After they deposited the gear at the top, Charlie seemed to perceive Drayden scrutinizing him. He flexed his bicep and recklessly jogged back down.

Catrice stood at the edge of the dock, taking in the splashing water below with discernable consternation. In her defense, she didn't know how to swim, and their track record on boats was abysmal.

"Hey, c'mon." Drayden took her hand and guided her up the gangway, wincing from her vice grip, as well as Sidney's prying eyes from the ship's deck. Once safely aboard, Catrice breathed a sigh of relief and Drayden verified that Professor Worth was coming up. Suitcase in hand, he was beginning to climb the ramp.

"Nice and easy," Charlie said behind him.

Professor Worth turned and glared. "Knock it off, Charlie. I'm fine."

"It's real shaky." He pressed himself against the professor's back, stabilizing his hips.

Professor Worth swatted his hands away. "Stop it!"

"Here we go, Professor." Charlie bear-hugged him from behind and hoisted him in the air, carrying him up the ramp.

Professor Worth flailed his legs like an angry toddler, trying to bash Charlie with his suitcase. "Put me down, Charlie! Right now!"

"Up we go," Charlie said.

Drayden closed his eyes. "Sweet Jesus, Charlie."

"Goddammit, Charlie! I run...my own...farm!" He battled mightily, but Charlie was too strong, even at less than 100 percent. The professor was still thrashing about when they made it up. "What—are—you—doing? I said put me down this instant!"

Professor Worth was glowing red and fuming as Charlie set him on the deck. He whirled around and stuck a finger in Charlie's face. "Do not do that again! I'm not that old!"

Charlie held up his hands, watching the professor storm off. "You're welcome, jeez." He soft-punched Drayden on the shoulder. "Old people, am I right?"

"Charlie, he's not geriatric. What's wrong with you? Stop treating the guy like some old fuddy duddy."

"What? Sorry."

Scruffy-looking men darted around the ship, tying and untying ropes, occasionally yelling commands. The teens and Professor Worth settled below deck at a round table with mismatched chairs. A single light bulb dangled above, illuminating a restricted compartment made of steel, from which white paint was peeling off in strands.

"This is nice," Charlie said, taking in the room.

Bud poked his oversized head in the doorway. "There's a bathroom around the corner, and life vests in a bin on the top deck. We should be there in about six hours."

The engines roared and the boat vibrated steadily after that. When they cruised out of the harbor, the swaying induced Drayden's nausea. Enduring the undulation on the windowless lower deck made him dizzy and filled his mouth with saliva.

"Anyone else feeling sick?"

Catrice covered her mouth. "Me."

"This is gross," Sidney said. "Let's go up top."

The group made their way to the main deck, needing some time to adjust to the blinding sunlight and blustery wind. Professor Worth explored the bow by himself. Lacking chairs or benches, the others stood against the metal railing, viewing the far-off Massachusetts coastline.

Catrice was green, taking shallow breaths.

"You all right?" Drayden asked.

She nodded quickly. "Better up here."

After they sailed through the narrow canal in Bourne and passed through Buzzard's Bay, they were in open ocean, eventually navigating along the south shore of Long Island.

Drayden noted that this boat motored much faster than the one they took to Boston. It also traveled further away from the coast, leaving little in the way of shoreline detail. Despite its ramshackle condition, the boat seemed to operate reliably.

The moment he completed that thought, it fell silent, as if the engines had turned off. While the ship continued gliding through the water, the formerly constant vibration ceased as well.

"What happened?" Sidney asked.

Drayden palmed the hull. "I don't know. Maybe they're trying to conserve gas. We're moving."

Professor Worth's concern was apparent. "That's not good."

"This isn't normal?" Catrice asked.

He shook his head.

Covered in sweat and smudges of black grease, Bud emerged from the deck level of the pilothouse, an embarrassed look on his face. "Just sit tight. Minor engine trouble, no big deal. Should be fixed in a few minutes." He climbed the stairs to the captain's chambers.

The ship gradually slowed and stopped, bobbing aimlessly in the gentle surf.

"Little help!" Charlie, having decided to tackle the dinghy, was lying on his side, panting, holding his thumb over its plug. It was partially inflated and starting to take shape. "Coach, I need a sub."

"I'll take a turn," Sidney said.

A few minutes became tens of minutes. The silence was broken by a far-off humming, growing steadily louder and higher in pitch.

"What is that?" Drayden asked.

Catrice pointed east, behind them. "Look, it's another boat. We could flag them down to get help."

"Good idea," Drayden said. "You guys do that, and I'm going to let Bud know in case he can signal them somehow."

Catrice and Professor Worth hurried to the opposite side of the ship, since the passing boat was further away from the coast.

In the cockpit at the top level of the pilothouse, Bud was in the puffy captain's seat, holding a tiny box with a coiled cable to his mouth. "Come in, dammit."

"Um, Bud?" Drayden said. "There's a boat approaching to the south of us. We thought they might give us a hand."

"Yeah, no kidding," he said. "They're not answering their radio. Strange." He peered out the window, watching it pass within a hundred feet.

Catrice and Professor Worth were visible below, frantically waving and jumping. The passing ship was a smaller craft, traveling swiftly. Nobody appeared to be outside on deck and it flew by without slowing.

Drayden got a funny feeling in the pit of his stomach as it whizzed past.

As the boat shrank into the horizon, Bud casually saluted it. "Hey, thanks for the help!" he screamed, muttering some curse words. He lumbered downstairs with Drayden behind him. When they hit the main deck, he said, "You stay here," as he continued lower, presumably to the engine room.

"I can't believe they didn't stop," Sidney said, rubbing her lips, while Charlie resumed inflating duties.

Professor Worth furrowed his brow. "Did Bud say what was wrong with the engine?"

"No," Drayden said. "He tried radioing the other boat and they didn't respond."

The professor removed his jacket and draped it over an empty metal drum. "Drayden, let's go to the engine room and see if we can help."

"Do you know anything about boats?"

"No. But I understand engines quite well."

Drayden felt they should leave it to the experts. He was familiar with the old adage of too many cooks in the kitchen. "I'm sure there's an engineer. Let's give them some time to fix it. I bet an engine big enough to power a ship this size is tricky."

Though he noticeably didn't agree, Professor Worth stuffed his hands in his pockets and paced.

Drayden swung by Charlie, who was lying face down with his arms splayed out to the sides and his lips wrapped around the dinghy's plug. His cheeks were puffed out and glistened with sweat from exertion. The dinghy was almost fully inflated.

"You good?"

Charlie replied with a sarcastic thumbs-up.

Minutes later, Professor Worth tapped Drayden on the shoulder and gestured toward the pilothouse. "Come now. We're going to the engine room," he ordered, before Drayden could object.

Multiple metal staircases led down to a heavy steel door, through which the air was thick and sweltering. The engine room was dark, brightened only by red lighting, and packed with jumbo pieces of equipment. After weaving through maze-like passages, they found Bud and another man engaged in a heated debate.

Bud jabbed his finger in the direction of the door when he saw them. "Hey! Get back upstairs."

Drayden raised his hands defensively. "Bud, I think the professor here might be able to help. He's an expert on engines."

He glanced at Professor Worth suspiciously before inviting him to enter. "Be my guest, then. This is Hector, the engineer, sort of." He stepped aside, glowering at Hector, and stood with Drayden to let the professor through.

Drayden had learned about engines from books, but this one was so gargantuan he couldn't even distinguish the different parts.

"Hello, Hector," Professor Worth said. "What's the problem and what have you tried so far?"

Hector tossed a wrench on the floor with a clank. "She's overheating so I shut her down." He counted each potential problem out on his fingers. "Cooling fans are working, thermostat is good, plenty of coolant, radiators are good, radiator caps are secure, air filters are good, gaskets are fine. I don't know."

Professor Worth touched a fat tube. "Forgive me, I've never seen an engine this size before. Where are the radiator hoses?"

Hector scratched his head. "There's a bunch of them." He walked Professor Worth around, highlighting them.

The professor scrunched each, eventually revisiting one. "This hose is a problem. It's crinkly when you squeeze it which means it's worn out. I bet it has a leak." He knelt and examined the floor in the darkness. "There's some coolant puddled here." He swiped his finger along the metal flooring. "Is there any way to pressurize the system without turning the engine on?"

Hector shrugged. "I don't know."

Professor Worth flashed him a look. "What about an overflow hose? And do you have an air pump?"

"There's an overflow, but no pump."

Professor Worth tapped on the hose. "You got tape?"

After Hector handed him a thick roll of black tape, Professor Worth wrapped it over the faulty tube, several layers deep. "If the leak was here, that should fix it until you get home and can replace this hose." He tossed the roll to Bud. "Let's start it up and see if it overheats."

Drayden and Professor Worth returned to the main deck, where Charlie stood proudly over the fully-inflated yellow dinghy. "Voila!" he said with a flourish. "Too bad we're stuck in the middle of the ocean."

"I think Professor Worth fixed the engine," Drayden said, eager to brag on behalf of the modest man.

"Good job, Professor!" Charlie shouted, deliberately enunciating each word.

Professor Worth pressed his hand against his forehead.

The engines started with a roar and, after a tense pause, they began moving.

"Woohoo!" Sidney hollered as she hugged Professor Worth. "Way to go, Professor!"

He blushed. "It was...no big deal," he mumbled, waving his hand.

"See? It's a good thing you came," Drayden said. It occurred to him that Professor Worth bore many similarities to Mr. Kale, his favorite teacher and mentor in the Dorms. Apparently, Drayden had some weird desire for a male advisor. Was that why he was so desperate for the professor to join them?

Professor Worth took in the vista of the Long Island shore. "You don't need to be an expert to help. If a job must be done, son, don't wait around for someone else to do it. Do it yourself."

After six hours, Drayden knew they were getting close. He retrieved his map from the wagon and tried to identify landmarks. Unfortunately, on this voyage, they'd taken a different route from their journey to Boston, which had carried them through Long Island Sound, between the Connecticut and Long Island shores. Since Bud's boat would be continuing south along the East Coast, cutting through Long Island Sound made no sense. Plus, it would have forced them to cruise down the East River, brushing by New America.

Bud approached Professor Worth and presented a hundred-dollar bill. "Here. I want you to have this back. We'd be floating in the middle of the ocean if you hadn't fixed my engine. You never have to pay to be on my boat again."

Professor Worth took the cash, folded it, and jammed it in Bud's T-shirt pocket. "Thank you, Mister Bud, but you keep it. You need to take care of your family, and I appreciate the ride. Instead, I have a request. I'd like to return to Boston on your next trip up. Do you know when that will be?"

Bud scratched his chin. "Uh...yeah, in a week. I can get you the exact day after I grab my calendar. But about a week. Where should I pick you up?"

"Wherever you drop us off."

Bud struck a match, cupping his hand around it, and lit a cigarette. He took a long drag. "You sure? I can get you in New America if you want."

Professor Worth checked with Drayden, who shook his head.

"I don't think that's a good idea. We have no clue what's going on there, or what will happen when we arrive." In the back of his mind, Drayden admitted that they couldn't bring Professor Worth inside New America in any official way. Unlike Boston, the city never allowed people outside the walls to enter. Aeru was allegedly the reason, but now he knew it was also to protect New

America's darkest secrets. They would have to smuggle the professor in somehow, perhaps with Kim Craig's help.

"Suit yourself," Bud said.

Drayden folded his map and shoved it in his pocket. "I don't understand. We were told in Boston that their boats couldn't come near New America without being attacked. Were they wrong?"

Bud puffed on his cigarette. "Probably not. They must not have a trade agreement with New America. My company does. Been there lots of times."

Drayden failed to make out any goods on the deck. "What do you transport?"

"Firearms."

Bud's disclosure threw a monkey wrench into Drayden's already loose plans. Would it make more sense to slide straight into New America? He'd never pondered it in his strategizing because, as far as he knew, it wasn't a possibility. Before finding Eugene's note, he'd wanted to head directly to the Bronx after they were dropped off in Brooklyn. While they were outside the walls, he could have searched for his mother. If he found her alive, he would rescue her, of course. They had a lot to talk about as well. Her affair, which had precipitated his involvement in the Initiation and expedition, was high on the list. She would be able to verify his suspicion that Nathan Locke was responsible for her exile. Assuming he would have a chance to go after Locke at some point, he needed to make sure he had the right guy.

In light of the threats to their families, he'd have to postpone that quest. He needed to get into the city and go right to the Palace to protect Dad and Wes from Eugene. If Bud was able to drop them at the front door, hidden inside a crate or something, they might want to mull it over.

That couldn't work though. With the surveillance, they would eventually be found. He required the capacity to roam freely around the streets, meaning he would need to report in public. As Bureau members who had been promised readmittance when they left on the expedition, the teens *should* be allowed to enter, provided they hadn't contracted Aeru. Even that was far from a sure thing, factoring in the extent of the Bureau's lies. Unable to think of any way to exploit Bud's access, they would have to stick to Drayden's original plan and make landfall in Brooklyn.

According to the map, they were passing Breezy Tip Point at the end of the Rockaways, on the precipice of New York Harbor.

Drayden headed to the bow to get a better look at the upcoming landmarks. A bulky shipping container rested at the front of the deck, so he went around it, coming upon a tight nook that offered an unobstructed view forward.

Catrice was sitting there, her legs tucked up to her chest with her arms wrapped around them.

"Oh, hey," Drayden said. "I didn't know you were up here."

"It's the best place for my seasickness."

"Makes sense." He unfolded his map and flopped beside her, leaning against the warm metal shipping container. "We're close. I just want to see the scenery coming up and figure out where we should be dropped off."

The ship advanced toward a hazy bridge in the distance. According to the map, it was the Verrazano Narrows Bridge, which connected Brooklyn to Staten Island.

"Do you have a plan?" Catrice asked.

"Sort of. Although, without knowing what they'll do when we show up, it's hard to have one. Do you?"

She surveyed the bridge, growing in the foreground. "Not really."

"I found out Bud can drop us off in New America because he delivers weapons there sometimes. But I think we should dock in Brooklyn and go from there."

Catrice sighed. "Drayden... We don't know what's going to happen next. We could be separated. We could be turned away. We could die. I'm not sure if we'll have another chance to talk in private, so I just want to say something. I want you to know how sorry I am about everything. How heartbroken I am over the way things ended up. I miss you and never meant for it to be like this." Tears pooled in her eyes. "It breaks my heart to see you and Sidney together."

There it was, his fear spoken aloud, echoing his own doubts. She hadn't made peace with the current situation at all.

Everything she had claimed after the expedition might have been true. She'd felt their relationship was so solid that she didn't have to constantly reassure him. Spending oodles of time around Eugene was her way of experimenting with sociability, and learning how to make friends was new for her. Due to the abuse at home, she had lived her life in solitude. The only two people she'd ever opened up to—Eugene and Drayden—both burned her. She had been betrayed by every single person she'd ever trusted.

Her continued interest in *him* was the baffling part, considering her beauty and endless potential suitors. Drayden attributed it to her life in a virtual bubble. She hadn't seen the world and simply didn't know who else was out there.

He took her hand. "I'm so sorry. I don't know what else to say other than to tell you how sorry I am, and I wish things on the expedition hadn't gone the way they did. But they did, and now I'm in a confusing place."

She gazed into his eyes. "Don't you still like me?"

His own tears came. "Yes, of course. It's just...it's not that simple."

"It could be."

Out of nowhere, Sidney emerged at the bow, peering at the rusty bridge overhead. "Dray, what bridge is this?" When she caught him cozied up to Catrice, holding her hand, tears in both their eyes, her face went blank. Her countenance bored holes in them both, before she ran off.

Drayden lowered his head. "Shkat."

Catrice snatched her hand away.

What a mess.

Drayden dabbed his eyes. Now they both probably hated him. Regardless of whom he ended up with—if either wanted him, which was questionable—it would never be free and clear. The relationship would always be cloudy, permanently damaged by the storms that preceded it. Even when he tried to do the right thing, he dug his own grave. It was only a matter of time before he'd be too deep to climb out. Maybe he'd be better off alone.

Drayden stood, leaning against the front railing of the ship.

The regal Statue of Liberty rose up far ahead, appearing every bit as majestic as it had been PreCon. Except it was no longer a symbol of freedom, a beacon for optimistic immigrants seeking a new life. Now her raised torch was a cry for help, hoping for someone to restore democracy to an autocratic land.

Drayden took a deep breath to reset his mind and dared to check on Catrice.

She refused his eye contact.

As he plodded back toward Professor Worth and the others, he was stopped by Bud, who touched his shoulder and pointed behind him. Towering above New America, the World Trade Center and its broken spire came into view.

CHAPTER 7

Without knowing the status of the docks in Brooklyn beforehand, it was impossible to plan where to be dropped off. Drayden had informed Bud that they desired their arrival to remain secret, so he preferred to be a little further away from the city rather than risk detection.

The ship had slowed to a crawl, hugging the Brooklyn coast. Governors Island lay ahead to the right, and the Statue of Liberty to the left, with Ellis Island visible behind it. At a minimum, they needed to stop prior to reaching any of those landmarks, because they would be in plain sight of New America otherwise. Brooklyn offered a plethora of docking options at first blush. A closer inspection revealed most were too damaged to use.

The ship veered right, toward one much larger than the rest that hardly resembled a traditional dock. Like a parking lot that extended out into the river, its girth allowed Bud to pull up alongside it, rather than having to turn into it, as a car would in a parking space.

Gathered on the boat's right side with ropes, the crew combed for anything reasonably sturdy to hold a line. The vessel drifted closer, bobbing and swaying, before crashing hard into the rotting wood and crumbling cement with a thud. Bud's cursing was audible all the way at the top of the pilothouse.

A deckhand descended a ladder attached to the ship's hull and jumped onto the dock to secure a rope. A few men followed him, and within minutes, they'd assembled the gangway. Drayden and team gathered their belongings, including the fully-inflated dinghy—suddenly an unnecessary burden—which Charlie lugged.

Bud jogged over from the pilot's tower and lit a cigarette, eyeing the city. "Looks like you got a hike left."

"It's only a couple miles," Drayden said. "Nothing compared to an eighty-mile walk to Boston."

Charlie dropped the dinghy on the deck, climbed into it, and reclined. "I'm so glad I spent an hour blowing this stupid thing up."

"We have to walk for a while," Drayden said. "Maybe we should deflate it."

Charlie's mouth hung open. "What? No. Uh-uh, I don't think so. I'm not blowing this up again."

"You'd rather carry it like that?"

"Yes." Charlie furrowed his brow. "Wait, why do I have to carry it?"

"If you're not strong enough, Charlie," Professor Worth teased, "perhaps the girls should take it instead."

"Not strong enough," Charlie muttered. "Pffft." He vaulted to his feet, using one arm to raise the dinghy above his head. With the other, he snatched the professor's suitcase. "I'll show you not strong enough!" He stormed down the gangway in a huff.

Drayden bit back a chuckle.

Professor Worth dusted off his hands. "Problem solved."

They said their goodbyes to Bud, and Professor Worth arranged to be picked up on the same dock in seven days, on the following Wednesday.

Drayden couldn't help but wonder if they'd be able to honor that commitment. Who knew what was to come?

Sidney and Catrice disembarked the ship without even glancing at him.

He vowed to focus on the task at hand, because it was critical, and it allowed him to ignore the Catrice and Sidney drama. It wasn't clear when he'd have a chance to talk to Sidney privately.

The ship made a sweeping loop through the harbor, black smoke streaming from the smokestack, and motored out to sea.

Map in hand, Drayden took stock of their surroundings.

Like other cities they'd passed through on the expedition, the streets and buildings were in ruins, shrouded in vegetation. They hadn't encountered anything on the scale of Brooklyn, though. Beyond its size, it was downright ghostly. Most of the structures here resembled warehouses, and the vast pier on which they stood was more a shipping graveyard.

Drayden's mouth was sticky and dry, and the faint smell of sewage from New America made his stomach turn. Getting home had been such a singular goal in Boston, he thought he'd feel more pumped about arriving.

For starters, he had to determine where they were. With no street signs around, he studied the coast, registering the shape of each pier, comparing them to those on his map. Only one mirrored theirs, easily identifiable by its breadth.

"This has to be the South Brooklyn Marine Terminal, which means we're in Sunset Park. It's about four miles to Brooklyn Bridge Park, right across from Pier Fifteen in New America. We should set up camp there."

"What should we do after that?" Sidney asked, refusing to look at him.

He hooked his thumb toward the streets. "I have some ideas, but let's talk while we walk."

Charlie dangled the suitcase out to Professor Worth. "Can you hold this for a sec?"

When he took it, Charlie plopped the dinghy on his head and strode away.

The five of them marched off the pier. Catrice lingered in the back, Sidney pulled the wagon, and Drayden hurried to get up front with the map.

"You gotta be kidding me," he said as he found himself, once again, on train tracks.

The rails were embedded into the asphalt, indicating they were old even before the Confluence.

"Are we following the tracks, or are they following us?" Charlie asked. "We can't escape these things. It's om...omin...it's creepy."

"I think the word you're looking for is ominous," Sidney said.

The dark, abandoned warehouses were so spooky it wouldn't have been a surprise to see zombies pouring out of them. Unlike New America, which had been cleared of vehicles soon after the Confluence, the Brooklyn streets were lined with rusted shells of cars and buses. Fully grown trees and thick grasses had sprouted through the asphalt in many places, making the hike just as difficult as it had been on the expedition. An elevated highway rose above the roads ahead, and a ramp before them appeared to lead to it.

"Guys, hold up," Drayden said. "I think we're gonna get on the highway here. I believe this ramp puts us on I-278, the Brooklyn-Queens Expressway. We can take it the whole way."

Catrice assessed the highway in both directions. "If any parts have collapsed, we'll be trapped up there."

"Good thinking," Professor Worth said. "But these streets are virtually impassable. Since the highway is elevated, it won't have all this bramble. Even if we have to backtrack an exit or two, I think it will be faster."

It turned out he was right. Mostly. They had to hug the edge of the highway, which was full of cars. Evidently an epic traffic jam had occurred at one time and never cleared up before life ceased to exist here. But it was, indeed, clear of overgrowth.

Drayden took a turn hauling the wagon, taking in the streets below, flush with townhouses, meager storefronts, and grand apartment buildings. As expected, they were abandoned, though it wouldn't have been out of the question to spot an indigent community of people given the scattered life they'd observed on the expedition.

Naturally, his thoughts gravitated to his mother. Where were all the exiles? Were they up in the Bronx, where they'd been banished? Encountering survivors in Massachusetts didn't automatically imply New America's exiles had endured. The villagers they'd seen may have been immune to Aeru. If those from New America weren't, they could have perished, as the city's residents had always suspected. It was a very real possibility his mother had died from it.

"Drayden," Professor Worth said, "I understand New America does not allow outsiders to enter. Have you thought about how we're going to get in?"

He *had* thought about it, but as with any problem that didn't have an easy solution, he figured he would worry about it later rather than do the hard thinking. Except "later" was now. They needed a plan, pronto.

"We know the walls are guarded. I'm pretty sure we could pinpoint some spots to crawl over in remote parts of the city. But I don't think that's the right way to do this. We need to be able to move around the streets openly to find our families. I have to locate Kim. The whole place is surveilled, so there's no way we would stay underground. I think we should enter legally, and then finagle a way to get you in."

"In that case," Professor Worth said, "I suggest two of you enter and two hang behind. For insurance, since you don't know what they're going to do."

"I'll go," Sidney blurted.

Drayden had to admit he was petrified. Even though he ultimately understood what bravery was all about during the Initiation, his default state continued to be scared. If the Bureau hadn't planned on their return, it was anyone's guess how they'd react when the teens suddenly turned up on New America's doorstep like uninvited guests. The possibilities were skewed sharply negative. Execution was much more likely than a homecoming party.

Acknowledging his fear was also part of what he had learned. Being scared was normal. Who wouldn't be? While Sidney may not have seemed frightened, she'd revealed that her love for her sister pushed her to do what was necessary in spite of her own dread.

"Me too," he said. "I have to go. Nobody else knows Kim. But I think Charlie should come with me instead."

Sidney threw eye daggers his way. "That better not be because I'm a girl."

Drayden couldn't deny that his instinct *was* to protect Sidney and Catrice. He cared deeply for them both. That they were girls was incidental. But his love for Sidney could put him in a compromising position. What if the Bureau used the threat of harm against her to break him? Although Charlie was his best friend, he wouldn't feel the same degree of responsibility to defend him, and if he was being honest, the fact that he was a boy may have been a factor. Sidney being pissed at him right now was a problem too. He wanted a partner who didn't currently hate him.

"No, Sid. If we were going to choose the two baddest, it would be you and Charlie. I know you're as tough as Charlie, if not tougher. But I can't be as tough with you as I could with him, if that makes any sense. Like, if they pit us against each other, or tell me they're going to hurt you. I would crack and sing like a canary. Charlie? Not so much. It's more about me than you."

She didn't look convinced.

Charlie was dripping sweat, the dinghy balanced on his head. "I'll go if I don't have to carry this cargo ship on my back anymore."

"There's an argument that Sidney should do it," Professor Worth said. "This male-dominated Bureau of yours may be less likely to harm a teenage girl. However, Sidney, if your priority is making sure you can take care of your sister, I would let Charlie go. Let's not sugarcoat it. This is a high-risk trip."

"Sweet, thanks," Charlie said.

Drayden consulted his map since they'd been on the highway for a while and he was feeling lost. "In about half a mile we get off I-278 and walk on this road beside it called Furman Street."

"Drayden," Catrice said, "you're going to take one of the batteries, right?"

"Yeah, that was a good idea. Prove we have batteries without showing how many."

"How do we get over there?" Charlie asked. "Walk across a bridge?"

"The bridges down here were blown up during the Confluence," Sidney said.

Drayden pointed at the dinghy. "We're taking that."

"Fine, but you're rowing, bro. I'm gonna enjoy the delightful ride."

They took Exit Twenty-Seven which put them on Furman Street, hiking alongside the imposing cement wall that bordered the highway. Combined with the thick foliage, the road approximated a cool, dark, medieval forest. A persistent breeze from the East River a block to their left carried the nauseating sewage smell, a consequence of New America's human waste.

"I see the Brooklyn Bridge!" Sidney shouted, pinching her nose shut. "Or what's left of it."

"That's where we're going," Drayden said.

They landed at an expansive intersection where several major roads met, bordered by endless storefronts and restaurants. Largely bereft of buildings, the waterfront offered an unimpeded view of New America's dazzling skyline. The lone exception was a two-story white house with reddish shingles on the roof and a miniature tower. Its sign read "Brooklyn Ice Cream Factory."

Drayden inspected the building. "I think we found our base camp."

Inside, the place was frozen in time, which, being an ice cream shop, he found appropriate. It was cozy, with cream-colored walls and old-fashioned equipment. A laminated white menu dangled from the ceiling offering flavors like strawberry and butter pecan. Drayden read them all, imagining each taste. Everything was covered in dust and cobwebs, the otherwise perfectly preserved tables and chairs eagerly awaiting patrons.

Drayden wiped off a seat and plunked down. "Let's have a quick snack and then it's go time."

Drayden wished the incident with Catrice and Sidney hadn't happened, because he needed their reassurance right now. Ordinarily, Sidney's belief in him was unwavering. Whenever he succumbed to self-doubt, she was always there to bolster him. His achievements in the Initiation and expedition notwithstanding, he had a feeling he wasn't up to the challenge and desperately craved their support, which didn't appear to be forthcoming this time.

Sidney halfheartedly hugged him, all but avoiding physical contact. Her body language spoke volumes. After a nearly identical hug from Catrice, he tried to refocus on the job at hand.

"Remember, if you don't see us in twenty-four hours, something's wrong. You'll have to go to Plan B."

"You guys are going to make it back," Sidney stated. Her hands clasped together, she regarded Drayden with pleading eyes. "Please, I'm begging you, make sure my sister is all right."

He nodded. "My first order of business is our families. If we can, we'll go right to them and try to move them somewhere safe."

Mentioning that the Guardians may have beaten them here would have caused unnecessary anguish, but that didn't mean it wasn't true. If Eugene had decided to fulfill his threat as soon as they'd arrived...well, Drayden couldn't even complete the thought. It was too agonizing.

He rubbed his hands along his body to make sure he was free of weapons, which would certainly be confiscated by the Bureau. To protect the confidentiality of the addresses in Kim's letter, he'd memorized them. He'd stuffed his Yankees hat in the wagon to ensure he didn't lose it. Rather than bring the Boston mayor's official letter to Holst, he was carrying a blank sheet of Boston letterhead. He'd eventually be questioned by the Bureau, and clearly couldn't have a letter from the mayor if he was going play dumb about New America's secrets. Without a doubt, the Bureau would know she'd have revealed the truth about their city. That letter was basically useless now.

Charlie and Sidney loaded one of the deep-cycle batteries into the center of the dinghy, which rested on the water's edge. The white flag for their hopefully peaceful arrival was already inside, plus rope to tether the dinghy to the dock.

Charlie flung a pebble into the murky river. "What happens if we fall in that water?"

"With the amount of bacteria in there," Professor Worth said, "you would most likely get sick and die."

Charlie pumped a fist. "Awesome."

Drayden picked up a paddle and hopped into the front of the dinghy. Charlie pushed it a few feet into the water and carefully climbed into the rear. Sidney gave it a gentle boost and they floated out into the river.

Charlie paddled on the left side, having relented about sitting back and enjoying the ride. Drayden, working on the right, noticed that his paddle fully disappeared in the brown sludge, exhibiting the true filth of the water. Both boys were weaker than normal, hampered by their nagging injuries from the grenade.

The late afternoon sun shone in their eyes, creating silhouettes out of the skyscrapers looming ahead. The external serenity of the city belied the turmoil inside its walls.

Drayden's mind was swirling, and he felt desperately unprepared for whatever might happen next, which he suspected would not be a straight shot to their families' apartments. The leverage he hoped the battery afforded them could prove meaningless. Boston's former mayor, Jason McCarthy, had cautioned that the Bureau's claims about failing power storage, and the resulting inability to generate enough power for food and water, may have been false propaganda. The Bureau might have spread it to conceal another reason why they were short on food, such as New America's isolation due to trade disputes. Or it was a blatant lie, and they were needlessly exiling people from the Dorms for maximum cruelty.

If the power issue was a ruse, their bargaining chip was worthless, their leverage vaporized. The Bureau would hold all the cards and the boys would be at their mercy.

That worst-case scenario wasn't the only contingency causing him stress, because at least it was out of his control. A potential interrogation by the Bureau, requiring him to think on his feet and save them, was equally worrisome. He couldn't prepare much in advance, since he had no clue what the Bureau knew about the expedition. If Eugene and crew had gotten back first, they would have spun some false tale about the journey, blaming Drayden and his friends for its failure. Knowing the truth about New America was extremely dangerous, and the Bureau might conclude the teens had learned New America's dirty secrets in Boston—ones they would never allow to get out.

Drayden stopped paddling momentarily. "Charlie, I don't know what's going to happen. But if we're taken in, let me do the talking, okay?"

"Afraid I'm gonna say something stupid?"

"No, chotch. I trust you. I may have to lie to them about what we know though, and I don't want them to catch us contradicting ourselves."

"Yeah, I would totally blow that. I'll keep my trap shut."

No guards were visible at the top of the wall, but somebody could have been covertly watching. About three-quarters of the way across the river, Drayden set his paddle inside the dinghy and picked up the white flag, waving it in a sweeping figure eight.

The twenty-five-foot tall cement barricade surrounding the city grew larger and larger as they neared the shore. Still, no Guardians were in sight.

Drayden would almost feel safer if they *were* being watched, so they didn't surprise anyone on the dock, leading to knee-jerk shots being fired. Harris von Brooks had mentioned that the expedition was secret, so the average Palace Guardian would not be expecting two teens to rock up to the shore in a rubber boat.

They were ten feet from the tip of Pier Fifteen. Perhaps they would make it without being detected after all.

Drayden tentatively rose up on his knees and hugged a mucky piling to stop them. Charlie tied the rope around it and secured the other end to the dinghy. The dock was relatively high off the water, presenting a minor challenge.

Drayden examined the pier's shadowy underside. "So how do we get out of the dinghy?"

"I assumed you knew," Charlie said.

He cursed under his breath. So many damn things to worry about, and he hadn't even considered how they would access the dock, lugging the hefty battery.

"Dray, you hold us steady, make sure we don't tip over. I'm gonna shimmy up the piling. Hand me the battery and I'll drop it up top. You'll have to scoot up after me."

The dinghy wobbling precariously, Charlie wrapped his arms and legs around the slippery wooden piling, like he was scaling a coconut tree. He extended a hand to Drayden. "Give it to me," he grunted. After Drayden passed the battery over, Charlie hoisted it onto the dock and climbed the rest of the way. "Ugh, my legs," he groaned.

Drayden followed his lead, astonished at how easy Charlie had made it look. The piling was cold, wet, and slick with algae. Each movement threatened splinters, but he struggled up and lifted himself onto the pier, battling through the same leg pain Charlie had groused about.

Charlie smeared brown and green sludge from his hands onto his pants. "What now?"

"Freeze! Get on the ground!" someone shouted from the top of the wall.

About ten Guardians aimed rifles at them, all screaming different orders. "On the ground!"—"I said get down!"—"Hands behind your backs!"—"Down down down!"

Charlie and Drayden promptly complied, lying on their stomachs facing the gate, hands clasped behind them.

So much for getting in undetected.

After the soldiers stopped yelling, Drayden felt the need to identify himself. "Guardians, we are friendly!" he hollered. "We are Bureau members, sent outside the walls by Premier Holst and Harris von Brooks!"

"Quiet!" one retorted. "Shut your mouth or you're both dead!"

The boys remained motionless for what felt like hours.

"What do we do?" Charlie whispered.

"Just do what we're told for now. They haven't killed us, and that's a good sign."

The gate opened to two people in glaring yellow protective suits, one training a rifle on them.

"Do not move until you are instructed, do you understand me? I'll blow your freaking brains out."

"Yes, sir," Drayden said.

"Identify yourselves," the Guardian ordered.

"I'm Drayden Coulson and this is Charlie Arnold. We're the kids who passed the Initiation. We were sent outside the walls by Premier Holst on a secret mission, and...well, we're back."

"What's in the black box? Is that a bomb?"

"No, sir. It's a special battery for the failing windmills. It's what we were sent out to get. I would not touch it if I were you, because if you damage it, you'll have to answer to Premier Holst." Drayden could not let these guys confiscate his only bargaining chip.

"Um," a quivering voice said, "can you each extend your left arm, with your palm facing up? I'm a medic, and I'm going to take a blood sample. You'll feel a quick pinch and it'll be over in seconds."

After the medic drew their blood, the Guardian expeditiously patted them down for weapons.

"You two stay right there. You move, you get shot."

Drayden gritted his teeth. "Officer, we're on a dock, surrounded by armed soldiers. We can't go anywhere. Can't we sit? This is really uncomfortable."

The guard laughed. "You think I care? You'll stay like that until I say otherwise. You're lucky we didn't shoot you already."

The medic and Guardian retreated behind the gate, which subsequently closed. After thirty minutes or so, Drayden groaned. The dock was wet, rough, and chilly on his face. An unrelenting itch surfaced on his leg and he couldn't scratch it without making a movement.

"Dray," Charlie whispered, "I have to pee."

"What, now? Why didn't you go before we left?"

"I forgot. I chugged all that water."

"You may have to go in your pants, dude."

"I can't go in—we didn't bring extra clothes. I'll be wearing pee pants forever after that."

"Then hold it, I don't know. Charlie, we got bigger concerns, man."

"This feels big at the moment," he mumbled.

They waited and waited. It felt like an eternity.

"It's happening!" Charlie whispered forcefully. "Oh—Oh God. Ahhhh. It's so horrible and yet wonderful at the same time," he said as he wet himself. "Why does this feel so good?"

Drayden closed his eyes. "Please stop talking about it, for crying out loud."

"Hey, can you not tell the girls I pissed myself?"

"I gotta be honest with you, Charlie. I'm going to have a real hard time not telling them."

A gaggle of Guardians poured through the gate and surrounded them. "On your feet, slowly," one ordered.

When Drayden stood, he glanced at Charlie's pants.

They were sopping urine, all over both legs.

A Guardian clutched Charlie by the shoulder, eyeing him up and down. "What the... Did you piss yourself, kid?"

Charlie blushed. "I...I—"

"Hey, Watkins!" the snickering Guardian yelled to his comrade. "You take this guy."

A look of disgust on his face, the Watkins fellow beheld Charlie's pants. He peered into Charlie's eyes and shook his head. "You done, or we need to find another bathroom?"

Charlie was expressionless. "I'm good," he said in a monotone voice.

"Let's go then, piss boy." The Guardian shoved him forward.

Two others carefully lifted the battery and followed the group.

Being pushed along himself, Drayden peeked behind. "Be very careful with that."

Someone slapped him in the back of the head. "Shut up. Move it."

The squad of Guardians escorted them into the city and onto Maiden Lane. Drayden caught a glimpse of their apartment building at 75 Wall Street. Were his father and brother inside? He hoped they were alive.

Being admitted into New America pointed to clean blood tests, so that was a minor positive. When frisking him and Charlie, the Guardians hadn't addressed their bulletproof vests. Drayden bet they didn't know what they were. He hadn't recalled ever seeing one during their Guardian training before the expedition. The Bureau would absolutely take them if they understood their value.

"Where are you taking us?" Drayden asked.

Somebody smacked him in the back of head again. "Quiet."

In truth, he didn't need to ask. He knew where they were going, and it was what he'd feared most.

They stopped directly in front of the golden Bureau headquarters on William Street, in the old Federal Reserve Bank. Even though it was early evening, the area was teeming with Palace residents, who were sneering at them and whispering.

Once inside the building, they were whisked into an elevator and down a long, familiar corridor. Without knocking, a mammoth Guardian manning the door opened it.

Waiting inside was a stern-looking Premier Eli Holst, who was holding something by his side that made Drayden shudder: a gun.

CHAPTER 8

The conference table was smaller than Drayden expected, given the grandiosity of everything else in Holst's office. It was situated in a room off to the side, sized for about ten chairs. He and Charlie sat on one end, with Holst at the other, flanked by Harris von Brooks and a man they hadn't met.

No words were exchanged when they'd entered; no pleasantries, no "nice to have you back," no smiles. The boys were ushered impetuously to the dark wood table. Thankfully, the Guardians had brought the deep-cycle battery along, which was just outside the room.

The three Bureau members stared, as if daring them to endure the tense silence without speaking first. Holst had set his pistol in front of him on the table, pointed at the frightened teens.

There was no chance Drayden would start this conversation. Each side had no idea what the other knew. This was a poker game, and he sure as hell wasn't going to show his hand.

Finally, Holst broke the stalemate. "Before we begin," he said, "and since this is such an important meeting, I've invited my chief of staff, Harris von Brooks, whom you know, to sit in."

Drayden wished he could punch the horse-faced man in the mouth, sitting there with his trademark black eye patch and his nose in the air. He'd lied about everything and set them up to die on the expedition.

"On my left," Holst continued, "is senior advisor Robert Zane."

Robert Zane...Robert Zane...

Drayden sought to keep his face from moving, to project no reaction to the name he recognized from Kim Craig. Robert Zane was the most senior figure in the insurgency, as well as the man tapped to take over for Premier Holst if it succeeded. Drayden had shared his name with the other teens, and he prayed Charlie either forgot it or was shrewd enough not to react either.

Perhaps Robert Zane would protect them. If Holst were going to do something malicious, Zane might be a dissenting voice, even putting a stop to it. Drayden hoped. He tried to get a read on the Zane fellow, but the man revealed nothing.

He was eccentric looking, with longish gray hair that puffed out to the sides, almost like a woman would wear it. Or a mad scientist. Thinking of men who resembled women and vice-versa, Drayden wondered if Kim Craig had seen them enter the city. She could have watched the whole episode on the surveillance cameras. She could be monitoring them right now, or ideally, plotting their rescue.

Holst tilted his head. "Tell us what happened on the expedition," he said, his tone the perfect blend of request and demand.

Sweat trickled down Drayden's cheeks. He was going to have to lie, and once you took that dicey path, it was easy to become mired in inconsistencies. One slip of the tongue and they were goners. As the long-time ruler of New America, Holst was a professional liar himself, and presumably an expert at sniffing it out.

Drayden cleared his throat. "Premier Holst, have the Guardians made it home?"

"We will be asking the questions," von Brooks snapped.

Drayden steeled himself. "Well, we—"

"Stop." Holst held up his hand. "I want him to tell it." He pointed at Charlie.

Oh shkat. No no no.

Two seconds in and he'd already been outsmarted, his whole plan blown to shreds. He needed to find a way to take the reins back immediately.

Charlie was shaking. "Um, I pretty much slept through the whole thing. I don't tell a good story either."

Drayden slammed his fist on the table, startling Robert Zane. "Goddammit! The Guardians tried to kill us! They tried to *kill* us, and you're playing games about who's telling the story? You sent us on a mission with murderers. You made *me* the leader of this mission," he said, jabbing his finger into his chest, "or so I thought, so I'm going to be just that. And no offense, but Charlie is an idiot. Sorry, Charlie." He would beg his friend to forgive him later.

Charlie nodded. "He's got a point there."

"Let me tell you what happened on your damn expedition," Drayden railed, as indignant as possible, before they had a chance to object. He recounted how the Guardians had immediately asserted authority, refusing his orders, even when they saw a boy on the Connecticut shore. Fuming about it, he let them know how Captain Lindrick had rejected his call to pull ashore during a storm, and they sank, eighty miles from Boston.

That brought Drayden to a juncture where he'd have to veer from the truth. If he was going to successfully convince them he wasn't aware of New America's secrets—its knowledge of existing colonies, its ongoing trade with them, and its place as the drug-producing capital of the world—he would need to inform them of "discoveries" they already knew, and act surprised about it all.

"There is life out there. We are not alone in New America. We started seeing camps of survivors throughout Massachusetts. Some friendly, some not, but they were generally living in squalor. We don't know how they survived Aeru, and they didn't either. The Guardians wanted to steal everyone's food, and we resisted. Eventually, we had a confrontation and split up, taking Corporal Eugene Austin with us. We know now that the Guardians were following us the whole way to Boston, and Corporal Austin was on their side all along. They attacked us in our campsite, stole our gear. They slaughtered an entire *village* of people. We defeated them near Boston, but left them alive, despite them trying to kill us. They claimed we didn't know the true purpose of the mission, and unfortunately, we never found out what they meant. We're just a group of teenagers. Nobody in Boston took us seriously, and the government denied us a meeting. We tried over and over." His first significant lie.

When Drayden slid his blank Boston letterhead across the desk, the three leaders barely took notice. "We did get proof we made it by swiping this paper from a government office. Since they let people come and go in Boston, we were able to find a windmill farm. You saw the deep-cycle battery we have. So, while we didn't get direct help, we delivered something."

Drayden tried his best to appear shocked, relaying information the premier obviously knew. "Premier Holst, not only are there people in Boston, but so much commerce was taking place. Ships coming and trading goods. I think an option for New America is to seek help, or food, from some of these other colonies out there."

Holst remained stone-faced.

"One last thing. The Guardians should not be readmitted into New America. Those are bad dudes. They killed a lot of innocent civilians, and our whole mission."

All things considered, Drayden was satisfied with his delivery, and portrayal, of the events.

Harris von Brooks leaned back in his chair and crossed his arms. Robert Zane dubiously shook his head.

What the heck? He's supposed to be on our side.

Holst picked up the gun. "Drayden." He fiddled with the weapon. "I don't think you're telling me the truth."

Adrenaline surged through Drayden's veins. Had he contradicted himself? What did Holst know?

The premier wandered to a window and peered outside, his hands behind him, one clasping the gun. "Tell me something." He gazed at Drayden. "Where are the girls?"

Drayden swallowed hard, his throat dry and scratchy. If he was honest—that the teens were unsure what would happen when they reentered New America—it would imply they had a reason to fear the Bureau. If they hadn't uncovered the truth, why would they have any qualms at all? He needed an answer.

"Premier Holst, I asked you at the start if the Guardians made it back yet. That's why the girls aren't with us. We were afraid that they would beat us here and lie about the expedition, and you would believe them over us. Charlie and I came in first to make sure you guys knew the truth. We had to know we'd be safe."

Drayden held the trump card in his pocket, but wouldn't play it until it was desperately needed. If they were in imminent danger, he would claim that he possessed enough batteries to save New America.

Holst fake smiled. "Oh, come now, this is your home," he said with some theatrics. "You would never be harmed in your own home, would you?" He flashed a look of disappointment and raised a finger. "But you are right that we need to find out the truth. From time to time, we must give people *encouragement* to be honest. I'm afraid we're going to have to do that here." He sauntered behind the boys and opened the conference room door.

A scrawny older man in thick glasses and a lab coat entered the room carrying a black briefcase. He dropped it on the table and unbolted it, revealing an assortment of...tools? He removed a hammer and set it aside.

Drayden went full panic mode, realizing what Holst was insinuating.

The man gripped a blowtorch and fired it up, the searing blue flame extending several inches along with a sound like blowing wind.

Drayden could hear his heartbeat in his ears.

Why wasn't Robert Zane doing something?

Holst retook his seat at the head of the table and leaned forward in his chair. Beads of sweat on his nose glistened from the light overhead. "You see, gentlemen, we have a little problem." His eyes flicked outside the conference room.

The door reopened.

Drayden practically fell out of his seat.

Captain Lindrick, having lost a great deal of weight, hobbled over to Premier Holst with the help of a cane. His left foot was gone, replaced by a peg leg.

They were back.

My family. Dear God, no.

Drayden tried to compose himself but he was starting to hyperventilate.

The meeting now spiraling out of control, Lindrick glowered at Drayden and Charlie. His presence clarified the "problem." His expression suggested he wanted more than death from them. He wanted them to suffer.

Holst's eyes narrowed. "Your job," he bellowed, "was to reach Boston with the Guardians' help, not to make poor decisions that led to your boat sinking, and then attacking them. None of the evidence supports your version of events. Captain Lindrick and his team do not miss when they shoot, yet you're in perfect health. I cannot say the same about him. And I don't think you're being honest about what you learned in Boston. So, let's see what you actually know."

The blowtorch man slowly approached, a twisted grin on his face.

Drayden was quaking, transfixed by the hot dagger of fire, anticipating the horror of it roasting his flesh.

Charlie shoved back in his chair. "No."

Holst motioned for someone outside the conference room, and seconds later, a Guardian barreled through the door to block them inside.

Captain Lindrick smugly crossed his arms. "What's the problem, Private Arnold?" he asked Charlie. "Don't worry. This won't hurt nearly as much as amputating your own foot with a hunting knife, without anesthesia."

If Drayden were waiting for the right moment to play his ace, this was it. He prayed it would work. He tried his best to exude confidence, despite his trembling. "You want the truth? Because there *is* something I didn't tell you."

Holst raised his hand to the blowtorch guy, who stopped short.

Drayden glared at the premier. "If you singe a single hair on my body, this city is finished. That's the truth. I have *fifteen* deep-cycle batteries. Yeah, you heard that right. Fifteen. Enough to power the Meadow and the Palace for the next twenty-five years. Did you really think we were so stupid as to only get one? Have you ever seen a windmill farm with only one windmill? We got them all. They're safely hidden with the girls, who are under strict instructions to destroy them if we don't return unharmed within twenty-four hours."

Holst stared back. His face twitched.

Robert Zane pointed at the evil doctor. "Turn that off."

Drayden internally breathed a huge sigh of relief, although he continued to mean mug Holst, since he needed him to bite on the batteries. If he had been disingenuous about their necessity all along, it was game over for the boys.

Holst glanced at Zane, before turning his attention to Drayden. He rubbed his chin.

Von Brooks leaned into the premier. "I'm sure we can locate the batteries inside twenty-four hours. *If* he's even telling the truth. No reason to stop this interrogation."

Drayden snickered. "Is that right? Do you have any idea how big Queens is?"

Von Brooks feigned a smile. "Nice try. So now we know they're not in Queens. Clearly, this young man lies. I doubt they have these batteries at all."

"I'm telling the truth. You won't find other windmill farms that haven't been looted. Batteries are a hot commodity in the outside world. Boston was grappling with power storage too, according to people there. We happened to go through a remote part of Massachusetts on the way to Boston and got lucky. We knew exactly where to go. Captain Lindrick may have even seen the same windmill farm."

Lindrick did not respond, hovering stoically beside his dear leader. He didn't deny it.

Holst set down his gun. "You have twenty-four hours to get me the rest of those batteries. After that, all bets are off. The continuation of this interrogation will just be the start. Do I make myself clear?"

"I need assurances," Drayden said. "Charlie, Catrice, Sidney, and I are not to be harmed. Our families either. Captain Lindrick's team threatened them when we were in Boston." He scowled at Lindrick. "I want some time here in the Palace to visit our relatives. As soon as we're ready to retrieve the batteries, we'll show up at the Pier Fifteen gate. We are not to be followed, because the girls will be watching and will destroy the batteries unless we are seen coming alone. Once our promise is fulfilled, I have to know we'll be safe."

"I think we could use him in senior management afterwards," Robert Zane muttered.

Holst appeared vaguely amused. "Fine, fine. Do not speak a word about the expedition to anyone. I'll know if you do. But you will have accomplished your mission once I have my batteries. You'll be perfectly safe here, as will your families." He smirked. "Provided, of course, they haven't been harmed already."

Drayden and Charlie sprinted down William Street, heading for Wall Street, hoping Holst was just trying to taunt them by hinting that their families had been victimized. Drayden was disgusted that the government of his own city would be so diabolical, prone to malice at every opportunity. Shouldn't leaders be principled role models? Was that too much to ask?

"Dray," Charlie said between heavy breaths, "how are we going to get—"

"Stop!" Drayden shouted, trying to cover Charlie's mouth but accidentally slapping him in the jaw instead.

"Ow!"

"Sorry, sorry. My bad." He touched his index finger to his lips and mouthed "Shhh," pointing up at the sky to remind him of the hidden cameras and microphones. Drayden wasn't sure if Charlie understood, but he damn well couldn't allow him to say out loud that they were not, in fact, in possession of fifteen batteries. Later, he would explain that he never had any intention of fulfilling his promise. The one battery and the claims of more were just to get them inside the walls. They would never see Holst again, as far as he was concerned.

They turned left on Wall Street, two short blocks from their apartment building. It was dusk, the evening air humid but cool. Scattered groups of people traipsing about the Palace thinned out the further they went, and by the time they crossed Pearl Street, nobody was around.

Drayden yanked open the door and darted into the spartan lobby, doubling over. "I don't suppose your parents mentioned which apartment they were in, did they?" Since their families had moved to the Palace on the day the teens left for the expedition, their exact location was unknown, beyond the building itself.

Charlie coughed. "No. Man, how are we gonna find them? This building is gigantic."

Drayden presumed they could go floor to floor, knocking on doors. If the Guardians had gotten to them, it would be pointless. Still, absent other ideas, it was the best option available.

"I think we'll have to check each floor. Wouldn't the Bureau put them near us? Maybe not, because they're horrible. Let's start on our floor."

The boys rode the elevator up to fifteen. The opening doors gave way to the bland, cream-colored hallway they knew quite well.

"Wesley! Dad! It's Drayden!"

"Hey, Pop!" Charlie called out. "Mama?"

Strangers poked their heads into the hallway, immediately retreating.

Charlie rested his hands on his hips. Numerous scabs had peeled away, the exposed skin an angry pink. "Keep going down?"

"Yeah. I mean, there's only two floors above this one, but I seriously doubt they gave our families killer apartments with great views. Let's try fourteen."

After striking out there, they proceeded to the twelfth floor.

"Wes! Wesley, it's Dray! Dad!" He jogged along, knocking on each door, fearing those parting words from Holst weren't an idle threat after all. Nor was Eugene's note. Since when were either of them known to joke around or be coy?

Provided they haven't been harmed already.

God, he wished he could have strangled Holst right then and there.

A door creaked opened behind him.

"Dray? Holy shkat! Drayden!" Wesley ran toward him.

Drayden clutched his brother, melting into his arms. He let out a whimper, the weight of the past few days and weeks revealing its damage. So much pressure, so much torment. He'd made it in time. Who knew what would come to pass next, but for now, he'd found his family safe and sound.

Charlie was hugging his parents a few doors over. Although he was fine, they were crying hysterically.

"Drayden!" Standing in the doorway, his father looked like he'd seen a ghost. "You're alive. Thank goodness." He embraced his son, baring the affection Drayden had been craving his whole life. "What happened? Where have you been? We were so worried, and the Bureau wouldn't tell us anything."

Drayden paused, conceding the authenticity of his father's warmth. "I'll explain everything, but first we need to find the Fowlers. Sidney's family. Do you know where they are?"

Wesley hooked his thumb down the hall. "Yeah, they're in 1208. Nice old people, cute little girl."

Thank God.

"Wes, go grab them. Have them come to your apartment, right now, it's urgent. Let them know Sidney is fine, and just outside the city." He jogged over to Charlie. "Come to my brother's apartment. Hey, Mister and Missus Arnold. Sorry for being so abrupt, but we don't have much time."

Charlie's father tapped his son's chest. "Your buddy's busier than a one-armed trombone player."

Charlie pointed at his dad. "See? That's where I get it from."

Joining everyone in his family's apartment, Drayden wondered whether Kim Craig was tracking his movement, assuming she'd witnessed the ruckus he and Charlie caused at Pier Fifteen. One alternative would be to wait here for a signal from her.

With Drayden's family, the Arnolds, Sidney's grandparents, and her sister Nora spread out across from him, Drayden prepared to write notes on a large pad of paper. If the apartment was bugged, he surely couldn't blab their story out loud.

Appreciating that the content would at best confuse her, and at worst terrify her, Drayden asked Sidney's grandmother to take Nora into the kitchen. None of this was appropriate for an eight-year-old.

His notes read:

> *The Guardians betrayed us on the expedition. We found a city full of people in Boston.*
>
> *There are people all over the world. The Bureau has deceived us.*
>
> *New America trades goods with other colonies. Our main export is drugs.*

That line drew gasps from the group.

> *The Bureau is exiling Dorm residents to shrink the population because power is failing here.*
>
> *You are all in danger. The Guardians made a direct threat against you.*
>
> *We've bought 24 hours to get you moved somewhere safe. I don't know where yet.*

Where was Kim, dammit? He needed help.

> *I have someone in the Bureau who may help us. Waiting to see.*

Drayden stood. "Hey, Nora can come back. We're going to wait here for, like, half an hour."

While they lingered, Charlie regaled the families with some of the more innocuous tales from the expedition: the boat sinking, the camps of people, the raging river they'd crossed, the wolves and bears.

Kim.

Drayden was stunned it hadn't occurred to him before. How in the world could he reconnect with Kim Craig if she didn't seek him out? He couldn't exactly stroll up to her office at Ninety Trinity Place. Either the Bureau would have someone tracking him, or they'd review the surveillance tapes of his movement. He would blow Kim's cover.

He guessed he could try the first address on Kim's letter: Forty Rector Street. And what, leave their families in the apartment, trusting the Bureau not to hurt them? If anything happened to him while he was searching for her, they were doomed. Because even if Holst kept his word about not harming them for twenty-four hours, he would absolutely make their families pay when Drayden failed to deliver the batteries.

After thirty minutes, he couldn't wait any longer and had another idea. The first time he'd met Kim, she took him to a location off the grid. She'd said it was one of the only places not surveilled besides the Meadow.

"Everybody, gather around," he said. "We're going to go on a walk." He snatched up the pad of paper and wrote:

> *You can't take anything with you. It would look suspicious.*
> *It's not far, just an alley off Broadway. There's no surveillance there.*

Charlie cringed. "Didn't you say the Bureau might have somebody following us?" he whispered.

Dammit, he was right. While the alley was a perfect spot, how could they get there without being followed? He rubbed his chin.

A lightbulb went off as he recalled the way they'd defeated the Guardians in the swamp at the end of the expedition. He wrote on his pad:

Question for all the men here. Does everyone have imitation jeans and hooded sweatshirts?

Drayden left the apartment building alone from the Water Street side, casually jaunting north—opposite the way he needed to go. Like the other males, he was wearing imitation blue jeans and a dark hooded sweatshirt, with the hood up. Each of them was at least six feet tall, with the exception of Charlie's father.

It wasn't as if it made them all identical. Charlie and Wesley were stocky, or the polar opposite of Drayden and his father. Sidney's grandfather was visibly an old man, irrespective of how he was dressed. Drayden didn't think it mattered much. The whole point was to obfuscate.

Charlie had ventured out first, followed by Drayden's father. Spacing each departure five minutes apart, Drayden had left, then Wesley would go, Sidney's grandfather, and Charlie's father after that. Sidney's grandmother and Charlie's mother had "taken Nora for a walk" much earlier.

Everyone had gone in different directions and planned to take circuitous routes to the alley between Broadway and Trinity Place, near the famous Wall Street bull. If anyone suspected they were being followed, they were to head back to the purposely unlocked apartment and await further instructions.

At a minimum, they were being watched on New America's surveillance cameras, which observed and recorded everybody. At worst, the Bureau had tasked someone with following Drayden around. By having the men dressed alike, leaving the apartment at different times, and taking nonsensical routes, that person wouldn't know whom to follow. It was also mostly dark now, save for a smattering of street lights and the glow of residents' interior lighting.

Drayden went six blocks the wrong way and took a left on Fulton Street, walking up a gentle slope in the direction of Broadway. While he wasn't far from Bureau headquarters, the streets were empty here and quite gloomy. Deserted restaurants lined the road; probably where Wall Street folks, Pre-Confluence, bought a quick lunch before returning to the office.

He found a confined park there, a speck of greenery in the middle of this concrete jungle, and plopped down on the remnants of a bench, immediately looking for anyone following him.

There were no signs of a tail. However, as Drayden noted, during the expedition they were trailed for dozens of miles without ever noticing.

After a five-minute rest, he continued up Fulton Street and passed a subway entrance, calling to mind the horrific Initiation all over again. When he reached Broadway, he turned left—due south—hoping Charlie had timed his walk correctly.

His unmistakable form, a shadow in the darkness, was approaching. Drayden had wanted some of them to pass each other, further confusing any follower.

Both boys kept their heads low as they passed without a word. Drayden took a left, then a right, gliding by the New York Stock Exchange, a glorious building even after all these years.

Right on Beaver Street, past a partially constructed office tower. Right onto Broadway a second time, in the opposite direction, coming to the iconic Wall Street bull. Behind it, at Twenty-One Broadway, was the office of Nathan Locke, the man who'd had an affair with his mother, and likely ordered her exile. Before Drayden left on the expedition, he'd threatened Locke, saying he'd be back to get him.

I haven't forgotten about you. I'm still coming.

Drayden crossed the street and slipped into the alley.

Everyone except Charlie was there already, huddling way too close to the Broadway side.

"Hey, guys, down to the middle of the alley," Drayden ordered.

Charlie breezed in shortly thereafter, flipping off his hood. "Looks like we're going to a football game."

His father fist-bumped him. "Finally made it, kid. Was gettin' worried. I wasn't sure if I should have timed you with a watch or a calendar."

Charlie slapped him on the shoulder. "Ahhh, good one, Pop. I'm gonna use that."

Wesley rubbed his hands together. "What now?" he asked Drayden.

"I need to g—"

Sidney's grandmother drew in a sharp breath, staring with bulging eyes toward the far end of the alley.

Someone was coming.

Oh shkat.

CHAPTER 9

It was Kim Craig.

Drayden kept hearing "sight for sore eyes" in his head, which, despite the circumstances, struck him as funny. Kim was a giant, burly woman who had threatened to kill him once and could have easily done so. Still, as she plodded up the alley, he instantly unclenched. He'd been under so much pressure to get his friends home, to save their families, and to survive the interrogation of New America's Premier. Seeing her in person, he felt some much-needed help was on the way.

Kim would know what to do and what would happen next. For the first time in ages, he'd be able to relax a smidge and let someone else handle it. He wouldn't have to face his fear that he never really was up to the challenge. He'd done his small part now, boldly choosing to drag their families to this alley rather than standing by for Kim to find him. Doing so went against his instincts, but like Professor Worth had said, he shouldn't wait for somebody else to solve his problems for him. Clearly, he'd made the right move.

Yet as she neared, her boy-cut red hair soaked with sweat, Drayden's nerves flared. She looked pissed off and stressed.

"It's okay, she's one of the good guys," he announced to the group.

Charlie whispered, "She?"

Drayden was so ecstatic to see her he was tempted to leap into her powerful arms, but she did not appear to be in the mood.

"Kim, thank God it's you. Thank you so much for coming. I wasn't sure how to contact you."

She smacked him over the top of the head. "What the *hell* are you all doing in here?"

Guess she wasn't as excited to see him. "I need your help. And I have a lot to tell you."

Drayden frantically recounted the highlights from the expedition, including the betrayal of the Guardians and the staggering duplicity of the Bureau. He concluded by elucidating their current dilemma and the necessity of ensuring protection for their families. What he did not mention was Professor Worth, her uncle, because saving that news would keep her focused on their immediate predicament.

She ran both hands through her hair. "For the love of God. That's so much worse than anyone thought." She took in the minute crowd behind Drayden. "It was *kind* of a clever trick you pulled getting to the alley, but I saw you all come in here. How many we got?"

"Me and Charlie aren't going into hiding," Drayden said. "That leaves seven of them."

Kim cursed to herself. "Listen up, folks. You don't know me, but I run surveillance. I shut off the cameras on Trinity Place just to get here, meaning you can go this way without being seen. I have a spot for you. It's a safehouse for those of us in the resistance after shkat goes down, which is imminent. It's off the grid, stocked with supplies. You're going to Forty Rector Street, on the tenth floor. There's nobody there yet. Make yourselves comfortable and don't plan on leaving for a while."

Forty Rector Street, Drayden thought. That was the first address on Kim's letter. "You guys know how to get there?" he asked everyone.

They exchanged confused glances.

Kim rolled her eyes. "At the end of the alley, go right on Trinity Place, your first left on Rector Street, and it's three blocks, on your right, before you hit the West Side Highway. Go, right now, and hustle."

While Charlie said goodbye to his parents, Drayden hugged his father, who seemed terrified. "I'll see you soon, Dad. Don't worry."

Wesley squeezed Drayden in tight. "Listen, man, can I come with you? I don't want to be holed up when you're out here trying to save the world."

"We have to go outside the city to get Sidney and Catrice." He stared at his feet. "Wes...while I'm out there, I'm going to search for Mom in the Bronx. I don't know if anyone's there, or alive, but I have to try. After that, if I can, I'll come find you. I need you to make sure everybody's safe, and kind of watch over things here. I love you."

"Wow, Mom? I can't imagine she's alive, but...please bring her back. You can do this. I love you too, little bro. Be careful."

Wesley whisked the family members down the alley, disappearing around the corner.

Drayden's entire body relaxed, knowing that regardless of what happened next, they were safe. For now.

"Kim, this is Charlie. He was in the Initiation and on the expedition with me, and he's my best friend. He knows everything. Given what went down on the expedition, and the fact that we never believed we'd survive or make it home, I had to tell him about the insurrection. But there's something else I didn't tell you. I asked about your aunt, Ruth Diamond. Nobody knew her. Remember the old man that saved us a few times I told you about? The professor? He was her husband. Professor Alan Worth."

Kim's jaw dropped. "*What*? Uncle Alan? I haven't seen him in...I never dreamed either of them was alive. How is he? Did he remember me?"

"He sure did. And he's here, outside the city with Sidney and Catrice. He came to help us, but mainly to see you."

Kim obscured her face, weeping quietly. "I don't have any family. He'd be the only one."

"We don't know how to get him inside. We also don't know what to do next and hoped you could tell us."

Kim dabbed her eyes. "I'm not sure I want him in the city for what's about to happen. I can't tell you every detail, but these are the broad strokes. The first objective in an operation like this is to cut off the head of the snake. Holst will be assassinated before anything else. After that, the walls between the zones will be destroyed. Then, well, all hell might break loose. If everything goes smoothly, Robert Zane will assume control, dissolve the Bureau, and have authority over the Guardians. If the Guardians answer to him, we've won."

She peeked behind her. "Here's the problem. In a perfect world, we'd have the Guardians ideologically on our side by now, but we couldn't involve too many people in this plot without risking Holst finding out. If we can't turn the Guardians against the Bureau, we may fail. They're big, and they're armed. We're not. This information you uncovered about the Bureau producing drugs, importing food, and trading with other colonies, while lying to everyone, might be enough to flip them. That we produce drugs for export instead of food isn't the main issue. I think being deceived about it will really get everyone's goat. Unfortunately, we have no way of spreading these secrets quickly. I need to deliver that info to Lily Haddad so she can blast it around the Dorms, which will naturally propagate it to the Guardians. Lighting a fire under the Dorm residents could lend momentum to our movement too. But I can't exactly call Lily. We haven't been able to communicate easily since Holst caught Thomas Cox."

Drayden had forgotten about that. Thomas Cox had been the Bureau rep for the Dorms, and the main go-between for Kim and

Lily. He'd been busted by the Bureau and executed during the Initiation.

Drayden rested his hand on Charlie's shoulder. "Why don't we go? We could get to the Dorms and tell Lily before we skip out of the city to our friends and your uncle."

Kim was shaking her head. "Remember, New America hasn't changed yet. Heavily guarded, walls between the zones—you couldn't even escape the Palace. Once the walls come down, maybe, but I can't say when that will be."

Drayden could think of a way. A route he knew, and virtually nobody else did. "We'll take the subway tunnels. We know the way; we've already done it."

Kim looked off into space. "Hmmm. I'm thinking out loud right now. There are cameras in there, but no one monitors them unless the Initiation is taking place. It could work."

Drayden tugged on his earlobe. "There's a couple of stations we wouldn't be able to make it through. We'd have to go up to the street."

"I can try and keep the cameras around the subways turned off. But that might not be necessary. It's dark. Most streetlights aren't working because of the power problem."

Drayden could serve the resistance on this one pressing task, abscond to Brooklyn, and let the professionals handle the heavy lifting. As he and Kim discussed the exact route and Lily's address, a few complications arose.

"We need flashlights. No chance we could make it through the tunnels otherwise. It's pitch black. A rope would be nice too."

She threw her hands in the air. "Wait here, I can get you flashlights. A rope, I'm not sure." She bounded down the alley and onto Trinity Place.

Charlie leaned against a stone wall with his arms crossed.

"What's up, man?" Drayden asked.

He avoided eye contact. "Nothing."

"Nice job timing your walk on Broadway. I even took a break in a park. You nailed it."

Charlie raised his brows. "Yup."

"Alright then. Good talk."

Minutes later Kim returned, short of breath, with two flashlights. "No rope. Sorry...you'll have to work that part out."

She rested her hands on her knees, gulping air. "You need... to tell Lily...she has to spread the truth to anyone who will listen. Hold a rally. The Guardians are the key though, I'm telling you. Like everybody else, they've been gaslighted by the Bureau. If we can turn them, we'll win."

Drayden took the flashlights, passing one to Charlie. "Thanks for everything. Please make sure our families are safe. When we sneak back inside, I'm bringing your uncle. I'm also going to take a trip up to the Bronx to search for my mother and see if the exiles are alive."

Her eyes widened. "Whoa, really? Listen carefully. If they happen to be alive, we may be able to use them." She scratched her head. "I'm not exactly sure how, but I bet people banished by the Bureau would love to see it dismantled. They've been exposed to Aeru, so they're effectively weaponized humans. See if they're willing to help and let me know."

Drayden recalled that New America's citizens were always told nobody survived outside the walls. It was, in fact, the very reason no one ever left voluntarily. If people expelled from the city were proven to be alive, it would be another powerful piece of evidence to showcase the Bureau's breathtaking dishonesty.

He nodded. "Got it. Figuring out how to locate you could be a problem, but I'll try Forty Rector Street."

She gave him an abrupt hug. "Good luck, kiddo."

"One last thing," he said. "What was the other address from your letter? Three Hundred Albany Street, 8I."

She whacked him across the top of the head again. "I told you not to open that unless I was dead!"

"Ow, sorry. I thought *we* were dead, and I wanted to know what it said. So, what is it?"

She looked away and side-eyed him.

"Kim..."

She shrugged. "It's Nathan Locke's home address. Use it wisely."

Drayden and Charlie ducked into the Rector Street subway station entrance and flicked on their flashlights. Immediately, the familiar musty smell of the tracks caused a sea of painful memories and a wave of emotion to come crashing back for Drayden.

"Hey," Charlie said, "I'm sure you already thought of this. But I don't really feel like redoing the Initiation."

"We don't have to pass it. We'll go around the challenges we'd have to complete to get through. And we only have to reach Thirty-Fourth Street."

One particular station stood out in Drayden's mind: Eighteenth Street, the bomb challenge. He needed to avoid it at all costs. He couldn't bear to lay eyes on the scene of his former best friend's demise. Luckily for Charlie, they'd started at Rector Street, a station up from the end at South Ferry, so he wouldn't have to relive Alex's death. Plus, at South Ferry, the chasm would have been impossible to cross.

The boys jogged in the narrow lane between the rail and the platform like they had during the Initiation, because it was free of railroad ties and the deep ditches between them. Besides the beams of their flashlights, the tunnel was lightless.

Drayden was beginning to be wary of the time. Even without a watch, he knew they'd entered New America in the late afternoon. It had to be 8:30 PM by now. The distance from Rector Street to Thirty-Fourth Street was around three miles, which would theoretically take only an hour or so above ground. Unquestionably, it would take them longer in the tunnels, despite jogging. He hoped to do it in under two hours. After meeting Lily, they'd need to flee the city to reunite with their friends before the self-imposed twenty-four-hour window expired. Otherwise, the team would move on to Plan B, and it would be impossible to rejoin them.

Since the ultimate objective of toppling the Bureau was both grand in scope and ambiguous in strategy, Drayden was relieved to hear the insurrection was on the horizon. He could sit back, watch it unfold, and hopefully weather the storm on the sidelines. It was comforting to have a small, very specific task—alerting Lily Haddad—in contrast with the monumental demands of over-throwing a government.

Getting through Rector Street, where the only "challenge" had been poison gas, was trivial. They were approaching Cortlandt Street, which would be chilling to revisit.

The tracks were blocked, forcing them onto the platform. Unlike in the Initiation, when the stations offering challenges had been lit up, they were now dark. Their flashlight beams illuminated the elongated poles, tipped with monstrous blades, dangling from the ceiling. Thankfully, this time they weren't swinging.

Drayden touched an axe-like blade, confirming its sharpness. The steel killing machine was several feet long and—even sitting still—terrifying.

"I can't believe we survived this challenge," Charlie said.

"I did it twice," Drayden replied.

"Yeah, that was dumb."

"Thank you. We gotta move."

They weaved through the inert blades and hopped down to the tracks, continuing their journey north. At Chambers Street, they officially left the Palace and entered the Precinct, the zone where the Guardians lived. It also marked the junction with the Two-Three Line of tracks, making the subway tunnel twice as wide the rest of the way. The Chambers Street station had housed the red and green hats challenge, an intellectual one, meaning there were no physical obstacles to circumvent.

Exhausted from running on recovering legs, Drayden slowed to a walk on the way to the next station. "I think being in Boston all that time, and laid up in the hospital, got us out of shape."

"Yeah, bro. I was hoping to drop ten pounds this year. Only twenty to go. I'm so fat I fell down and rocked myself to sleep trying to get up. I'm fatter than—"

"Charlie, Charlie, I get it. You ready to start up? I'm a little worried about making it back to the others in time."

"I feel like a turtle trying to run through peanut butter, but fine."

They sailed through Franklin Street, remaining on the tracks. Drayden had beaten up Alex there, unleashing his latent jiu-jitsu skills. Reflecting on it now, the skirmish had marked a legitimate turning point in his fighting ability. He'd since used his jiu-jitsu on several occasions.

Eighteenth Street is getting closer.

Within minutes they arrived at Canal Street, which posed their first major problem.

"Even though we know the way through, I don't think I can do this again," Drayden said. The maze of pipe-like tunnels had pushed his claustrophobia to the limit. "I think we should go up to the street and reenter the station at the opposite end, past the tunnel maze."

Charlie rested his hands behind his head. "We're in the Precinct, dude. For all we know we're right next to a Guardian station. Could be crawling with them. I don't know, man. It wasn't that bad."

"We're on the west side of New America. Nobody lives over here. Everyone's on the east side, so there's no reason for Guardians to be patrolling in this part. I can't do this, Charlie. Can we go up, please?"

Charlie squatted and peered inside the tunnels. "Fine."

The boys turned off their flashlights, emerging onto Varick Street, silent except for their own breathing and shrouded in blackness like the tunnels.

"Let's go," Drayden whispered. "At the next block, there should be an entrance back into the station." He hugged the crumbling buildings, trying to walk without his footsteps making any sound. When he hit the following street, he breathed easier, until he found nothing there.

"Where is it?" Charlie asked.

"I don't know," Drayden whispered, scoping out all four street corners. "Did we miss it? Let's try the next street."

That one had no entrance either.

Drayden smacked his forehead. "This is a minor station. It only had one entrance. Dammit. We have to make it to Houston up here at street level. Not ideal, I know. Tap my shoulder if you see or hear anyone."

They set off, moving alongside the abandoned storefronts, restaurants, and office buildings, employing extreme caution as they crossed intersection after intersection.

"Jeez, how far is it?" Charlie asked.

"I have no idea."

What if they couldn't reenter? They might have to backtrack and do the damn tunnel maze.

Drayden didn't have his map and was unfamiliar with this area. Crossing King Street, he was starting to feel lost. The longer they spent above ground, the more likely they would be discovered.

Finally, they reached Houston, a much bigger road. They crept down the stairs and jumped onto the tracks. At this station, they'd been given the option of continuing or quitting the Initiation, so it hadn't contained an actual challenge.

After a short-lived jog into the tunnel between stations, Drayden had to walk again. He was drained and hungry, having barely eaten all day. Something else had been vexing him too.

"Hey, Charlie... Listen, I'm sorry about what I said in the meeting with Holst. I only had like one second to think of a way to bail you out of telling the story of the expedition. Obviously, I didn't mean it. You're not an idiot. Far from it, in fact." Drayden shined his light on Charlie, who was walking directly across the tracks.

He pursed his lips and stared at the ground. "It's okay, I know you didn't mean it."

Oh wow. He *was* upset by it. "Charlie...no, man, don't do this. I swear to God I didn't mean that. If I hadn't concocted something and you had to tell our story—"

"I would have screwed it up. Because I'm stupid."

"No, you would have screwed it up because we didn't talk about what to say and you weren't prepared. I had scripted the whole thing. It's not that I'm smarter."

"Dray, let's not go overboard. I know you're trying to make me feel better and all, but you're definitely smarter than I am. It's like, if you'd called me ugly, it wouldn't bother me. I know I'm not ugly. I'm dashing with a side of dangerous. But you called me stupid and I *am* stupid. I'm not mad at you; I'm mad that I'm stupid."

For as long as they'd been friends, Charlie cracked endless jokes about his intelligence, and it had always troubled Drayden. The humor belied his hidden pain. Nevertheless, because Charlie laughed about it so often, Drayden didn't think he would take the comment so personally. Perhaps having someone else confirm your deepest fear about yourself, even one you joked about publicly, was more damaging than he comprehended. He bounced onto the tracks and snagged Charlie's arm, stopping him.

He was on the verge of tears.

Drayden clutched him by the shoulders. "I'm sorry. I shouldn't have said that. I should have been quicker and come up with another way to save you from telling the story. I feel terrible for what I said. I promise I did not mean it. Who figured out how to get across that narrow channel in New Bedford on the expedition? Who knew how to snag the bowl of boiling water off the fire? Who got the battery out of the dinghy? Dude, you're smart. I would never, *ever* have said that if I thought it was true."

"I hear ya," Charlie said.

Drayden punched him on the shoulder. "Attaboy."

Charlie smiled. "Now we're even for that time I tried to kill you in the Initiation."

"You know what?" Drayden nodded. "We *are* even. Not because of this. Because you've saved my butt over and over. You always said you had my back, and you always do."

"Aw, shucks." Charlie ruffled Drayden's hair. "Let's go before you try to kiss me."

The Christopher Street station had presented a challenge in which they swam underwater in a frigid pool for an unknown length, navigating maze-like walls. Drayden grew nauseous, recalling how he'd nearly drowned. While lit up during the Initiation, it was now frighteningly dim.

"Nope," he said when they walked in. They climbed the stairs to Seventh Avenue, again finding this station too inconsequential to maintain a separate entrance on the other side.

"Charlie, we have a problem. We have to get to Fourteenth Street to enter the tunnels. But that's where the wall between the Precinct and Lab is. I'm pretty sure there will be Guardians, even this far west. What should we do?" He also knew they were nearing the station that haunted him.

"I gotta be honest, Dray. I don't feel like going back there for a swim. Let's get to the wall and check it out."

Under the cover of night, the boys slinked through the decaying streets, occasionally hiding around building corners. Two flashlight beams came bobbing down Seventh Avenue, around Thirteenth Street.

Drayden dragged Charlie into an old deli on the southeast corner with a missing door and shattered front window. Ironically, a dangling sign read "Subway."

The flashlights panned back and forth across the avenue, presumably a routine patrol by the Guardians.

"Charlie," he murmured, "get on the floor."

Both boys went belly down on the dusty tiles. A beam of light illuminated the front window briefly before disappearing. The officers were having a conversation about whether it was preferable to have a uniform that was too big or too small.

"Too big, ya flunks," Charlie whispered.

"Shhhh, chotch."

After a minute, Drayden peeked through the window.

The coast clear, they scurried out, chancing upon an entrance to the subway right there on Thirteenth Street. They descended the stairs and hurried onto the tracks, only to find them blocked halfway through the Fourteenth Street station. A staircase took them through a door onto the platform.

"The two-guards riddle," Drayden said. "I seem to remember you losing your freaking mind on this challenge."

"Wasn't one of my finer moments, no."

Having resumed their jog on the tracks, they soon came to the Eighteenth Street station, the site of the disastrous bomb challenge. Although Drayden didn't want any part of this one, the staircase to the street was inside. During the Initiation, a white wall halfway into the station had impeded their progress, and a second steel wall had fallen behind them, trapping them inside a room. Assuming it remained lowered, the steel barrier obstructed the station, leaving no choice but to use the street. The white one, despite its door, would prevent Drayden from seeing into the room where the bomb had detonated. Thankfully.

Yet as he stepped onto the platform, glimpsing the white wall in the distance, his morbid curiosity about Tim's body resurfaced. They would have removed it, right? Of course.

Something overcame him. *He had to know*. Like an accident scene, not only did he find himself struggling to look away from the wall, he was drawn toward it.

Charlie tugged his sweatshirt. "No, bro. Don't. Let's go up to the street."

"I have to see. I have to know if he's there." Drayden's eyes moistened.

"If he is, you don't want to see it!" Charlie hissed.

Drayden shook Charlie off and dashed to the wall, perplexed by his own behavior, operating almost unconsciously.

"Dray!"

He covered his eyes as he pushed through the door, cracking his fingers enough to see. After navigating around the charred wreckage of the table which had held the bomb, he fell to his knees. Tears immediately streamed down his cheeks as he recollected how he'd failed the person who loved him as much as any friend could. His best bud, who'd constantly protected him, had died right here.

Tim's body was gone. But a deep crimson stain of dried blood grimly tainted the cement floor.

Why? Why would he come here and relive this? What was wrong with him? Since the Initiation and expedition had been such a whirlwind, he supposed he'd never really come to terms with Tim's death. Perhaps stopping at this station was part of the grieving process he'd been avoiding.

No matter what Drayden achieved in life, he would never recover from a failure that now defined him as a person, coloring his identity forever. He was the one who came up *just* short when it mattered the most. He was the kid who enjoyed the loyalty of his friends but could never equally reciprocate it—a fact reinforced by failing to protect Charlie from the grenade.

Charlie hoisted him to his feet and embraced him.

Drayden sobbed into his chest. He would give anything to have those few seconds back. It was so hard to accept that mere ticks of a clock could represent the difference between life and death. If he'd grabbed Tim and ran, instead of running away alone, Tim would probably be alive. If he'd been less of a klutz and his hands hadn't slipped on the detonator, he would have disarmed the bomb, and Tim wouldn't have died.

Charlie forced him the other way to the exit.

Just because they were in the Lab now didn't mean Guardians wouldn't be policing the roads. They would have to be on high alert, seeing as they needed to make it all the way to Twenty-Eighth Street to reenter the tunnel. Twenty-Third Street marked the colossal den of rats and cockroaches and they wouldn't even dare look inside.

Drayden wiped his tears on his sleeve. He touched Charlie's shoulder. "Thank you."

Charlie nodded.

The boys snuck up Seventh Avenue without incident and descended a staircase at Twenty-Seventh Street. This station had been deserted, so they zipped through it and eventually arrived at Thirty-Fourth Street. It had featured the three hanging boxes brainteaser, which he'd solved before Charlie and Alex blew it.

Drayden punched Charlie on the shoulder. "This wasn't one of your finer moments either."

"Let's just say the whole Initiation wasn't one of my finer moments."

"Ah, c'mon, you were huge on the rock wall at Times Square."

After they exited the station onto West Thirty-Third Street, they huddled under ramshackle scaffolding. Drayden somehow felt a little more at peace with the Initiation now. It hadn't been so scary seeing it a second time, and knowing Tim's body had been removed was a sign the Bureau had taken care of it in some way, which gave him a degree of solace.

The boys were in the Dorms but hardly safe, above ground the rest of the way, at risk of a Guardian confrontation at any time. However, outside of the Palace, nobody *should* be pursuing them, in theory. If they were stopped, they could try claiming to be Dorm residents out for a leisurely stroll.

"Do you know where Lily lives?" Charlie asked.

"Kim gave me the address. But we need to make another stop first."

CHAPTER 10

Drayden gently knocked on the door at 240 East Twenty-Ninth Street, praying he was home.

"Why would Mr. Kale be here?" Charlie asked. "I don't understand why he's not in the Lab." Regarding the shoddy micro-townhouse, he pretended to gag. "Or why he'd want to stay in this dump."

The building, which abutted an old firehouse, looked like it should have been condemned. Ratty blue shutters adorned some of the windows, giving the impression it may have been charming at one time.

Teachers, by virtue of their intellectual expertise, lived in the Lab alongside scientists and doctors. Those who worked in the Dorms typically rode a bus to and from.

"Rather than commute between the Lab and Dorms every day, he stays here sometimes," Drayden said. "The Bureau set him up with this place because he essentially runs the school, and he's there doing stuff even during the summer. Remember, the guy isn't married, has no family." Although Drayden had seen the house before, he'd never been inside.

A tiny window in the front door revealed nothing except a staircase leading upstairs. The real windows started on the second floor, which inferred that Mr. Kale might not hear them knocking. If he was there at all.

Please, please be home.

Drayden glanced both ways down Twenty-Ninth Street to make sure they hadn't attracted any attention. He reached up and inspected the rusty metal fire escape that blighted the face of the building.

"Stand back," Charlie said, reading his mind. He gripped the bottom of it and, using his impressive strength, lifted himself onto the first landing.

As he went to knock on the window, Drayden blurted, "Not too loud!"

He softly tapped it and pressed his face against the filthy glass.

A light turned on and Mr. Kale appeared in the window, his expression a combination of confusion and shock. After he put on his glasses, he looked at Charlie, then down at Drayden, and back again. A flashed index finger later, he vanished into the room.

Mr. Kale was indeed a sight for sore eyes, no equivocation required. He had been one of Drayden's oldest and dearest friends, as well as a smart man and great role model. Mr. Kale was the true father he never had. In fact, his father's lack of involvement in his life was probably the reason he longed for a male mentor, now that he thought about it. Drayden had so much to tell Mr. Kale.

Charlie gracefully hopped down to the street, like an oversized Spiderman.

Mr. Kale flung the front door open and lunged outside in his pajamas. "Drayden! Charlie!" He grabbed Drayden into a warm embrace.

A feeling of serenity washed over him, realizing now how much he'd missed Mr. Kale. As with Kim, yet even more so, he felt supported by him. Protected and safe.

When his favorite teacher pulled back, he held Drayden by the shoulders. "What are you doing here? And how?"

"Can we come in?"

Despite Drayden's genuine elation at reuniting with Mr. Kale, he was bewildered by seeing him so out of context. More than a teacher and authority figure, he was a distinguished-looking fellow—African American, graying hair, always well dressed. In his defense, he'd awoken minutes earlier, but here he was, before them, in pajamas. Not just any pajamas either. He was sporting some kind of full-body fuzzy suit, like you'd envision a child wearing.

Mr. Kale waddled up to the second floor and into the drab kitchen, where he immediately set a pot of water on the stove. He closed the curtains on the front window, because lights were strictly forbidden after 10:00 PM, and pulled out two chairs at the wobbly kitchen table for the boys.

"I want to hear everything," he said, "but please allow me to make you some tea. Are you hungry?" He set out fruit and crackers.

"We don't have much time," Drayden said over his growling stomach. Apparently, Charlie was starving too. They both inhaled the food.

As Mr. Kale was pouring the tea, Charlie noticed his pajamas and asked, "What's with the getup?"

Mr. Kale looked down his body, as if suddenly remembering his fluffy sleepwear. "Oh, jeez. Didn't know I'd be having visitors tonight. It's one of the few things I still have from before the Confluence." He set three mugs on the table and sat. "Let's hear it."

Drayden summarized the events and revelations of the past few weeks, whispering to counter any possible recording devices, as well as omitting key names.

While Mr. Kale's face twisted repeatedly, the astute teacher was mindful never to interrupt him with questions, appreciating the urgency of their visit. His cup of tea untouched, steeped beyond drinkability, he held his head in his hands. "I'm shocked, but I'm not. Nothing surprises me about the Bureau."

Drayden couldn't stop tapping his foot. "Do you know what time it is?"

His eyes flicked up at a shelf. "It's eleven-thirty."

"So, do you have any rope?"

Mr. Kale rummaged through a kitchen closet. "I'm happy you boys decided to stop here. Absolutely, go visit Lily Haddad and tell her everything. She has the loudest voice in the Dorms. But I know some people too. I'm going to spread the word, and I know you're aware how instantly gossip can mushroom." He paused to wrench something out. "I certainly hope this plot succeeds. Even if it fails, that doesn't mean we can't take down the Bureau. We have the power right here."

He returned with a hefty coil of orange cable, raising his index finger when he sat. "Never forget: An educated public is the greatest weapon against tyranny."

Drayden understood his point, in theory. How an educated populace could *literally* depose the Bureau wasn't so clear.

Mr. Kale tugged hard on the cable. "I don't have rope, but I have this extension cord. It's long, around fifty feet."

Drayden touched it. "Hmmm. You think it could hold our weight?"

"Well, if I'm right that you guys are thinking about using it to escape over the border wall, you only need it to descend. The walls have ladders up, so the Guardians can monitor the outside world."

Charlie looked back and forth between the two of them. "If we tie that and shimmy down...how do we untie it after?"

"We don't," Drayden said. "We'll have to leave it behind."

"Actually," Mr. Kale said, "you can make what're called quick-release knots, including one known as the getaway knot. There's a whole subset of mathematics called knot theory. It's not about tying knots exactly, but if you have a mathematically curious mind, knots are a cool thing to learn about. Quick-release knots produce two lengths of cable. One you descend. The other you yank and it unties the knot."

Mr. Kale chopped off the plugs and taught them to tie the getaway knot, leaving enough slack to slip out the release side from the bottom of the wall.

Learning about the getaway knot just reminded Drayden of how much he didn't know. He was tired of being the person who had to solve every problem and yearned to stay with Mr. Kale. But they had to get going.

He nudged Charlie. "Let's do it."

They hugged Mr. Kale and thanked him for his help.

"I hope we see you soon," Drayden said, a chill running down his spine.

"You can count on it. I'll be here. Good luck."

Carrying the extension cord in a plastic bag, Drayden and Charlie hustled west on Twenty-Ninth Street in the direction of Third Avenue. This part of the Dorms was heavily populated, meaning it would be unusual, though not unheard of, for two kids to be prancing around at night. It was also highly probable they'd encounter Guardians. Taking into account her status as the leader of the Dorms, Lily Haddad's apartment might even be guarded.

At Thirty-First Street, a pair of Guardians strode across the avenue, forcing the boys to duck behind a stoop.

These two guys barely resembled the Palace Guardians, who were all Special Forces. One was scrawny with a pencil neck, and the other was rotund, his shirt untucked out of necessity.

Once they were gone, Drayden and Charlie raced up Third Avenue and took a right on Thirty-Third Street, promptly arriving at number 203, an unassuming gray townhouse with a red door. It was quite a slum for the unofficial mayor of the Dorms. In spite of the light restriction, a first-floor room's glow illuminated half the block. Luckily, no Guardians were posted out front.

Drayden knocked and stepped back.

The darkened vestibule was decrepit, like nobody lived there. Given what Drayden knew about Lily, it made sense. She was a humble woman of the people, right there in the trenches along with everyone else, fighting for real equality. His mother had always spoken highly of her.

A shadowy figure in a long nightgown and robe unlocked the door, only cracking it an inch. "May I help you?" she asked coldly.

"Ms. Haddad, it's Drayden Coulson."

Her visibly shocked face popped out the door. "Drayden?"

"Maya Coulson's son?"

Lily came onto the stoop and shut the door behind her. "Why yes, Drayden. What are you boys doing here? And at this hour?"

"We're sorry to bother you. But it's dire. May we come in?"

She glanced behind her and clutched her red robe tight. "I don't know, it's very late. I don't usually allow guests into my home. I try to keep my work separate from my private life. Can we talk right here?"

Not the reaction Drayden was expecting.

"Ms. Haddad, this is immensely important. I have critical information and...a message, from someone you know. We're not even supposed to be in the Dorms. We snuck up here through the subway from the Palace just to talk to you. Me and Charlie would be in serious trouble if a Guardian walked by."

She touched his arm. "Yes, yes, of course. Come in. Please, call me Lily." She extended her hand to Charlie. "Hello, Charlie."

"Pleasure to make your acquaintance," he said, shaking it.

Drayden gave him a look.

Their tour through the dingy vestibule made Drayden suspect she was embarrassed by the apartment because of her stature. That would be silly, since everyone in the Dorms lived in relative poverty. When she opened a second door to the main house, the boys stopped in their tracks.

"Whoa!" Charlie rotated around, his eyes skyward. "I want to be mayor of the Dorms."

Drayden was more confused than amazed. A two-story tall living room with a spiral staircase? The entire townhouse to herself? All city infrastructure was aging and this apartment was no exception, with snaking cracks in the walls and chipped countertops. Still, the place was stunning. Now he understood her reluctance to let them inside.

Lily blushed. "You boys are too young, but right after the Confluence I sort of took on a leadership role here in the Dorms, and the early Bureau gave me this apartment. That was back when they were genuine about their aspirations for a better New America. Things are much different these days. Over the years I held onto this apartment though, and yes, I'm ashamed of it. I'm aware it doesn't gel with my public image and I'd appreciate it if you wouldn't expose me."

Charlie waved his hand dismissively.

"No, no," Drayden said. "We're happy for you that you got a nice place."

She gestured toward the kitchen. "Can I make you kids tea?"

"No," Drayden said. "We ju—we're fine, thank you."

Lily invited them to sit on an L-shaped white couch in the sprawling living room, while she plopped down across from them in a leather chair. "So...what do you have to tell me?"

Drayden could recite this in his sleep by now. He recounted the discoveries and secrets of the expedition, as well as the events since. Yet this time, he omitted some details. He didn't know Lily well; not like he knew Mr. Kale. Not everybody needed to hear they'd lied about the excess batteries, or find out where the girls were waiting. Lily was one of the good guys, but he'd learned the Bureau had ways of "encouraging" trustworthy people to spill their secrets. He did, however, disclose that Kim herself had sent him to relay the truth about New America, so Lily could start circulating the news, especially to the Guardians.

She cursed under her breath. "This government. I've been saying for years how corrupt they were, but I never imagined anything like that. I'm shocked our primary export is drugs. The deceit is staggering."

"Yeah, I mean, we have no idea how much stuff the Bureau's receiving in compensation. I think the notion is that they're keeping most of it while the Dorms wither away. The fact that the Bureau has an Aeru vaccine, and nobody knows about it, is a big deal too. Can you spread the word here? Hold a rally or something? Kim believes the insurrection hinges on the Guardians' loyalty. If everyone's gossiping about it, they're bound to hear. Plus, it can't hurt the cause to rile everyone up."

"I agree with her. In the morning, my team and I will engineer the best strategy to get the news out." Her eyes softened as she leaned forward in her chair. "You boys are incredibly brave and have already done so much for the future of this city. Please, let me help you now. It's astonishing how much you've been through. You relax, I'll be right back." She stood and left the room, disappearing up the stairs.

"Don't we have to go?" Charlie whispered.

"Yeah. I just don't want to be rude. I didn't tell her we have to leave because I don't want everyone to know where we're going." He surveyed the massive ground floor, noting it extended all the way to the rear of the townhouse, where a door led to an outdoor patio and alley between the buildings.

A few minutes later Lily returned with a tray containing two glasses of milk and a cup of mixed nuts. In the Dorms, milk was a scarce and coveted treat. That she would share two whole glasses was incredibly generous.

Unable to help themselves, the boys greedily guzzled the milk and devoured the nuts.

Drayden wiped his mouth with the back of his hand. "Lily, thank you. We really can't stay."

"Are you sure? There's nothing left for you to do. The grownups can take it from here. You two look exhausted. Wouldn't you feel better after some sleep?"

He couldn't deny he'd love a little rest, but napping was out of the question due to time.

Lily rearranged the pillows on the L-shaped couch to make space for them to lie down. "I'm going to fetch blankets for you in case you change your mind, and the bathroom is around the corner if you need it."

Charlie frowned at Drayden.

Right after she climbed the stairs, both boys leapt to their feet and Charlie made a beeline for the bathroom.

"What are you doing?" Drayden whispered.

"I'd like to use a proper bathroom for a change."

Drayden scowled at him. "What? No, man, let's go. I feel bad doing this but we gotta hightail it before we run out of time. Go in your pants again."

"These jeans are clean!" he whisper-yelled, balling his fists and grudgingly following Drayden to the door.

Lily came down the stairs with an armful of blankets. "I'm sorry you have to go, but I'll make the beds up. If you need a place to stay, you're always welcome."

Drayden felt like a jerk. "That's so generous of you. We're sorry to run out, but we're in a bit of a rush. Thanks for your hospitality."

They stepped outside and froze.

Two Guardians were heading their way on Thirty-Third Street.

Without any other option, Drayden and Charlie started walking west toward Third Avenue, as if walking was the most natural thing to be doing at this hour. The Guardians were approximately a hundred yards behind them.

Drayden had briefly considered jumping back into Lily's apartment, or hiding, but they were in plain sight of the Guardians the moment they stepped out the door and it would have appeared highly suspicious.

"Dude, what do we do?" Charlie muttered.

"I don't know. Just walk normally, like we're not doing anything wrong."

His heart was pounding. This was bad, and he knew it.

"Hey!" one of them called out. "You two! Stop right there."

Oh shkat.

"Run, Charlie."

They took off, hauling down the road.

"Freeze!"

Drayden turned north up Third Avenue, the rapid footsteps of the Guardians audible behind them. "Right on Thirty-Fourth!" he shouted.

Upon reaching it, with their pursuers now turning onto Third Avenue a block behind them, more Guardians came at them on Thirty-Fourth Street.

The boys hesitated, while Drayden processed the scene, before continuing north up Third Avenue. He led Charlie to the west side of the avenue and then left on Thirty-Fifth Street.

Drayden's legs hadn't fully recovered and were fatiguing. He was gasping for air and growing a cramp in his side. Having to lug the extension cord in a bag wasn't making running any easier either.

"Dude, which way?" Charlie asked.

"South, left!" Drayden answered when they neared Lexington Avenue. Two of the Guardians were trailing them on Thirty-Fifth Street, but the gap had increased.

Drayden racked his brain trying to think of somewhere to hide. Nobody ever won a footrace with the police.

They approached Thirty-Fourth Street again, this time from the north, where more Guardians surfaced on Lexington Avenue to the south.

"Jesus," Charlie said.

Drayden cussed. "Left on Thirty-Fourth!"

They made the turn. Like a beacon, the old Dumont Hotel, known to all teenagers as the "Hookup House," rose up ahead, towering above everything nearby. It was their only hope.

"Charlie, the Hookup House."

They'd have to make it inside before their pursuers made it to Thirty-Fourth Street, because if they were seen going in, it would only be a matter of time until they were found.

Charlie shoved open the shattered door. They hurtled up the darkened stairs, clearing two and three at a time.

"Third...floor," Drayden said, totally winded.

The dilapidated hotel hallway featured identical rooms on each side. They needed one with a window on the front of the building so they could watch the Guardians on the street. Drayden darted into room 306, shut the door, and hunched down by the windows.

Charlie started to cough and slapped his hands over his mouth, grimacing to suppress it.

Two Guardians flew by on the sidewalk, followed by another trio shortly thereafter. Two more emerged across the street, angling their flashlight beams inside the abandoned storefronts.

"Shoot," Drayden whispered. "They know we hid. Everyone knows about this place too. It won't be long before they come in here."

Three other Guardians returned, flashing the lights inside the buildings on their side of the street, eventually passing by. Just as Drayden was feeling relieved, two more entered the Hookup House.

"Dammit," Charlie hissed. "What should we do?"

Drayden sighed. "Look, if we're caught, we're caught. We'll have to deal with it. But we're not giving up."

Charlie took cover behind the bed. "Let's hide here in case they peek inside the room. And, like, close our eyes and listen. See if we can hear them climbing the stairs."

Drayden joined him. "Good call."

"I hear doors opening and closing," Charlie whispered.

The noise was outside in the hall now: doorknobs turning, doors creaking.

Heat flushed Drayden's cheeks. "Don't move."

The door to their room flew open.

He was shaking.

A flashlight beam flitted around the room.

The sound of their steps drifted down the hall. "I'm telling you, they're not in here. We're wasting our time."

"What do you think, they evaporated into thin air? Let's check a couple more floors. Those are the kids though."

Those are the kids.

Footsteps faded away up the stairs.

Charlie yanked Drayden's sleeve. "We gotta go. Now. We have a tiny window while they're upstairs. As long as it's not a trap." He hurried to the door and scouted out the hallway, waving Drayden ahead. After tiptoeing to the stairwell door, Charlie gently turned the knob and ever so slowly cracked it, when it squeaked.

He drew in a quick breath and paused.

Drayden cringed.

They waited for the sound of footsteps. Not hearing anything, Charlie snapped the door open and eased it shut. They tried their best to descend the stairs silently. If Guardians were outside on the street, they were screwed.

His heart pounding, Drayden peered both ways down Thirty-Fourth Street and opened the front door. "We're clear," he whispered. "We're shooting for Park Avenue, where we should be able to move easier. If we see Guardians, we might want to split up and try to meet around Fifty-Ninth Street."

"No!" Charlie protested, like a frightened child. "I want to stay with you."

"Okay, fine."

He and Charlie sprinted to the corner of Thirty-Fourth and Lex, stopping short to stay out of sight.

Some Guardians were milling around a few blocks north. Nobody was behind them.

Drayden rested his hands behind his head. "I think we have to run across and hope they don't see. It's dark. We should be able to make it."

"Let's go for it," Charlie said.

They bolted across Lexington Avenue and didn't relent until they reached the relative safety of Park Avenue. No one lived this far west, so the Guardian presence should be thinner. They worked their way north, swiftly crossing at each intersection. At Fiftieth Street, they were in the vicinity of the Meadow, and the wall that separated it from the Dorms at Fifty-Ninth Street.

"We should start going east soon," Drayden said. "We don't want to get anywhere near the wall, which probably has tons of security. Especially now that we know what's being grown in the Meadow."

After the once-majestic Waldorf Astoria Hotel, they took a right on Fifty-First Street, passing by soaring office buildings before the area became full of untouched townhouses. Ultimately, they intersected the border wall at First Avenue and holed up inside an old restaurant called Ethos.

"If I'm correct," Drayden said, "there's another block of streets past the wall this far north. It's not the river on the opposite side. We can scale it here and walk outside to the Fifty-Ninth Street Bridge."

"How do we get on the bridge?"

"One thing at a time, man. First, we gotta climb the wall. There should be ladders leading up to little watch stations at the top. We just need to find the closest one, make sure it's clear."

Drayden had no clue how many Guardians protected the border at a given time. Surrounding the entire perimeter of New America, the wall was nearly thirty-two miles long, so without question much of it went unmonitored. It also required many watchtowers.

A block north, he saw an unoccupied metal platform near the top of the wall.

They darted over, coming upon steel rungs built into the cement. Drayden followed Charlie up, and within a minute, both were standing on the narrow metal grating, enjoying a bird's-eye view outside the city. As he'd suspected, First Avenue gave way to one more block of abandoned apartments and a highway beyond that.

Drayden rapidly unraveled the extension cord, praying he remembered how to tie the getaway knot. It was fairly simple to do if you made the release side short. But their circumstance necessitated both sides be long, so they could untie it from the bottom of the wall.

He got to work securing it to the platform, having to slide twenty-five feet of cable through loops several times.

"I feel like a sitting duck." Charlie scanned the surrounding blocks.

Drayden tried his best to finish the knot quickly, although this wasn't the kind of task he wanted to be hasty about. If he flubbed it, they would plummet twenty-five feet onto pavement.

"Dray, I don't want to alarm you," Charlie said softly, "but we have company. You want to tie off that knot?"

Two flashlight beams were speeding up First Avenue.

With a final squeeze, both cables extended down the outside of the wall—the climbing one, and the release cable to undo the whole thing. Drayden tugged on the climbing side to make sure it was sound. "Charlie, go!"

Charlie, having always wanted to join their ranks, had befriended some Guardians and trained with them years before entering the Initiation. Thankfully, he'd know how to do this. He climbed on top of the wall, clutching the cable.

"Jeez, it looks so high from up here."

"Freeze!" a Guardian shouted. "Don't move or you're dead!"

"Now, Charlie!" Drayden said.

He slung the cable under his butt with one hand and began to walk down the wall, backwards. Releasing the cable in bursts, he rappelled down.

Shots rang out and bullets ricocheted off the cement, splintering fragments around Drayden.

He cowered, but there was nowhere to hide. He was totally exposed.

The Guardians were running, only a half block away. "Get down, now!"

Pop...pop pop. More shots in a flurry.

Even though the cable most likely wouldn't sustain them both, Drayden had to move. Sure, these guys weren't exactly sharpshooters, but they wouldn't miss from directly beneath him. He hopped on top of the wall, trying his best not to observe the perilous drop.

He lowered his legs and then his body over the exterior until he was dangling by his fingertips. Many of the techniques in jiu-jitsu relied on the strength of your grip, and his was solid. Still, he'd never hung like this before and had no idea how long he could hold on. The second Charlie touched the ground, he would snag the cable. Except...what if he grabbed the quick-release side by accident?

"Dray!" Charlie called out, nearing the bottom. "Jesus, hold on, buddy, I'm almost down."

The Guardians were climbing the ladder.

"Charlie, wiggle the correct side of the rope for me!"

"I'm down!" He whipped the climbing one around. "Go!"

Drayden grasped it and tried to slide but it burned his hands too badly. He paused, a quarter down, to bundle the rope beneath his body and rappel the same way Charlie had. He pushed off the face with his feet, descending in sweeping arcs. As soon as his feet touched the ground, Charlie yanked the release side of the cable.

The Guardian at the top of the wall caught it before it fell.

Turning into a tug of war, Drayden joined Charlie and pulled. They lifted the officer off his feet and, as he was about to tumble over, he released the cable, causing both boys to crash to the ground.

A gun extended over the edge, firing shots blindly around them, shattering the asphalt.

Drayden and Charlie pressed their backs against the wall, creating an impossible angle for the Guardians to shoot them. Drayden coiled up the cable amidst continuous, ineffective gunfire.

Despite their desire to head north, they scampered south along the wall to throw the Guardians a curveball. At Forty-Ninth Street, they ran east toward the river.

The Guardians fired a few more shots, meaningless as the boys were well out of a realistic range.

Drayden and Charlie went north on FDR Drive, which was the highway bordering the East River. With a second to breathe, they whooped and high-fived, elated over their successful breakout from New America. Drayden's heart sank though when he caught a glimpse of the Fifty-Ninth Street bridge.

It was the only path back to their friends in Brooklyn. The ramp started all the way back on Second Avenue, inside the border wall. Here, it stood at least a hundred feet off the ground.

Drayden and Charlie loafed on Sutton Place and Fifty-Ninth Street, beholding the bridge, having cut back into the city a block. The thought process was that further west, in the direction the ramp began, the bridge might be lower. They couldn't cross over First Avenue because of the border wall, but investigating it had been worth a shot. Although it was indeed shorter here, it was still too high.

"Yo, check it out." Charlie roamed along Fifty-Ninth Street. Halfway down the road, an old restaurant with a sign reading "Guastavino" was wedged beneath the bridge, encased in stone blocks that led up to the bridge's underside.

Drayden clenched and unclenched his fists, thinking their rock-climbing experience from the Initiation was about to come in handy.

Charlie dug his fingers into a crevice between the stones. "All we need to do is climb to the top of the restaurant and lift ourselves up. It's not that bad."

He showed the way, again doing his best Spiderman impersonation, and with some sweat and achy fingers, they were on the lower level of the bridge. It offered excellent protection from any Guardians who might be overseeing the upper level, which contained the gate. Drayden was confident they wouldn't pursue the boys outside the walls because they hadn't taken the Aeru vaccine, but they could fire their weapons with ease.

The roadway was in surprisingly good condition and free of cars. When the quarantine had gone into effect during the Confluence, the government must have blocked off the bridge on both sides. At the far end of the bridge over Queens, Drayden stopped to strategize and take stock of the roads below.

One hugged the river.

"I don't have my map," Drayden said. "We're going to have to wing it. We could easily get lost and not make it back in time. If we can see the river, or the New America skyline, we should be able to zigzag our way."

Charlie saluted. "Roger that."

After getting off the bridge, they backtracked to an overgrown road by the East River. A mile or so later, likely in Brooklyn, they switched to a different street to remain alongside the water.

A dim glow to the east diffused in the blackness of the sky, implying it was around 5:00 AM. They didn't need to reunite with their friends until 5:00 PM-ish, so provided they didn't become disoriented, they were golden on time.

The chaos of the prior twelve hours hadn't allowed Drayden a chance to digest everything that had happened. None of it had gone quite according to plan. Nevertheless, he was kind of proud of himself. They hadn't died or been imprisoned, and most importantly, they'd saved their families.

Almost. One family member was waiting to be rescued: his mother, assuming she was alive.

Now that Dad and Wes were safe, and the insurrection was imminent, he could revert to his original plan. Once they rejoined the girls and Professor Worth, they'd make the long trek to the Bronx to search for the exiles. In addition to the primary goal of locating his mother, he needed to report back to Kim on their status and willingness to participate in the overthrow plot if warranted. It was anyone's guess if his mother had survived, but given the abundance of life they'd seen on the expedition, he thought it highly probable they would find a community there.

After passing by the ruins of the Williamsburg Bridge, the road turned, leading away from New America. The boys followed it a little longer until they began to feel off-course. Then Drayden saw it—I-278, the Brooklyn Queens Expressway.

The BQE took them in the right direction, and before long they could see the Brooklyn Ice Cream Factory from the highway. An exit and a short walk later, they'd made it. Finally.

Charlie groaned as they closed in on the building. "I'm so tired. When are we going to sleep?"

"I think we can grab a quick nap here."

For a second, Drayden contemplated announcing their arrival in advance, so he wouldn't startle the others into firing a weapon.

His jaw dropped the moment he opened the door.

The place had been ransacked. And his friends were gone.

CHAPTER 11

Drayden instinctively reached for his gun. Unfortunately, he'd disarmed before entering New America.

He stumbled back and crouched outside the doorway. This building hadn't been the best choice because it was out in the open with nowhere to hide.

Charlie squatted beside him, surveying the area.

"Shkat," Drayden whispered, his heart pounding.

The color drained from Charlie's face. "What if they were captured?"

Dear God.

Drayden couldn't bear to imagine what they'd be going through right now. "I can't believe the Guardians would've come out here. I never thought they would go outside the walls."

"What about Eugene and crew?" Charlie asked. "They got the Aeru vaccine too."

Drayden peered through the doorway. "Good point."

"I don't think there's anyone in there, bro. They would have fired or something." Charlie inched into the Brooklyn Ice Cream Factory with his fists up, as if a brawl were a possibility.

It was empty. Tables and chairs were overturned, and the area behind the counter had been trashed.

Drayden nosed around for any signs of a firefight.

There were no shell casings or blood, and the windows weren't broken.

He found it hard to believe the trio wouldn't have defended themselves if they were threatened or surrounded. Unless they were so overwhelmed that a gun battle would have been suicide.

Charlie raised his hands. "What are we supposed to do now?"

Drayden tugged on his left ear. "I don't know."

"Should we sneak back into the city and search for them?"

This was a scenario for which Drayden hadn't planned. Never even crossed his mind. His belief that they were untouchable outside the walls had been presumptuous. After all, they weren't the only ones vaccinated for Aeru. Why had he been so foolish to pick the most conspicuous building for their base camp? Directly across from Pier Fifteen, it would literally be the first place the Bureau would explore. He scrutinized the room once more before leaving.

Something caught his eye.

The glossy white menu hanging from the ceiling had been vandalized, but not in the same way as the rest of the shop. Words were scrawled across it diagonally in black pen, and they positively hadn't been there before. They could have been mistaken for graffiti if he hadn't seen the unblemished sign earlier.

This was no random doodling. It was a code.

wous aurt ltm kha sfn

He recognized the pattern immediately, and only one person would have left it: Professor Worth. He'd used Eugene's cipher.

"Charlie, look at this. It's a code, like Eugene's note. I wish I had a pen."

"What's it say?" Charlie asked.

"Guess I'll have to do it in my head." He visualized the first word, *wous*, going down a page, and then the next, *aurt*, beside it. Basically, he needed to read the first letter of each word, then move onto the second letter, and so forth. W-a-l-k-s...

walksouthfurmanst

"Walk south Furman Street," Drayden sounded out. "Thank God. That means they're safe, hiding somewhere down the road."

Charlie scratched his neck. "If they saw Guardians coming, how the heck did they have time to scribble this code?"

Drayden shrugged. "I don't know. Maybe Professor Worth came back after they left just to write the note for us. C'mon."

Charlie touched Drayden's shoulder as they departed the shop. "Dude, apparently there's Guardians out here. We gotta be careful. Especially since we're unarmed."

They were an easy target in the middle of this broad, open expanse, so they hurried into the lush tree cover on Furman Street. The boys plodded along, studying each building, counting on their friends to be watching for them.

Drayden's head was pounding now, likely due to sleep deprivation. He and Charlie had been awake for twenty-four hours. The world seemed to be spinning, and it felt like a cloud was enveloping his brain. Two blocks later, a noise startled him out of the fog.

He stopped and jerked Charlie's sleeve. "You hear that?"

It was a high-pitched whistle.

"What?" Charlie asked.

Drayden closed his eyes, attempting to amplify his audio perception. "It sounds like a bird. A trilly whistle. You don't hear it?"

"Oh, I do. I thought it was in my head."

The sound was intermittent, and grew louder as they passed 130 Furman Street, a sleek four-story apartment building. Although run down like other structures, its style was more modern.

Sidney's head protruded out of a third-floor window, her cheeks red. "Over here!" she whisper-shouted.

They made their way inside, where Sidney emerged from a staircase in a dark hallway and rushed Drayden, embracing him. "We were so worried. What happened to you guys?" When she pulled away, the heightened color of her face and her forlorn eyes were asking a different question.

"Your sister's fine." He nodded. "We got them all moved somewhere totally safe."

Sidney burst into tears.

Drayden held her. Despite what he and Charlie had been through, he couldn't fathom the stressful night of uncertainty she must have had.

"Thank you," she said over and over, squeezing him until it hurt.

He rubbed her back. "Let's go upstairs and we'll tell you guys everything."

After a joyful reunion with Professor Worth and Catrice in a dusty but furnished apartment, Drayden ran them through the previous twelve hours, which felt like twelve years. He did point out that just because their families were safe for the time being, they couldn't stay in Kim's safehouse forever. Once Holst realized he wasn't getting his batteries, Drayden bet he would hunt high and low for their relatives.

"Well done, fellas," Professor Worth said from the couch. He looked at Drayden questioningly. "You starting to believe yet?"

"All I did was react to whatever was thrown at me. Anyone could have done it. I just hope Lily Haddad is rallying the troops as we speak. What about you guys?"

Professor Worth encouraged Catrice to tell the tale.

"We saw three flashlights," she said, "far away, but headed toward us for sure. We barely had enough time to escape into a safer building, without being seen. Then we eventually made our way here, which was better."

"Was it Eugene?" Charlie asked.

"I don't know. We couldn't see their faces. We took the weapons and as much as we could from the wagon and had to run for it."

"They got the other battery?" Drayden asked.

"I assume," she said.

He appealed to Professor Worth. "I guess it doesn't matter, right? Hell, it kind of bolsters our claim that we had more batteries, and they'll think we have the rest hidden somewhere else. How did you leave that note for me, by the way?"

Professor Worth appeared perplexed. "What note?"

Goosebumps spread across Drayden's arms. "The coded one on the ice cream menu? It said to walk south on Furman Street."

The professor shared a look with the girls. "Drayden, we didn't leave you a note. We could see the ice cream shop from here, so we saw you go in. We figured you would come this way, but if you didn't, we would've come out to get you."

"Eugene," he muttered, incredulous that they were back on this rollercoaster with him, as if being at war with Holst wasn't enough. "Eugene left it. What, is he just toying with me?" He shook his head. "Wait, if he wanted me to believe you guys had left the note, and take Furman Street…they were setting a trap for me and Charlie." He jumped to his feet. "They might be close by right now."

"I doubt it." Professor Worth waved him down. "Sit, you're exhausted. We've been here around six hours. They must have given up and left, because otherwise you would have been ambushed. We never saw them after they left the ice cream shop. We should still be discreet when we leave, of course."

He plopped down. The professor didn't get it. Eugene really had his number. Drayden never understood the degree to which he would take his defeat by the teens in the marsh so personally. He was hungry for revenge, to prove his superiority. During the expedition, Drayden had constantly been a step ahead of him, but the advantage had flipped. Eugene was owning him, which was one more reason he'd prefer to avoid a second confrontation with him and the other Guardians.

He stretched out on a bed. "If we stay here for a while, that should guarantee they're gone, and that happens to jibe with our desire for a nap. We've been up for twenty-four hours. Then we have to hike to the Bronx to see if the exiles are there. If so, Kim might want to use them as part of the insurrection."

"You guys get some rest," Sidney said, staring at her shoes.

He'd eventually have to address the Sidney situation, but for now he was too damn tired. He began fading before his head hit the musty pillow, giving him time for one final thought.

I'm coming, Mom.

The most practical route to the Bronx wasn't the shortest. They needed to stick to highways to skirt the worst of the overgrowth on the regular streets. Their path took them along I-287 to the Grand Central Parkway through Queens, over the unstable RFK Bridge, and up I-87 into the Bronx. At nearly nineteen miles, they would be lucky to make it in one day.

They had fled their hideout in Brooklyn without incident, confirming Professor Worth's suspicion that the Guardians were gone. Regardless, Drayden remained wary of Eugene.

Having surrendered the wagon, the group was a touch low on food and water. They'd shared a paltry meal before heading out, and everyone lugged supplies in their pockets. Back at 75 Wall Street, Drayden and Charlie had ditched their Guardian uniforms for jeans and sweatshirts, which lacked cargo space, plus the scalding, early afternoon sun forced them to carry the sweatshirts.

Three hours into their hike, they were roughly halfway, traveling west on the Grand Central Parkway. The monotonous slog reminded Drayden of the expedition.

Charlie was marching beside Professor Worth in the rear, carrying his suitcase for him. "Prof, let me know if you need a piggyback ride. It's gotta be tough hiking twenty miles while old."

The professor wiped sweat from his reddened cheeks with a handkerchief. "I might take you up on that this time."

Drayden ran his fingers through his sweaty hair and stopped in his tracks, both hands on his head. "My hat!"

Sidney, walking in front of him, spun around and rifled through her pocket. "I got it." She wriggled out the green cap and tossed it to him.

"Oh my God, thank you." He pulled it on snugly and sidled up to her. Even pissed at him, she had his back.

She continued staring straight ahead, refusing him the dignity of a glance. The hot sun apparently hadn't melted the frost between them.

"Hey," Drayden said, "I know it must have been pretty crazy when you guys had to run from the Guardians. I appreciate you snagging my hat."

For a few seconds she didn't say anything. "Why do you care about that hat so much?"

"I told you, my mom gave it to me a long time ago." He touched it, acknowledging privately that it was almost an emotional portal to her. "It's like a small piece of her that I can hold onto."

"I get that. But why are we so desperate to hold onto old things? You remember your mother. You don't need a hat to remind you."

"There's something to be said for history, and good memories. She held this hat in her hands. In a way, it connects us."

"I think you should find a new hat and start creating some new memories. You can't do that when you refuse to let go of the old one."

"Sid...I'm sorry about the thing on the boat, but it wasn't what it looked like. It—"

"It was *exactly* what it looked like," she snapped. "I don't want to talk about it, Drayden. And I don't want to always be wondering what's happening at the front of the boat."

He pressed his lips together to forcefully shut himself up before he dug the hole any deeper.

Sidney glowered at him and sped away.

She was right, he thought. He hadn't fully committed to her and was trying to play both sides. It wasn't fair, even if the incident hadn't occurred. But the current plight in New America demanded he put it on the back burner. His hat in its rightful place, he was searching for his mother, and that was plenty to focus on right now.

Three and a half hours later, having successfully passed over the rickety remains of the RFK Bridge, the group trudged through the heavily overgrown I-87 into the Bronx.

Drayden buried his face in the map, reading as he walked. "We should get off the highway soon and explore these streets. If I'd been exiled, I'd probably wind up in this area, which is called Kingsbridge."

He blazed the path through the endless and desolate Bronx streets, knowing they needed a strategy. They could wander around aimlessly for days and still overlook an existing community.

Drayden stopped, letting his arms flop by his sides. "Anyone have a thought about how we might locate a survivors' camp here?"

Professor Worth and Catrice both went to speak at the same time. The elderly man demurred. "You first."

Catrice wrung her hands. "Remember how we found the backpacks at our camp in the woods? I think we should hike over to the Henry Hudson Bridge, where the Bureau dumps off the exiled. If there is a community, you'd think it would be set up so that anyone who was freshly exiled couldn't help but stumble onto it."

Professor Worth nodded. "Outstanding. Well done, Catrice."

They made their way to the Henry Hudson Parkway. Their exile simulation kicked off a number of blocks past the end of the bridge, so they wouldn't draw the attention of any Guardians manning the gate.

Drayden visualized his mother making this exact walk, except cold and alone, in the dark. Recreating the steps of an exile cast a fresh light on the unconscionable cruelty of the Bureau and reinforced its depravity.

At first, nothing unusual stood out. Then evidence of life started cropping up. A recently used fire pit. Garbage. They took the next exit for 232nd Street, turned right, and abruptly stopped.

A modest cluster of people, dressed in little more than rags, huddled on a curb around a pile of wet clothes. Further down the road, others gathered around a bucket holding long sticks.

"Keep your weapons holstered," Drayden said.

The survivors immediately took notice of the strangers treading hesitantly along their street. Some of them gawked through hollowed out eyes. Many remained expressionless, their faces reduced to grimy skin over jutting cheekbones.

A rail thin elderly woman, her hair sloppily chopped off, hobbled their way.

As she got closer, Drayden realized she wasn't old at all, just emaciated. She also looked vaguely familiar.

"Hello," she said softly.

He'd seen her before. "Miss Vester?"

"Drayden?" Squinting, she eyeballed the teens. "Sidney, Catrice? My goodness, you kids are late for class. Detentions all around!" She muttered something unintelligible. "Where were those lesson notes?" Wrapping bony arms around her body, she inspected the pavement.

Baylee Vester had been an English teacher at Norman Thomas High School. Drayden now remembered hearing she'd been exiled months ago.

"Miss Vester!" Sidney went in for a hug.

The frail woman pulled back and raised her guard. "No, no, no! No touching. We have strict rules here. If you break the rules in school, you get detention." She grinned. "You touch, you get sick. Call me Baylee. I don't know Miss Vester."

"Sorry." Sidney fumbled with the buttons on her uniform.

Drayden opened and closed his mouth, unsure of how to proceed with someone quite clearly in a diminished mental state. "Baylee, there's a revolution starting in New America. We're here looking for survivors, who we had a hunch might be alive."

"We're thriving, as you can see." She fanned her arm out behind her. "Sure, most become sick or starve. There are hundreds of us now. More every day."

"What do you eat?" Charlie asked.

Her eyes bulged. "We have delicious food. You should try it! We have fish. And new people joining us from the city usually come with vegetables or potatoes." She wagged a finger. "We don't let them eat it," she whispered. "We plant it."

Drayden felt Sidney looking at him, and he knew why. He was suddenly afraid to ask about his mother. While it had only been a month and change, finding her had been his primary goal for what felt like years. With news of her fate at hand, he wasn't ready. He stared at his shoes and started to tremble. It was too agonizing. He couldn't bear the wrong answer, so maybe he wouldn't even ask the question.

"Miss Ves—Baylee," Sidney said, "do you know if my parents are here?"

"They are."

Sidney covered her mouth with both hands. "My God," she whispered.

"Drayden," Baylee said.

He swallowed hard, unable to respond or look up.

"Your mother is here too."

CHAPTER 12

Drayden wanted to seek out his mother alone, but Charlie insisted on coming. Sidney was off tracking down her own parents, while Professor Worth and Catrice were resting under the shade of a sprawling tree on 232nd Street with all the weapons.

Why was he nervous? This was his *mom*. He hoped she would be proud of him for making it this far, even though entering the Initiation had gone against her last wishes. Words couldn't describe everything he'd been through to get here. She would know; she'd see it in his eyes.

Baylee had directed him to the former Intech Academy, which was a public middle and high school before the Confluence, a few short blocks away. Amidst her ramblings, she'd remarked that a number of people were staying in the gymnasium, and she believed his mother was among them.

Drayden couldn't resist picturing their reunion, imagining them locking eyes across the gym, his mom's face a vision of blissful shock. They would run to each other and embrace, full of laughter and tears, flouting the community rules about touching but not caring one bit. After he caught her up on recent events, he expected that she would be a substantial help on whatever came next, given that she'd discussed aiding the resistance with Lily Haddad in the past.

Perhaps they could smuggle her into the city. Her alleged reluctance to fully join the insurrection was not likely due to a lack of approval. It was probably because she didn't want to risk exile and be snatched from her kids. And *finally*, Drayden would gain some clarity on her sordid and consequential affair, and the individual responsible for her exile.

An uninviting blockish cement structure, Intech Academy resembled many of the schools in the Dorms—three stories tall, long, with rows of broken windows. When he and Charlie passed through the front door, they were almost knocked over by the smell, a combination of sewage, urine, sweat, and vomit. What was his mother doing here?

Charlie pinched his nose shut. "You were right, I shouldn't have come," he croaked.

The foul smell was emanating from the gym, so it wasn't hard to find.

Drayden's stomach knotted. This was a makeshift hospital.

It was dim inside, the air thick and dank, reeking of death and sorrow. People were lying on the floor in rows, filling the entirety of the former basketball court. A few were on blankets, though most were curled up directly on the warped hardwood.

It wouldn't have been unlike his mother to risk her own life taking care of the infirm. She had done exactly that when she helped an injured woman at the Food Distribution Center, getting herself covered in the poor woman's blood. Brave and selfless was just who Mom was. Except Drayden didn't see any doctors or nurses, or anyone tending to these patients, which made perfect sense because doctors and nurses were never exiled. Only Dorm residents were.

With Charlie in tow, he paraded up the first row of people, taking in each face. Some of them appeared deathly sick. Most were asleep, or unconscious, though a handful were moaning.

"Dray," Charlie said, his voice nasal. "I gotta take off. I'm sorry, man, I can't handle it. I'll be right outside."

Drayden nodded and continued his search, down the second row. Then up the third. So far, not a trace of her.

"Drayden?" someone whispered behind him.

He spun around, his heart thumping in his chest.

What? It can't be.

He'd walked right past her. "Mom?"

She was tucked into a ball, her knees up to her chest, struggling to lift her head off her blue New York Knicks hoodie, now a surrogate pillow. She was skin and bones; barely recognizable, as if she'd aged twenty years.

Drayden dashed back to her. "Mom!" He dropped to his knees and held her tight, noticing her hair had thinned too.

"Is it really you? No, sweetie, don't hug me." She tried to push him away.

"I don't care. Oh my God, I can't believe I found you." He buried his face against her shoulder and sobbed.

She rocked him. "Baby, how are you even here? You can't stay. You have to get out of here."

He couldn't stop crying, overcome with herky-jerky breath spasms, spewing gibberish. "Mom, I entered the Initiation, and I passed it and moved to the Palace, and then they sent me on this expedition to Boston, and, and we made it there, and we found out all these horrible secrets about New America, and I couldn't get back, but this old man, this professor, he helped us, and we got a boat back, and I got here in time to save Dad and Wes, and then...I...Mom?"

She had dropped her head onto the pillow, regarding him with glossy eyes. "That's amazing, honey. I'm so proud of you. You didn't have to come find me though. I want you to stay where it's safe."

"It's not safe there. There's a whole revolution going on now. People trying to overthrow the Bureau. I'm kind of a part of it. But I needed to find you. I had to find you."

"Dray, I'm sick. Very sick."

"I'm going to get you help. I can bring medicine. Let's get you out of here first."

"No, baby. It's too late. I have Aeru. We all do. That's why we're in the gym. And I'm not going to let you catch it too."

"I took a vaccine. I'm fine, I can't catch it. There's that vaccine and other treatments. I can get them. Mom, you wouldn't believe the things I've been able to do the past few weeks. I can make you better, trust me."

She smiled. "That's my boy. You've grown up so much." She rubbed his cheek. "If you keep yourself healthy and safe, that's all I want. And I'd love some water if you have any."

He immediately brightened. "Yes! I do. You stay put, and I'm going to fetch you water and figure out how to get you medicine. I have friends here, and between us, we can solve this. Okay?"

She touched his knee. "I love you."

"I love you too. I'll be right back."

Having sprinted from the school, Drayden and Charlie reconvened with the others by their spot on 232nd Street. Sidney was fuming.

"What's up, Sid?" Drayden asked.

She crossed her arms. "Oh, nothing, I was just reminded why I wasn't *that* upset when my parents got exiled. All they wanted to know about was Nora. Is she okay? Where is she? Why am I not taking care of her?" She groaned. "As if I haven't been killing myself to make sure she's safe, and they have the nerve to imply I'm slacking off or something."

"I know what it's like to be disappointed by your parents," Catrice said softly.

Sidney put her hands on her hips. "Is that right, Catrice? What do you know, huh? You don't know anything about my parents."

"Sid," Drayden warned.

"Take it easy," Charlie told her. "She's just trying to help."

"Well she's not helping, because she never helps. All she does is get sympathy from you guys for being weak."

Catrice ran her fingers through her hair and looked away.

"Sid, go take a walk." Charlie pointed down the street.

"Of course, take her side like always." She rolled her eyes. "No, I want to know what's going on with Dray. Did you find your mom?"

He grew an instant lump in his throat. "I...I did. She's...she has Aeru."

Her face softened. "I'm sorry. I'm so sorry, Dray. Here I am ranting and raving about my stupid parents." She dropped her arms by her sides. "I'm sorry, you guys."

Catrice was glaring at her.

Sidney pressed her hands together as if in prayer. "What can we do?"

Drayden thought he should confer with Professor Worth. "She asked for water, so I'm going to take her a bottle right now. After that I want to sneak into the city and see if I can get some medicine for her. Like the Aeru vaccine, or another treatment."

The teens exchanged uneasy glances.

"I'll go alone if you guys don't want to come."

"No, bro," Charlie said. "We'll obviously come, if that's what you want to do."

Professor Worth slung his arm over Drayden's shoulders. "Come." He motioned toward the street.

"What?"

"I want to talk to you alone for a minute," he said, forcing Drayden over to the curb, away from his friends. He eased himself down, extending his hand for Drayden to join him.

"Drayden, I believe in you more than you'll ever know. I want you to believe in yourself too, because you're capable of so much. But this is one thing you cannot do."

"What, go into the city? Find medicine?"

"No. Save your mother."

Drayden jerked his head back. "That's shkat! I could head to the Palace and track down the scientist who did our training before the expedition. Her name is Sam. She would help me. I'll bet she can get me some of the vaccine, or an experimental medicine they have. I'm sure they've been working on it for years. I was prowling around the streets for the whole day yesterday with no problem."

Professor Worth gazed into his eyes. "There is no treatment for Aeru, son. The vaccine only works if you haven't caught it yet. Boston is supposedly more advanced than New America and they have no cure either. If you went into the city, creeping around labs, looking for this scientist, you would be killed. I'd suspect that is the last thing your mother wants."

"But—"

"No." He shook his head. "If you want to help your mother, go be with her. Stay with her. We can plan on remaining here as long as we have to. We're going to hit pause on everything else. Don't forget, I lost my wife Ruth to this awful disease. The best thing you can do for her is to maybe say a prayer, and give her all your love."

Drayden burst into tears, burying his face in his hands.

The professor hugged him until he pulled himself together. "Stay here. I'm going to grab you a water bottle. I'll let the other kids know what's going on."

A minute later he returned. Drayden took the water and hugged Professor Worth one more time.

The professor patted him on the back. "Go on now."

Drayden ran the few blocks to the school, enduring the horrific smell again when he set foot in the gymnasium.

His mother was asleep.

He sat and gently shook her shoulder. "Mom? It's me."

She opened her eyes with a faint smile. "Hi, honey."

"Here, sit up. I brought you water." He slinked his arm underneath her and tilted her forward.

She sipped it. "That is so good. Thank you."

"This bottle is yours, and I can bring more."

"You're the best son, you know that?" She laid down.

Drayden reclined beside her and held her hand. "Unfortunately, I don't think I'm going to be able to get that medicine."

"I know."

They remained like that for a while. "Hey, Mom? I need to talk to you about something. Did you ever figure out why you were exiled?"

"No, I still have no idea."

"Was it possibly Nathan Locke?"

She furrowed her brow. "What about Nathan Locke?"

"Mom, I know. I know you two were having an affair."

His mother tried to prop up on her elbows and smack Drayden on the arm. "We most certainly were not. Where did you get that idea?"

"Wesley. He saw you, in the FDC."

She scowled at him. "I was being *harassed* by Nathan Locke. It was not some sort of affair, although he wished it was. He'd been chasing me for years. What could I do about it? Who could I complain to? I had to put up with it."

Drayden blew out a long breath. Throughout the expedition, he'd been blaming his mother's affair for every iota of suffering he endured. He'd even come to terms with the fact that his mother was flawed like everyone else and couldn't have foreseen the drastic consequences. That it was entirely untrue was the gift he didn't know he needed. None of this was his mother's fault. "Oh, thank God. What a creep. I confronted him. He said he invited you to move to the Palace with me and Wes and you said yes."

She laughed a little. "He did ask, all the time. The answer was always no."

"Do you think there's any chance he was the one who had you exiled? Because I was sure it was him, until talking to you."

"I don't think so."

"What if he got tired of you saying no?" Despite her clarification, he wasn't convinced. Locke was a proven scoundrel, if for no other reason than he'd blatantly lied, most likely to antagonize Drayden.

"I mean, anything's possible in that hellish city," she said. "But there would be no reason for him to suddenly do that. It's not like something had recently changed. Every day he hounded me, and every day I tried to run away."

"Now I'm back to square one. No clue who's responsible."

Mom wrapped her arms around his. "I'm going to close my eyes for a bit. Can you tell me about the Initiation and this trip to Boston?"

"Yeah, definitely." He recited everything that had happened since her exile, from the Guardian stalking him in the Dorms before the Initiation to his white-knuckle escape over the border wall a day earlier. His mother seemed to be asleep for parts of it but perked up occasionally, reacting to something he'd said.

"So...I kind of have a girlfriend now." He snickered. "Actually, I sort of have two. Or, zero, depending on who you ask."

She opened her eyes slightly and squeaked, "Two girlfriends? Do tell."

Drayden filled her in on the teen drama, and she nodded and smiled every so often. After that she fell asleep, and he did too. In the middle of the night he awoke, the gym pitch black and silent. He really had to pee but he didn't want to leave her side. He squeezed her hand and dozed off again.

It was dawn when she roused with a startle, waking him up.

She stared at him, fear in her eyes. They both knew.

Through all the investigating, and the wondering and the Initiation and the expedition, he'd been to hell and back to find her. But as always, like with Tim and Charlie, he fell short. He should have gotten here sooner. Once more, he was too late. He would remember this feeling for the rest of his life. This was his greatest failure and he'd be damned if he would ever fail this way again.

He hugged his mother, kissed her, and told her he loved her. Tears flowing down his cheeks, he said goodbye, never letting go of her hand.

He made sure she knew he was right there with her and felt loved in her final moments.

And just like that, releasing his hand, his beloved mother died.

CHAPTER 13

Drayden sat cross-legged, staring at his mother's lifeless body. With a whimper he surveyed the gym, looking for anyone to help. Why wasn't someone with medical training around who could try to resuscitate her? What a pathetic mockery of a real community this was, allowing its residents to die, helpless in a room, like passengers on a plane with no pilot.

Neither her neck nor wrist showed a pulse.

Drayden touched her cold lips, and gently closed her mouth. Then he closed her eyes, before lying down beside her, feeling lost in a timeless void.

When daylight brightened the gym through the frosted block windows near the ceiling, he sat up and wiped his eyes with his shirt. Kneeling, he lifted his mother's head and slid out her Knicks hoodie. Carefully, he eased it over her head, slipped both arms through, and pulled it down snug.

With her water bottle tucked under his arm, he lifted her, shocked at how light she was.

As he approached the doors, an old lady jabbed her finger at him. "The sick must remain in the gym!"

Drayden ignored her and made his way to 232nd Street, seeing his friends under their usual oak tree.

Their expressions somber, they watched him near, carrying his mother's body.

He walked straight past them, another block, until he reached Ewen Park, a hilly patch of intentional greenery amongst the ruins. At the top of the hill, he set her down in a pleasant nook surrounded by vibrant yellow flowers.

Drayden's friends were congregated in a solemn bunch behind him.

He spent a few minutes finding an appropriate rock and returned to the grassy alcove, where he started digging.

The dew-soaked grass offered little in the way of resistance, but it became much more difficult mere inches lower.

He slammed the tool into the unforgiving soil, assaulting it over and over.

Within minutes, Professor Worth joined him, and the others did too.

Drayden stepped away into the woods, foraging for a broad, flat stone. Although he failed to find the ideal one, he came back with the best available. Hands shaking, he carved "Maya Coulson" into it with his hunting knife.

The girls had collected some colorful wildflowers, which they'd arranged on the grass. Charlie and the professor left for a stretch, reappearing with a sheet and various wooden boards, likely from a disassembled cabinet. Once the grave was deep enough, Professor Worth placed the boards on the sides and bottom.

Drayden climbed inside and picked up his mother's body, compelling everyone else to stand back. Charlie was turned away, obscuring his face. The girls were teary, clutching each other. Professor Worth stood with his hands clasped and his head bowed.

Drayden held his mom momentarily then laid her down inside. He knelt, tidying her clothes, and folded her cold hands over her stomach. He tried to say something, but nothing came out.

After setting her water bottle beside her, he removed his green Yankees cap and placed it on her chest. "I've been wearing this so I could always have a piece of you with me. Now I want you to have it so you'll always have a piece of me with you." He draped the sheet over her and climbed out, wringing his hands.

Professor Worth whispered something to Sidney and Catrice. They locked arms with Drayden, one on each side, and led him away down the hill.

He peered back.

Charlie and Professor Worth were on their hands and knees, refilling the grave.

He steeled himself, trying to believe he was ready to tackle the next challenge in their quest to vanquish the Bureau.

"I'm so sorry," Sidney said at the bottom of the grassy knoll.

That was all it took. He broke down, falling to his knees. Nothing would ever be the same. It wasn't clear he'd be able to go on, or that he even wanted to.

Inside the Kingsbridge branch of the New York Public Library, which was serving as the "headquarters" of the exile community, Drayden stood alone in the out-of-order bathroom. While his friends were speaking with the ragtag council that had commandeered a semblance of leadership over the camp, he wanted to be by himself.

He leaned over a sink streaked with old, hardened soap in pastel colors and glared at himself in the dusty mirror.

He hardly recognized the person looking back. The puffy eyes, dirty skin, stiff hair, and sunken cheeks were a mask, projecting toughness that belied the weakness lurking underneath. Sure, he'd had a couple of big wins in the Initiation and expedition. But he was indecisive. A *hesitator*. The inaction caused by his lack of confidence in himself, even if cursory, often made all the difference between success and failure.

With his mother gone, a new, sinister goal took shape in the darkness. *Revenge.* An individual, probably Nathan Locke, bore personal responsibility for his mother's death. Drayden was going to find him and kill him. Then he would stop being a witness to the insurrection and start being a player. Waiting for Kim to do her thing and hoping for the best wasn't enough. It was passive, and he needed to be active. The Bureau had blood on its hands and had to pay.

His mother's passing was a paradigm shift—a rift in a universe he'd always assumed tended toward fairness. He knew all along her exile likely guaranteed her death. Yet deep down he'd maintained a glimmer of hope that she was alive, which drove him through the Initiation and expedition. Something told him she was managing to endure. With her death, the hope was gone. Extinguished. In the remaining vacuum, a new emotion had swooped in: *rage*.

When Drayden rejoined the group, Professor Worth and Catrice were holding court, trying to prepare the survivors for an eventual entry into the city once the revolution began. Whether they would form some sort of army as Kim hoped was doubtful, in view of their condition. Nonetheless, he felt the survivors still had some role to play in the Bureau's downfall. Catrice was talking about monitoring the gates, which would hopefully be opened or destroyed, and the possibility of sending someone to retrieve them.

"Charlie? Charlie Arnold? Well, I'll be damned." A scruffy, darker man strolled up, tugging on his unkempt beard.

It was Alex's father.

"Mister Sarole?" Charlie asked incredulously. "Holy cow. I didn't recognize you with the beard. How's...how's it going?"

The father of Drayden's nemesis was a notorious drug dealer in the Dorms, forcing his kids to deal as well, before he was exiled. His random trace of warmth summarily vanished, replaced by his trademark frown. He scrutinized the fivesome and narrowed his eyes. "Where's my son?"

Charlie swallowed hard. "He didn't make it through the Initiation. I'm sorry."

He grabbed a handful of Charlie's shirt. "What do you mean he didn't make it? He failed or something?"

Charlie glanced at his hand and flushed. "He fell. He died."

"Why didn't you save him, Charlie? I thought you were his friend."

Drayden wrapped his fingers around his Glock.

"I tried, Mister Sarole. I almost died myself."

He stroked his mangy beard. "Alex always was weak. That loser." He eased away, eyeing them suspiciously. "What are you all doing here anyway?"

"We just gave a rundown to your comrades," Charlie said. "Basically, there's a revolt starting in New America. We're trying to bring you guys back into the city so you can help. Even if the gate is blown out, you should wait till we send someone to come get you, when we know it's safe."

Mr. Sarole licked his lips. "Yeah, yeah. That's good, Charlie. Very good. I have to get back in there. And these people here," he said, waving his hand casually, "they do whatever I say. We'll be ready to go. You give the word, you hear?" He pointed at the pistol on Charlie's hip. "I'm gonna need you to give me one of those weapons."

Drayden raised his chin. Alex's father was a bully like his son, and Drayden wasn't about to take it from another Sarole. As he pushed forward, Charlie gestured for him to stop.

"Sorry, Mister Sarole. Can't do that. We'll be back real soon. You guys be primed to go."

He puffed his chest out and crossed his arms. "I see. Okay, Charlie, have it your way. I'll remember this. We'll have to sort it out next time."

Drayden was proud of Charlie for standing his ground. He'd forgotten about Alex's father, and what a horrible person he was, beating Alex and forcibly indoctrinating him into the family business. It was disconcerting that returning the exiles back home meant including those who actually deserved their expulsion. They would have to sort it out all right.

Reconnecting with Alex's sadistic father spurred Drayden to draw comparisons to his own. While his father had been emotionally absent, he wasn't a monster. Drayden had always resented that his father hadn't done more to stop his mother's exile. Now he understood the powerful forces behind it, and how little his father could have done. In the Dorms, adults were helpless to protect their families. Dad had also stepped up since, trying to fill the emptiness left by Mom's banishment. He deserved credit. It was time to forgive his father and repair their fractured relationship.

Drayden and his friends left the exile camp, embarking on the long trek back to New America. Most of their food and water was gone. Besides their weapons, they lugged Professor Worth's suitcase, the flashlights, and the extension cord.

Drayden didn't even know where they were going. Regardless, they needed to head south down I-87.

Professor Worth ambled next to him, holding the orange cable, now fitted with some sort of hook on the end. "Drayden, we spent the past day hammering out the details of our entry into the city. It's not trivial. First, we have to access Manhattan, which is an island. Then we need to get over the wall. Here, up north, the Harlem River is less than two-hundred feet across in many spots. An easy swim. Except...Catrice can't swim. So we must take a bridge."

"Sure," Drayden mumbled. "I think we have to use the Fifty-Ninth Street bridge, because it has a lower level that provides cover."

"Yes, that's what we thought as well. Charlie briefed me on your escape. We're going to need one of those Guardian watch stations for our climb. Charlie and I raided a number of stores and houses, and found a few items that could be useful. Ultimately, our best shot is with this hook we fashioned. We'll have to catch it on the watchtower on the inside of the wall, like a grappling hook, and lift ourselves up. We need to find the one you used, given we don't know where any others are, and you can't see them from outside the wall."

Drayden nodded. With new business to attend to, he absolutely did need to get into the city.

Sidney slowed until he caught up to her. From a pants' pocket, she removed her Guardian baseball hat, which was gray camouflage with a flat top. "I want you to have this."

He forced a smile. "Thanks." After adjusting the band in the back, he pulled it on tight.

"I'm really sorry, Dray. There are no words. But we're going to make some new memories now. Good ones." She rubbed his arm. "I'm also sorry about how I acted yesterday. I lost my temper. It was a bad look."

Drayden's focus drifted to Catrice, who bore the brunt of Sidney's tantrum. "It's fine. It was emotional seeing our parents."

"Don't worry, I'm going to talk to Catrice too." She jogged to catch up with her.

"Catrice?" Sidney said. "I need to apologize. I'm sorry about what I said. I was angry and I took it out on you. I didn't mean it."

"It's all right. Thank you."

She rested a hand on Catrice's shoulder. "You were right too. I guess I'm just getting a taste of what you've had to deal with your whole life. I can't imagine what you must have gone through. You're the last person in the world I should be lashing out at about parents."

Catrice wiped her eyes. "Thanks."

Sidney smiled. "Maybe you can help me figure out how to deal."

"I wish I knew. I wish I knew what it's like to love someone as much as you love your sister."

Sidney stared at her for a moment. "Yeah."

Three hours of hiking later, the group crossed the Fifty-Ninth Street bridge, with the midtown skyscrapers looming in the distance and the afternoon sun in their eyes. They slowly and deliberately descended the stone walls of the restaurant Guastavino, landing on Fifty-Ninth Street.

"Where was this Guardian watch station?" Sidney asked.

"On or around Fifty-Second Street," Drayden replied.

Charlie signaled toward the East River. "Let's do it."

They proceeded south along Sutton Place, a block east, to elude any Guardians on the border wall. At Fifty-Second Street and First Avenue, after a short jaunt west, they crept into a restaurant near the base.

"I see it," Charlie whispered. "Where we came over."

"How can we tell if anyone is on the other side patrolling?" Catrice asked.

Professor Worth stepped outside and kicked the crumbling stone facade of a nearby restaurant, dislodging a hunk of cement. "We'll have to throw this over," he said as he returned. "If anyone's there, we'll know posthaste."

Charlie took the block from him. "I'll do it. You guys get your weapons prepped in case this starts a firefight. Or just Sid."

Drayden fought off a smile. Charlie and Sidney were assassins. He and Catrice? Not so much.

Their rifles high-ready, everyone trailed him into the shadow of the wall. Charlie lobbed the stone block over it like he was tossing a baseball and aimed his rifle skyward.

After five minutes, no Guardians had appeared and Charlie unwound the extension cord. "Assuming I can get this bad boy locked on the tower, we're gonna climb it. I'm going to show you how. It's not hard. You don't have to pull yourself all the way up, which would be crazy tough. You're gonna do a move called the brake and squat. Basically, you wrap your foot around the cord and stand on it. Then you lift yourself a foot or so with your arms, scrunch your legs up, wind your foot in again, and stand. You only need to move yourself up an armlength at a time. As long as you can do a pull-up, you can make it the whole way." He paused. "Is there anyone who can't do a pull-up?"

Catrice sheepishly raised her hand.

"Shoot." Charlie scratched the back of his neck.

"I have an idea," Professor Worth said. "After Charlie and someone else goes, we tie a loop at the bottom. Catrice puts her foot in the loop, and we hoist her up."

She chewed her nails. "I'm sorry, you guys. Should I go last then?"

"No," Drayden said. "Somebody who can shoot will have to stay at the bottom for cover in case we get ambushed. I think Sid, because we need Charlie on top to pull."

"That's cool," Sidney said. "I don't mind going last."

"Everybody stand back," Charlie ordered. He handled the cord a foot shy of the hook and whipped it around in a circle like a lasso. Grunting, he hurled it up at the top of the wall. It fell a good amount short. Around twenty tries later, using various throwing techniques, he'd still failed to latch the grappling hook onto the watchtower, causing him to make obscene gestures at the cement.

"Lemme try." Sidney held the hook, took a running start, and launched it over, instantly snagging it on the other side. She dusted off her hands.

Doubled over, Charlie stared at her. "Beginner's luck." He shook his arms out. "I'll go first. Watch me, especially what I'm doing with my feet." He leaped and gripped the extension cord, flailing his legs around for a second, eventually intertwining the cable and his right foot. He set his weight down on it, letting go with one hand to demonstrate. "See?"

He reached higher, lifted himself, releasing his foot, and wound it up once more. "Up we go, right, Professor?" He cackled and continued until he made it all the way. Safely on top of the wall, he brandished his rifle and scanned the area below.

Charlie jumped down onto the Guardian platform and waved his hand forward. "We're clear!" he hollered. "Let's go, Professor Worth next."

He grabbed his suitcase. "First this." With a simple knot, he secured it and gave Charlie the go ahead.

Charlie expeditiously reeled in the suitcase and lowered the cable. Professor Worth rubbed his hands together and got started, impressing everyone with his surprising strength and youthfulness. He expertly worked his way up and joined Charlie on the platform.

"Drayden, you next!" Charlie shouted, craning his neck over the edge.

"See you guys in a sec," he said to the girls. Grasping the cable wasn't a problem, although he fumbled around with his foot, trying to create the loop. After he figured it out, he inched up, slowly getting the hang of it. His arms started fatiguing near the top, but it wasn't too difficult. As he scoped out the abandoned streets below, he felt an expected tinge of anxiety. He hopped onto the metal grating of the platform, joining Charlie and Professor Worth.

Charlie leaned over the wall. "Catrice, tie a loop and we'll pull you up!"

While Sidney nervously paced, her rifle high-ready, Catrice formed the loop and tested it out. Placing one foot inside, she clasped the cable with both hands. "All set!"

Charlie cracked his knuckles. "Ready, Dray? We're gonna do this together. I'll be behind you. Professor, keep your weapon live and watch for Guardians."

Drayden tugged the cord right where it came over the wall, employing every ounce of muscle, and Charlie pulled directly behind him. It was insanely hard, not so much because of Catrice's weight—she was akin to a feather—but due to the friction between the cable and the cement, which was rectangular with sharp edges.

Charlie bore the brunt of the work, groaning each time he heaved.

Drayden eased up and peeked over the edge. "It's working."

Charlie paused, wiping sweat from his brow. "Holy crap."

When Drayden grabbed the cable to continue, his eyes widened. "Uh-oh."

The extension cord's orange casing was shearing off with each tug, ripping over the rough cement.

"Charlie, wait," he said. "The cable's tearing."

"Keep going," Professor Worth said. "You have no choice. It's the only way to get her over. Quickly now."

"What's wrong?" Catrice yelled, her face a question mark.

"Nothing, it's all good!" Drayden replied.

"Drayden," Professor Worth said, "grab her as soon as she's close."

He and Charlie picked up the pace, shredding the cable enough to expose the metal fibers inside.

Drayden let go and leaned precariously over the wall, extending his arm. She neared the top. "Catrice, give me your hand! Grab it!"

Keeping one hand around the cord, she seized Drayden's hand with the other.

The cable snapped.

Catrice shrieked. Connected to Drayden by sweaty palms, she dangled twenty-five feet above the asphalt, flailing her legs. Charlie slammed backward into Professor Worth, almost knocking him off the platform.

Drayden clamped onto Catrice's wrist with his free hand, feeling her slipping away. "Charlie, help!"

He sprung to his feet and snagged her other hand. The two of them dragged her to safety on top of the wall.

Drayden breathed a huge sigh of relief, albeit a fleeting one.

Professor Worth peered down at Sidney, stranded on the wrong side. "This is a problem."

CHAPTER 14

As miserable and selfish as Drayden felt leaving Sidney behind, he was confident Professor Worth and Catrice could find a way to rescue her. They would likely need to explore nearby residences for helpful equipment. Luckily, no one lived this far north and, with the exception of the period immediately following the Confluence, the area had remained relatively untouched.

Drayden had a job to do and needed to do it before the insurrection started. After that, the city might be on lockdown. It also had to be a solitary endeavor, because his friends would not approve. This unplanned delay was his only chance.

"Sid!" Drayden called out one last time. "You're going to be okay. We're going to get you over. Just stay out of sight on the other side of the street. I'll see you in a jiffy."

She responded with a thumbs-up.

"I don't understand, Drayden," Professor Worth said, furrowing his brow. "This doesn't make sense. We should stay together. You're inserting a variable into our plan with a high degree of volatility around it."

Drayden clearly couldn't tell them the truth. "I need to get my brother and I have to deliver this information about the exiles to Kim. It'll be too hard to move undetected if there's a group of us.

Trust me, I'll be fine. And you guys all have to work together to help Sidney. Once you have her, I'll meet you at Mr. Kale's house in the Dorms. Charlie knows where it is." He did, in fact, want to retrieve Wesley and report to Kim, so it wasn't a flagrant lie. Nor was it the full story.

He unslung his rifle and handed it to Charlie. "Move cautiously out there and tuck your weapons away. Whatever you do, make sure you don't get captured. The regular old Guardians in the Dorms aren't quite the Special Forces guys in the Palace. You can evade them."

"I don't like this, Drayden," Catrice protested. "I have a bad feeling about it."

He hugged her. "Thank you, I appreciate your concern. I do. I...I have to go." He bro-hugged Charlie and Professor Worth.

The professor held him by the shoulders. "Be careful, son."

Drayden raced down the ladder, carrying his flashlight and wearing his pistol on his hip. Navigating the streets was so much easier alone. Since the ones in the Dorms were a perfect grid, he could see miles in every direction at each intersection. The over-abundance of abandoned buildings made the potential need for an urgent hiding place a negligible matter.

Drayden worked his way to the Fiftieth Street subway station on the One Line, which was a track he knew from the Initiation. Inside, he felt safe, ironically, considering how dangerous the Initiation had been.

Like on his trip up to the Dorms with Charlie, he sought to avoid certain stations. The first was at Times Square Forty-Second Street, home of the skyscraping rock wall. He'd fallen off it the first time, and he wasn't about to seek redemption.

The further south he went, the riskier heading up to street level became, because he was traveling through increasingly populated areas. Once he hit the Fourteenth Street station, he was leaving the Dorms, crossing beneath the wall that separated it from the Lab.

As far as he knew, the walls were intact, and he couldn't help but wonder why. Kim had said the plan involved assassinating Holst first and then levelling the walls. What were they waiting for? Had something gone wrong? If the insurrection had already been foiled, he was a dead man. Between breaking his promise about the batteries to Holst, being at war with Captain Lindrick's crew, and running amok all over the city, he was an enemy of the state, as were his friends and family for that matter. His very survival hinged on the success of the overthrow plot.

Approaching the Palace, his nerves flared. His mother deserved vengeance, and he absolutely planned on delivering it. Yet even on the expedition, a trip flush with combat deaths, he'd *personally* never killed anyone. In fact, he'd gone out of his way to spare the Guardians' lives—when they were trying to murder him, no less.

Despite his mother's belief in Nathan Locke's innocence, Kim Craig possessed evidence of his guilt, in the form of his name beside the sealed computer file on Mom's exile. Without question, the guy would never open the door to Drayden—not after he'd threatened Locke before he left for the expedition. He'd need a disguise, which wouldn't be a problem and required only a quick stop.

Drayden made it, exiting the subway tunnel at Rector Street into a pitch-black neighborhood. Though the darkness provided excellent cover for him to move stealthily, he would exercise extreme caution. His apartment building, and a change of clothes, weren't far, but he couldn't saunter down the middle of Wall Street.

After his eyes adjusted, he walked briskly along Trinity Place, traveling much further south than necessary. His route would follow a sweeping loop through the uninhabited sections of the Palace, allowing him to enter his building from the south on Water Street.

He was about halfway when he heard voices.

Drayden scoured the area for a place to hide, cursing to himself. In this exact spot, unlike the entirety of his journey thus far, there weren't many options. Battery Park on his right, being wide open, was useless. A mammoth Greek-styled building on his left was the only alternative. His hand on his Glock, he bounded into the doorway and crouched, concealed solely by the darkness.

Two young Guardians in camo pants and T-shirts stepped out of the park, yapping about girls.

He tried to calm himself and remain perfectly still, since he was in plain sight.

A few minutes after they passed without incident, he ventured out, zigzagging through the narrow roads to reach Water Street, about four blocks south of his building. Crossing Broad Street—site of the New York Stock Exchange due north—he glanced back, as he often did, and drew in a quick breath.

Was he being followed? It appeared like someone had ducked into the shadows.

He flattened himself against a building, searching for another hiding spot. Surrounded only by towering offices here, he scurried around the corner, drawing his pistol.

His heart was pounding. He wasn't prepared for a fight right now. Not to mention, a gun battle would draw so much attention that his demise would be assured. How could anyone have trailed him? Where had they caught up? Both trembling hands on his gun, he peeked around the edge.

Nothing.

Maybe it was his imagination; his anxious mind playing tricks on him.

He wasn't sure why somebody would follow him anyway. If it was a Guardian, or someone from the Bureau, he expected they would either arrest or shoot him. Could it have been Eugene? Drayden was going to remain here until his tail revealed himself. Except, standing on the wide-open corner of Broad and Water wasn't exactly safe either.

Dammit.

One more look.

Nobody there. He guessed it was nothing other than a stress-induced hallucination.

Drayden ran the rest of the way to his building. After flinging the doors open, he jumped into an elevator and repeatedly slammed the button for the fifteenth floor, before remembering he needed to go to his brother's place where he'd changed outfits. He pressed twelve, squeezing his gun, nervously anticipating an unavoidable confrontation with his pursuer.

"C'mon," he muttered, impatiently willing the elevator doors to shut. When they did, he exhaled and rested his hands on his knees.

Drayden zoomed out of the elevator and into the apartment, fortunately unlocked from the day of their family jaunt to the alley.

He chugged a glass of water, used the bathroom, and donned the Guardian uniform he wore on the expedition. Combined with the military cap from Sidney, he resembled any Palace Guardian, provided no one looked too closely.

Drayden recited the address in his head—300 Albany Street, 8I. He pulled his Glock, made sure it was fully loaded, and cocked it.

Lingering outside the beige door to Locke's apartment, Drayden wasn't sure he had the guts to go through with it. Then he pictured his mother on the floor of the ghastly gym and, just like that, the doubt vanished.

He jutted his jaw and knocked on the door. "Mr. Locke, Guardians!" he shouted, altering his voice by making it much deeper.

He turned his back, hiding his face, and continued a pretend conversation with his imaginary partner.

"So this girl, she walks right up to me, starts talking to me like we know each other. And I'm racking my brain, like, where have I met her before? Betting I was drunk and don't remember. But I let her keep talking, you know, to buy myself time to figure out who the frick she was. Next thing I kn—"

The door opened inward a touch, and peripherally Drayden observed a head stick out.

"What are you guys doing here at this hour?" Locke asked, noticeably irritated at having been disturbed.

Drayden spun around and forcefully kicked the door open, smashing it into Locke's body, sending him tumbling to the floor. He stormed inside the apartment, whipped out his pistol, and closed the door behind him.

His fat belly protruding through his now-untucked shirt, Locke was holding his lower back and groaning on the hardwood, piercing Drayden with bulging eyes.

Drayden trained his weapon on Locke's face. "Surprise. Didn't think you'd see me again, did you? I told you I'd be coming for you."

"Wha...? Drayden, what are you doing?"

"Get up." He waved his gun toward the ceiling.

Locke, in fancy trousers and a collared shirt, stared at him with his mouth agape. His normally coifed gray hair was disheveled.

What kind of flunk dressed so formally at home? Drayden lurched closer, the gun in Locke's grill. "I got nothing to lose, tubby. Get up. Now."

Locke labored to his feet, his hands above his head.

"First things first." Drayden sized up the apartment. "I'm looking for a rope. A long one. You got a rope?" If the others hadn't been able to rescue Sidney, he needed to bring some help.

The guy was a blubbering mess. "I...I, no. I...uh...no, I don't think so. No. No rope."

Drayden slouched. "For crying out loud, someone should start a rope business in this city. You got a long extension cord?"

He raised his eyebrows. "Uh, yes, yes I do." He flicked a finger to his left. "In the kitchen."

Drayden motioned that way. "Let's go, nice and easy. You get it for me." He followed Locke into the spacious kitchen.

After he dug the cable out of a cabinet, he followed Drayden's orders to drop it on the table in a bag.

"Now into the living room. On the couch." Drayden swiped the cord and watched the fat old bureaucrat plop down on the couch with his hands folded over his lap.

He was fidgeting. "Drayd—"

"Quiet." Drayden sat on the edge of a chair opposite the couch. "I'll be asking the questions. No more lying. There're no Guardians here to protect you. If you're honest—even if I don't like your answers—you might make it out of this alive. But if I suspect you're lying, I'm pulling this trigger. I just buried my mother and I don't care about you. Understand?"

He nodded quickly. "Your mother?"

A lump formed in Drayden's throat. He took a moment to gather himself. "She...died, this morning," he said, his voice shaky. "There's a whole community of exiles living in the Bronx. Did you know that?"

Locke's shock was evident. "No."

"Did you know New America is producing drugs instead of food and trading with other colonies?"

"Yes."

"How many people know?"

Locke's arms flopped to his sides. "I don't know."

"You have to do better than that."

He cocked his head. "I don't know," he said, his aggravation flaring up. "The senior leadership. Some of the Palace Guardians, because they're the ones who process all the shipments."

"Before she died, my mother told me she wasn't having an affair with you. You were harassing her. True?"

Locke lowered his eyes. "Drayden...there're two sides to every story. I was not harassing her. Pursuing her, yes. It wasn't all resistance. I'm sorry, that's the truth."

Drayden didn't believe him, of course. He was going with his mom on this one. He also realized he should have compiled a list of pressing questions in advance. Now his mind was swirling to catalogue everything he needed clarified.

"What do you know about the expedition? What was the purpose of it? Were they sending drugs?"

Locke shrugged. "Wasn't involved in it. I only know what I heard. We used to have a trading relationship with the Boston government, and the Bureau wanted to reestablish it. As for the drugs, I wouldn't be surprised if they sent them as a gift to restart that business with distributors in Boston. I don't know for sure."

"Why send me and my friends along?"

"I don't know, Drayden. My guess is you were insurance, to make sure the Guardians succeeded. I'm sure the Bureau felt you were expendable."

Drayden scoffed. "Unbelievable. Were the Guardians instructed to kill us at the end?"

"I have no idea." He rubbed his eyes. "Knowing Holst, he probably gave them authority to decide."

"I was given a fake Aeru vaccine before the expedition. Who ordered it? Was it you?"

Locke drew his head back. "What? I don't...I don't know anything about an Aeru vaccine."

Drayden shot to his feet and paced. "Everybody got the same one, except me. Mine was different, and I believe, fake. Someone wanted to guarantee I died. Was it you?"

"No! I didn't even know you were receiving a vaccine. I told you, I knew very little about your expedition."

Drayden jabbed the gun at Locke, feeling himself losing control. "Why was I given a different vaccine, goddammit?"

"I don't know, maybe...maybe they gave you a placebo. I doubt it had anything to do with you specifically. Do you know about placebos? I imagine they were being scientific about it, and some-body needed a placebo to prove the real vaccine worked. Perhaps you were unlucky. I don't think anyone in the Bureau has a vendetta against you."

Hmmm. It was actually a reasonable explanation. Drayden hadn't thought of that. He gazed into Locke's panicked eyes. "I'm going to ask you this once. And you better think about your answer. Because if I even catch a whiff of a lie, someone will be burying you very soon. Did you have my mother exiled?"

"No, I did not. I already told you that, and I was telling the truth."

He'd withheld this damning info from Locke last time to protect Kim, but they were far past that now. "The file. Your name was listed next to it. Why?"

"What file?"

Drayden stomped his foot. "The computer file!" he shouted. "About my mother's exile. Your name was listed beside it."

Locke laughed dismissively. "You don't know much about computers, do you? Electronic files record the name of the last person to view them. That has nothing to do with who ordered the exile. Anyone who's fairly senior can read any file."

"So, you looked at it?"

"Yes. I was outraged by her exile. I told you that. I wanted to know who was responsible."

It hit Drayden then. Locke knew. "You saw it. You told me she was part of this population-reducing program. Was that the truth?"

Locke went to speak and stopped. He pursed his lips.

Drayden raised his Glock and held it inches from Locke's brow. He'd had enough of this man's games. His mother was dead, someone was going to pay for it, and the bill was due.

Images flashed through his mind, like a slideshow on fast-forward. His mom's sickly head on his shoulder. Her dead body in his arms. The fresh dirt, his wet shoes from the dew, his hat on her cold, withered body.

Tears streaked his cheeks. He pressed the muzzle against Locke's forehead.

"It wasn't the truth," Locke whispered.

Drayden clenched his jaw. "You have five seconds."

Locke regarded him with moistened eyes. "You may not believe this, Drayden, and you very well may kill me, but I'm not the monster you think I am. I didn't tell you for your own good. I was trying to protect you. You didn't need to know. It would hurt you too much."

Instantly Drayden was back in his apartment on the night of the exile. Something hadn't been right. The screaming and crying... everyone had broken down. Except one person.

Oh God.

It couldn't be. Suddenly, he didn't want to know. This was a mistake. He couldn't bear to hear it. His finger fluttered on the trigger. He could end it right now and spare himself the pain.

Sweat was pouring down Locke's reddened face.

"It was your father."

CHAPTER 15

Drayden was recklessly wandering the streets like a zombie, trapped inside his own mind. He'd backpedaled out of Nathan Locke's apartment without a word, leaving him alive in a pool of sweat. Drayden knew he never had it in himself to kill a person, especially if it wasn't in self-defense. Although he thought he wanted revenge against the one individual responsible for his mother's exile, he wasn't a murderer. His threats had been vapid and meaningless, like his life felt now, with his mother dead and his father implicated in her exile.

The darkness of the streets approximated a movie theater, replaying the exile over and over again on an imaginary screen in his mind. While Drayden had begged the Chancellor to reexamine the facts, and Wesley tried to wrest a gun from the Guardians, his father had remained silent and obsequious in the corner. Even for the king of all pushovers, it was a shocking reaction and Drayden had been outraged at the time.

Yet the most peculiar and incriminating incident had occurred when his mom said goodbye. Drayden and Wesley were both a puddle of tears. Dad? He wouldn't look at her. *Wouldn't even look at her*, as she hugged him and whispered in his ear. His wife of twenty years, the mother of his children, was being unjustly cast out to her death for the ludicrous claim that she'd conspired against the Bureau, and he registered no objection, surprise, or grief. Drayden had rationalized it away as shock, but alas, there was another plausible explanation.

Dad must have discovered the "affair." Drayden recalled his parents fighting days before the exile, which was unlike them, particularly his father, who ostensibly didn't care enough about anything to fight over it. Apparently, he *did* still care about some things, like being shown up or humiliated. All he'd needed to do to exact retribution on Mom was contact a Chancellor and say she was plotting against the Bureau. New America would jump at the chance to exile someone. The morning after, his father had delivered a pathetic little speech about moving on with their lives, which had enraged Drayden for its capitulation. Everything, all of it, made perfect sense now.

Except...Dad? Really? His father was neither rash nor illogical. Would he take away the mother of his children, killing her in the process, because he believed she was having an affair? Drayden had to concede, it did not seem like him. He would have bet all the money in the world that Dad couldn't have cared less about an affair.

Nathan Locke was also a veritable liar. If he were indeed culpable, of course he would have lied under the threat of execution, blaming someone else for the exile. The guy was intelligent as well as devious. If he was the true culprit, pinning it on Dad was a brilliant ploy.

Drayden's next move was clear. He wanted to hear it from the horse's mouth, so he would ask his father straight up. If he was guilty—and Drayden would see it in his eyes—he would never speak to Dad again. Nor would Wesley. They would ostracize the coward and never look back. Their father's failure in life would be complete. Total and utter disgrace.

Drayden had been planning on stopping at Forty Rector Street anyway to get Wesley and relay the status of the exile community. Even if Kim wasn't there, he'd leave the info with the others. Nobody knew what was going to happen next or what might be asked of them, but they could use Wes on their side. He was brave, tough, and always had his brother's back.

In stark silence, Drayden was meandering on West Street when he snapped out of his trance, realizing he'd made a mistake. West Street was expansive like a highway, lacking cover if he sensed danger. Cursing, he hopped the median and darted to the east side of the road, which was lined with a sidewalk and the occasional large building.

He turned left on Rector Street, winding up right in front of number Forty, and froze. Something was off. He pressed his back against the brick facade and listened.

Footsteps. Behind him.

Drayden's heart was beating in his ears.

Shkat.

He took off down Rector Street, leaving behind the safehouse that sheltered his family. If he was seen going in, they were toast, and he could blow the whole insurrection. His mind frazzled, he only had only seconds to figure out where to go next.

The subway.

He was within spitting distance of the Rector Street station, his escape route.

A glance behind him revealed nothing, only darkness.

One block away from the subway station, panic set in. Two Guardians were posted outside, their flashlight beams easily visible.

Dammit!

He hooked a hard right on a street the block before it, now unsure where he was. He needed to maintain his orientation, so he could keep track of his general direction. At present, he was going south. His speed was hampered by the damn bag holding the extension cord which banged into his leg with each stride.

At the end of the block, the road curved to the right, running beneath a garage of sorts, and deposited him on West Street again. He looked both ways. The median here between the northbound and southbound lanes was a jungle of overgrowth, so he lunged inside it. He briefly debated lying low in there, until deciding he would eventually be found. *You can run but you can't hide* flashed through his mind.

Drayden crossed to the other side of West Street and went north at the next opportunity, thinking the zigzagging might throw off his pursuer.

The border wall was visible on his left, a block away by the Hudson River.

Though challenging at night, he spied it as he ran, seeking a Guardian watchtower. Before long, he was back on Albany Street, smack dab where he started, in front of Nathan Locke's apartment building.

Then he saw it. At the end of the road, a ladder led up the wall, presumably to a platform obscured in the shadows.

He raced down the block, his heart pounding. Closing in on the border, he leaped onto the ladder and scampered up, peering behind him.

A hundred yards away, in the middle of the road, a glint of metal shimmered for a split second. He was coming.

Drayden climbed onto the platform and, with shaking hands, whipped out the extension cord from Locke's kitchen.

God, he needed a simple knot. He tied a thumb knot, the most basic one in existence, hoping it held.

A gunshot rang out, the pop reverberating throughout the streets.

The bullet struck the wall, blasting a cloud of cement dust in his eyes.

Drayden screeched. Temporarily blinded, he clutched the cable and hurtled over the edge. Rappelling down in sweeping arcs, he slid way too fast, burning his hands.

He crash-landed on his butt in muck, instantly soaking his pants with freezing water from the Hudson River, only feet away. Dropping the cord, he bolted to the wall and pressed his wet back against it.

A flurry of gunshots splattered mud and water all around him.

He shielded his head with his arms. Hugging the cement barrier, he scrambled south and didn't stop until the gunshots did.

Mud up to his knees, Drayden leaned against the border wall, his face buried in his hands. He was somewhere outside Battery Park, where the Guardians maintained their training facilities. The adrenaline had subsided, allowing his achy legs to make their presence known. Cold, wet, and exhausted, he took a breather to reflect on his current predicament.

He'd had such momentum. He'd boldly left his friends, successfully navigated the subways alone, and found a way into Locke's apartment to interrogate him. He was even starting to think that maybe, just maybe, his success in the Initiation and expedition hadn't been mere luck. Then it had all unraveled.

Drayden wondered if his chaser had been Eugene before dismissing the thought. Eugene could have shot him in the dark, blindfolded, from a mile away. Eugene would have caught him effortlessly in a foot race. The Bureau probably tasked people to track him down, like bounty hunters. He really needed to drop this obsession with Eugene, his boogeyman.

Regardless of who was stalking him, here he was, outside the wall, miles from the Dorms, without equipment to reenter the city. He had no way to contact his friends and ask for help. His only passage to the Dorms involved a dangerous journey along the border wall, which was monitored in multiple key places. Here in the Palace, it also abutted the river, leaving scarcely any room to walk, except through marshland.

He felt like crying but staved it off. What good would it do to feel sorry for himself? He called to mind Professor Worth, and the way his ability to survive under an extreme resource shortage was tested after the Confluence. He endured and thrived, because he had no other choice besides death. Drayden simply had to believe he could do it.

For starters, he needed to inventory his assets: a flashlight and a gun. Hmmm. Neither were much use at the moment. Was that all he had?

No. He was close to Pier Fifteen. The dinghy!

It had been tethered beneath the dock. Although a bit of a Hail Mary, it might still be there. When he and Charlie were detained, the Guardians had ignored it from what he remembered. Assuming he made it to Pier Fifteen, he could paddle to the Dorms, safely away from New America's shoreline. With some luck, Sidney wouldn't have been rescued yet. If she had? He was kind of screwed.

He sucked each foot out of the mud and plodded through the sludge, keeping a hand on the wall for balance, and to ensure he didn't stray too far away. The excursion to Pier Fifteen was likely less than a mile but given the conditions, it could take a while.

After thirty minutes, he was totally spent and his legs were cramping. The remnants of an old, abandoned dock, and the sewage stench of the river, signaled he was on the east side of New America now.

Provided he found the dinghy, how in the world could he get to it undetected? The safest way, with respect to the Guardians, would be to swim. The idea of traipsing down the pier, in full view of anyone watching, was laughable. However, Professor Worth had argued the water was deadly from the bacterial content. One problem at a time.

Fortuitously, the wall cut into the city streets and he was walking on dry land, albeit in cinderblock-like boots encased in mud. Past another abandoned dock, Pier Fifteen was visible, illuminated by a spotlight.

First, he checked up for Guardians, but the border wall was far too tall to see over. Squatting about fifty feet away from the pier, he glimpsed beneath it.

The dinghy was bouncing around between the pilings like a pinball, at the end of a wooden pier a good hundred feet long. If anyone happened to be watching his protracted race to the tip, he would be little more than target practice.

One thing was certain: he couldn't allow himself to be captured. He'd rather die in a gunfight on the dock, his subpar marksmanship notwithstanding. Being delivered to Holst would mean savage torture and death anyway.

He had to go for it. What choice did he have? His back against the wall, literally and figuratively, he shuffled closer until he was standing on the wooden planks.

If Guardians directly overhead witnessed him hauling down the dock, they might hesitate to shoot at someone dressed like one of their own. Even if their confusion bought him adequate time to reach the dinghy, though, he'd be a sitting duck paddling away at one mile per hour, at which point they'd know he wasn't a Guardian.

He considered aborting and walking the rest of the way. But he and his friends might need the dinghy, and this was his only shot to retrieve it. If New America went into lockdown and they sought to make an exodus, the dinghy could be their only way off the island.

Enough waffling. Drayden drew his Glock and quietly kicked mud off his boots.

Mom, if you're watching, please protect me.

He took a series of rapid breaths and sprinted his heart out. His footsteps were so damn loud! Fifty feet to go. Forty. Thirty. He wasn't going to look back. Ten. The dinghy was floating off the end. In his excitement and haste, he vaulted off the tip of the pier, immediately regretting it midair.

He splashed down inside, his gun slipping out of his hand as he braced himself on the sides, trying to keep from plunging into the water or capsizing.

It wobbled dangerously then stabilized. Luckily, the gun had fallen inside.

He hunched over, as if that would make any difference, and waited for the shouts of the Guardians, or the sound of the gate opening.

Nothing happened. They hadn't seen him.

Go!

He needed to paddle away from the pier ASAP. Further out in the water, in the darkness, he might be in the clear.

Drayden unmoored the boat, wishing this rope were about forty feet longer. He grabbed a paddle and shoved off the piling. As noiselessly as he could, he paddled until he was swallowed up by the shadows. Slumping over, he observed the pier.

Nobody was there.

Thank you, Mom.

He floated into the middle of the river and worked his way north, which was surprisingly challenging against the current. At times, it seemed he wasn't moving at all.

The night sky began lightening, fading from black to violet, with a hint of pink in the east.

Gradually, he made progress, passing by the Brooklyn Bridge, and clearing the remains of the Manhattan Bridge. Ignoring the horrific smell, it was peaceful out on the water alone. He felt like the only person on the planet.

Drayden decided he would boat to Fifty-Second Street and pull ashore there. If Sidney had been rescued, he would rest and think about his next steps.

He closed in on the Fifty-Ninth Street Bridge at dawn. The rising sun cast a gorgeous glow on the midtown skyscrapers, still dignified in disrepair.

Just then, a huge explosion rocked the morning silence, the deafening boom echoing for seconds. Then another. And another. Smoke billowed from different spots all over the land. Massive blasts continued, causing the ground to shake.

It was starting.

If Kim's crew was blowing up the walls, something else had already happened. They'd cut off the head of the snake.

Holst was dead.

CHAPTER 16

Drayden hurriedly paddled the dinghy ashore at Fifty-Second Street, his senses on high-alert. Distant explosions rang out, as if the city were under continuous attack.

In most spots along the East River, a cement wall formed the barrier between the water and FDR Drive, the highway that flanked the eastern coast of New America. In a rare stroke of luck, an elevated pedestrian walkway bordered the highway here, and beneath it, the water lapped up against a gravelly shore. The walkway overhead provided cover, like a garage, allowing Drayden to drag the dinghy onto the dirt and leave it well hidden. He weighed taking the rope, but it was too damn short.

After kicking more clumps of mud off his boots, he worked his way down Fifty-Second Street, trying not to fret about the prospect that Sidney had been rescued until it was warranted. At the border wall, he slipped into the same restaurant in which they'd hid prior to their previous attempt to reenter the city.

Sidney was nowhere to be seen. That didn't mean she wasn't around, lingering inside a nearby building, awaiting help. If she were hiding, she'd unquestionably reveal herself if she saw him, although it wouldn't be prudent for him to zip around shouting her name.

Drayden rushed to the base of the wall, finding the busted orange extension cord haphazardly coiled on the ground. With no sign of her, he waited five minutes, then jogged up and down First Avenue, peering into the abandoned shops. Eventually he gave up and returned, deflated, to the restaurant on the corner.

On the positive side, his team had found a way to rescue her. On the negative, he was in trouble, and he knew it. He collapsed on one of the dusty chairs, letting his head slump on a table.

Believe in yourself. You can do this.

Drayden sat tall, taking deep breaths through his nose and out his mouth to settle himself, like he'd learned in jiu-jitsu. Closing his eyes, he visualized a particularly serene time, when he'd sat alone atop a skyscraper, allowing his legs to dangle over the ledge. It was a month or so before the Initiation. He'd just completed an epic mathematical proof—over seventy-five pages long—with Mr. Kale. Being Drayden's idea rather than a school assignment, the project had taken weeks to complete, and the only reward was the knowledge that he could do it. In that rare moment of mental peace, with New America laid out before him, and the blustery wind tickling his cheeks, he'd felt like he could conquer the world.

He could paddle across the river to Queens and rummage for equipment. Obviously, that strategy had proven successful in recovering Sidney. His friends had found a rope or something. Despite the time and effort required, it was probably his only choice.

Before venturing out, he racked his brain for any other ideas, trying to strongarm creativity into existence, which rarely worked. He'd love another option that didn't involve many hours of—

A gigantic explosion, extremely close by, rocked the restaurant, rattling the windows and rumbling the floor.

Drayden fell off his chair and hunched down, his ears ringing. *What the hell?*

He burst out the door.

Black and gray smoke was mushrooming above the wall a few short blocks north.

As he watched it billow, he questioned why the insurgents would have razed any part of the border wall, particularly this far north. To his knowledge, they only intended on destroying the barriers between the zones.

The gate.

At Fifty-Ninth Street, the gate to the bridge afforded one of the only ways off the island. The other was the Henry Hudson Bridge to the Bronx, where the exiles were deposited. The rest of the bridges and tunnels were either damaged or had been intentionally demolished after the Confluence. Technically, the RFK Bridge, which they'd crossed to reach the Bronx—and also connected to New America—remained standing but it was terrifying and not fit for practical use.

Drayden hustled up First Avenue, noting both smoke and fire above the wall at Fifty-Ninth Street, supporting his suspicion that the resistors had bombed the gate. He took a right and scaled the stone facade of Guastavino once again, emerging onto the lower level of the bridge.

The border wall was visibly intact here on the bottom level, though the gate was on the upper level.

After a glance at the lofty drop below, he climbed a rusty column on the outside of the bridge, repeatedly telling himself not to look down. With sweat greasing his palms, he gripped each strut extra tight. His feet thumped on the asphalt of the upper level, allowing him to expel the breath he'd been holding.

The gate in the wall had indeed been blown to shreds, the sides of it on fire, spewing a steady stream of smoke into the sky. Right in front of it, a deep smoldering crater sat in the roadway.

Drayden tiptoed semi-crouched, hugging the edge of the bridge, until he was twenty yards away from the mangled gate, beyond which was an entrance ramp to the bridge.

No one was there—no Guardians, and thankfully, no bodies. None that he could see anyway.

Perhaps it had been unguarded when it blew. In light of the earlier explosions, the Guardians may have extracted their people from the walls. Or, body parts were strewn everywhere and not evident yet. He hoped not. Either way, the gate was wide open, free and clear.

He would not hesitate this time. He'd witnessed the fruits of his indecision too many times. With his chest out, he sprinted down the roadway, wincing from the heat and smoke as he closed in on the gate. He navigated around the crater and through the gap, consumed by a coughing fit. Following the ramp, which curved to the left and marked his official reentry into New America, he swiped at his watery eyes. He slowed at the bottom, landing on Fifty-Eighth Street between First and Second Avenues.

"What are you doing up here?" somebody called out.

Drayden spun left, coming face to face with three Guardians, all panting and sweaty.

He recoiled, until he noticed they weren't drawing their weapons or approaching urgently.

My outfit.

"You believe this?" Drayden asked, at once thanking his lucky stars he'd changed into his Guardian uniform and also trying to think of a reason why a Palace Guardian—dressed in gray fatigues rather than in black like regular officers—would be way up north in the Dorms. "The Bureau is sending some of us out for backup. After the first bombs went off, they had a feeling these rebels would attack the gates. You guys all right?"

"We ain't dumb," a lanky young Guardian said. "As soon as we heard the first blasts, we got the heck out of Dodge. We didn't want to be anywhere near the wall. What's happening?"

Drayden figured it wasn't too early to start turning them against the Bureau, one-by-one if necessary. "There are some rumors that the Bureau's been deceiving us. That there's actually a lot of people out in the real world and the Bureau's been trading with them for years, keeping all the spoils for themselves. Word is getting around and apparently residents are pissed."

A grizzled older officer with a silver mustache eyed Drayden skeptically. "You look a little young to be a Palace Guardian."

Drayden shrugged. "Guardian in training, sort of. I actually have a special role, kind of like a detective, because I'm a Bureau member too." He pointed at the Bureau pin on his chest.

They shared a group nod, impressed.

"Wow," the younger one said.

"That's why they sent me up here. Had to see if everyone was safe, and they wanted me to make sure this hole in the wall stays guarded at all times. We can't let anyone just wander in or out of the city. I'm heading downtown now and I'll send reinforcements your way. Can you guys hold the fort for the time being?"

"Yes, sir," the older Guardian said, saluting him.

Drayden saluted back. "Carry on." He strolled away, west on Fifty-Eighth Street, praying they didn't holler after him. He didn't want to give them another chance to ask basic questions, like how exactly had he gotten up to the northern Dorms from the Palace so fast? Or, why were his boots caked in mud?

Luckily, they didn't. He journeyed straight down the center of Second Avenue, suddenly relishing the power of his Guardian uniform. If he'd been forced to sneak all the way to the Thirties, slinking from building to building, risking a confrontation with some tense, trigger-happy Guardians, he would be in grave danger. Now he could strut around with swagger.

He passed by other squads of officers, far from the populated areas of the Dorms, offering each a salute and tip of his cap. Besides a second glance, nobody said a word to him.

Drayden first heard a commotion around Forty-Second Street, and by Thirty-Fifth Street the avenue was overrun with protestors. Many were carrying signs such as *Down with the Bureau!* but the protest seemed like it had been spontaneous for most people, who were in their work clothes. Plumbers, FDC workers, and electricians all stomped about, clogging the road until it was nearly impassable.

He'd gotten his wish. Lily Haddad had rallied the troops. The insurrection hinged on the Guardians turning against the Bureau, not on Dorm residents protesting en masse. Still, he surmised the backing of the people couldn't hurt.

Several chants resounded simultaneously, rendering them almost indecipherable. Drayden heard, "The Bureau must go, we'll make it so!" and "We want the truth! We want the truth!"

That was the instant he became apprehensive about his attire. No other Guardians were around. While formal protests hadn't taken place in many years, fiery rallies led by Lily were common. The Guardian presence was typically heavy to ensure order or keep tabs on the pulse of the Dorms, which made their absence here noteworthy.

At Thirty-Third Street, the crowd was so thick Drayden could barely weave through it. There, on a makeshift podium, stood Lily, a megaphone pressed to her mouth. Despite its ineffectiveness in reaching anyone except those directly around her, the megaphone was standard equipment for a rally. They lacked adequate technology to address a sizable gathering. The accepted protocol was to spread the message back through the audience.

"Please, everyone, you must remain calm! We are demanding answers from the Bureau as we speak. We must remain peaceful! I urge you to resume your jobs to prevent any retaliation from the Bureau. Please, I need you go to home! Let us handle this. We will hold the Bureau accountable."

She did have a point. The Bureau, via the Guardians, was armed. The protesters were not. This was not a fair or just society. No safeguards existed to guarantee the Bureau wouldn't send troops to open fire on the protestors, killing everybody. Lily, although undoubtedly in favor of the protests in spirit, had lived through the Inequality Riots and the revolts in fledgling New America. She'd witnessed the Bureau's sheer disregard for human lives.

Four blocks away, at Twenty-Ninth Street, was Mr. Kale's apartment. Negotiating the masses, Drayden bumped shoulders with a man walking in the opposite direction, each of their torsos getting twisted back. He turned around to give him the customary apologetic wave, even though it was equally the other guy's fault.

A rather stocky fellow, dressed like a janitor, he spun around with his hands balled up. "What are you looking at, punk?" He rubbed his fist into his palm. "We don't want your kind here." He inched closer. "You're not welcome!" he roared.

The kerfuffle drew unwanted attention. More and more eyes were on him, the lone "Guardian" in the crowd—in gray Palace fatigues no less.

"You're one of them!" someone yelled.

"Hey, we got a Bureau person right here!" from another.

Within seconds, it felt as if the entire crush of protestors were surrounding him, hurling slurs and obscenities.

Drayden raised his hands above his head. "I'm on your side! I'm a Dorm resident. This is a disguise. I'm not a Guardian, I swear!"

Someone shoved him from behind and he nearly toppled over.

He reached for his gun and thought better of it. That would not end well for anyone, including him. He unbuttoned his camouflage shirt and whipped it off, leaving him little more than a skinny boy in a white T-shirt. "I live in the Dorms!"

His cries were in vain. Nobody was listening, and they had no interest in the truth. They wanted vengeance, a scapegoat. They were closing in. He was pushed from the front, then shoved in the back. Someone threw a punch but he ducked it.

It was so loud, the air filled with howls and laughter. They were laughing at him. No one was going to stop this.

He gripped his pistol for real this time, his adrenaline skyrocketing.

Somebody bear-hugged him from behind before he could pull it out.

"It's me!" she shouted in his ear.

Sidney.

Charlie burst into the melee, ferociously shoving people away. "He's one of us!"

Sidney whirled around and hugged Drayden from the front, her head turned back at the aggressors. "Leave him alone!" she screamed.

The crowd was roaring, but for the moment, not assaulting him anymore.

Professor Worth was right on Charlie's heels. He threw his arm back, like he was about to pitch a baseball, and flung a wad of bills in the air. The mob instantly forgot Drayden and focused on the cloud of money dancing its way down to the asphalt. Protestors were jumping and trampling over each other to snag it.

Sidney took Drayden's hand and dragged him away, east along Thirty-Third Street. Charlie hovered over him, with Professor Worth close behind. Catrice was waiting on the sidewalk in tears, tugging on her hair.

She dashed over and into his arms.

"I'm fine," Drayden mumbled, lying through his teeth.

Professor Worth slung his arm around Drayden's shoulders, smirking. "Let's get you a change of clothes, shall we?"

Mr. Kale embraced Drayden in the kitchen. "I was worried about you, Drayden." He pulled back, gripping him by the arms. "When Catrice told me you'd ventured downtown on your own, I'll admit I thought it was a terrible idea."

Drayden dropped his hands by his sides. "You were right. Everybody was. It was stupid and I was lucky to survive." When would his luck run out? Here, with his two mentors together—his two surrogate fathers—he finally felt safe. As dangerous as the journey had been, the closest he'd come to dying was minutes earlier in the protest. He resisted the urge to be angry and annoyed that it had come at the hands of the very people on whose behalf he was fighting.

Sidney rubbed his back. "What happened?"

He plopped down in a chair, resting his elbows on the table, with everyone else huddled around him. "I actually made it down—" Drayden stopped, really taking a gander at them for the first time, leaning back. "Are you guys wearing costumes?"

While Charlie and Professor Worth were dressed the same as before, Sidney looked like she was about to teach a college course in English Literature, and Catrice appeared to be heading to a kid's birthday party, as one of the kids.

Sidney glanced down her body. "We had to change out of our camo too. Mister Kale doesn't have any women's clothing—"

"That he'll admit to," Charlie interjected.

Sidney waved him off. "He borrowed some clothes from a woman who has a daughter. I only fit into the mom's stuff and

Catrice had to wear the daughter's, so, yeah." She grinned at Catrice, who was wearing polka-dot leggings, a way-too-short skirt, and a mini pink T-shirt.

Catrice blushed. "I feel silly."

"You look...studious," Drayden said to Sidney, in her beige slacks and gray blouse.

"Is this what it's like to be smart?" she asked Catrice.

"Why are you asking her and not me?" Charlie said.

Sidney cocked her head. "Are you serious? She's a freaking genius, and you're...you know, you."

"Touché."

Drayden filled them in on his Palace adventure, although he omitted everything about Nathan Locke and the visit to his apartment. He was ashamed and didn't want them to know about his father.

"You *are* lucky to be alive," Mr. Kale said. "The Bureau obviously has people hunting for you, and they know you've been using the subways. I don't think you can do that anymore."

Drayden rubbed his temples. "What's going on here? How did these protests start?"

Mr. Kale sat across from him. "I told everyone I knew about the info you gleaned from the expedition, and it just took off. Lily Haddad must have blasted it through her network too. She didn't hold a rally, but the news spread like lightning. The protests started yesterday, and then blew up today with the explosions. No pun intended."

Drayden raised a hand questioningly. "What's the plan now? Lily was out there trying to quash the protests. I think it's the time to push. These protests will only help the overthrow plot in the Palace. According to my source," he winked at Professor Worth, "the assassination of our dear leader would have preceded the wall explosions. Holst is dead. The Bureau is probably in disarray."

Sidney's jaw dropped. "I can't believe Holst is dead."

"Thank God." Charlie strode over to the fridge.

"Stop!" Mr. Kale practically tackled him, immediately looking contrite. "Sorry, power's out. I want to keep that closed." He retook his seat. "I think Lily wants to avoid a riot, because there's nothing to stop the Guardians from shooting everyone. Even without direct orders, they have the authority to fire at any time. I'm assuming Lily's team needs time to formulate a plan."

Drayden tugged on his left earlobe. Despite being armed, the Guardians were vastly outnumbered by the Dorm residents. Of the roughly 100,000 people in New America, 75,000 lived in the Dorms, outmanning the 15,000 Guardians five to one. He had experienced firsthand the uselessness of a weapon in a sea of people.

"Professor, what do you think?" he asked.

"I think you should go meet with this Lily woman. No one has more intimate knowledge of the Bureau's crimes, or direct information about the insurrection, than you do."

"It's a good idea," Mr. Kale said. "I can take you. As soon as we get you some new clothes." He stood, nodding toward his bedroom. "Follow me."

Minutes later Drayden emerged in olive green dress pants, a white linen shirt, and a sweater vest.

Everyone tried to contain their laughter, but the effort lasted only a fraction of a second before they lost it.

Mr. Kale covered his mouth and stared at the floor, stifling a laugh.

Drayden put his hands on his hips. "I don't know why *you're* laughing. They're your clothes." Besides the duds being "grown up," they were also extremely baggy, even with his bulletproof vest underneath, because Mr. Kale was a heavier man.

"That looks totally natural," Charlie said. "You'll absolutely blend out there now. You look like a librarian intern. You look like a kid going as his dad for Halloween. You look li—"

"Let's go," Drayden said to Mr. Kale, shoving Charlie away. He stretched the sweater vest down to cover the pistol on his hip.

When they set foot inside the pint-sized lobby of Lily's office, bustling with people and activity, Drayden had flashbacks to the day he hid there before the Initiation. Her receptionist, who he instantly recognized, had chased him out the door. He wondered if she recalled him.

"May I help you?" she asked, giving no sign she remembered.

"We're here to see Lily," Mr. Kale replied. "It's important. Tell her Gavin Kale and Drayden Coulson need to speak with her."

She muttered something unintelligible and headed down a long corridor.

Mr. Kale rested his hand on Drayden's shoulder. "The incident in the crowd sounded terrifying. Are you sure you're alright?"

Drayden leaned against a wall. "I'm still a little rattled, to be honest. I didn't know what to do. They wouldn't listen to me. People were starting to throw punches. I was a second away from using my gun."

"I don't blame you, but thank God you didn't. You would have been swarmed and possibly killed."

The receptionist returned and waved them ahead to Lily's office, where Drayden followed Mr. Kale inside.

Lily was seated at her desk, with six others Drayden didn't recognize around her. Two were sitting in chairs facing the desk.

"Gavin, Drayden, come in please," Lily said. "I'm glad you're here. We're talking strategy." She fanned her arm across the assembled crew. "In addition to my advisors, we have the unofficial heads of some of the various workers organizations. Lou Ricci leads the carpenters, Joe Kelly runs the plumbers, and Paula McSweeney speaks for the seamstresses."

"Hey, Joe," Mr. Kale said with a wave. He extended his hand, urging Drayden up front.

Drayden awkwardly grinned. "We want to help. I'm happy to share what I know from my contacts in the Palace about this insurrection, or anything about the secrets the Bureau's been keeping."

"Drayden and his friends are responsible for breaking this news about the Bureau," Lily said to the group.

"Great job, kid," one of the men said.

Lily stood. "I was just telling everybody that I've heard nothing from the Bureau since the protests and explosions. I'm waiting for them to contact me. We've confirmed there's a large hole in the wall between the Dorms and the Lab, around Third Avenue, which is being protected by the Guardians. In the meantime, I want peaceful protests. Peaceful being the key. Our voices need to be heard loud and clear by the Bureau, but I don't want to provoke them."

Joe Kelly, dressed in utility clothing standard for plumbers, grew red in the face. "I think we should pour through these holes and march right to the Palace."

"The Bureau is like a wounded cat right now," Lily countered. "We don't want them to lash out, all claws and sharp teeth, because that could entail a major loss of life."

"Miss Haddad," Drayden said, "I was told that the walls would only be destroyed after Holst was assassinated. The explosions should mean he's dead. The Bureau might be at war with itself. I'm not sure it's time to sit back."

The room came to life at the news of Holst's possible demise.

"Wow," Lou Ricci said.

"Game changer," said Joe Kelly.

"Nobody here knows the Bureau better than I do," Lily said. "Even without Holst, if they sense an inkling of rebellion, they'll try to set an example. They've been warning me for years there would be a severe crackdown."

"Lily," Mr. Kale said, "I think some good old-fashioned civil disobedience is warranted. Nothing violent, but a work stoppage. New America will grind to a halt if Dorm workers stop doing their jobs. The Dorms are the backbone of this city, and it can't function without us. It wouldn't be an act that should draw violence in response."

"I'll second that," Paula McSweeney said.

"Miss Haddad," Drayden said, "do you have any contacts inside the Guardians? Like I told you the other night, my person in the resistance told me they're the key; the only thing standing between the Dorms and the Palace. As long as they're loyal to the Bureau, we have no chance. If the Guardians were to turn, perhaps by being educated about the truth, we'd have a real shot at crushing the Bureau."

"There is a small contingent of Guardians led by a sergeant who are on our side. Unfortunately, I have no way of contacting him to share the information you uncovered. The Guardians have all but retreated from the Dorms. I suspect they're fortifying the Lab to protect against any kind of revolt. What I'm saying is, I cannot go to him but he can come here, so all I can do is wait to be contacted. Given the scrutiny right now, I'm sure he's having a tough time reaching out."

"Maybe we could send somebody to find him."

"That's not possible," Lily snapped.

"I mean, I might be able to do it."

Everyone turned around, regarding him as if he'd gone insane.

"I'm not saying I want to, but I have a Palace Guardian uniform from the expedition. I used it earlier and bumped into three officers who thought I was a Palace Guardian. I even passed teams of other guys who didn't bat an eye at me. It's an option, if we're desperate."

Lily pressed her hands together. "Drayden, I appreciate everything you've done so far. We wouldn't know the Bureau's secrets without you, and I applaud your bravery. But that is out of the question. It's far too dangerous for you and not what we need at this time. This is serious business and people's lives are at risk. Why don't you leave this to the adults?"

Joe Kelly pointed at him. "I'll take that kid any d—"

The broadcast siren blared, signifying a public address by the Bureau in thirty minutes.

CHAPTER 17

Drayden and crew, Mr. Kale, and Professor Worth sat before the imposing video screen on the soft grass in Madison Square Park, amongst thousands of fellow Dorm residents. Although numerous screens were scattered throughout the Dorms, this was the one most people used for broadcasts from the Bureau, because it was centralized and in a spacious park.

Typically, everyone ignored the inconsequential broadcasts, since the Bureau rarely reported anything of substance. Not this time. Many of the protestors, seething and wielding their signs, packed the park. Anti-Bureau chants periodically cropped up in corners.

While the Dorm residents were probably expecting a speech from Holst to address the rumors, protests, and explosions, Drayden was hoping for something else. He caught himself, "hoping" again, swearing he wouldn't get lured into the passive version of hope. Regardless of the result of this broadcast, he would be active, pressing forward, doing whatever was required. Still, he was aware that this could be the moment Robert Zane took control of the Bureau, portending a rebirth of their entire way of life, remaking New America into an inclusive, fair, and truly equal society. Not that it would happen overnight, but they had to start somewhere.

Charlie, wearing his sweatshirt to cover up the gun on his own hip, leaned back to Drayden. "This must have been what it was like on election night before the Confluence. I'm so nervous."

Drayden's own heart was racing. "Let's be optimistic," he said, taking Sidney's hand.

The screen turned on, temporarily filled with white static in the frame and a buzzing sound.

Eli Holst appeared.

Oh no.

The leader at once looked smug and defiant, his sweaty nose gleaming, a faint smile on his lips.

Charlie and Catrice made eye contact with Drayden, their mouths hanging open.

His face grew hot, the adrenaline coursing through his veins like an assault. Sidney squeezed his hand with such force that it hurt.

"Citizens of New America, good afternoon," Holst said, striking an insolent tone. "I've called this broadcast today to talk about a *situation* that's come to my attention. I know you all heard the explosions throughout our great city this morning as well, and I want to assure you that everything is fine and under control."

Drayden contemplated what that meant. Was it over?

"There is a minor band of troublemakers—bad actors, rabble-rousers—who thought it would be fun to cause great damage to our infrastructure today and spread false rumors about the Bureau. I can promise you, these rumors are fake. The Bureau, alongside our terrific Guardians and scientists, has served to save humanity. We are a wonderful organization, which is but a small part of the incredible world of New America. We are here to serve you, the people, and ensure you are always safe and protected. Anything you might hear to the contrary is just the desperate words of a few disgruntled citizens."

The audience came to life with boos and expletives.

Drayden shook his head in disgust. Lie after lie after lie. At least the residents weren't buying it.

"Don't believe these bad actors. They have no proof to substantiate their outrageous claims. Believe what you have seen with your own eyes for many, many years! As the leader of all people here, I know I shouldn't wish harm on any citizen of this great land. But I do wish these troublemakers were instead thankful and appreciative for everything we do, including feeding, educating, and housing them. That's not enough for them, though. Instead of allowing everyone to lead peaceful, happy lives they are trying to disrupt and agitate. Let's not let them get away with it."

This was Gaslighting 101.

"These evildoers put every one of you in danger today. Not just with the explosions themselves, which did, in fact, injure several Guardians. No, they also blew holes in the border walls, potentially allowing the deadly Aeru bacteria into New America. In their selfish effort to be a nuisance, they jeopardized our entire civilization, and therefore the survival of the human race. These are not heroes. They are the enemy. But have no fear, my dear citizens, the Bureau will protect you as we always do."

Holst wiped his forehead with a handkerchief. "The protests happening in the Dorms must come to an end. The zones have been at peace with each other for decades. Let us not return to the dark ages of rioting and violence. We don't want anyone to get hurt. If the protests continue, and there are casualties, it won't be our fault. You were deceived by these bad actors with false information and I can understand how that would make you angry. But I can assure you everything they said is ridiculous and without merit. As you know, we will hear your *legitimate* concerns. Your voices are, and always have been, important. Please bring any issues to the attention of your local representatives in a civil fashion. I promise we will address them. However, we will not be bullied by an angry mob, inspired by false accusations."

On the bright side, the fact that Holst felt compelled to address the truths Drayden had disseminated throughout the land indicated the effort itself was somewhat successful. The premier was evidently worried people would believe the news. Nevertheless, with each of Holst's dishonest words, the wind was slowly leaving Drayden's sails. The entire speech was a gut punch that felt like it was fired straight at him, to cause maximum damage. He knew the Bureau was deceitful, but the scope of their duplicity was staggering.

"This piddling rebellion by a handful of insignificant actors," Holst said, with an annoyed swish of his hand like he was swatting a fly, "is now over. Most have been captured, proving no match for our excellent counter-intelligence operatives. I want to personally thank the Guardians, who work so hard to protect us, for their valiant service. Their loyalty and sacrifice are a model for all citizens to follow."

The crowd booed, louder this time.

Immediately thinking of Kim Craig, Drayden gazed at Professor Worth with pleading eyes.

He gave a subtle nod, not appearing the tiniest bit swayed or troubled.

When Drayden looked back to the screen, his heart just about stopped.

Instead of Holst's enlarged cranium and thick glasses, it now displayed a still photo—a snapshot from a security camera. Taken at night, it showed him and Charlie, in their jeans and hooded sweatshirts, advancing down a brightened sidewalk.

Holst continued speaking in the background over the photo. "We are searching for these two young men who are part of the syndicate of troublemakers. We have reason to believe they are hiding out in the Dorms. I'm asking each and every one of you to help us end this threat by catching them and turning them in. You will be handsomely rewarded, with money, extra food allocations, and possibly a job promotion. All for the simple task of helping New America restore law and order by punishing the evildoers."

Drayden was shaking. *That snake.*

Charlie slowly flipped up his hood. Mr. Kale, without looking away from the screen, casually removed his glasses and passed them over to Drayden.

He put them on, doubting they would mask his identity any better than Superman was disguised as Clark Kent. Thankfully, he was wearing Mr. Kale's clothing, unlike Charlie, who was sporting the exact same outfit from the photo. Drayden stared at the screen, terrified to accidentally make eye contact with anyone there.

Holst resurfaced, smiling. "You can even feel free to rough them up, and it'll be fine by me." He chuckled before growing stern. "Thank you, citizens of New America, for joining me today. We will work tirelessly to rebuild the walls and everybody can resume their daily lives. Remember our motto: Bravery, Intelligence, Equality. Good day."

The screen flicked off.

The group walked briskly on Lexington Avenue in a protective circle around Drayden and Charlie. Charlie's hood was up, and Drayden's eyes were down. He tried to have faith that Mr. Kale's glasses, combined with his schoolteacher outfit, would obscure, if not conceal, his identity. Once they were inside Mr. Kale's apartment, he might need to take it a step further.

As soon as the screen had shut off, the audience erupted into anti-Bureau chants. Drayden was proud of his fellow residents for not biting on Premier Holst's gaslighting. Every word of his speech, spewing lies and veiled threats, had been vile. Urging people to stop protesting for their own safety was a lot like an abusive husband telling his wife it wasn't his fault for hitting her if she continued making him angry.

Drayden hadn't fully grasped the degree to which the populace had been brainwashed. Hearing a Holst speech after finding out the truth about New America and the rest of the world was eye-opening, not just for the dishonesty, but the gall and arrogance. The premier was deliberate about thanking and praising the Guardians, knowing they were the key to the Bureau retaining power. He probably suspected the Dorms were a lost cause, so he'd pander to the only ones he really needed. It was a smart move.

The rowdiness of the crowd and the immediate resumption of the protests, in the form of an epic march up Second Avenue, gave Drayden some solace. If the residents hadn't believed what Holst said, perhaps they would also ignore his plea to capture him and Charlie.

"What do you guys think?" Drayden asked. "Are me and Charlie screwed?"

"Absolutely not," Mr. Kale said. "These people will be cheering you, not turning you in. Just to be safe, I'm going to stop by Lily's office. We need to counter their messaging with our own, spreading the word that you boys aren't to be touched, making sure Dorm residents know the promise of a reward is a lie."

"I think it is best if we alter your appearances," Professor Worth chimed in. "Let's see what we can do at Mister Kale's apartment."

Sidney hooked her arm inside Drayden's. "We're not gonna let anybody get you."

He smiled at her. "Thanks."

Something about that security camera photo bothered him. It was a nighttime photo and they'd been wearing jeans and hoodies, so it was the evening they'd snuck through the subways up to the Dorms. For one, Kim had said she would turn off the cameras. He supposed she had implied only the ones lining the subway. But the other thing was the lighting. They were plainly visible, suggesting they must have passed through a lighted area. He didn't recall any. It had been pitch-black. How had the Bureau gotten that shot?

Mr. Kale stopped short, pointing down Twenty-Eighth Street. "I'm going to take care of this right away. Hopefully Lily's there. I'll meet you guys at my place," he said, wandering off.

Drayden noted a few packs of residents traveling up Lexington Avenue having left the broadcast. None were noticeably paying him any attention.

Despite everyone's reassurances, he couldn't help but feel slightly defeated by Holst. He remained resolute about supporting the insurrection, yet it had become infinitely harder after the premier had exposed him in front of the whole city. While he'd love to believe his fellow citizens would defiantly stand by his side, people in the Dorms were desperate and hungry. Not everyone knew that Holst was not a man of his word, and that the rewards he offered were almost certainly bogus.

He peered back.

Two men were walking half a block behind them with their heads lowered.

"Professor," Drayden said, "I gotta be honest. I'm worried about Kim."

He sighed. "Me too. Let's look on the bright side though. They did implement their plan to blow up the walls. So, the fact that Holst survived the assassination attempt, if one was made, doesn't automatically mean the whole plan has been foiled. Given how many lies he told in his speech, there's no reason to believe he's telling the truth about rounding up all the plotters."

He made a good point. "True. I just hope she's okay." His unease carried over to their families. Even if Kim had been snared, the safehouse hadn't *necessarily* been discovered. Drayden's anxiety running countless layers deep, another distressing thought arose.

The broadcast siren had curtailed their meeting with Lily Haddad, so he hadn't had time to chew on her last words. *Leave this to the adults.* It was the second time she'd made that appeal. She may have been right too, him being a sixteen-year-old kid, but he was still offended. He felt he deserved a little more respect for uncovering the Bureau's secrets and risking his life to propagate them.

"I think we have company," Catrice whispered.

The pair following them had become a burgeoning gang of men and boys, treading closer and closer.

Drayden and his friends hit Twenty-Ninth Street and turned right, now two long avenue blocks away from Mr. Kale's place.

"Uh oh," Charlie said.

A second group of men was bearing down on them from the front, heading away from the populated section of the Dorms, insinuating that they weren't merely on their way home from the broadcast.

"What should we do?" Catrice asked.

"Whatever we have to," Sidney replied.

They slowed to a stop, coming face to face with the band of boys in front, who were pointing and whispering to each other. The gang behind caught up, looking like they were hungry and had found their next meal.

Drayden instantly tensed.

They were surrounded.

CHAPTER 18

"Luke?" Charlie said.

"Hey, Charlie," one of the boys in the pack said, staring at his feet. "Um, I recognized you on the screen."

"What are you doing, bro? Holst is full of shkat. We're not a danger to New America. We're the ones who discovered the truth and let everybody know. I hope you guys aren't planning on collecting this phony reward."

Drayden gripped his Glock beneath his sweater, cognizant of the fact that, despite their weapons, they were greatly outnumbered. He also didn't want to have to shoot anyone.

"Gentlemen!" Professor Worth shouted to both groups, as if he were giving a lecture in a grand hall at MIT. "Premier Holst's speech was full of nothing but lies. Every rumor currently circulating about the Bureau is true. Not only have they deprived you of food and livelihoods, they've shrouded the truth. The world outside the walls is full of people, nearly three hundred million. Boston, Massachusetts, is a thriving city, where everyone is free and nobody lives in zones. The Bureau trades with other cities behind your backs, and their main export is narcotics. They don't even grow food in the Meadow. They import it. And they are reaping all the spoils and hoarding them in the Palace."

He began walking in a circle around Drayden and his friends, addressing the wannabe kidnappers. "These two boys are the heroes who uncovered the truth, which is why the Bureau wants them captured. They should be celebrated, not punished. The leaders in the Dorms know how much they've done for New America. In fact, should you apprehend them, you have no one to turn them in to. There are no Guardians here. If you were to present them to Lily Haddad, she would just release them. She knows the truth. I ask you, if Premier Holst would lie about everything else, why would you think he is telling the truth about a reward? There *is* no reward."

He stopped and clasped his hands. "What we need to do is focus on protesting the Bureau and working together. Don't let this demagogue trick you into turning against one another. Now is the time to unite."

What a great speech, Drayden thought. He was biased, due to his current predicament, but he felt it was extremely persuasive.

"Maybe he's lying about the reward, and maybe he isn't," a burly man up front said. "I'm willing to take my chances. We can turn them in and still protest the Bureau."

"What is wrong with you guys?" Sidney yelled. "We're all on the same team. We're fighting for you!"

The guy shifted uncomfortably on his feet. "Look, you want to do this the easy way or the hard way? Nobody needs to get hurt."

Sidney drew her Glock and pointed it at the man's head. "The hard way. And you're the first one going down."

Catrice sidled up to Sidney, pulling her gun as well.

Drayden followed their lead, panning his weapon over the pack, as did the others, including Professor Worth.

The men, their faces in shock, slowly backed away. "Whoa, okay, okay!" someone cried out.

"We're already enemies of the state!" Drayden shouted. "If we're caught, we're dead. If we kill you all and get caught, we're dead. It's the same for us either way. So, do *you* want to do this the easy way or the hard way?"

Backpedaling, the brawny man held up his hands. "Take it easy, man."

"We're all on the same team, dammit," Drayden said, losing patience. "You tell your friends. Tell everyone. We're fighting for you. We can beat them, but we have to work together."

Drayden exhaled as the gang of men and boys ran off. "Thanks, you guys," he said to his crew.

"Idiots." Sidney holstered her pistol.

With the excitement over, they made it back to Mr. Kale's apartment, finding him inside.

"You guys all right?" he asked.

Drayden yanked off his sweater vest. "Yeah. A posse of thirty dudes tried to abduct me and Charlie. Had to draw our weapons."

Mr. Kale shook his head. "I spoke to Lily. She's launching a counter propaganda campaign through her network, by word of mouth, to make sure people in the Dorms know the truth about you boys. She confirmed that, even if somebody were to capture you, you'd be released. Doesn't mean we shouldn't be careful. You shouldn't go out alone."

A propaganda campaign.

Why hadn't he thought of that earlier? "I have an idea. We need the Guardians to turn on the Bureau, right? That's the key to winning this fight. They've been gaslighted by the Bureau and believe its lies."

Mr. Kale pressed his lips together. "Lily requested that you guys stay inside for the time being. She wants to minimize the risk someone comes after you and wants to coordinate the effort against the Bureau herself. If you remember, she kind of said the same to you in our meeting. I don't know if I agree, but I do want to keep you safe."

Professor Worth was side-eyeing Drayden.

His words from the boat, after fixing the engine, were ringing in Drayden's ears. If a problem needed solving, he shouldn't wait for somebody else to handle it. He should do it himself whether he was the most qualified or not. This felt just like that. He knew he tended to hesitate, costing him dearly in the past. This time would be different.

"I don't think it makes sense to wait around for Lily to drive this. I'm sure she knows what she's doing, and her intentions are in the right place. But I think we should all be doing everything we can, small or not. Do you guys want to join me?"

"Does a one-legged duck swim in circles?" Charlie asked.

Sidney groaned. "Why can't you ever just say yes? I'm in, all the way."

"We're with you," Catrice said.

Charlie pulled off his hoodie. "I probably shouldn't be marauding around the Dorms in the same getup I was wearing in the photo. Mr. Kale, you got anything besides sweater vests?"

He smirked. "I have the perfect outfit for you, Charlie. Although, you're a big boy, so it'll be a little snug. Follow me."

Minutes later, Mr. Kale emerged solo. He turned back, waving Charlie forward. "You look great. Don't be shy."

His eyes glued to the floor, Charlie inched out wearing tight khaki pants, a green linen shirt, and a maroon cardigan buttoned to the top. He looked up, revealing the icing on the cake—glasses with thick black frames.

"Wow," Drayden said.

Catrice giggled. "I wish we had a camera."

"I'm ready to take on the Bureau now," Charlie whispered.

The following morning, on Park Avenue and Thirty-Third Street, far away from the crowds, Mr. Kale unlocked a side door to Norman Thomas High School, Drayden's former stomping grounds. He led Drayden, Charlie, and Professor Worth into a dim hallway.

Drayden had never been in the building during a school break, and the unfamiliar silence and coldness was creepy.

Mr. Kale faced them with a slight smile and clapped his hands together. "So...where to?"

Drayden chewed a nail. "We need paper, quills, and ink wells. Like, a lot of them. A few hundred sheets of paper, and...thirty quills and ink wells? Let's stockpile all that stuff while we wait for the girls."

At Drayden's behest, Sidney and Catrice were out and about, rounding up every friend who came to mind, meaning primarily Sidney's pals, to join them in the school.

Mr. Kale rubbed his chin. "Um, okay. We should be able to do that." He waved his hand forward. "Let's go."

They ascended a staircase to the third floor, where they passed by many of their old classrooms, currently in a state of hibernation.

Drayden nudged Charlie. "Have I mentioned you look ridiculous in that outfit?"

He lowered his glasses, eyeing Drayden back. "Have I mentioned you look perfectly normal like that? I think that's worse, ya dork."

After everyone gathered the items from a supply closet and ferried them to a classroom, Mr. Kale went downstairs to wait for Sidney and Catrice, while Drayden, Charlie, and Professor Worth settled into chairs.

"This brings back memories," Professor Worth mused, taking in the sparsely decorated classroom. "Good ones."

Charlie coughed. "Speak for yourself."

"Professor," Drayden said, "I'm sorry for dragging you along on this trip. I feel bad now. What if we can't reunite you with Kim, or she's been caught? Don't get me wrong, I'm so happy you're here. I don't think we would have made it this far without you. I feel guilty though."

He touched Drayden's shoulder. "I made the right decision joining you. This has already been the experience of a lifetime for me. I told you I don't believe in fate, yet I also can't help but feel there was a reason we connected in Massachusetts. I believe I must have a role to play in this battle. It just hasn't been revealed yet."

"I'm going to get you to Kim. I promise."

His gaze veered past Drayden. "I believe your friends are here."

The buzz of chatter and laughter grew louder as the mass of teenagers converged on the classroom. Catrice and Sidney popped into the doorway with a huge crowd behind them.

"Hey, we got everybody we could," Sidney said, using the back of her hand to wipe her forehead.

Drayden clumsily stood, extending his arm toward the rear of the room. "Great, thanks, Sid. Bring everyone in."

He recognized many of the faces filtering through the door as former classmates whom he'd never gotten to know personally. They were, in short, the cool crowd. Sidney's people. With thirty of them dawdling in the back, and Mr. Kale watching him from the doorway, he broke out in a cold sweat. These were the same flunks who teased and tormented him throughout school, and they were all here at his request to do work. He had no clue how they'd react. They might laugh at him.

Drayden cleared his throat. "Um, thank you, everybody, for coming. I'm going to explain what's going on, and what I need you all to do. For star—"

"Charlie?" someone called out.

"Oh, hey Zack."

"What are you wearing, dude? I think you've been spending too much time with Drayden."

Everyone cracked up.

Charlie grinned and pointed at him. "Good one. Can you shut up and listen now? This is important."

Drayden took a deep breath and summarized the myriad ways the citizens were being deceived by the government.

He studied the dubious eyes of his classmates. "The Bureau must be stopped. These protests are important and should continue. Dorm residents need to resist, and demand change. But the real problem is the Guardians. Even though we dwarf them in number, they're armed and we're not. They're loyal to the Bureau because they don't know the truth. We have no way of letting them know."

As the words left his mouth, Drayden realized the Bureau probably withdrew the Guardians from the Dorms to insulate them from the rumors. He snatched up a sheet of blank paper. "I have an idea. It goes back to some of the stuff we learned in history class," he said, adding in a lowered voice, "if you guys were paying attention."

Catrice snickered.

"In wars, one of the things governments do is spread propaganda. Often false, but sometimes they try to enlighten people who have been living under a dictator, controlling the news, where state-run media lies to them and they have no way of discovering the truth. The United States government would literally drop pamphlets from airplanes around countries like that, so their citizens would find out what was really going on. We're going to do the same thing."

He waved the piece of paper. "We're going to write a number of phrases on each sheet. Then we're going to take them to a tall building, right by the wall between the Dorms and the Lab. We're going to make paper airplanes. I know it might sound dumb, but from a decent height, they should travel far into the Lab. It's not as good as dropping them in the Precinct, except we have no way of getting them there. According to the Dorm leaders, the Guardians are all clustered in the Lab anyway, to counter protestors who might come at the gate."

Drayden swiped a piece of chalk and faced the chalkboard. "This is what we're going to write." He scratched:

The Bureau has deceived you
The exiles are alive
The world is full of people
The Bureau trades with other colonies
Our main export is drugs
We no longer grow food in the Meadow
The Bureau is hoarding the spoils in the Palace
Guardians, rise up!

"Everyone understand? We'll make the paper airplanes after we're on the roof of a building, because it's easier to transport unfolded paper. Let's get to work."

Much to Drayden's surprise, the teenagers enthusiastically collected their paper, quills, and ink wells, taking seats in the classroom. He watched with amazement, almost to the point of choking up, as they all took him seriously. No one was laughing anymore. Even specific boys who had bullied him were furiously drafting their notes.

Once everyone was finished, Mr. Kale and Professor Worth stacked the papers in a box. Charlie and Sidney were mingling with their former friends, joking around, telling stories about their adventures. Catrice and Drayden awkwardly stood alone, immediately reminded of why they hated high school.

Drayden clapped to get their attention. "We've got kind of a long walk, over twenty blocks, and a difficult hike up stairs. I appreciate you all helping." He hooked his thumb at the door. "Let's do this."

Professor Worth winked at him on their way out of the room.

To steer clear of the protestors, already going strong this morning, the group slipped down Park Avenue, much further west than all the action. Thus far, the protests centered around the

Bureau office on Second Avenue and Thirty-First Street, not at the wall between the Dorms and Lab, where the Guardian presence was likely heavy.

After a twenty-minute hike, they cut left on Fifteenth Street—a block shy of the wall—to avoid the surveillance of the Guardians who would be monitoring the activity on the Dorm side.

Within three blocks, they found the ideal building: 145 East Fifteenth Street. An immense white brick structure, occupying an entire block, it appeared to have been part offices and part apartments. The apartment side rose up twenty-five stories, extending above the surrounding buildings. A tower with a clock soared even higher, providing the perfect launching spot.

Drayden and his friends distributed the notes to their classmates and led the arduous climb up the stairs. The earlier zeal about this effort notwithstanding, there was no shortage of groaning and whining along the way. On the top floor, Drayden, Professor Worth, and Mr. Kale located the path to the main roof, and a staircase up to the tower. Leaving the teenagers on the sprawling roof, the three of them ascended the stairs to check it out.

A miniature concrete room, exposed to the open air and surrounded by Greek columns, sat directly above the giant clock.

"What do you think, ten of us in here?" Drayden asked.

Mr. Kale examined the space. "Um, sure, and everybody else can remain on the roof."

Braced against a column to peek over the ledge, Drayden observed fifty or so Guardians protecting the gaping hole in the wall at street level.

Back on the main roof, he addressed everyone. "Guys, listen up! I'm gonna take a couple people up to the tower but most of you will stay here on the roof, where there's more room. Make any kind of paper airplane you want, as long as it's not the type that requires you to tear the paper. Don't launch them until we give the word. Just get them ready to go. We'll have a countdown, and then start tossing them, one after another. Everyone good?"

Sidney and Catrice remained with the majority of their class-mates, while Drayden rounded up six of them to join him, Charlie, the professor, and Mr. Kale in the tower.

Drayden sat cross-legged on the cement, constructing various styles of paper airplanes. Being so high up, the tower room was windy, making it a tad challenging to corral both the unfolded papers and the finished planes.

Professor Worth was working deliberately, but his airplanes were advanced.

"Not your first rodeo?" Drayden asked.

He smiled. "We used to have contests at MIT to see who could build paper airplanes that flew the farthest. I think these will soar from this height."

Although some of the others' paper airplanes resembled toddler art, everyone finished with ten planes each.

"This is a great idea, Drayden," Mr. Kale said, giving him a pat on the back. "Well done."

"Thanks. I hope it works." He hurried downstairs to give Sidney the go ahead to commence a countdown within minutes, loud enough to hear in the tower.

When he returned upstairs, the others had situated them-selves between the columns, a mere foot from the precipitous drop to the street.

"Be incredibly careful, please," Mr. Kale cautioned. "Don't throw your paper airplanes with such force that you lose your balance."

Drayden squished between two of the students, doing his best to keep their airplanes separate.

"On three!" Sidney yelled in the distance. "One...two...three!"

With a gentle shove, Drayden tossed one plane after another off the ledge. In seconds, he was finished, stepping back to enjoy his handiwork.

A boundless cloud of paper airplanes sailed and swirled through the air like a flock of doves, dancing and playing. Because of wind gusts, some even flew upward. A few were duds of course, nosediving down to the street, while others turned too far right or left. Several blew back onto the roof. But most floated the right way, and a handful were on a trajectory to travel extremely far.

Drayden wished he'd remembered to warn everyone to remain quiet. Nevertheless, he couldn't suppress a smile when all the kids started cheering.

That was the moment gunshots rang out, the Guardians firing up at them from the streets below.

CHAPTER 19

Coated in sweat, Drayden practically tumbled down the narrow staircase from the tower with the nine others.

"Go go go!" someone yelled.

When he hit the main roof, it was pandemonium.

Kids were screaming, shoving, and running over each other to retreat into the interior stairwell, where they were racing downstairs. Some had fallen and were in tears.

A heavyset boy, who Drayden recognized from school, was among those injured, squeezing his ankle. Charlie scooped him up, wrapped the boy's arm around his shoulder, and held him by the waist. "You're all right, Tony. Nice and easy."

Tony hobbled along, bearing almost no weight on his right foot. "Thanks, man," he said.

"Everyone, calm down!" Mr. Kale shouted. "Meet in the lobby! Don't run."

His pleas fell on deaf ears. The shots fired were fleeting, and perhaps a reflexive reaction to the mass of paper airplanes, mistaken for some sort of aerial assault. Still, Drayden couldn't believe the Guardians had fired their weapons. It was a major escalation of the incipient battle between the soldiers and the civilians.

He also felt responsible for putting his classmates in harm's way. To his knowledge, nobody had been hit. He didn't see any blood. But it wasn't hard to imagine that someone would plummet down the stairs, given they were twenty-five stories up and it was a stampede. People had already gotten trampled. This was his idea and he'd dragged them into it.

Drayden pushed past the others, hoping to hit the ground floor first in case Guardians were waiting outside. He couldn't allow anyone to recklessly bolt out of the building.

Although he was not the first one in the lobby, the teenagers were congregating there, awaiting further instructions.

"Everyone, please, remain calm." Mr. Kale hustled into the center of the room. "We're going to get you all out of here."

Catrice, helping a visibly shaken girl, and Charlie, bracing Tony, were the last ones down.

Drayden dashed to the front door onto Fourteenth Street, squinting to see through the dusty glass.

The massive hole in the wall around Third Avenue was crawling with Guardians. Fortunately, none had crossed into the Dorms.

Drayden looked over the frightened and frazzled faces of his classmates. "Everybody, listen up. Thank you. I can't tell you how much I appreciate your help. That went awesome. Except for, you know, the gunshots at the end."

A few people chuckled.

"I think those shots were a hair-trigger reaction to the swarm of paper airplanes. I don't see any Guardians on the streets. Just to be safe, let's try to get out of here quietly. We'll exit the same way we came in, on the Fifteenth Street side. We'll go west, and then up Park Avenue."

While his last word echoed in the cavernous lobby, a switch flipped in his mind. His need to protect those whose lives he'd endangered was suddenly overpowered by his will to inspire them to fight. The protesting shouldn't be left to the adults. Technically, in New America, they *were* adults, having graduated high school and taken job assignments. New America was their home, and would be for years longer than the older protestors. It was their future at stake. They needed to be the voice that called for the kind of society in which they wanted to live.

"Don't be afraid of them," he said, his tone modulating to impassioned. "New America doesn't belong to the Guardians and the Bureau. It belongs to us. The people. They're not going to shoot a bunch of scared, unarmed kids. You should see what it's like in Boston. Anyone can go anywhere and have any job they want. Why can't it be that way here? It can be. We just have to demand it. Citizens in New America outnumber the Bureau a hundred to one. Why is this small body of aristocrats making all the rules, which happen to benefit them? It's time to change this shkat, and this might be our only chance."

He paused, realizing he'd strayed off topic. "If you want to continue helping, you don't need an invitation from me, or Sidney, or Charlie. The more we work together, the more powerful we are. There's power in numbers."

Drayden glanced at Professor Worth, having stolen his line.

Both he and Mr. Kale were grinning back, beaming with pride.

Drayden felt this would have been the opportune moment for hoots and hollers from galvanized vigilantes, but they remained silent, ostensibly unmoved by his call to arms. "Let's move out," he grumbled.

The sizable group moved stealthily in tense silence until they were far enough up Park Avenue, walking beside a stunning patch of wildflowers, and everyone unclenched.

Catrice was bringing up the rear with Charlie, who continued to help Tony stumble along. Sidney was ambling alone.

Drayden picked a daisy, hiding it behind his back until she reached him.

Sidney tilted her head and smiled when he handed her the flower.

"I'm sorry about the boat," Drayden said. "I'm stupid. Will you forgive me?"

She wrapped her arms around his neck. "Oh, I suppose. You're the dumbest smart guy I know."

"That's the nicest thing anyone's ever said to me."

She laughed and kissed him on the lips.

As Charlie and Tony passed by, Tony cracked up at one of Charlie's jokes.

"Hey, Dray, this is Tony," Charlie said. "He and I were boys in middle school, but kinda lost touch, I guess because he hated Alex. I didn't know."

"Kindred spirits, you and me," Drayden said, walking next to him. "I bet I hated him more."

Tony spat. "What a flunk that guy was."

Charlie scoffed. "Hey, can we not stomp on his grave? Kid's dead. How about a little respect?"

Sidney snickered. "There's either a special place in Heaven or a special place in Hell for you, Charlie, being friends with that winooze clown."

He made a face at her. "I told you guys. He was misunderstood."

"Pffft," Tony said. "I think I understood him perfectly when he used to call me 'macaroni Tony.' Or 'no jawbone Tone.' Or how about 'overgrown Tone.'"

Charlie was trying and failing to contain his laughter. "Sorry. C'mon, 'overgrown Tone' is pretty funny." He lost it quietly with his face turned away. "He likes a scone, Tone," he mumbled. "Thyroid hormone Tone."

"You'll have to excuse him, Tony," Drayden said. "He has a problem. Alex used to make fun of me for being too skinny. I guess, in a way, he wasn't prejudiced, he was just a jerk."

A few blocks from the Bureau office in the Dorms, the roar of the protests came into earshot. Without seeing them, it was obvious they had grown.

"Drayden, how are we going to rescue our families from their hideout?" Sidney asked. "This feels like it's becoming serious. The longer they stay, the more risk there is that they'll be found."

"Especially since Holst has a hit out on me and you, Dray," Charlie said. "Plus, your relatives have to be getting sick of my dad by now. You think I crack too many jokes?"

Drayden grew nauseous at the mere mention of his own family. He wanted to lock his father *in* and throw away the key, conceding the irony that he'd always believed his family was the "normal" one among his friends. Sure, normal minus the part where his mother may have had an affair and his father had called in her exile. Just a minor blip.

"I have no idea how to get them out of there," Drayden said. "We have to work on it."

Catrice, unsurprisingly, remained aloof.

Sidney clutched her arm. "My God. It just dawned on me. Your family is here, in the Dorms. Have you seen them? Or do you have any plans to?"

That detail had escaped Drayden as well. He knew the answer before she responded.

"No. To both questions." Catrice carried on with her head down.

"You entered the Initiation to get away from them," Sidney said, her demeanor suggesting she was beginning to understand Catrice. "Was that the only reason?"

"Yes," Catrice said softly, growing teary eyed.

Sidney went to speak and was lost for words, nodding instead. "I'm sorry."

At Twenty-Eighth Street, the caravan of teenagers ventured east, where the protestors' chanting, in unison, became clear. "We want our food! We want our food!"

Although Drayden hadn't received a spirited acceptance of his appeal to take up the protests, he noted that the long line of former classmates remained a unit as they reentered the demonstration. Second Avenue, for endless blocks north, was a standing-room-only crowd, packed to the gills. They flanked the periphery, watching the angry mob pump their fists to their updated rallying cry. "We want our food! We want our food!"

An older woman, dressed like an electrician, brushed by Drayden, ferrying a sign that read *The Bureau Sucks!* in red ink.

"Excuse me, ma'am!" Drayden shouted. "What's going on today? What's the deal with the food?"

"Take a look," she said, fanning her arm over the disorderly assemblage. "Nobody is working. We found out the Bureau's cut off all food deliveries to the Dorms, and is limiting water too."

In the center of the chaos, Lily Haddad rose up on a podium, energizing the masses, whooping along with them. "We want our food! We want our food!"

Drayden tapped Mr. Kale on the arm and pointed.

Mr. Kale nodded. "I saw her! I'm happy she's come around on the protests. It's the right move. If the Bureau did stop the food allocations, this just got a lot more dangerous."

With limited options, what else could Dorm residents do but protest? Trying to negotiate with a tyrant who had his fingers on all the city's levers meant arguing from a position of weakness. It would fail. The peoples' power didn't reside in their ability to control municipal functions. It lay in their sheer *size*. Drayden was finally comprehending what Mr. Kale had said in his apartment when he and Charlie first reunited with him. They had all the power they needed to overthrow the Bureau right here in the Dorms.

The will of the people cannot be denied.

While the work stoppage was a smart tactic, placing a stranglehold on the entire city which effectively shut it down, the Bureau's move trumped it. Dorm residents would die from a lack of food far faster than the rest of the zones would suffer from a denial of services the Dorms provided. The Bureau was playing a deadly game of chicken.

Witnessing his fiery fellow citizens exercising their rights to protest, Drayden felt it wasn't enough. They were getting mired in hope—the bad kind—by praying the Bureau would capitulate to their anger and give them what they wanted. They were *asking*, not insisting, not forcing their hand. Without resorting to violence, they needed the Bureau to feel their pressure. To be a bit scared.

He also watched with pride as his fellow schoolmates eagerly joined the protest, chanting amongst everyone else. Perhaps his speech had lit a fire inside them after all. If he could rally them once, why not again?

Drayden huddled with Charlie, Sidney, and Catrice, shouting to be heard.

"I have an idea! I think this protest is great. I love seeing everybody unite like this. But I don't think this message is being heard. Not clearly, anyway. We need to take this demand, this fight, directly to the Bureau. Why don't we try to turn this into a march? See if we can motivate people to hike it to the wall, at the hole where the Guardians are on Fourteenth and Third. The protest will feel a lot louder there."

Charlie fist-bumped him. "Right on, bro." He licked his lips. "How?"

He shrugged. "You got me."

Catrice digested the scene. "Why don't we start with our class-mates? Move to the end of the protest down Second Avenue, kind of like the front of the line if we were marching south. We start walking, but try to get everyone's attention, so they see what we're doing. We can send kids into the crowd to spread the word."

"Me and Charlie can do that," Sidney said. "They look really into it now."

"Let's do this," Drayden said.

He and Catrice navigated along the outside of the throng until they stood alone down Second Avenue. They spied Sidney and Charlie mobilizing their schoolmates, many of whom subsequently joined the nascent procession. Others approached random protes-tors to let them know about the new plan.

At first, with the citizens engrossed in the protest, nobody noticed the would-be march leaders.

Drayden cupped his hands around his mouth. "Guys! Let's start walking. Do *anything* you can to draw attention. Jump, yell, cartwheel, whatever." He led the way, bouncing, waving his arms. "March to the wall!"

Sidney performed a perfect backflip. One boy climbed on his buddy's shoulders and power whistled.

Slowly, word got around, akin to a giant game of telephone. The kids working the crowd only needed to light a few matches and their plan spread like wildfire. Some citizens followed them. Then more.

"Let's get the chant going!" Drayden hollered. "We-want-our-food! We-want-our-food!"

His classmates joined in, continuing their histrionics.

A palpable shift in the mass of people occurred, as if the cluster of teens were a magnet and the protestors were metal filings. The gap in the crowd they created by their march south naturally filled in with bodies, imparting momentum in their direction.

Drayden glanced back and made eye contact with Lily Haddad, who had spotted him and his former classmates. He then caught sight of Mr. Kale and Professor Worth parading alongside them, way over on the sidewalk.

It worked. Everyone was coming. Thousands of people were undertaking the mile-long trek to the wall. Drayden wasn't leading the way anymore, having been swallowed up by the pack. The crowd was guiding itself, like a fluid organism with one collective mind.

As the wall loomed larger ahead, Drayden wondered if his propaganda attack had worked. It was probably too soon to tell, plus it wasn't the kind of scheme that would immediately cause the Guardians to flip allegiances. He was planting the seed of doubt in their minds about the Bureau. Even if they consciously dismissed it, since it contradicted everything they'd always believed, they couldn't unread it. The idea was in their heads. The question then was, what irrefutable piece of evidence would sway them?

After fifteen minutes, the rowdy cavalcade rumbled onto Fourteenth Street, hanging a right to end up at Third Avenue. Guardians, some wielding high-powered rifles, formed a human barricade across the lengthy gap in the wall.

When Drayden reached an angle from which he could see down Third Avenue into the Lab, he gasped.

On the paper airplane tower, he'd counted about fifty Guardians manning the gap. Now hundreds flooded the space. Many were wearing SWAT gear with helmets and facemasks.

The protestors leading the march stopped feet from the Guardians in the gap, screaming in their faces, jabbing their fists, shouting, "We want our food! We want our food!"

The officers showed no reaction and stood their ground.

A bus turned up Third Avenue in the Lab, several blocks away. More followed.

Nearing the gap, the first one slowed and the sea of Guardians parted. It lurched forward, crossing into the Dorms.

The protestors in front backpedaled and pushed to the sides, hurling obscenities at the bus, which was packed with Guardians in SWAT gear.

It steadily advanced, executing a slow-motion right turn onto Fourteenth Street, appearing judicious not to hit anyone, although it never stopped.

A second bus followed, hugging its bumper, and turned left. A dozen more alternated right and left turns after that. The first one, having cruised past the protestors, went up Second Avenue. The second swung onto Irving Place. Subsequent buses parked all over Fourteenth Street.

The chants petered out. Nobody knew what was happening. The buses were just idling there, while the Guardians on foot reformed the human chain in the gap.

At once, as if someone had given a signal only they could hear, the Guardians poured out of the buses.

From the other side of the wall, hundreds of Guardians plowed into the Dorms with their batons ready.

CHAPTER 20

Drayden watched in horror as one defiant protestor, a slight, middle-aged man, stood his ground in the face of the rushing Guardians.

Get out of there, dude.

The horde of soldiers hit him like a tank, flattening him to the ground with an awful thud. Even worse, some paused to beat him with batons. The wailing man curled up on the asphalt, protecting his head.

The amorphous mass of protestors attempted to recede, but could only go so far, restricted by the thousands behind them. Some plainly had no intention of backing down.

Once the crush of Guardians met the frontline of protestors, something had to give. It was the irresistible force versus the immovable object.

The Guardians swung their batons violently, yelling "Disperse! Disperse!" while smashing the unfortunate souls up front. It was bedlam after that. Many of the protestors buckled with bloodied heads and shrieks of pain. Others pushed and elbowed to retreat. Scores of valiant warriors among them, however, resisted.

Thoroughly outmanning the Guardians, they swarmed individual soldiers, handily disarming them and turning the tables. For every officer who tried to rescue one of his comrades, five additional protestors were waiting to thrash him. The noise of the Guardians' commands, the screaming of the injured and frightened, and the roar of the crowd was so loud it hurt Drayden's ears.

Cowering beside Charlie, Sidney, and Catrice, he was frozen, paralyzed by his racing heart and indecisive mind.

What do I do?

Slowly, the pushing and shoving of the throng was forcing the friends apart.

"Keep your weapons holstered!" Drayden ordered.

"Drayden!" Catrice reached for him as she was muscled away.

He looked both ways, realizing he'd lost Mr. Kale and Professor Worth.

The battalion of Guardians beating their way through the crowd was nearly upon him.

Drayden spun away and crouched, struggling to flee, failing to escape the yelps of the victims.

A sharp pain ripped through the back of his head with a thump and he fell to the street face first.

"Disperse! Disperse!"

He moaned in agony.

His head was throbbing, his ears were ringing, and he was disoriented. Blood flowed down the side of his face. People stepped on the backs of his legs, already tender from the grenade injuries, causing him to cry out.

Get up!

Drayden scrambled to his feet, finding Guardians all around him swinging wildly. One whipped his baton at Drayden's face.

He ducked it, and bulldozed his way deeper into the crowd, managing to scuttle west along Fourteenth Street, eluding the assault. Dizziness rocked him, making him curious if getting cracked in the head after a recent concussion would cause brain damage.

As he neared the fringes of the mob, where other Guardians were attacking from the perimeter, he turned back.

The Dorm residents, God bless them, were most certainly not dispersing. Only a miniscule percentage on the frontlines were under attack, with thousands of reinforcements behind them. More and more were forcing their way to the front. Disparate bands of people were working together like gangs, staging their own counterassaults.

Charlie! He was among a crew of his classmates and plumbers who were prowling around, defending those under attack, and putting a beatdown on the Guardians.

An officer came at Drayden from the side, his bloody baton cocked.

Having faced this scenario in jiu-jitsu practice many times, he didn't have to think. His muscle memory took over. On autopilot, he backed up slowly with his hands raised, as if he was pleading for the Guardian to stop. In reality, he was preparing his counterattack.

Gazing into the guy's narrowed eyes, what he saw was *anger*. This was not a man simply following orders. He believed in what he was doing. He was sick of these ungrateful protestors complaining about his beloved government, and wanted to punish them.

The Guardians had been deceived for ages by the Bureau on so many levels. Somehow, someway, the all-powerful government had convinced them that the city's woes were due to those with no power. The ruling-class had convinced the middle-class that the lower-class was the problem. It was the greatest trick they'd ever pulled. How could he ever persuade these perfectly programmed drones to turn on their puppet masters?

The Guardian swung the baton in a sweeping motion at Drayden's head.

He lunged forward, driving both hands into the Guardian's arm, forcefully blocking it. With his left, he seized the man's wrist. With his right, he thrust his shoulder back, knocking him off balance. He propelled his right leg in reverse to kick the Guardian's leg off the ground and slammed him down.

The officer crumpled to the pavement on his back, falling victim to a basic leg sweep.

Drayden applied a wrist lock, causing the Guardian to howl in pain and drop the baton.

He picked it up and disengaged, this no longer being a case of self-defense. He was a martial artist and would not beat the Guardian with the baton, which would have been an assault. Just because someone had attacked him didn't require him to harm them; an epiphany he'd had on the expedition. He didn't need to stoop down to their level of depravity. Not that he would hold it against anyone else. That was their choice.

Breathing heavily, Drayden flaunted the baton like he was going to use it. "Back off!"

The Guardian slinked away. He only made it a couple of feet before a pack of protestors tackled him.

Drayden snickered and straightened out his bloody dress shirt.

It occurred to him that the Guardians were not using their guns. Even assaulted by protestors in a justifiable self-defense circumstance, they weren't pulling their weapons. Without a doubt, they'd been given explicit instructions not to fire on the protestors. It was something for which to be thankful, despite the brutality of their offensive.

Once again, Drayden was proud of his fellow citizens. He never imagined they had this fight in them. Where was it hiding all these years? That was just it though. It had always been there, simmering beneath the surface. Dissatisfaction. Anger. Resentment—the true motto of New America.

The secrets that he'd uncovered in Boston and exposed weren't the cause of this uprising. They were the catalyst. The bomb was already built; all he did was light the fuse.

The Bureau and the Guardians had misread the situation. They believed the threat of firepower was enough. When it wasn't, they assumed violence through savage beatings would do the job. Likewise, they were mistaken. People who have been oppressed for decades see such threats differently. They were scared, sure, but fear of the Bureau's weapons and violence paled in comparison to the threat of never-ending tyranny.

Catrice.

Right in the middle of the action, she was aiding an older woman who was bleeding profusely, trying to get her to safety. A Guardian hovered over her, raising his baton.

Oh no.

"Catrice!" he shouted.

Out of nowhere, Sidney sprung up and walloped the guy from behind, knocking him to the ground. He was buried under droves of people after that. Drayden never saw him get up.

Sidney assisted Catrice and the woman, successfully dragging them out of the line of attack. Guardians were retreating now. Only a trivial number at first, but gradually more and more raced back to the safety of the Lab.

A bus full of protestors barreled past, moving erratically, the inept driver honking the horn. Dorm residents were diving out of the way to dodge it.

Drayden chuckled at the sight, when something else caught his eye.

To his right, a handful of Guardians were *assisting* the protestors, shuttling them from danger. It was easy to miss amongst the chaos, but real, nonetheless. Some of these officers weren't on board with this assault. Or was it even more significant than that?

Before searching for his friends, Drayden paused. Sure, this was only one battle, but he'd led his fellow Dormers down here and they'd won. He didn't hesitate or overthink.

I did it.

After a string of disappointments, he would allow himself a moment of pride—an acknowledgement that his bold push forward made a difference in this fight. His brief pat on the back finished, he budged his way into the tumult to reconnect with Sidney and Catrice.

Cheers and roars commenced as more and more Guardians deserted with their tails between their legs, evacuating on foot to the Lab, abandoning the buses.

Charlie was high-fiving Tony and other kids, all of them bloodied.

When he saw Drayden, his smiled faded. "Jeez!" He grabbed Drayden by the cheeks, tilting his head, trying to locate the wound. "That looks terrible, dude. You okay?"

"Yeah, I'll be fine. I saw you out there, kicking butt and taking names. Nice job."

"That was awesome. Old-school brawl. Even better that we won. Thank God they kept their guns holstered."

Lily strolled through the protesters to applause, whoops, and whistles. They parted to make way for her, like a queen visiting the battlefield after the enemy had been vanquished.

The chants resumed, even louder. "We want our food! We want our food!"

Lily was glowing.

Drayden and Charlie had successfully reunited with Sidney and Catrice, and the four of them were standing in the packed crowd still buzzing over their apparent victory. Professor Worth and Mr. Kale were nowhere to be found.

"We need volunteers at the Thirty-Third Street hospital!" Lily shouted into her megaphone. "The doctors are stuck in the Lab. All the injured, please go to the hospital and we'll do our best to get you treated!"

Drayden gingerly touched the bruised egg on the back of his head, which had mercifully stopped gushing blood. Hospital or not, at the very least he had to clean it, plus he was nervous about a second concussion.

"I commend you all for your bravery!" Lily continued, to uproarious cheers from the gallery. "I think the Bureau hears us loud and clear now. We're not going away!"

While she likely remained concerned about everyone's safety, it was a relief that she seemed to grasp the urgency and gravity of the current state of affairs. She knew they were doomed without food and needed to make audacious moves.

"There have been some reports of attempted looting at the FDCs. Please, everybody, I know you're hungry and worried about food. We're going to have to ration and it isn't fair to steal it for yourself. I understand you're scared—believe me, I do—but remember your fellow citizens who are feeling the same way."

Lily considered the gap in the wall, currently unattended, though Guardians were reassembling in the Lab. A smattering of protestors lingered on the precipice of the cavernous hole. They were the same men and women, a cabal of plumbers, who had been roaming around with Charlie. Joe Kelly, the leader of the plumber's group, who Drayden first met in Lily's office, was among them.

"Ladies and gentlemen, please!" Lily pleaded. "I urge you to continue your peaceful protests right here by the wall. We were fortunate the Guardians didn't retaliate with firearms. We don't want to test them again. We must remain peaceful. Let's not give the Bureau the excuse they need to escalate this conflict!"

Charlie poked Drayden. "Those plumbers are nuts, man. Look at 'em, just aching to bust into the Lab. They think we should, bro, and I agree. We beat the Guardians. If we all plow through there, we could push them back to the Precinct. And maybe the Palace after that. What do you say?"

Drayden pressed his lips together. "I don't know. The Guardians made a conscious decision not to shoot. This time. If we get close to their homes, or, God forbid, the Palace...I'm not sure we'd be so lucky."

As much as he believed in himself and his fellow citizens, who were they kidding? For unknown reasons, the Guardians had engaged in a rare display of humanity—an unprecedented respect for human lives. Pushing into the Lab would be a provocative move, and if it worked, a significant victory.

However, Drayden was scared, and worried his luck would run out. He'd had a great run and knew it couldn't last forever. If the plumbers wanted to take a shot at it, he wasn't about to stop them. Perhaps he would forgo this round. He didn't have to do everything himself.

Charlie rubbed his hands together. "You said it yourself, Dray. This is the time to push. I mean, we've got the Bureau on its heels."

"I agree with Drayden," Catrice said.

"Everybody should take a deep breath right now," Sidney chimed in.

Drayden admired Charlie's courage. Whatever he lacked in other departments, he'd never been short on bravery.

Drayden grimaced. "I gotta take care of my head. It needs to be cleaned out before it gets infected. And I think we should try to find Mister Kale and Professor Worth. I have no idea where they are, or if they're safe."

The mob noise rose to a fever pitch. The plumbers were waving their arms, riling everyone up. "Let's go!" Joe Kelly was shouting. "We want our food! We want our food!" He stepped through the hole into the Lab as if piercing an invisible membrane which, once penetrated, blew wide open from the pressure built up behind it.

Nothing could stop it now and it couldn't be undone. The protestors poured into the zone.

"Please, people, stop!" Lily cried out, barely audible over the raucous crusade.

Charlie lunged ahead, turning back to shout, "C'mon, you guys! Everyone's going."

Drayden exchanged a glance with the girls. "You go, Charlie, if you want. We're gonna head to Mister Kale's and recharge."

He wore the disappointment on his face. "Okay. Yeah. I'll meet you guys there in a little while."

"Be careful!" Catrice yelled, watching him run off.

They were hardly the only ones walking the opposite way. Many of the injured were presumably going to the hospital. Although Drayden should have joined them, he wanted to make sure his mentors were safe, which was impossible in this congested crowd. Logically, the two men would try to reconvene with them at Mr. Kale's apartment.

Once inside, Drayden collapsed at the kitchen table with the girls. His head was pounding, and he could feel bruises and bumps on his legs, courtesy of the adrenaline subsiding.

Sidney fetched a wet washcloth and soap from the bathroom. "This might hurt, but I'm gonna help you clean out that cut."

"Thanks." He scrunched his face, the soapy water making his entire body shake when it touched the wound.

"Sorry. You have a huge bump."

"Hey, Catrice," Drayden grunted, trying to distract himself, "I don't know if you knew, but while you were helping a woman who was hurt, Sidney saved you from getting throttled by a Guardian. She pushed him over right as he was about to whack you with his baton."

Her jaw dropped. "No, I had no idea. Thank you, Sidney. My God, I can't believe that. I was helping an injured old lady. Why would he try to hit me?"

"Because he was a flunk," Sidney said. "Those guys were enjoying beating people. It made me so mad." She pressed the cloth with force.

"Ow!" Drayden cried out.

"Sorry, Dray. Getting worked up over here. Don't worry, that guy got his. After he fell over, he got trampled."

The front door clicked open downstairs. "Drayden?" Mr. Kale called out.

"We're here! In the kitchen."

"Thank God," Professor Worth said, rushing up the stairs.

Mr. Kale tilted Drayden's head forward. "My goodness, are you okay? That's a terrible cut."

"I'm fine. I got cracked by a baton. Were you guys all right?"

Professor Worth patted him on the back. "Yes. Mister Kale and I were kind of in the rear, never in any danger. We're a tad old for a fistfight."

Mr. Kale stepped around the table to address the three teens. "I've never been prouder of you kids—*my* kids—watching you lead that march to the wall. You made all my years of teaching worth it. I hope you know that."

"If I'd known the Guardians were going to attack, I'm not sure I would have done it," Drayden admitted.

"No way you could have known," he said. "Speaking of which, I tal—"

The front door opened and slammed shut. "You guys here?" Charlie yelled, shuffling up the stairs. "Oh, good," he said when he saw them.

"How'd it go?" Sidney asked.

"It was easy. Too easy. That's why I'm back already. I didn't even go down to the Precinct because the Guardians folded like a tent. No resistance at all. With the mob coming, they pulled back. As far as I know, we're just outside the Precinct now."

"Great job I guess," Drayden said.

He wasn't sure what to make of it. The fact that this heavily armed military force was allowing the protestors to advance without opposition made him more nervous than anything. While the victory in the brawl had felt real, this concession of the Lab seemed suspicious.

Mr. Kale sat across from him. "Drayden, I spoke to Lily. She said she has information that confirmed the Guardians were under orders not to attack the protestors, but did it anyway. They wanted to beat people. She thinks it's more important than ever to make contact with her sergeant on the inside." He paused. "She said if you're still willing to help, she has a top-secret assignment for you. She asked for you to go to her apartment, alone. And to bring your Guardian uniform."

CHAPTER 21

The Bureau had to be taken down, and Drayden would not allow his mother's death to be in vain. This wasn't the time for hesitation or cowardice. So why was he scared? Why hesitant?

The evidence was all there. Whenever an obstacle presented itself, even a monumental or dangerous one, Drayden succeeded *if* he was bold. Throughout many of the challenges in the Initiation and expedition, and the battles in New America since they'd returned—including the most recent one—he'd found a way to come out on top.

All he needed to do was believe in himself. It was that simple. He was capable of accomplishing anything he wanted if he'd just make the leap and believe. Everything he desired was on the other side of the chasm of his self-doubt.

In fact, his only failures manifested when he hesitated or questioned himself. Tim, Charlie, Mom. What did he have to fear? Death, he supposed. Except, what was he saving himself for? His family was in tatters, his world broken. The Bureau was on the ropes, and the opportunity had arisen for him to play his role, perhaps delivering the knockout punch. Everything was on the line, right here. If there was ever a time for him to dauntlessly believe in himself, it was now. *This* moment.

Drayden faced Mr. Kale, standing with his chest out and shoulders back. "I'll do it. I'll go see Lily and take the assignment."

Mr. Kale adjusted his glasses. "I don't know. It feels like an unnecessary risk to me. The Dorms are doing well. I'd even say we're winning."

"He's right," Catrice said. "It doesn't make much sense."

Sidney touched his arm. "Please don't do this. It's not that I don't believe in you, Dray. I do. But she's going to send you into the Precinct. Someone will figure out you're not a Guardian. It's suicide."

Charlie leaned against the doorframe. "I think you should do it. If I go with you. We got this, bro."

Drayden tugged on his ear. "What do you think, Professor?"

He tilted his head. "We're all speculating. Why not find out what she wants you to do first? Once you hear about this secret assignment, then decide. You two can come back here and discuss it with us if you need to."

Drayden already knew. Lily had reached the point of despair in her inability to contact her inside man within the Guardians. She wanted Drayden to seek him out, since he'd foolishly volunteered to do it without thinking it through. The odds would be stacked against him.

That was precisely why he had to go. He lived inside that narrow margin between success and failure. Beating the odds in the Initiation and expedition wasn't due to luck, but knowing how to leverage his strengths to tip the scale in his favor. Nothing precluded him from doing it again if he acted without timidity or hesitation.

"It's a good plan," Drayden said. "Charlie, let's do this."

Charlie fist-bumped him.

Mr. Kale raised a finger. "Let's get you boys clothes that aren't covered in blood."

After they changed into equally embarrassing "teacher" duds, including sweaters to cloak their pistols, the two of them collected their Guardian uniforms in a bag.

Sidney hugged Drayden and kissed his cheek. "Be careful."

The streets were dark, save for the occasional dim glow from someone's inside lights. Behind them, Second Avenue was quiet and abandoned, the protests having shut down for the night. Would they be back on the streets tomorrow? Surely. Why would they let up now?

"Hey," Drayden said quietly, "let's stay alert for people who might be angling to kidnap us. And Guardians, of course."

"Roger that."

They hurried up the pitch-black Third Avenue and turned right on Thirty-Third Street, immediately coming to Lily's townhouse at number 203.

While the surrounding residences and storefronts were darkened, suggesting they were vacant, her interior lights shone bright, illuminating the street.

On her stoop, bathed in the glow, Drayden froze.

The photo of them from the broadcast.

His face flushed. He squeezed Charlie's arm. "Charlie. The pho—"

The door opened and Lily emerged, wearing a long, flowing dress. "Drayden, I'm so happy you decided to come. I knew you would. I see you brought Charlie, which is totally fine." She extended her arm. "Please, come in."

"Well...I..."

She flashed a sly grin. "I have some milk and chocolates for you boys. It's the least I can do considering what's next."

Charlie made a silly face at Drayden. "Milk and chocolates, wha? Don't mind if I do."

Drayden sighed and followed him through the foyer into the spacious dining room, which featured a gorgeous rectangular glass table.

Lily proceeded into the kitchen. "Have a seat at the table. Make yourselves at home."

Drayden plopped down and touched his pistol to make sure it was there, wondering if he was overthinking the light outside her townhouse. "Should we be scared?" he called to Lily.

She was pouring two glasses of milk. "You wouldn't be human if you weren't scared right now."

When she presented the drinks and a bowl of chocolate truffles, Charlie giggled. Lily took a seat at the head of the table, resting her chin in one propped up hand.

Drayden sipped the cool milk. He reached for a truffle before changing his mind.

How exactly did she have chocolates? It seemed like a minor detail, except they were not available in the Dorms, even during normal times. Their first *ever* taste of chocolate had been in the Palace. What if they were poisoned?

Charlie, meanwhile, was stuffing his face. Streaks of chocolate were smeared all over his lips and fingers.

"Not hungry, Drayden?" Lily asked.

"No, I'm all right. Thanks."

Charlie gazed at him in a sugary bliss. "So good," he said through a mouthful of truffles.

Guess we'll find out if they're poisoned.

"You kids have done such an amazing job," Lily said, "which is why I've summoned you here today. I've been astounded at how *effective* you've been. Uncovering the Bureau's secrets. Getting the word out. The little paper airplane stunt you pulled." She smirked. "But the most impressive thing I witnessed was you leading the

Dorm residents on that march to the wall. So extraordinary for kids your age."

"Thank you," Drayden said flatly. While he may have been over-analyzing it, as he so often did, something felt…off. He couldn't put his finger on it. Maybe it was the combination of the incriminating lights outside, the mysterious chocolates, and the effusive compliments that felt like they were leading up to a "but."

Lily glanced at the door. "Now, I wish you'd consulted with my office before your paper airplane trick. Not that it was a bad idea. Far from it. It was very creative. I hope you can appreciate that we needed to have a united front and a, sort of, central command."

Needed.

Past tense. So far, this was smacking of a rebuke, and a recap of an effort that was over. She hadn't said anything about a top-secret assignment. His heart beating faster, Drayden flashed his eyes all around the vast space of her townhouse.

"During the hand-to-hand combat with the Guardians," Lily said, "you both held your own well. I was watching. You boys aren't only brave, you're very skilled."

"So," Drayden said, his neck tensing, "what is it that you need us to do?"

She stood and paced, wringing her hands. "That's just it, Drayden. As I said, you two have been so effective. Almost too effective."

Oh no.

Drayden should have trusted his instincts at the door. He'd walked right into this against his better judgment. He pinched Charlie's leg beneath the table.

He burped and furrowed his brow.

Drayden tried to subtly nod at the door.

Lily clasped her hands in front of her. "You see, now we have a problem."

Drayden sprang to his feet and gripped Charlie by the arm, dragging him up to standing. "Let's go," he muttered. They hustled to the door, barely noticing Lily's crossed arms and faint smile.

When Drayden swung it open, he found himself face-to-face with two pistols.

Drayden and Charlie were confined to the couch in Lily's luxurious living room, while she sat across from them in a chair with her legs crossed. Two nervous Guardians flanked her, training their pistols on the boys.

These guys weren't Special Forces or Palace Guardians. They were beat cops. Both were middle-aged, skinny, and shifting uncomfortably on their feet, as if they'd never drawn their weapons before.

On the plus side, they evidently had no idea Drayden and Charlie were armed, which made sense because Dorm residents normally had zero access to weapons. On the negative, they'd blindsided the teens, denying them an opportunity to whip out their guns. Had they tried, they'd likely be dead. Sitting here now, Drayden worried Charlie might go all "Rambo" and start blasting at any moment. Clearly, they couldn't talk it over.

"What is going on?" Drayden asked.

Lily peered at her front door. "There's a van coming from the Palace to pick you up."

"How could you?" Drayden hissed. "You're a fraud."

"No, Drayden," Lily retorted. "I'm no such thing. I care deeply about the Dorms, which is why I'm trying to keep everybody safe. I'm in contact with Premier Holst. If I cannot get the Dorms under control, the Guardians will massacre everyone. You think they were defeated withdrawing to the Precinct? No. They're creating a scenario where the use of deadly force will be justified. And our people just walked right into it as I feared."

Her allegation confirmed Drayden's suspicion about the real victory at the wall to the Lab versus the simulated one allowing the protestors inside. But what jumped out was her claim to be in touch with Holst. How?

"You have to understand," she said, "I'm doing what I must. In this case, buying us some time and goodwill from the Bureau by delivering what they want: you two."

Drayden jutted his jaw. "You're sacrificing us? You're no better than the Bureau, exiling Dorm residents to save everybody else. Can't you see how hypocritical that is? It's not right! Everyone's lives matter. My life matters. We have the upper hand. You don't have to give them anything. You're a coward."

She shook her head. "I'm sorry. I don't want to do this. As I said earlier, you kids have proven to be shockingly effective leaders. The Dorms don't need that right now. What's best for the residents is to go back to the way things were. They might not know it's the best, but it is. I will see to it that everyone gets their anger out and this misguided effort to unseat the Bureau fizzles. The Bureau isn't going anywhere."

"Why are you so loyal to the Bureau? They've been lying to us for decades. There's a whole world of people out there. New America is one giant facade. Don't you think it's right to expose it?"

Lily scooted forward in her seat, her eyes softening. "I want you to understand, so you don't think I'm some kind of monster. Don't you realize that the Bureau is trying to protect everybody? When they set me up as the leader here during the Confluence, it was my job to keep the peace. I don't want to see people killed en masse like they were back then, with all the rioting. How does it help anyone to know the truth? What would it change? Are the seamstresses suddenly going to be living a life of luxury because they know we aren't the only ones in the world? No. Little would improve for them. Right now, their expectations and reality are matched. They don't have false hope. Their wants are simple and the Bureau supplies everything they need. It's for the best."

"You're out of your freaking mind, lady. People's hope is not your decision. You're a puppet for the Bureau. I've never been more disappointed by someone in my life. How are you in contact with Holst anyway?"

"We have a direct phone line." She gestured upward. "Here, and in my office. The only working telephones in the entirety of the Dorms," she said, as if bragging.

"You've been cooperating with the Bureau all along. I can't believe it. You're probably the one who gave up Thomas Cox."

As the former Bureau representative for the Dorms, Cox's execution had resulted from an allegedly intercepted conversation with Lily about destroying the Bureau. Kim Craig had attested that he was overheard on a hidden microphone, and Drayden had expressed concern at the time that the Bureau would have discovered Lily's involvement. Kim had reasoned the Bureau couldn't touch her because of her importance in the Dorms. Come to find out, the explanation was much simpler. She was a spy for them.

"Indeed," she said. "These plots against the Bureau spring up from time to time. Everyone assumes I'll be on board, making it easy for me to reveal them to the Bureau."

Kim had been in touch with Lily many times regarding the insurrection. In fact, Lily was the one who had originally connected he and Kim.

"What about Kim Craig? You turn her in too?"

"The Bureau knows about Kim. I can't say what's happened to her, since I'm not in the Palace. But if you're friends with her, I would expect the worst."

My God.

If Kim were unmasked, what about their families? Drayden's mind was a mess. Too many thoughts, too many questions. He needed to spew them all out before it was too late.

"Why did you send me to Kim Craig in the first place?"

"Honestly? To get rid of you." She looked down. "I knew Kim would figure out that you were aware of her plans, and I thought she would eliminate you because of it. I never intended for her to recruit you."

Now he was really confused. "If you weren't on board with her plot in the first place, and intended on tipping off the Bureau, then why would you want me killed?"

Lily wagged a finger at him. "You're very clever, Drayden. You see, Holst needed this plot to advance. To stay alive. He wanted to draw out as many traitors as possible. If you had leaked it, either on purpose or by accident, he would've caught fewer people."

Drayden hoped Kim had planned for a contingency where they had been busted. She was smart. There was no reason to think she hadn't prepared for this eventuality. Even if Holst had gotten the upper hand, she'd managed to raze the walls, so he hadn't foiled her completely.

"But," Lily continued, "please understand, that wasn't the only reason. I'm not a callous murderer. My priority is always the Dorms, and making sure I'm here to protect the residents. You had been hiding in my office. I didn't recall what you'd heard. Hearing me discuss Holst's ouster was one thing. If you'd heard me talking about *working* with Holst, or God forbid speaking to him on the phone, I couldn't let that get out. Then I would've been exposed, to the insurgents, and possibly to the Dorm residents. So, you needed to go. I've survived this long for a reason. If anyone has ever mused that I might be in cahoots with the Bureau, they've found themselves mysteriously exiled."

Mysteriously exiled.

Drayden's jaw dropped.

Oh my God.

"It was you. *You* had my mother exiled."

"Yes, and I'm sorry. She was lovely, and I wish I didn't need to do that. In her defense, I tried to lure her into this overthrow plot to see if she'd bite, and she declined. The problem was, I had a feeling she accidentally overheard a conversation with Holst in my office. I couldn't exactly ask her about it, could I? I had no choice. She had to go."

Drayden's eyes teared. "You *are* a monster. My mother just died. I buried her myself, up in the Bronx, where all the exiles are living. Living in hell, because of you and your duplicity." He wiped his cheeks with his palms. He didn't want to let her know how much she'd hurt him, but he was burning with rage. "She didn't know anything about you and Holst! I asked her if she had any idea why she was exiled, and she didn't. You exiled her for nothing. For nothing at all."

"I'm sorry. I never wanted it to be like that."

He squared his shoulders, trying his best to exude strength. "Why did her exile file say that it was my father that had her exiled?"

Lily drew her head back. "I'm surprised you know about that. Think about it, though. My cooperation with the Bureau is known to Holst and a select few others. It can't say my name in there. Any Bureau member can access those files. I knew of the problems at home between your parents. Your father was a perfect choice. I can see now that you believed it."

Drayden stared at the floor. "No, I didn't." He didn't want to give her the satisfaction. All things considered, it was an enormous relief that his father was innocent.

Was there anyone alive who wasn't corrupt? It seemed to be a flaw in human nature that even honorable and well-intentioned people were prone to malfeasance. Give someone a damn whiff of power and instantaneously he became a liar, a thief, and a cheat.

Nobody was coming to save them either. Their friends would assume they'd accepted the secret assignment from Lily. If he and Charlie never returned, Drayden supposed they would conclude the boys had been captured and killed. It would be true too, except in a much more sinister way than they would believe.

Charlie's inquiring eyes were boring holes in Drayden.

Unfortunately, he hadn't the slightest idea how to break out. He studied the Guardians, mere feet away. If he and Charlie went for their weapons, they'd be blown away. Time running out, he had to come up with something.

Think, dammit!

Lily stood and checked her watch. "Your ride should be here any moment now."

CHAPTER 22

Accepting his own death as a virtual certainty, and debating the optimal way for it to happen, was a horrifying mental exercise. Drayden had faced this dilemma before, on Pier Fifteen. Like then, he refused to be taken alive to meet his demise at the hands of a torturous Premier Holst. They needed to make an escape here or die trying. Although he wasn't able to confer with Charlie, he knew his buddy would agree.

What was the downside of going for it? They were headed for death anyway. Still, busting out *alive* held a lot more appeal than dying of gunshot wounds on the spot in the next five minutes. He couldn't think of a tactic that wouldn't seriously injure or kill these two Guardians. That would be wrong. They were only doing their jobs, following orders. Judging by their jittery guns, they weren't crazy about it either.

Wait. That was the key. The Guardians' responsibility was to deliver the boys—alive—to Holst. They weren't mentally prepared to kill.

Drayden had to make a move right now. He stood, as if about to walk out of the room.

The nearest Guardian lunged forward, jabbing his weapon. "Hey! What are you doing? Sit back down. Now!"

Drayden exhaled a deep breath, his hands on his hips. "I'm going to the bathroom. Look, we're getting on this damn van in a few minutes and I have to pee, okay? Let's be honest, Dave, you can't shoot me. We both know it. Premier Holst wants us detained alive. If you shoot me, you're as good as dead yourself."

"Bob. Not Dave. And I *will* shoot you if I have to."

"Whatever. Don't worry, we're caught, we know it, and we're getting in the van. It's over for us. But we both know you're not shooting me." Drayden sneered at Charlie. "Hey bud, you chugged all that milk. Don't want you peeing your pants again."

He scowled. "I told you not to talk about that. But dammit you're right, I gotta go." He leaped to his feet.

"Whoa, whoa," the other Guardian said. "What are you guys up to, huh?"

Drayden shared a glance with Charlie. "We're peeing, Ron. I'm gonna go, and when I'm done, Charlie'll pee. Then we'll hop in the van. Relax."

"Nice and easy," Bob said, right on Drayden's heels.

Charlie was walking behind Bob, with the second Guardian shadowing him. Lily remained in the living room, appearing highly suspicious.

The microscopic bathroom sat between the dining nook in the kitchen and the front hallway. Drayden went in and shut the door, while Bob and his twitchy gun stood on the other side.

What now?

He wished a brilliant plan lay in wait, but his strategizing ended at the bathroom door. He could easily shoot Bob through it. Even if he nailed him in the leg though, in an attempt to spare his life, Bob would likely die from infection.

"I'm not hearing any pissing!" Bob shouted.

"You're giving me stage fright, Johnny," Drayden replied. "I can't go with you standing right there, pointing a gun at me."

Think!

Drayden ran the water in the sink—the standard move if you're having trouble peeing, or pretending to. Luckily, Lily's place wasn't too affected by the water restriction. Yet another perk of her loyalty to the Bureau.

The plug in the drain was stuck in the down position, causing the sink to rapidly fill with water. Being an antique sink, it offered no overflow protection.

Hmmm.

He flushed the toilet.

The sink was almost full. Once the toilet stopped running, he reflushed it.

The sink overflowed. Water cascaded down the front and sides of the vanity, pooling on the floor.

Drayden continued flushing the toilet, and scooped out handfuls of water from the sink. There was no plan here, no endgame. He was mostly buying time to devise something else, but if his tactic had any objective whatsoever it was to sow confusion; to distract and give the illusion that he was in the midst of a scheme to which the Guardians weren't privy. Much like repeatedly calling them by the wrong names, he wanted them unsure of themselves and a little intimidated. They might momentarily lower their guard in befuddlement.

"What the hell's going on in there?" Bob asked.

Drayden didn't answer. He shoveled more and more water onto the floor, where it was nearly half an inch deep now, on the verge of pouring out the door.

"Hey!" Bob screamed.

Drayden faced the door, stooped low, his hands up. He made gagging noises, and took strained inhalations, pretending to choke.

Water flooded out of the bathroom into the dining room.

"What the...?" Bob jerked the door open, his pistol now at his side.

Drayden pounced, wrapping his arms around Bob's waist and driving him into the hardwood floor.

His pistol tumbled away.

"Bob!" The second Guardian hurtled over to assist his partner and secure his weapon.

Charlie tackled him from behind.

Drayden effortlessly slid into the mount position on Bob, straddling his hips, and smashed him in the nose with a brutal elbow strike.

Bob covered his face, his nose leaking blood, and rolled over onto his stomach.

Drayden surfed on top of him, winding up on the small of his back. He slinked his arm underneath Bob's neck and applied a rear-naked choke.

"Get off me!" the other Guardian yelled at Charlie, who was sitting on his chest, pinning his arms to the floor.

When Bob fell unconscious, Drayden hopped off, swiped the guy's pistol, and slipped it in his waistband.

Bob would be asleep for a spell and rouse with a headache, but otherwise be fine.

Charlie gnawed on his bottom lip. "Yo, what do I do now?"

"Knock him out," Drayden said.

The Guardian recoiled. "Wait! Don't! Please. Just...just handcuff me or something."

Drayden peripherally caught Lily trying to tiptoe through the kitchen. He pulled his own pistol and aimed it at her. "Where do you think you're going?"

She froze, her hands raised.

Shaking, the Guardian stood and cowered in front of Charlie.

Drayden lined up shoulder-to-shoulder with him, comparing their heights. "Hey, um, take off your uniform. Then Charlie's gonna cuff you to the fridge." Who knew if a Dorm Guardian uniform would come in handy at some point?

After the Guardian stripped to his underwear, Charlie snatched his gun and dragged him over to the refrigerator, where the man clasped his hands behind his back. Thanks to his Guardian pals, Charlie knew how to work the handcuffs and locked him to the handle.

Bob was regaining consciousness, moaning and trying to get up.

"Charlie, we gotta go." Drayden hurried over to Lily and waved his pistol toward the rear. "You're coming with us." He ushered her through the living room to the glass door at the far end of the townhouse. "Charlie, get our Guardian gear and let's go!"

They fled the building into a shadowy, dirty alley and veered right, dodging rats. Many of these glorified courtyards behind apartments had no exit.

"Is this closed in?" Drayden asked Lily.

"I...I don't know."

Charlie pointed ahead. "This building on the left is huge. Bet it has a back door."

They forced Lily to the gargantuan brick apartment tower and found a steel service door, which was locked.

"Damn." Charlie yanked it to no avail.

"Shoot it out!" Drayden ordered.

He stood back and blasted three shots at the knob, completely obliterating it.

"Miss Haddad!" Bob squawked in the distance. "Miss Haddad, where are you?"

Drayden shoved her away. "I'm going to expose you. Everyone will know you're a fraud, working for the Bureau. You're finished."

She held her nose in the air. "Nobody will believe you. I have twenty-five years of goodwill behind me. Feel free to try."

Drayden raised his pistol. Finally, he knew without a doubt this woman was responsible for his mother's death. All because of a "might" which turned out to be a "didn't." The arrogance, selfishness, and cruelty of it rendered her unfit to be a member of society. The image of his dead mom flashed in his mind. Right here, Drayden could exact the revenge he sought; an eye for an eye, street justice. With one pull of the trigger, he would also remove this cancer from the Dorms.

She furrowed her brow. Her mouth twitched.

"Dray, let's go man!" Charlie heaved the door open and dashed inside.

Drayden would not become her. He wasn't a murderer who killed people for self-serving reasons, or a vigilante who deemed himself the arbiter of the greater good, committing homicide in the name of integrity. Like anyone else, like his mother and father, he was flawed. It had taken ample failure and pain to get to this point, but Drayden knew exactly who he was. He lowered his gun and followed Charlie.

Under the cover of night, the boys were walking west on Thirty-Fourth Street, taking a lengthy, circuitous route back to Mr. Kale's apartment. They hadn't seen any Guardians—regular or Palace variety in vans—out prowling for them. Still, they felt it was best to flee the general area.

"I can't believe Lily Haddad is a double-agent," Charlie said. "Did not see that coming."

Drayden slouched. "I'm sorry, I should never have let us go inside. I knew we were in trouble as soon as I saw the brightened street outside her apartment. It hit me—that's where the photo from the video screen was taken. Lily must have been the one who told the Bureau to analyze the footage there. Plus, remember that night, she disappeared upstairs for a while? Where she has a phone to Holst? When we left her place, it was swarming with Guardians."

Charlie whacked him on the arm. "Why'd you let us go in then?"

"Chotch. Two seconds after she opened the door you made a beeline for the milk and chocolate. It was too hard to leave after that."

Charlie threw his hands in the air. "Oh, so now it's my fault. You know what? That whole mess back there was worth it for those truffles. Mmmmm."

"How would she have chocolate? We don't get chocolate in the Dorms. That was the other indication something was amiss. I thought they might be poisoned. That's why I didn't eat them."

Charlie gagged, spitting over and over. He smacked Drayden even harder this time. "What the hell, man? For Christ's sake." He spat again. "And you let me stuff my face like it was my last meal? I had chocolate up my nose. I had chocolate in my hair. You couldn't be like, 'Hey bro, ease up on them poisoned truffles?'"

"Charlie, you're not dead. They obviously weren't poisoned. But I should never have let us go in."

"Dude, you're not responsible for what everybody does. You're the one who always gets us out of jams. Bad luck hits, and you bail us out. How many times did it happen on the expedition?"

Drayden's failures notwithstanding, what if his successes hadn't been luck after all? He'd never challenged his assumption that he'd been lucky to survive the Initiation; fortunate to best Eugene and the Guardians. In reality, he constantly pushed, strategized, and fought. Wasn't he in charge of his destiny rather than fate or luck?

Drayden smirked. "See, I said you were smart."

"Dray, the bad guys are the bad guys, and the good guys are the bad guys. What are we gonna do now?"

"I don't know. I need to think." As if there weren't enough powerful forces working against them, the Dorm leadership was compromised. Lily actually defended the Bureau's intentions, which suggested the decades of gaslighting had been so successful that the people responsible for it had even gaslighted themselves. She was probably right about no one believing him about her treachery. Since he was already known for making outrageous—albeit true—claims about the Bureau, accusing Lily of being a Bureau plant would just paint him as a conspiracy theorist and weaken the credibility of his earlier allegations against the Bureau. He was also sixteen and it was his word against the longtime leader of the Dorms.

The problems didn't stop there. What about Kim? Lily had been duping her this whole time. According to Kim, the insurrection involved senior Guardians, scientists, and Bureau members. What if Lily knew everyone's identities? Hopefully Kim and her allies had been prescient, decentralizing the names and details, preventing a single snitch from implicating everybody.

Fortunately, Lily's presumption that Holst was a step ahead of the insurgents crumbled much like the exploded walls had. Based on their destruction, he wasn't. Drayden wished he could slip away to the Palace to uncover the truth.

If he did, he could attempt to rescue his family from the safe-house. Although distressed about Lily's exile of his mother, he was so relieved his father was off the hook. Drayden was ashamed for how impulsively he'd turned on his dad.

It came down to goodwill, he supposed. *Equity*. Just as Lily argued she had too much goodwill built up for the residents to believe the truth about her, the opposite was true of his father. Love, kindness, and good deeds cultivated a positive equity bank between people. In the case of a negative event, the equity bank might take a hit, but it wouldn't destroy the relationship. Dad had been absent throughout Drayden's life. Their account was empty. Claims that he had exiled Drayden's mother were enough for him to light the relationship on fire.

"I thought you were gonna shoot the Guardian," Charlie said. "When you went to the can."

"I didn't know what I was going to do. I did think about shooting him, but he would've died. He didn't deserve that."

Charlie inclined his head. "Arguable."

"Not really."

"Well, I would have done something earlier, but I figured you had a plan."

"Nope. I literally went with the flow when the sink flooded."

Throughout the Initiation and expedition, Drayden realized, he'd learned to trust his gut. It hadn't come naturally, and he wasn't sure it ever would. He was logical and evidence-based, like a scientist. Acting on instinct went against his nature. His gut had told him something was off at Lily's front door. And if he was being honest, their previous meetings had been suspicious as well. Her stellar apartment, her incessant appeals for Drayden to step aside in favor of the adults... All of it had felt wrong.

Instead of listening to his gut, he'd forced the narrative that he had to believe in himself. Perhaps he could indeed achieve anything he wanted with self-belief. But what he couldn't do was rely on it to make a desired result magically come to fruition. Life would be easy if it worked that way. Some events were out of your control, like the leader of the Dorms betraying you.

They were traveling east along Twenty-Ninth Street now, in the vicinity of Mr. Kale's apartment. Post Lily's betrayal, Drayden succumbed to those familiar feelings of defeat. He had no clue what to do next.

Charlie opened the door to a darkened ground floor. "Hello?" he yelled.

Mr. Kale appeared at the top of the stairs with his mouth agape. "You guys are back so soon? What happened?"

The boys looked at each other. "It didn't go well," Drayden said. "And we have a big problem."

•

CHAPTER 23

The next morning, Drayden and Mr. Kale sat in Joe the plumber's quaint kitchen, the faded green walls featuring a baseball-sized hole stuffed with a dirty sock.

"Get outta town," Joe said. "Lily? Can't be. Twenty years, I known her."

Drayden wasn't surprised at his reaction. Lily's deception was unthinkable. The expressions on Mr. Kale and Professor Worth's faces when he'd told them were of shock, if not disbelief.

Thankfully, Professor Worth had rallied everyone, reminding them that even if the Dorm leadership was treasonous, the numbers remained in their favor. The autocrats of both the Dorms and Palace represented a tiny fraction of the population, the will of which could not be denied. As he had pointed out, however, they needed to seize the moment. Eventually, Dorm residents would grow hungry and tired, making it much easier for them to regress into their old lives, accepting their new reality with resignation.

Every time Joe leaned on the kitchen table it wobbled and Drayden was resisting the urge to jam paper underneath the faulty leg. It wasn't his place.

He rested his elbows on it, reclaiming the lean in his direction. "Joe, it's the truth. The only reason she told me so much was because she believed I was about to be killed and felt bad. Guess it never crossed her mind that we would escape. She's responsible for my mother's exile, Thomas Cox's death, and God only knows how many more. Remember how she was trying to keep you from storming the Lab? She's a puppet for Holst."

A girl of about four tottered up to Joe. "Daddy, look at my picture." She unveiled a paper covered in jagged lines.

"Gorgeous! What is it?"

"It's you, Daddy!"

"Oh, oh yeah, I see." He kissed her forehead. "Margherita, sweetie, Daddy's having a meeting. Run along now."

His son, around two years old, was playing with a toy truck on the linoleum floor. He hopped to his feet and banged it into Joe's knee.

"Ow! Giovanni!" Joe rubbed it and smiled at his guests. "For the love of God," he said under his breath. "Victoria! Come and get the kids!" He pointed at them. "Angels, these two. Such a blessing."

Victoria, apparently his wife, leaned against the doorframe between the kitchen and living room, a cloth diaper dangling from her fingertips.

"There's no water, Joe. I thought you were a freakin' plumber. What kinda plumber can't even get water in his own house?" She wadded the diaper into a tight ball.

"There's a water shortage in the Dorms," he said in a lowered voice through gritted teeth. "It don't matter if I'm Albert *freaking* Einstein, I can't make water out of thin air! What do I look like, a water god? Do I look like, like Poseidon to you?"

"You look like a crappy plumber is what you look like."

"Do you mind? I'm tryin' to have a meeting here. It's important."

She flashed a fake smile and ushered the children out of the kitchen.

Joe chuckled, visibly embarrassed. "Family. Listen, let's say you're right. What are we gonna do about it?"

Mr. Kale snickered. "I don't know these leaders in the Dorms besides you. That Lou fellow who heads up the carpenters and the others. I think we need to spread the word that Lily can't be trusted. We should strategize on our own. She told Drayden nobody would believe him over her, and she may be right about that. But he's telling the truth, and if the residents hear it from you, and Lou, and Paula, it'll carry a lot more weight."

Joe cracked his knuckles. "Yeah. I don't know if they'll believe me either. I'll talk to Lou about it. A bunch of us should get together and confront Lily. She can't have us all arrested."

"I don't know." Mr. Kale shrugged. "Honestly, I'm not sure what the best approach is here. We clearly shouldn't tell her about our strategy going forward. Just cut her out of the loop."

Why stop there?

The trace of a scheme was percolating in Drayden's mind. He couldn't elucidate it, but something was there.

Joe frowned at Drayden. "You're supposed to be this wizard who passed the Initiation and cracked all the Bureau's secrets. What do *you* think we should do next?"

"I...I have an idea, sort of, but I'm not sure yet. Something you said gave me a thought." He grimaced. "Can you guys keep talking?"

Joe gawked at him like he was some sort of exotic creature. "Yeah, um, sure thing. I'll try and find Lou this morning but me and my guys aren't gonna be part of the protests today. I'm taking everybody uptown on a little adventure. A secret mission, you could say."

Mr. Kale raised his eyebrows. "Secret mission?"

"The Bureau believed they pulled one over on us by cutting off the food and limiting the water, thinking those are the most important things in New America, right, and they control them? The thing you gotta understand is they store the Dorm's water in this giant tank. They probably flipped a switch to slow down the flow, but the water's still there. I'm taking my boys on a trip to the Fifties to see if we can undo what they did. Turn the tables on the Bureau. All we gotta do is make sure we don't get busted sneaking a group of people up into the northern Dorms."

The most important things in New America...sneaking people up into the northern Dorms...

The lightbulb went off. Just like that it clicked, in the same way it had on the expedition when Drayden concocted the plan to defeat the Guardians in the marsh. Leave it to Joe and his verbosity to be the catalyst.

He stared at the table. "I got it," he said quietly. "I know how we're going to beat the Bureau." He wasn't sure why it had taken him so long to recall what he brought to the table, literally and figuratively. Armed or not, neutered of power or not, obstructed or not, he always possessed the strength of his mind. It didn't matter that they were outmuscled. Brains were more powerful than brawn. What resulted from Kim's plot almost didn't matter either. The real insurrection was right here in the Dorms, and they had all the power they needed.

Joe regarded Mr. Kale, then Drayden, before crossing his arms. "Well, what is it?"

Drayden ran his fingers through his hair. "You may have to put your secret mission on hold. Don't confront Lily. Go talk to her, but don't let her know you spoke to me. Pretend like everything is normal and you don't know her dirty secret. She wants everyone to give up, to withdraw from the Lab, because she claims she doesn't want anyone to get hurt. She's talked to Holst and they're planning on slaughtering us if we should dare invade the Precinct. I don't think she cares about Dorm residents. She's doing Holst's bidding."

He pointed at Joe. "You tell her that enthusiasm for protesting is starting to fade. Some people want to get back to work, but you don't know if you'll be able to stop the remaining ones from storming the

Precinct. You have the momentum and the Bureau on its heels. She'll tell you that you must and you say you'll try your best."

"Um, sure."

Drayden rubbed his temples, trying to sort it all in his mind. "After that, go talk to Lou, and everybody else who has a voice with their people. Tell them everything, about Lily and the Bureau's plans, but make sure they don't let Lily in on it. If you have even an inkling that one of them is loyal to Lily and will run and tell her, then exclude them. It has to remain a secret. She *must* believe she's safe."

Joe nodded. "No problem. I can do that. Lou and Paula are good folks, plus Dustin with the janitors, Jeannie and the electricians..." He looked off into space. "I ain't so sure about Randy." He speedily shook his head, snapping back to the present. "And then what?"

"Tell everyone to await further instructions, which we'll bring to you here in your apartment this afternoon. You and the other Dorm leaders will let the people know what they need to do. It *has* to come from you guys. Nobody would listen to me. After that? Prepare them to invade."

Protests had already started for the day around the Bureau office in the Dorms and presumably down into the Lab. Negotiating the mass of citizens, the glare of the morning sun reflecting off buildings into his eyes, Drayden noticed Lily Haddad was nowhere to be seen. He was curious what would transpire the next time they ran into each other.

"Drayden, can you fill me in on this plan?" Mr. Kale asked. "Maybe we should talk it over."

"Yes. Let's review it with everyone else, though, because it involves them too."

The plan required an epic level of coordination. It requested a lot of many people and called for bravery. But as the architect, it also relied on Drayden to believe in himself again. It demanded he overcome his recurring fear that his luck was about to run out.

He'd been waffling about luck ever since the Initiation. He hadn't been lucky. Luck was merely a matter of perspective. He could call himself lucky for having survived the expedition. Another observer might equally deem him *un*lucky for being forced by the Bureau to undertake it. Sure, he was unlucky for being on a boat that sank, but lucky he didn't die. It wasn't luck that he'd defeated the Guardians on the expedition. "Luck" didn't exist. The universe presented situations beyond his control and he carved his path through them. His successes and failures were all his, and despite his tragic downfalls, he'd claimed some damn big victories too. There was no reason he couldn't pull this off.

Inside Mr. Kale's apartment, everybody huddled around Drayden at the kitchen table to hear a rough sketch of his idea and how he thought it would play out. His friends were fidgety, while Professor Worth was jotting down notes and Mr. Kale was listening intently.

Drayden looked over the faces of the teens. "So...we need someone to travel to the Bronx. Or two people."

Sidney raised her hand, as if they were in class. "How would we get there?"

"You change into your Guardian uniforms after you're out of the Dorms to avoid being attacked like I was. Walk up to the Fifty-Ninth Street Bridge and straight out the gate. With the uniform on, and your Bureau pins, nobody will stop you. You'd have to climb down from the bridge outside the wall and fetch the dinghy, which is hidden at Fifty-Second Street, right on the shore beneath a pedestrian walkway. Then paddle up to the Bronx."

Everyone exchanged dubious glances.

"I'll do it," Catrice said quietly.

Drayden furrowed his brow. "Really?"

She wrapped her arms around herself. "Yes. I know I haven't been any help since the Initiation. I want to make it up to you guys, and prove that I can add value too."

Sidney fist-bumped her.

"I'll go with her," Charlie said. "This is a two-person job. Catrice has the brains. I have the muscle. Together, we're like a superhero. Plus, I wanna put my Guardian duds back on. No offense, Mister Kale, but your clothes make me look like a member of the young Bureau's club. I look like the guy who got cut from the football team and had to become an accountant."

Drayden smiled. "Remember what I said about reentering. You'll probably need brains and brawn."

Charlie winked. "One outta two ain't bad."

"And the rest of us will do what?" Sidney asked. "Join this protest we're planning at the Precinct wall?"

"Yes. We can't be in our Guardian gear, but we may want to pack it in a backpack for later."

Mr. Kale scoured his cabinets and refrigerator. "Getting low on food here. Assuming we're going to move forward with this plan, we need to set the wheels in motion pronto. If my own apartment is any gauge, we're on the verge of a food crisis."

"I would add," Professor Worth said, "if what Lily Haddad said is true, the Guardians are preparing their own assault. They may be waiting for our invasion of the Precinct, but we shouldn't presume they'll call it off if we don't invade. They may launch an offensive either way."

If they were going to implement Drayden's grand plan, this was the pivotal juncture. It would require the word to be spread to many people. Once the train left the station, it couldn't be pulled back. People would have to be in their respective positions and primed to go—some before dawn.

Mr. Kale crossed his arms. "Listen, we have a lot of people to alert. We're going to have to wait for Joe to meet Lily and warn her about a Precinct invasion. And then we need him to tell the other leaders about our plan. I'll take care of that part. I'll go to his apartment and give him the details."

Drayden informally saluted him. "Sid and I will rally the students. We'll start with her friends. I'm just nervous we won't be able to have everyone ready by tomorrow morning."

"We can totally do it," Sidney said. "We may have to round people up and go door to door, but you know how quickly gossip balloons. I think they're hungry for this fight."

"Well said, Sidney." Professor Worth nodded. "I agree. This is your chance. It's a good plan."

Drayden would not hesitate this time. He'd learned his lesson. In the face of growing consequences, the pressure of expectations, and fear of failure, it was easy to shrink away from the moment, to curl up and hope someone else took care of it. How many times had he fallen prey to that version of hope? Life had a way of passing you by while you were sitting there stewing about what would happen. He would never be that person again.

CHAPTER 24

The next morning, Drayden, Sidney, and Professor Worth lingered near the front of the crowd, centered around the gaping hole in the wall between the Lab and Precinct. Although Drayden was still wearing Mr. Kale's clothes, he was armed with both his own pistol on his hip and the Guardian's stolen gun in his waistband. He was also lugging a backpack containing his and Sidney's Palace Guardian uniforms, plus the extra uniform he'd poached from the guard at Lily's apartment. Sidney continued to wear her middle-aged woman ensemble.

Thousands of people had turned up, and by the looks of it, were raring to go. Their anger was not feigned for the purposes of deceit. It was real and palpable. The air was tense, electrified. Many carried makeshift weapons, such as kitchen knives, wooden posts, hammers, and metal chains. Drayden had beseeched them to be equipped for war, and they'd obliged.

Up front, standing on a stool, Joe the plumber was pumping a plunger above his head, which Drayden found hilarious. He couldn't fathom how Joe would hurt someone with a plunger, but he figured the plumbers knew how to wield their own tools for maximum effect. Joe certainly didn't fit the mold of a classic leader, with his potbelly and scraggly beard. Sometimes in a crisis the true leaders were unmasked, unlikely as they may be.

He was leading a rallying cry of "Down with the Bureau! Down with the Bureau!" Residents shook their fists and weapons in the air.

The Guardians were well prepared for this attack, unsurprisingly, since Drayden knew that Lily would have notified them. The hole in the wall was almost as wide as the avenue, affording a snapshot of a battalion that went a hundred deep, plus countless more out of sight. Many were in SWAT gear, packing rifles. Snipers lined the top of the wall in both directions for blocks.

Drayden noted these were all Precinct Guardians, clothed in black uniforms. Palace Guardians only wore gray, which would have made them stand out. That was perfect, because he didn't want them working together. Eventually, he would need the regular Guardians to assail the Palace ones.

"Down with the Bureau! Down with the Bureau!" The chants were growing louder.

He glanced both ways down Houston Street and behind him up Third Avenue, known as Bowery down here in the Lab, attempting to estimate the crowd size. There had to be ten thousand people, maybe more. While a solid turnout, it was smaller than recent protests, particularly the brawl with the Guardians.

That was by design. One, the Bureau needed to think the protests were shrinking; that the Dorms were losing their resolve in this fight. Ideally, it would be enough to dissuade the Guardians from launching a proactive assault. And two, many of the protestors were currently elsewhere, in hiding, provided everything went according to plan. Mr. Kale was with them, ensuring the effort unfolded smoothly.

Drayden caught sight of Lily Haddad, flitting to his left through the masses, her megaphone in hand. Periodically, she would stop to chat with people.

Nervous heat rushed through his body. He averted his eyes, staring the opposite way down Houston Street. What was he doing? *She* was the one harboring a deep secret; the traitor who should be avoiding *him.*

He glowered at her, daring her to make eye contact.

She was speaking with an elderly woman, tilting her head and nodding, doing a spectacular job pretending to care.

Watching her do so gave Drayden pause, his pulse quickening. He was confident that Joe, Paula, and the other Dorm leaders would withhold their plan from Lily, heeding his request. But what about ordinary Dorm citizens who were out here at the behest of those leaders? Would all ten thousand people be able to keep a secret from someone they'd trusted for decades?

He supposed it didn't matter now. Even if she discovered their true intent, whom could she tell, and how? It wasn't like she was carrying a phone and could ring Premier Holst. She couldn't slink over to the Guardians in full view of everyone and strike up a conversation to let them know. The real risk was his plan falling apart and his fellow citizens paying the price.

He gripped Professor Worth's arm. "What if this doesn't work? What if everybody dies and it's all my fault?"

The professor patted him on the shoulder. "Regardless of what happens, it's not your fault. People are here by choice. They know the risks. I'm sure much of this won't go as planned, but that's okay. We'll react and adapt. Give it a chance, Drayden."

"What if we can't get you downtown to Kim?"

Per Drayden's forecast of future events, they would secure an opportunity later to journey into the Palace, hopefully reuniting with Kim and their families.

Hopefully.

"That's not our concern right now. One thing at a time."

"It's gonna work, Dray," Sidney said.

Drayden tugged on his left earlobe.

Lou Ricci, the carpenters' head and a tall, strapping man, sidled up to Joe, brandishing a hammer. "Down with the Bureau! Down with the Bureau!"

Besides the carpenters and plumbers, the other recognizable groups here were the janitors, electricians, and bus drivers, distinguishable by their attire. Paula and the seamstresses were noticeably absent. They were with the second crew, far away. Given the time constraint in organizing this offensive, the easiest way to decide who would go where was by occupation.

Drayden observed activity on the Guardian side of the wall too. Soldiers were in motion, switching positions and marshalling into formations. While they could have been fortifying their defenses, he worried they were setting the stage for their preemptive strike, as Professor Worth had warned. The Dorm residents needed to make their move right away. However, he wasn't leading this.

A young man Drayden didn't know tapped him on the shoulder and leaned into his ear. "Hey, you guys know the real plan?"

"Yup. We're all set. Thanks for checking."

"Cool, bud. Just making sure everyone knows." He moved on to the protestors beside them.

Professor Worth nudged Drayden. "I think the plumber is trying to get your attention."

He made eye contact with Joe, who raised his eyebrows and flashed a thumbs-up.

Drayden gave him a double thumbs-up back. Peripherally, he caught Lily Haddad witnessing the exchange. Drayden faced her with crossed arms.

Joe jumped up and down. "Are we gonna reclaim our city?" he hollered.

"Yes!"

"Yeah!"

"Are you ready to do this?" he shouted.

"Booyah—Yeah—Woohoo!" the crowd responded.

Joe faced the gap, which was plugged up with too many Guardians to count. He thrust his plunger, screaming, "It's time! It's time!"

The mob roared, pushing in even closer, weapons raised. The noise reached ear-piercing levels.

The Guardians braced themselves, calling out their own commands, decidedly ripe for this battle.

Joe and Lou locked eyes and shouted, "Now!"

Just like that, everyone spun around and ran the other way. Away from the wall.

CHAPTER 25

Sitting beside one another on a bus speeding up Sixth Avenue, Sidney clutched Drayden's hand. Professor Worth sat calmly across the aisle, whistling a tune Drayden didn't recognize. The bus was packed to the gills; every seat taken and protestors standing shoulder-to-shoulder in the aisle.

It was only the third time ever Drayden had ridden on a bus. In spite of the circumstances, he loved the thrill of traveling through the city so fast. The protestors had hijacked the buses abandoned by the Guardians, plus the ones already in the Dorms to transport workers. This part of the plan had required the bus drivers' presence at the wall protest.

With a normal capacity of sixty, each cramped bus now carried around seventy-five people. Twenty buses followed Drayden's, meaning, at most, they were transporting 1,600 protestors. The vast majority would have to walk several miles to the Meadow, where they were headed.

At a minimum, the buses would arrive at the heavily guarded hole in the wall between the Dorms and the Meadow an hour before the pedestrian protestors. With a mere 1,600 people, this would seem like a problem, though it wouldn't be, since Drayden had accounted for that.

Obviously, invading the Precinct would have been suicide. That was a head fake. It was also what the Bureau both wanted and expected. They sought an excuse to quell the protests by force, and an ill-advised attack of the Precinct would have provided it.

What the Bureau didn't see coming? An attack on the *Meadow*, which had two distinct goals. One was to seize the drugs being grown in the tents and hold them hostage. The other was to divulge them to the Guardians, who should be arriving shortly after the protestors.

Therein lay the beauty of faking an attack on the Precinct. The Guardians were certain to be confused and follow. What good would it have done to infiltrate the Meadow if no one knew about it?

When Drayden and Mr. Kale had met Joe in his apartment, his words were the key. He'd said the Bureau restricted the food and water because they believed those resources were the most important things in New America. What was more important than that? *The drugs that paid for them.* Capturing them was a way for the Dorms to one-up the Bureau, to turn the tables once more. Revealing them was an elegant solution too, furnishing the evidence needed to convince the Guardians of the Bureau's deception. Clearly, they weren't swayed by words or rumors. They were too far gone, too brainwashed. Only indisputable proof would demonstrate they were defending the wrong people.

The bus slowed, now only a block away from the former gate in the twenty-five-foot wall to the Meadow. Guardians hastily formed a barricade of bodies in the gap. Some held up their hands at the bus, imploring it to stop, while others aimed rifles. More armed officers could be seen on watch towers behind the wall.

Drayden pushed up out of his seat and scanned the surrounding blocks. "Where are they?" he asked Sidney.

She craned her neck to get a better angle out the window.

A sea of people emerged on Fifty-Eighth Street and behind them on Sixth Avenue.

Drayden watched in amazement, pride, and relief as hundreds—and then thousands—of Dorm residents converged on the buses, chanting "Down with the Bureau!" He caught a glimpse of his former classmates, the ones from the paper airplane stunt, among those in the crowd.

Before dawn, under the cover of darkness, this second crew of protestors had clandestinely journeyed up through the Dorms, congregating in the vicinity of the wall, out of sight. The arrival of the buses was their cue to spring into action. Besides the students, the crew included seamstresses, administrative staffers, food service workers, street cleaners, and many others.

Drayden wiped sweat from his brow. Until seeing it himself, he couldn't verify that they'd complied with his request, via their work leaders, to amass there. If they hadn't, the 1,600 people on buses would be in serious jeopardy, facing off against dozens if not hundreds of heavily armed Guardians.

With the weight of the pedestrians behind him, the bus driver accelerated toward the gap in the wall.

His back pressed up against the seat, Drayden's heart was pounding.

"Get down!" The driver ducked beneath the dashboard.

Gunshots rang out and bullets shattered the windshield. Screams echoed throughout the bus.

Drayden dropped to the floor and blanketed Sidney, who tried to reciprocate.

More bullets penetrated the side windows, showering them in glass, as the bus plowed through the gap. The driver sat upright and cut a hard left turn, tires screeching, onto Fifty-Ninth Street.

Brushing off the shards, Drayden dared to peek out the window, now open to the air, and shuddered in horror.

The Guardians weren't just firing at the buses. They were shooting the protestors, many of whom were dropping to the ground with grisly gunshot wounds. Even so, due to their sheer numbers, the protestors overran them, relentlessly streaming through the gap alongside the other buses.

Despite covering his eyes, Drayden couldn't avoid seeing through the cracks between his fingers.

A mob of people tackled an officer, savagely beating him. Someone snatched the Guardian's weapon and pressed it to his temple.

Drayden turned away but heard the shot. He started hyperventilating. This battle had escalated, past the point of no return. How was he not responsible for those deaths? This was all his idea.

Once the bus hit Columbus Circle, the massacre at the gate was mercifully no longer in view. They sped up Central Park West, with the park on their right side. The trees in this section had been cleared, leaving only the towering wind turbines and the massive white bubble-like agricultural tents. After five blocks, the bus ground to a halt.

"People!" Professor Worth shouted. "We must remain on the bus until most of the buses get here! Then we storm these tents!"

Drayden sat frozen, nearly catatonic, having witnessed the bloodbath at the gate. Closing his eyes only made the image of Tim's brutalized body flash through his mind. His lower lip quivered.

The professor touched him on the shoulder and said in his ear, "Every single person made their own decision to be here."

Drayden heard Tim's voice at first. He clenched his fists to bring himself back to reality.

"There was no way this battle would end without bloodshed," the professor continued. "It would have taken this turn no matter what. Let's not allow their deaths to be in vain. We have a chance to win."

"What happened?" Sidney asked. "I didn't see."

"The Guardians were killing people coming through the gate," Drayden muttered. "And...and I saw some protestors shoot one of the officers in the head."

She wilted and rested her cheek on his shoulder.

Drayden knew they'd never fully escape the trauma of death from the Initiation and expedition. He wrapped his arms around Sidney, and she held him back.

More than half the buses were lined up near Sixty-Fifth Street, and many of the pedestrian protestors that survived the gate carnage were steamrolling through the rocky terrain of the park, gunning for the tents. "Time to go," Professor Worth said. "Drayden, see this through. Come now."

The professor eagerly clapped. "Everyone, let's go!"

The residents raced off the bus and went for the closest tent, having to traverse titanic boulders and circumvent the fenced-in bases of the windmills.

Running beside Sidney and Professor Worth, Drayden couldn't resist staring up at the 350-foot tall wind turbine, powerfully spinning overhead, dizzying him as he passed beneath it.

Facing an onslaught of protestors, the few Guardians on foot patrols around the tents offered zero resistance, holding their hands up in surrender.

When the crowd breached the first tent, Drayden contemplated how they would open it enough to "expose" it. It wasn't literally a canvas tent that could simply be torn down. Steel framing fortified the structure, while the walls and roof were a puffy rubber material. The whole building was hundreds of feet long and a good eighty-feet tall.

The protestors were storming through a regular-sized door. Before Drayden followed them, he noticed the side of the tent featured garage-like doors all the way to the end.

A skunky scent inside, which was almost as arresting as the sight, permeated the soaring space. Easily an acre of impressive marijuana plants, identifiable by the trademark starfish leaves, stretched from wall-to-wall.

Scores of men and women in white lab coats cowered in response to the endless stream of protestors through the door. The rowdy Dorm residents were yelling and screaming about the startling discovery, which confirmed the rumors about drugs in the tents. Many of them had followed instructions to bring matches as a threat.

"We need to get those giant garage doors open," Drayden said.

Professor Worth nodded at the scientists. "I'm sure they know how to do it."

Drayden scrutinized the cluster of white-coat-clad men and women, zeroing in on one with red hair and glasses who looked familiar.

Lucy Ravenna. She had been their guide for the tour of the Meadow before the Initiation.

Drayden took Sidney's hand and led her over to the woman. "Hi, Miss Ravenna?"

She furrowed her brow. "How do you know my name?"

"Because you gave us a tour of the Meadow a couple weeks ago. My name is Drayden Coulson." He motioned toward the side of the tent. "I need you to show me how to open these big doors."

Lucy Ravenna crossed her arms. "I'm sorry, I can't do that. I don't know what's going on. Unless my superiors tell me to open them, I cannot."

Drayden recalled hearing that the scientists were treated quite well by the Bureau. He imagined the ones privy to its deepest secrets were particularly pampered and didn't support the insurrection. The inequity of it coalesced into a ball of rage in the center of his chest. "This revolution can't be stopped!" he shouted at her. "You know better than most about the Bureau's deception. We're going to pull back the curtain, once and for all. Which side of history do you want to be on?"

"I...I'm afraid to cross the Bureau. I'm sure you could figure out a way to raise those doors if you really want."

Drayden pulled his Glock and dangled it by his side. "Miss Ravenna...Lucy...we have to open the doors ASAP. I was asking nicely, but I can ask a different way. Please raise them right now."

She recoiled at the sight of his weapon. "Follow me," she said quietly.

Lucy brought them to a compact equipment room, basically a closet, near the main entrance to the tent. She entered a key into a lock and flipped a switch.

Drayden poked his head out the door.

Generating a sound like grinding metal, the dozen or so garage doors were slowly rising.

"Thank you." He waved his pistol. "Let's do the next tent." He collected Professor Worth and the four of them weaved through the thousands of people outside chanting "Down with the Bureau!"

"Whoa!" Sidney marveled at the contents of the adjacent tent, replete with magnificent red and pink flowers. "What are these?"

"Poppies," Lucy said. "*Papaver Somniferum*, also known as the opium poppy." She took them to a similar utility closet and opened the garage doors to that tent.

"How many more tents are there?" Drayden asked.

"There are twenty in all," Lucy said, putting her keyring away. "Are we done now?"

Drayden appealed to Professor Worth. "I think two tents gets the job done, no?"

"Yes. It's time to prepare for the next stage of this battle, when the Guardians arrive."

"What are your names?" Lucy asked. "I want to make sure I can let the Bureau know who ordered me at gunpoint to raise the doors to the tents."

Drayden jutted his jaw. "I told you, my name is Drayden Coulson. The Bureau knows me. Feel free to tell them. You should get on board with this effort. The Bureau's going down. If you don't evolve, you'll go down too. Your privilege won't save you."

She laughed dismissively. "I'm sure you think you're a hero, Drayden. You and your fellow agitators here." She surveyed the angry crowd. "Someone might want to let them know their matches are useless. These plants are far too wet to burn. Nice try, though."

Lucy pointed at the plants behind her. "Do you know what would happen to New America if you destroyed these crops? We're dead. This is our currency with the rest of the world. And you may not like the idea of growing drugs instead of food, but for the record, did you know that we could never feed all of New America with our food-growing capacity in these tents? Not even close. Let me give you some perspective. There's about an acre of marijuana in the first tent. Say we grew corn instead for comparison. Do you know how much more an acre of marijuana is worth than an acre of corn? About two thousand times as much. In other words, an acre of marijuana allows us to import two thousand acres of corn. This 'revolution,'" she said, using air quotes, "is idiotic. You're going to kill us all."

Drayden had to admit he was stunned by the numbers, although given Lucy's condescension, he didn't want to give her the satisfaction. It also missed the point. That drugs were an illicit vice wasn't the crux of the problem. The deception was, as were the spoils the Bureau was reaping in compensation—and keeping for themselves—while everyone else starved. "This is about more than the tents. This is about the truth. Nobody's saying we have to destroy the crops and replace them with corn. What we're saying is the Bureau needs to be destroyed because they've been lying about everything in the world for over twenty years. They've made everyone suffer, *except* themselves."

Lucy defiantly pursed her lips.

"How nice is your apartment?" Drayden asked. "Enjoying the chocolates?"

She blushed, looking away.

Professor Worth peeked out the door. "Drayden, the citizens from the wall protest are arriving."

Drayden glared at Lucy Ravenna one last time before following Professor Worth and Sidney outside. They walked until they were far enough away to see the entirety of both tents, which was nearly back to the buses, to make sure they were fully surrounded.

The battle was just beginning, but Drayden was thrilled that the Dorm residents were perfectly executing their plan, encompassing the tents and threatening to destroy their contents. With the pedestrians from the Precinct wall protest arriving, their numbers would be insurmountable, even if every single Guardian followed. Tens of thousands occupied the Meadow already, and thousands more were streaming into the park by the minute. It was an astonishing sight.

There *was* power in numbers, like Professor Worth had said.

Drayden had never seen so many people in one place. Half of the entire Dorm population seemed to be there. It was standing room only in Central Park, for crying out loud. The chants were deafening. "Down with the Bureau! Down with the Bureau!"

Right on cue, as Drayden expected, the mass of Guardians from the Precinct showed up on the heels of the pedestrian protestors. Dressed in their trademark black uniforms, thousands of them poured through the gate into the Meadow.

The big question was, what had they been ordered to do? Perhaps they were sent to the Meadow to slaughter everyone. Whatever was to happen, he would know within minutes.

CHAPTER 26

Drayden agonized over how they might reconnect with Mr. Kale. Having been overburdened by weightier issues, they'd overlooked the need to arrange a place and time to reconvene. He'd be impossible to find in such a populous crowd.

The Guardians were assembling into a formation just south of the protestors in the park. In row after distinct row, with soldiers in SWAT gear up front, they were indisputably preparing for... something.

Drayden's stomach was in knots, knowing that, despite his strategizing, the Guardians had their own game plan. He would be foolish to believe they were exclusively playing defense, solely reacting to the maneuvering of the protestors. A physical confrontation was their bread and butter, after all.

Small teams of officers were flanking way out to the sides, which made him fear an imminent attack. Although dramatically outnumbered, the Guardians were armed. At present, Drayden and the rest of the protestors were bunched together in a giant oval, enclosing the two tents. The soldiers were a mere hundred feet away, the two sides facing each other as if on a medieval battlefield.

Drayden glanced at the tents, realizing the Guardians may not be able to see inside. Too many people were standing in the way.

A major purpose of this whole exercise was to reveal the tents' shocking contents to them.

"Sid, we gotta clear people away from the doors. They can't see in. Can't see the drugs."

"How?"

"I don't know. Let's try." They weaved through the unruly throng, bumping citizens out of the way every so often.

At the first garage door, Drayden cupped his hands around his mouth. "Hey! You guys! We gotta clear space here so the Guardians can see inside."

Nobody budged. Either they couldn't hear him or ignored him, though some classmates nearby acknowledged his pleas. They sprang into action, going person to person, imploring protestors to step to the sides. In truth, the area was too cramped to move much. Word gradually got around and rough lanes formed through which the doors would theoretically be visible.

Drayden continued along the remaining garage doors, trying his best to shuffle people around. It wasn't perfect. At the very least, the Guardians should get a glimpse of the plants. He and Sidney returned to Professor Worth, who was watching the Guardians and rubbing his chin.

"What is it?" Drayden asked.

"I'm trying to figure out what they're up to."

Drayden held his hands behind his head. "I don't get it. They still have their weapons engaged, like they're gonna start blasting. Don't they see what's in the tents? Why aren't they reacting?"

"Maybe they need time to process it," Professor Worth suggested. "Remember, they're under orders."

What more proof did they require? They were fighting for, and at the behest of, a government that had deceived them and everyone else. The logical question—which the Guardians should have been asking themselves—was, if the Bureau would lie about what they were growing in the tents, what else were they lying about? Of course, the answer was everything.

Absolutely everything.

If one acre of marijuana was worth two thousand acres of corn, the Bureau was receiving substantially more goods in payment than he'd ever dreamed. New America was always short on food, especially in the Dorms. Even though Drayden's food allocation in the Palace had improved, it wasn't overflowing or luxuriant in any way. The lion's share of the bounty was probably reserved for Holst's inner circle, who were living like kings.

A new chant materialized, slowly at first in the corners of the crowd, then swiftly gaining steam. "Holst is a liar! Holst is a liar!"

The Guardians were unwavering, weapons locked and loaded, positions taken. The fact that they hadn't yet attacked, and the protestors were not planning on throwing the first punch either, meant this was a stalemate. They were at an impasse. What would break it?

Just as the thought drifted away, a teenage girl stepped forward from the crowd, strutting with confidence toward the Guardians and coming to a stop midway between the two groups. Drayden recognized her. She was one of the former classmates who'd participated in the paper airplane launch.

What is she doing?

"My God, it's Zoe." Sidney had both hands in her hair.

Mesmerized by her baffling move, the protestors fell silent, the chants petering out.

"What is wrong with you guys?" she screamed, her face contorted in disgust. She pointed behind her. "These tents are full of drugs, not food! I know you all can see it. The rumors are true! They get everything while we starve? Why are you fighting for them? They've been lying to us! To you! Put down your weapons and join our fight!"

Drayden stared in amazement at her bravery. Someone needed to step up, to call out the Guardians for following morally compromised orders from corrupt leaders. Zoe had evidently decided it would be her.

The crowd roared behind her, cheering and clapping.

An officer emerged from the soldiers' ranks carrying a megaphone. "Step back! Disperse! Everybody go home!"

"We're not going anywhere!" she shouted. "You either join us or we're destroying these crops!"

More cheers and applause erupted from the assembled citizens.

"This is your last warning," the Guardian said, now flanked by another man with his rifle raised.

The chants started up again. "Holst is a liar! Holst is a liar!" The girl pumped her fist, taunting the Guardians, in concert with the fellow protestors behind her. Drayden, Sidney, and Professor Worth joined in too, the noise growing to thunderous levels.

A gunshot rang out.

Zoe dropped to the ground, eliciting gasps from the crowd.

Drayden drew in a quick breath.

My God.

Everyone fell quiet, in apparent shock. "Hold your fire!" multiple Guardians bellowed.

A small band of protestors darted out to aid the wounded girl. Others appeared on the verge of charging the Guardians.

Then a second gunshot resounded.

The officer up front, presumably the gunman who'd fired the first bullet, collapsed to the ground himself.

What the...?

Drayden checked to see if Sidney or Professor Worth had discharged their weapons, but they hadn't. Sidney was holding both hands over her mouth and Professor Worth was frozen, wrinkling his forehead.

Off to the side, a tiny faction of Guardians was now wrestling one of their comrades to the ground, trying to pry away his weapon. Other officers came to his defense, and before long, they were brawling. More gunshots sounded out and the formerly well-formed lines of soldiers promptly broke apart. Guardians scattered in all directions, some ducking behind boulders, some firing their weapons. Isolated groups engaged in hand-to-hand combat.

Cries of terror emanated from the mass of protestors, trying to elude the budding internal war breaking out within the Guardians, but finding nowhere to run.

The infighting, which sparked chaos on both sides, was isolated to a few packs of officers who were surely having trouble identifying friend from foe, because they were all dressed identically. Everyone else was standing back, taking cover.

Drayden wrapped his fingers around his pistol and he noticed Sidney and Professor Worth doing the same.

"This is good," Professor Worth said, nodding.

"Is it?" Sidney asked.

"Some of these guys aren't on the Bureau's side anymore," Drayden said. "There's a resistance internally. And they're making their move."

A handful at a time, Guardians joined the protestors with their arms up, reciting "Holst is a liar! Holst is a liar!" Apparently, they wanted the citizens to know they were sympathetic, to avoid being assaulted. While the number of defectors was trivial, the significance of their disloyalty was huge. The Guardians were not united in their defense of the Bureau. Perhaps they'd been given orders to kill the protestors and refused on moral grounds. Or they were on the fence and "turned" when they saw the drugs in the Meadow, confirming a primary rumor about the Bureau.

One such soldier entered the crowd near Drayden, standing alongside the protestors, watching his comrades duke it out.

Drayden rushed over to him. "Excuse me, Officer? Thank you for joining us." He pointed at the warring Guardians. "What's going on?"

The guy cursed. "A lot of us are on your side. A lot. But you gotta understand how hard it is to be the first to walk away, branded a traitor and executed if nobody joins you. Some of us have had enough. The Bureau needs to go down."

"Looks like plenty of your buddies are on the Bureau's side. Don't they see the drugs in the tents?"

"They see what they want to see. They'd rather not believe the truth."

The body of protestors was reduced to murmurs and chatter, witnessing an event no one had ever dreamed possible: the Guardians fighting each other, in some cases to the death.

A faint sound surfaced in the distance. At first, Drayden thought he was imagining it. People began glancing and gesturing toward Central Park West. It sounded like...a rally?

The noise grew louder and louder, to the point that it was impossible not to watch in anticipation. Once the sound became decipherable, even the Guardians stopped fighting and waited.

"We are the exiled! We are alive! We are the exiled! We are alive!"

Drayden's smile grew wide. It was a risky move, without a doubt. Nevertheless, he felt it was a risk worth taking.

Charlie and Catrice led a parade of several hundred of the exiled citizens from the Bronx. They were marching down Central Park West, announcing their presence for all to see. Everyone in New America had been told—implicitly or explicitly—that the exiled died outside the walls, since the Bureau had always claimed nobody could survive outside.

Instantly, the protestors in the park applauded, cheered, and laughed. The Bureau's lies were crumbling like a house of cards. Nobody even seemed to care that an assemblage of people who had been exposed to Aeru were storming the streets. Regardless, Charlie and Catrice would keep them away from the masses.

Then the unthinkable happened. The Guardians lowered their weapons, talked amongst themselves, and broke up, intermingling with the protestors. Not all of them. Yet many took off their gear, even removing their uniform tops, and joined the crowd in white undershirts. Piles of discarded clothing and equipment dotted the grass.

Some may have initially refused to accept the truth about the drugs, or dismissed the revelation as one white lie from the Bureau. There was no denying a second debunked claim, however. The exiles were *alive*, and that contradicted the core of everything they'd ever believed about their world. *Finally*, it had come to pass. The Guardians had turned.

Now it was time to go to the Palace.

CHAPTER 27

Charlie engulfed Drayden in his arms and lifted him off the ground. "Woohoo! Attaboy." He set him down, a hand draped over Drayden's shoulder. "You know, in another life, you woulda been a military general."

"I don't know about all that." He hugged Catrice. "You guys okay?"

She and Charlie made eye contact. "We got it done," she said. "That's the important part. It didn't go quite as planned, though. We only brought those who had been outside a while and hadn't gotten sick. It's still risky and we need to isolate them, like we talked about. We're sending them down to Norman Thomas High School for now. Someone will have to care for them."

"At least we got Sid's parents," Charlie said.

While Sidney was reconnecting with them, a commotion broke out by a tent, the heated shouts of Dorm residents attracting considerable attention. Several Guardians raced over.

The overall scene could be best described as chaotic. This part of the story was unscripted. Drayden hadn't planned anything past the exiles returning and the Guardians switching alliances because, frankly, he hadn't been sure it would work. They were in uncharted territory now and, clearly, nobody had any idea what to do. He craned his neck, trying to figure out what was happening.

A smattering people were trampling through the towering marijuana plants, wreaking havoc.

Drayden smacked himself on the forehead. "Oh God. We can't let them destroy these crops. Lucy was right. If they do that, we're all dead."

He and his friends hustled over to the first tent, where some of the Guardians were training their weapons on the offending protestors.

"I said get down!" a burly young officer barked.

A swarm of residents surrounded him, threatening to reignite the tensions.

"Officer, we need a megaphone!" Drayden yelled. "Where's your megaphone?"

He dropped his gun to his side. "Hey, Bobby," he called out to one of his comrades. "See if you can grab a megaphone, will you?"

"Drayden!" A sweaty Mr. Kale came forth from the crowd to hug him. "Thank goodness, I've been looking for you guys."

"We couldn't find you either," Drayden said, immediately comforted by Mr. Kale's presence. "So many people. Guess our plan worked, huh?"

He overlooked the tumultuous backdrop. "It sure did. Not without some loss of life, unfortunately. I'm sure you recognized the young woman who got shot. She was a former student. I'm so proud of her."

"Did Zoe make it?"

"I don't know, honestly. She's being cared for and was alive, last I heard. With a wound like that, the odds are not good. I'm willing to bet the Bureau has some secret treatments these days to fight infections. If we can overthrow them, we might be able to save her."

A team of Guardians reappeared with a megaphone and handed it to the bulky young guy who'd requested it. He went to speak and stopped. "You want to do it?" he asked Drayden.

"People don't seem to be in the mood to listen to us, and I can't really blame them."

"I'm sixteen years old. I'm not sure they'll listen to me either."

"Gimme that." Professor Worth nudged Drayden out of the way and took the megaphone. "Citizens! We must protect these crops! Without them, we will all starve. They are our currency with the rest of the world. In time, we can grow other things. If you destroy these plants now, New America is broke! Please, come down from there. Everyone, please!"

Many of the assembled crowd, having heard the professor's words, howled in anger at the hellions rummaging through the crops. Eventually, they relented and climbed out to taunts and jeers.

"Listen up!" Professor Worth continued. "We need some of you to remain here with the crops to ensure the Bureau doesn't send people here to destroy them in a last-ditch effort to screw over New America before they are toppled. The rest of you, start making your way down to the Palace. Let the Guardians take the buses because they are armed! Let's go, people!"

"I think you should be the new premier," Charlie said. "You got this leadership thing nailed. May I?" He took the megaphone. "Look alive, people! You're not getting paid by the hour. Move it! Let's get this show on the road! Let's—"

Professor Worth snatched the megaphone away. "Charlie. That's...that doesn't help."

"No good? Sorry."

Protestors and Guardians streamed south out of the park, while some Guardians rallied around the buses.

Sidney rejoined them and wrapped her arm around Drayden's waist. "I sent my parents to Mister Kale's apartment instead of the school. We need to rescue the rest of our families from the safehouse before the Bureau gets them."

Drayden had been waiting for a window of opportunity to reenter the Palace and extricate them, assuming they hadn't been captured. That time was now.

"Professor, we have to take one of these buses. I'm not sure the Guardians will let us on, since they have no idea who we are."

Professor Worth considered the lengthy line of vehicles. "Come, quickly."

Hundreds of officers were flocking around the buses, several of which remained empty. The professor approached the same one they'd taken to the Meadow, finding the driver sitting inside with his legs on the dashboard. Professor Worth stepped aside and ushered the teens on board.

Drayden stopped himself and snagged Mr. Kale's arm. "You shouldn't come. We all have to go. Our families are there, and I need to get Professor Worth to Kim Craig. But there's no reason for you to go to the Palace. This could be bloody too. Doesn't it make more sense for you to stay here?"

"Well...I...I was hoping to watch over you kids. I'm worried about you."

"Mister Kale, we have to guard these tents. If the Bureau's on its way out, there's no reason to think they won't try to burn the house down before leaving. Plus, we amped up the Dorm residents to destroy these crops and now a bunch of them believe we should go through with it. We can't. The city needs the food these drugs will pay for. I'm worried that people will go rogue. I think a person with some sense should stay behind. Everyone knows you from being a teacher for so long."

Mr. Kale's eyes softened, and he nodded.

He was, indeed, the father Drayden never had. And there was no way Drayden was going to let him be killed by the assassins in the Palace, which would be fiercely defended by a limited but elite fighting force.

Mr. Kale hugged him. "I love you, Drayden. Be careful, son."

Drayden fought back tears. For some reason, this felt like goodbye. "I love you too. We'll come find you once this is over and we'll have a crazy party."

"Go on now."

After Drayden and Professor Worth boarded, Mr. Kale briefly hopped inside. "You kids be careful. Don't be heroes. I expect to see you back at my place in a few hours." He shook Professor Worth's hand and returned to the park.

Professor Worth touched the bus driver on the shoulder. "What do you say we visit the Palace?"

The driver crossed his arms. "The Palace? No thanks."

"Sir," Sidney said, "this is our moment. Everyone's going down there."

The guy shook his head. "Uh-uh. Nope. Almost got my face shot off coming into this Meadow. These Guardians might not shoot good, but I betcha those Palace Guardians do." He stood and moved to the side. "You can take the bus if you want. I'm staying out of it."

The teens exchanged wary glances and Professor Worth slid into the driver's seat.

"You know how to drive a bus?" Charlie asked. "I could, you know, give it a shot."

The professor waved him off. "I don't, but I know how to drive a car. It can't be that different." He fiddled around with buttons and switches on the dash.

The bus driver sighed. "Lemme give you a hand." He ran Professor Worth through the basics before lumbering away. Other buses were blowing by, proceeding north a block and heading left to turn around.

Catrice peered out the shattered window, riddled with bullet holes. "Drayden, shouldn't we pick up some people? Like, Guardians? Seems a waste to take an empty bus when so many are walking."

He shrugged. "We can't. We're taking a detour, going off the grid. We need to drive there, because I don't think we should be sauntering through the Palace on foot. Especially me and Charlie."

The electric bus purred to life. Professor Worth took off and slammed the brakes, causing everyone to fly forward. He started and stopped multiple times, inching the bus up Central Park West in herky jerky movements. Eventually he got the hang of it and they trailed a long caravan of buses down Seventh Avenue. Somewhere in midtown, they crossed east and continued on Third Avenue, passing through the gap in the wall at the Precinct, providing a visual of a zone they'd never seen.

Drayden turned back to Charlie and Catrice, seated behind him and Sidney. "Hey, you guys should change into your regular clothes. I don't think you want to be wearing Palace Guardian uniforms while we're in the Palace attacking the Palace Guardians."

Charlie groaned. "I hate Mister Kale's clothes. I look like a motivational speaker who secretly lives at home with his parents."

Catrice blushed. "I'm going to change in the back of the bus. Nobody peek."

Charlie undressed right there. "We've already seen each other in our underwear."

Sidney faced forward, shielding her eyes. "Doesn't mean we want to see it again."

"I gotta say," Charlie said, "the Precinct looks kinda like the Dorms. In other words, a dump."

To be fair, it wasn't exactly the same. The streets in the Dorms were a grid, and this being "downtown" New America, it featured random zigzaggy roads and mostly short buildings. It was dingy though, unlike the manicured Palace.

The buses had made a number of turns and were now speeding along Broadway, bearing down on the wall at Chambers Street, which marked the entrance to the Palace.

Drayden expected to see a lethal presence at the hole in the wall but to his surprise, no one was there. The buses were cruising straight through.

"That's a shock, isn't it?" Professor Worth said.

Drayden rubbed his chin. "We don't know what's been going on down here this whole time. Maybe the resistance inside the Palace has gotten the job done."

Kim Craig could have had a few tricks up her sleeve.

As the first buses neared Zucotti Park on their right, a blaze of gunfire tore through the air. The deafening, rapid-fire streams of machine guns ripped into the front bus, obliterating it until it appeared to smoke and blur.

"Oh my God!" Sidney shouted.

Guardians in the buses behind it were leaning out the windows, returning fire from pistols.

"Professor, turn right!" Drayden yelled. "Get us out of here!"

They zoomed onto Cortlandt Street and sped to the end, where they could turn right or left on Trinity Place. Gunshots reverberated to the left, on the west side of Zucotti Park a block south.

"Which way?" Professor Worth asked.

Drayden cursed to himself. "We have to go left, but that takes us into the danger zone."

The professor pulled out his pistol. "Get your weapons ready."

His heart thumping in his chest, Drayden drew his Glock and knelt by an open window on the bus's left side. Hopefully, the Palace Guardians wouldn't be expecting a lone bus at the far end of Zucotti Park.

Sidney and Catrice joined him, lining up beneath windows that had been shot out earlier. Charlie zipped to the front and perched behind Professor Worth, who made a wide left turn and floored it, the engine whining as he barreled south on Trinity Place.

"Get down!" Professor Worth screamed.

Charlie stuck his arm out the driver's side window and blasted round after round toward the park.

Adrenaline stiffened Drayden's muscles, almost to the point of paralysis.

Palace Guardians swarmed the park. The bulk of them were on the east side, dug in, engaged in a vicious firefight with the regular Guardians. Some on the west side noticed the bus flying by and pounded it with semi-automatic weapons. Bullets smashed the remaining windows and penetrated the metal exterior of the bus.

The teens ducked, cowering on the floor.

Within seconds they passed the park, withstanding a continuous stream of bullets on the rear of the bus. Two loud, strange pops later, the vehicle swerved to the left, nearly crashing into a brick wall. Professor Worth regained control and steered it back onto the roadway, despite a visceral grinding noise emanating from below.

"They shot the tires out!" Professor Worth yelled.

The bus slowed to a crawl, limping clunkily down Trinity Place.

Drayden looked out the now-missing back window.

A considerable number of Palace Guardians were following on foot, rapidly gaining on them.

He ran to the rear with Sidney and emptied his magazine with a flurry in their direction.

The soldiers scattered, taking cover behind buildings.

"Professor, go!" Drayden shouted.

He stepped on the gas, the friction between the metal rims and the pavement generating billowy smoke. Another round of bullets riddled the back of the bus.

The teens hit the floor again, although Sidney responded with gunfire from her elevated arm. Her shots, which pinned the Guardians down, bought them just enough time to pull away and escape down Rector Street.

CHAPTER 28

The smoking carcass of the bus in a sad heap behind them, Drayden and crew sprinted west down Rector Street. Random gunshots still boomed far away like a warning, reminding them of the unknown dangers of the Palace.

After checking both ways to make sure they weren't being followed, Drayden flung the doors open to Forty Rector Street and dashed into the dim and decrepit lobby.

"What floor?" Sidney asked, huffing and puffing.

"Ten." Drayden hurried to the elevators, hoping they worked, and pressed the "Up" button.

Nothing happened—no lights, no gears turning.

"Stairs it is," Charlie said.

"You're sure this is the right building?" Catrice asked Drayden.

"Yeah. It definitely is."

Spotting the staircase across the lobby, Sidney excitedly climbed in front, boiling over with anticipation at the prospect of finally seeing her little sister. Occasionally, she needed to pause to let everybody else catch up, particularly Professor Worth, who was struggling in the rear.

Drayden's neck tensed when they reached a door containing a faded "*10.*" Until now, he hadn't seriously considered facing the possibility that their families were no longer here. He knew some parts of the insurrection had failed, because Holst hadn't been assassinated. If the premier, in his disgraceful speech to New America, had been truthful about apprehending many of the insurgents, their families could have been found too. Given how badly Holst wanted him and Charlie, Drayden didn't dare speculate about the consequences for his father and brother.

Sidney gripped the doorknob.

"Sid," Drayden said, "let's be quiet. I don't know, just in case the Bureau knows about this place and has people stationed here to catch any resistors."

She nodded and opened the door, revealing a bland hallway lined with glass doors on both sides. They proceeded discreetly, peering inside each door, finding nothing other than dark, abandoned offices. The hallway turned left and ultimately made a loop around the whole building, bringing them back to where they started.

Sidney wrung her hands. "I don't understand. They should be here."

Not only were they missing; there was no evidence anyone had *ever* been there—no signs of life or habitation. It seemed untouched, yet their families had allegedly been hunkering down there for days. Had they changed locations right away?

Drayden groaned in frustration. "Hell, let's try making some noise." They repeated the loop around the building. "Dad? Wes? You here?"

"Nora? It's Sidney!"

"Mama! Pop!" Charlie called out.

Drayden was beginning to lose hope. If their families weren't in this building, and hadn't been for a long time, what did that mean and how would they find them?

A door opened behind them. "Can you be *any* louder?" Kim Craig's familiar ginger-topped head protruded into the hallway, along with her enduring snarkiness. "They can probably hear you over at Bureau headquarters."

"Kim!" Drayden shouted, a wave of relief washing over him.

Her gaze strayed beyond him and she froze. "U-Uncle Alan?" she said softly.

A broad smile on his face, Professor Worth slipped past Drayden and took her hands. "Kimberly."

She swallowed him up in her strong arms. "I can't believe it...I..."

Then, much to Drayden's surprise, big, tough Kim Craig wept. She was suddenly a child again, clutching the beloved uncle she hadn't seen in decades.

Sidney nudged by Kim and peeked through the door. "Are our families in here?"

Kim wiped away her tears. "Yeah. Come on in."

Sidney bounded inside and everyone else followed her into a sprawling, loft-like room littered with boxes, tables and chairs, and blankets over the floor. In addition to Kim and their families, several other people milled about—presumably associates of Kim's. They all appeared ragged and exhausted.

Everything after that was a blur for Drayden, seen through teary eyes. The reunion that was a long time coming, particularly for Sidney and her sister, didn't disappoint. Wesley hoisted Drayden in the air, as he always did, squeezing him so tight he couldn't breathe. Dad teared up, his closed eyes revealing a mixture of relief and gratitude.

Charlie's parents were both emotional wrecks, fighting like siblings to embrace their son. Sidney, likewise, was crying joyfully, refusing to let her sister Nora go even for a second. Although Catrice was somewhat excluded from the event for obvious reasons, Sidney invited her into the celebration. She introduced her to Nora, who greeted her with a warm hug, the kind only an innocent child would give to a stranger. It melted Catrice, who soon found herself wiping her own tears.

"Dray, we were so close to leaving," Wesley said, looking scruffy after many days in the safehouse. "I don't know how much longer we could have stayed in here. Totally in the dark, no idea what was happening. Kim came a few days ago and since then, we've been cut off from the world."

Drayden fumbled with the cuff on his sleeve, lost for words. "I need to talk to you guys for a sec. Let's sit." He recounted the story of finding Mom and holding her when she died, along with his profound regret over getting there too late.

Wesley hid his face in his hands while Drayden spoke. His father stared at the floor.

"You did the most wonderful thing for her," Dad said, lifting his head. "You did not fail. You were with her when she passed. She wasn't alone and she was with her favorite person. I'm so thankful you were able to do that for her."

Drayden obscured his face, his lower lip quivering. "I found out who exiled her, Dad. It was Lily Haddad." He was haunted now by the ephemeral belief that his father had been the guilty party, feeling intense shame for it.

"Lily?" Wesley furrowed his brow. "I don't understand. Why would Lily exile Mom?"

Drayden went to speak and stopped. "Everybody needs to hear this part."

Wesley gathered Drayden's friends and their families, and Nora snuggled in a blanket on his lap.

Drayden choked up at the sight, realizing that while Wesley hadn't been out in the trenches, he'd been a hero in his own right, watching over everyone as Drayden had asked.

Drayden rehashed the events of the prior week, including Lily's treachery. Their expressions morphed from disbelief to horror to elation when he touched on the success of the Dorms' revolt and the current attack on the Palace by the Guardians.

"Kim, what about you? What's been going on in the Palace this whole time?"

She lowered her head. "I assume you saw the broadcast from Holst, so you know the assassination attempt failed. Much of what he said was true. The Bureau launched a ruthless counter to our insurgency, capturing many of the plotters, and it became clear we had a rat. I'm pretty sure now that it must have been Lily, which is incredibly disappointing."

A slight twinkle appeared in her eyes. "But this plan of ours was in the works for a long time. No single person knew the full plot or all the people involved. For taking out Holst, which was our main objective, we had a backup plan, and even a backup to the backup. The thing is, once it became clear the Bureau knew about me, I had to go into hiding. I've been here a couple of days and don't know if they've gotten him. We've been talking about leaving here and taking our chances. Then you guys walked in."

Sidney sipped water. "So, what do we do? Just wait it out?"

Professor Worth raised his index finger and cringed. "I have a little problem. Now that I've reconnected with Kim, there's nothing left for me to do. And...I have a boat to catch. Tomorrow. If I miss this ride, I may never get home."

"Why don't you stay here with me?" Kim asked. "You don't have to go back. We're each other's only family."

Professor Worth took her hand. "It's always been my plan to finish my days at my farm and be buried beside your aunt. I have crops that need attention. Why don't you come with me?"

She chewed on her lower lip.

"In fact," Professor Worth said, "*none* of you need to stay here. You are more than welcome to join me in Massachusetts. Boston is not far away and would also take you. It's a far better place than

New America, which, even if this revolution succeeds, will take many years to rebuild and restructure."

Drayden tugged on his left earlobe. The professor was right. Boston *was* better. Even under the most favorable scenario, New America would need to reorganize, reengineer its economy, rewrite the entire form of government, reassign jobs... Not only was the task monumental, starvation was a real possibility, since the original issue that prompted the expedition remained a problem: power storage. Wouldn't it be easier just to bail? He didn't have any loyalty to New America, nor did he owe it anything. There was no hometown pride or history on which to cling. It had always been a despicable place. Except...

"*We* can leave," Drayden said, tapping his finger on his chest. "And you can, Professor. But our families can't. They haven't taken the Aeru vaccine."

"Hmmm." Professor Worth nodded. "You're right."

Charlie cracked his knuckles. "I don't know, I kinda want to stay."

"I'm not saying we have to go," Drayden said. "But we need the option. If the Bureau ends up surviving, even in a reduced capacity, they could make life here miserable. And we'd probably be executed. We only have a way out if we can take our families along."

Kim leaned forward in her chair. "We have some senior scientists in the resistance. I know where they keep backups of the Aeru vaccine. The building, anyway. It looks half-built, so nobody would ever suspect anything of value is inside, which is why everything of value is in there. Aeru vaccine, new experimental antibiotics, painkillers. You name it. It's purely a backup facility, in case the main science lab, where the lion's share of that stuff is officially kept, burns to the ground or something.

"No one would ever go into this building, so it's not guarded or locked, because a locked door would draw attention. I'm guessing the medicines themselves are secured, and I think the Bureau keeps guards around them, although I'm sure they've abandoned that post now. With so few Palace Guardians, the Bureau needs every single one on the front lines."

Drayden knew what he had to do. No hesitation, no fear. If he could defeat the Guardians in the marsh on the expedition, and eradicate the whole Bureau, he could do anything he wanted, as long as he believed in himself. His role in this conflict wasn't quite over yet. If he delivered on this final task, he would guarantee the safety and survival of his friends and their families, whether the Bureau was ousted or not.

He stood. "I'll go. I can get it."

"No," his father said. "It's too dangerous. I'd rather leave without the vaccine and roll the dice on getting sick."

"Dad, Mom caught it. Half the exiles were dying of it. Despite the lies from the Bureau, Aeru is still a big risk out there. You cannot leave here without the vaccine. Plus, with all the chaos in the Palace, nobody will even notice me."

Charlie twirled his pistol. "If you're going, I'm going with you. You're my boy."

Drayden fist-bumped him.

"I'm coming too," Wesley said. "I can't stay in here another minute."

"Count me in as well," Professor Worth said. "That makes four of us. In a building that must be searched, we can do it four times faster."

"Okay," Drayden said. "Kim, what's the address?"

"Sixteen Beaver Street. Unfortunately, it's right in the heart of the Palace, a block or so from the New York Stock Exchange. I've never been inside, but I know some floors are little more than steel framing. It's like ten or fifteen stories. You're looking for a floor that's finished, with a refrigerated section. That's where you'll find the meds. Watch out for Guardians or even booby traps."

Sidney hugged Drayden and pulled back with her hand rested gently on his cheek. "You can do this. I know you can." She kissed him.

Drayden faced his brother. "You ready to stick it to the Bureau?"

"I've been ready since they took Mom."

"Let's do this," Drayden said.

CHAPTER 29

Drayden, Charlie, Wesley, and Professor Worth strolled down Trinity Place, trying to avoid arousing any suspicion. In addition to Mr. Kale's clothes, Drayden wore his military baseball cap low to conceal his identity, since he was persona non grata in the Palace. He also lugged his backpack to retrieve the medication and carried the extra pistol in his waistband. Although Wesley didn't know how to shoot a gun, he'd borrowed Catrice's, figuring an enemy wouldn't know he had no clue how to use it.

Random gunfire resounded in the distance, albeit significantly less frequent. A team of frenzied Palace Guardians had run past them without a glance, preoccupied with the assault from the regular Guardians.

Sixteen Beaver Street was in the "downtown" of the Palace, mere blocks from Bureau headquarters. The foursome crossed over to Broadway at the last possible place to steer clear of major thoroughfares. They stopped to get their bearings, winding up face-to-face with the famous Wall Street bull statue, a stone's throw from Nathan Locke's office.

"Which way?" Wesley asked.

Drayden walked onto Broadway, observing the fork in the road to the right. "We go left at the fork and it's there." In the opposite

314

direction, north toward Zucotti Park, the firefight between Guardians persisted.

Drayden's hat flew off his head, as if someone had forcefully swatted it away. "Whoa! What the...?" He scooped it up, noting the lack of wind.

Charlie pulled his Glock. "Dude. Look at the front."

The rounded brim contained two holes, indicating something had passed through it.

"That's a bullet hole." Professor Worth drew his own pistol and whirled around, scanning their surroundings.

The streets were deserted, and the buildings as outwardly abandoned as always.

"Stray one?" Wesley asked.

Drayden's stomach sank. Nobody was firing guns anywhere near them, weakening the stray bullet theory. He could rule out a miss from sniper too, because that person could freely take another shot right now. Yet he hadn't, meaning someone had intentionally shot the hat off his head. A marksman. No gunshots had been heard either, which made him especially uneasy. *A silencer.*

He pulled the hat back on. "We gotta move." His pistol in hand, he hustled down Broadway with everyone else in tow and turned left on Beaver Street.

He spotted the building right away. The narrow sliver of a road was full of short townhouse-like structures housing vacant shops. An office tower, however, soared above the rest, seemingly under construction when it was abandoned.

Drayden hurriedly tallied the floors, counting twelve. He yanked open the unlocked door and entered a lobby which was half-built but neither dusty nor dirty. The framing for a security desk sat in front of an elevator bank.

"Let's take the stairs," Drayden said. "There are twelve stories, so we can each comb three floors."

Wesley jogged in place. "I'll do the top three. I'm fresh."

Drayden gave him a thumbs-up. "Fine, you do ten through twelve. Charlie, can you do seven through nine? I'll do four, five, and six. Professor, you do the bottom floors. If you find the Aeru vaccine, grab some but not all of it. If it's guarded or looks like a trap, come get the rest of us. How about we reconvene in the stairwell at the sixth floor when we're each done. Plan?"

"Boo-yah," Charlie said.

Parading up the unfinished cement staircase, Professor Worth stopped on the third-floor landing. "I'll begin on three and go down. I have a feeling the key floor is much higher. See you boys in a bit." He opened the door, beyond which Drayden spotted a bare room with exposed steel beams.

On the fourth floor, Drayden decided to get started. "I think I'll go here first, then work up to five and six."

Charlie saluted him. "Roger that." He and Wesley continued up the stairs.

Drayden emerged into a bleak lobby outside the elevator bank. A glass wall on one side gave way to a finished—though clearly never used—office. Passing through the glass door, he felt confident they would be out of here in fifteen minutes. Most of these floors were unused, and with four people would be a breeze to canvass. If the Aeru vaccine was defended in some way, he could consult Professor Worth on the best way to extract it.

Behind the receptionist's desk, an expansive main room contained two long rows of cubicles, and lengthy open walkways on the sides of the room. Drayden schlepped down the one by the windows, noting the cubbies lacked chairs or desks. At the end of the aisle, he turned right and found modest glassed-in offices. Past that was a lunchroom filled with tables and chairs.

With no refrigerators or storage facilities in sight, he retraced his steps, glancing out the floor-to-ceiling windows to the street below. Compared to Boston—a superior city in every way—it was ugly here, even in the Palace. He might seriously weigh moving if he could procure this vaccine for everyone else.

Back at the start of the walkway, near the receptionist's desk and the main door to the office, he poked his head inside another glassed-in office to ensure he wasn't overlooking anything.

Totally empty.

He shrugged. Up to five.

A gun cocked behind him.

Goosebumps spreading down his arms, he spun around.

Eugene stood there grinning, adorned in his full Guardian uniform, training a pistol on him. It was fitted with a silencer. "Hey, boss."

Adrenaline coursed through Drayden's veins.

"I was going to shoot you in the back, but that seemed cowardly. Like something you would do. Plus, I could have shot you in the back about five different times over the last six days. I wanted you to know who it was that got you."

Drayden swallowed hard and slowly reached for his own gun.

Eugene tilted his head. "Hands up, dummy. I see you moving."

Drayden's mind always working, he promptly determined he had zero options. Eugene was only twenty feet away and his finger was on the trigger. Peripherally, Drayden could see the main door, which was way off to the right between them. On his left, only ten feet away, was the first cubicle by the windows. Could he dive behind it?

"Hands. Up." Eugene's piercing blue eyes practically glowed, like a demon's. "You're not making it to the door or behind that cubby. Jesus Christ, Dray, I was training at this while you were sucking your thumb and playing hopscotch. You're done, kid. It's over."

Drayden raised his hands. "What's your problem, man? It *is* over. The Bureau's finished. We're all going to get a fresh start. You too. We don't have to be enemies."

"Me and you are enemies no matter what. We have unfinished business."

"No, we don't," Drayden said. "Why are you after me, anyway? I never had a problem with you until you tried to kill me and my friends. I'm willing to let it go. Why can't you?"

"You're willing to let it go." Eugene laughed. "That's rich, Dray. Yeah, you're willing to let it go because you're about to die."

He *was* about to die. Drayden couldn't believe it. After everything he'd been through, he was inches from the finish line in this battle against the Bureau, only to be murdered by this psycho? Eugene had indeed been toying with him this whole time, knowing he could kill Drayden whenever he wanted.

Eugene cupped his left hand beneath the pistol in his right. "I was always better than you. So long, boss."

Drayden was trembling. He closed his eyes.

The door creaked. "Eugene!" Professor Worth shouted.

Drayden gawked at him.

Oh, thank God.

The professor hovered inside the door, eyeballing the two of them, his mouth hung open in shock.

Eugene wrinkled his forehead, holding his weapon firm on Drayden. "The professor? Thought that was you earlier. This must be my lucky day. Two birds with one stone."

Professor Worth stood tall, a smirk on his face. He winked at Drayden.

What is he doing?

"Drayden. Run." Professor Worth went for his gun.

Eugene swung the pistol around and shot him in the chest. The professor collapsed backward with a grunt.

"No!" Drayden screamed. He sprinted along the walkway by the windows, ducking low enough for the cubbies to shield him.

Bullets whizzed overhead and smashed into the windows.

Breathing heavily, Drayden pulled his gun and crouched behind the last cubby by the far end of the room. The thud of Eugene's footsteps was audible coming down the opposite walkway.

"Dray! You're next. Man, you're just making this harder on yourself. You already got your hero professor killed."

Drayden was doing his best to compose himself, to stifle his whimpers. *Professor!* In a panic, he took stock of the room, searching for an alternate way out.

An exit sign! It was on a small plastic placard dangling from the ceiling above a steel door near the lunch room. To access it, he'd have to cross in front of Eugene. Drayden considered firing a few shots to stymie him, but that would give away his location. Still, he needed to move. This room wasn't very big, so Eugene would eventually find him.

You can run but you can't hide.

He crawled along the cubbies and stopped short of the other walkway to listen.

Eugene was methodically advancing through the room. "Show yourself, you coward!"

He made a break for the exit, passing in front of Eugene for a split-second to his right.

Bullets shattered the glass office on his left. Eugene, his reflexes like a ninja, had managed to squeeze off two rounds, but Drayden had the advantage of surprise and went by in a flash. Now he was around the corner from Eugene, who was running after him.

Drayden remained low and rammed the exit door open. He dove onto the stairs and raced up, leaping three and four at a time.

More bullets ricocheted off the door while it swung shut. He was coming.

Drayden hauled open the door to the fifth floor.

Eugene's footsteps were rumbling up the stairs.

Floor five was only partially finished, featuring a cement floor, lots of steel beams crisscrossing everywhere, and scattered construction equipment. With only seconds to spare before Eugene came in, he scoured the area for a place to hide.

Where, dammit?

The cement mixer. He stooped down behind it, straining to catch his breath and be quiet. Despite the fact that the bulky piece of machinery camouflaged him, its irregular shape allowed him to peek through the gaps.

Eugene burst into the room, panning his weapon back and forth.

Drayden poured sweat, clasping his gun so tight his fingertips turned white. He glanced behind him, hunting for another hiding spot, because Eugene would bust him here, fast.

Then what? What was his endgame? He could not beat Eugene. The guy was a sharpshooter, a trained fighter, and this was a gunfight to the death. Drayden couldn't hit the side of a building. He'd always known his first victory against Eugene had been tainted, a fluke. Eugene *was* better than him. Nobody would be coming to save him either. Eugene was using a silencer. They wouldn't hear the shots.

Unless Drayden fired his own gun. Doing so could disrupt Eugene enough to retreat further into the room. If he dragged this out and Charlie registered the gunshots, he might have a chance.

"Dray." His pistol in his right hand, braced beneath with his left, Eugene was moving cautiously along the interior wall. "Remember that time I stole your girlfriend?" He chuckled. "There's literally nothing you're better at than me. And unfortunately for you, the thing I'm *most* better at is this."

If Drayden was going to fire his gun and slip away into the room, he needed to do it right now. Eugene was closing in. Any closer and Drayden would be an easy target when he ran for it.

The only other object for refuge was a towering pile of unused steel beams further back. Drayden aimed his pistol in Eugene's general direction through a narrow gap in the cement mixer. Steel beams that ran the length of the hallways, forming the structural framing for the building, obscured the firing line. Sections of Eugene, like his stomach and knees, weren't blocked by the beams, but Drayden had little chance of hitting him anyway.

Drayden clenched his jaw. He pulled the trigger twice in rapid succession, the gun firing with two booming pops, and made a break for it.

Eugene dropped to a knee and returned fire.

Drayden blasted bullets haphazardly behind him, squeezing off round after round, if only to hinder Eugene's accuracy.

Fortuitously, the steel framing running along his side of the room also blocked much of his body and head. Eugene's shots rattled and clanked off steel, causing sparks to fly.

He made it safely behind the stack of steel beams right as Eugene really began to unload on him, the bullets leaving his gun silently but striking the metal like someone pounding it with a crowbar.

Drayden's chest was heaving. He wasn't sure how much longer he could hold Eugene off, and he was fresh out of hiding places. The next move would have to be through the front door of the office, but he would be easily picked off if he tried. Even if he miraculously escaped, Eugene was faster and would catch him.

Eugene clicked in a fresh magazine. "Quit stalling! It doesn't matter if your friends come. I can take them all out, no problem. Don't get them killed too. You're only prolonging the inevitable."

Goddamn this maniac. He was right. Who was Drayden kidding? Nobody was coming to save him anyway. Given the size of the building, Charlie couldn't possibly hear the shots. If he somehow did, as good a marksman as he was, he was no match for Eugene, who had trained his whole life for this moment.

Maybe he should give up, heeding Eugene's request. Walk out, kneel before him, accept his inferiority and his fate. He'd had a good run, but his luck had finally expired. Drayden thought about his mother, and the consolation of joining her in Heaven. He pictured Sidney and Catrice receiving the news that he'd been killed. Hopefully, by sacrificing himself, he would convince Eugene to spare his friends.

Eugene was lurching closer and closer on the opposite side of the room. "Dray, I'll make this real easy for you, buddy. Bullet to the head. You won't feel a thing."

Bullet to the head. Bullet to the head.

Drayden started to hyperventilate at the crazy thought running through his mind, the tiniest spark of an idea that might be his only hope.

Don't hope. *Act.*

You beat him once before. You can beat him again.

Drayden peered down the barren hallway on his side of the room.

The steel beams that framed it were at head height and waist height.

He had to do it. It was his only chance. He was going to let himself get shot.

Drayden closed his eyes for a hot second and took a long, slow inhalation to calm himself.

Do it. *Now!*

He sprung into the hallway and pointed his Glock at Eugene, unable to see him because of the steel beam in his face.

A rapid flash.

He heard the double-clink of Eugene's silencer-tipped weapon discharging at the same time as the bullets struck him in the chest. Drayden crashed face first on the ground in agony, clutching his torso. When his gun hit the concrete floor, it tumbled away.

His eyes bulged. He couldn't breathe. The pain ripping through his midsection from the broken ribs felt like an elephant standing on his chest. Radiating in waves through his body, it nearly made him vomit.

He was quickly going into shock and gasped, trying to regain his wits. He had one more job to do.

The nonchalance of Eugene's footsteps, casually approaching from behind, suggested he was unaware that Drayden, while hurt, had been saved by his bulletproof vest.

Lying flat on his stomach, moaning, Drayden extended his left arm, as if attempting to retrieve his pistol, which was just out of reach. Simultaneously, using his right hand, he removed the other gun from his waistband, keeping it buried beneath his body.

"I'm going to put you out of your misery in a sec. But I want you to admit I'm better than you first."

Drayden groaned.

"C'mon, kid. I know you're in pain. Admit that I won."

"You...didn't win," Drayden grunted.

"What?"

Drayden rotated his head to the left so he could see Eugene. "I'm better than you...and I always was."

Eugene scoffed. "Oh, you're talking some metaphysical mumbo jumbo, like you're better because I'm the bad guy who killed the good guy?" He appeared more amused than anything.

"No. I mean, I won." He placed his finger on the trigger.

Eugene's smile faded. His eyes flashed to Drayden's back, perhaps noticing the lack of blood.

In one motion, fighting through the pain, Drayden whipped the pistol around and shot Eugene in the chest.

He stumbled away and fell onto his back, still wielding his gun.

Drayden lumbered to his knees and then rose to his feet, crying out in pain.

Eugene was wide-eyed, blinking repeatedly, his mouth open. He coughed, and blood spurted out. He tried and failed to prop up on his elbows, unleashing an angry grunt.

Drayden hobbled toward him.

Eugene managed to raise a shaky arm and point his gun at Drayden.

Drayden charged him and soccer-kicked it out of his hand, sending it across the room. He stood over Eugene, holding the Glock at his head.

Eugene smiled, blood running down his cheeks. "You don't... kill people. Remember?"

Thinking about his mother's death, and now Professor Worth's, at Eugene's own hand no less, Drayden felt his rage building. He knew that what a person would do when no one was watching, and when there would be no consequences, revealed a lot about his character. Here, on this empty floor, in this abandoned building, it was only him and Eugene, in a moment that could haunt him forever. The weight of it wasn't lost on him in real time. When he'd spared Eugene's life in the marsh during the expedition's final encounter, he thought he was being true to his values, refusing to become the murderer Eugene was. But he'd failed to acknowledge they were in a one-on-one battle, and it was to the death. Eugene would never stop until he was stopped. It would end here.

"Just this once."

He pulled the trigger.

CHAPTER 30

Tears streaming down his cheeks, Drayden cradled Professor Worth's head, panicked over his devastating wound but relieved he was alive. "I'm gonna get you help. I promise. You saved my life and now I'm going to save yours."

The professor was shaking. He nodded, and even tried to force a smile. "Now I know...what my role was," he whispered.

Drayden wiped his tears on his shoulder. "No. You shouldn't have done that. But thank you. You've saved me so many times. I..." He scanned the room, wishing he knew what to do.

"Charlie!" Pain cut through his chest like a hot knife when he screamed. "Help!"

"Drayden. My only request...is that you find a way to bury me... on my farm. Can you do that?"

"No!" The tears returned. "Don't say that. Yes, I'll make sure of it in thirty years, when you die of old age. We're getting you fixed. Just hold on." He gently lowered his head and burst out the main office door into the lobby by the elevator bank.

Footsteps echoed in the staircase.

"Charlie?"

His brother pushed through the stairwell door with Charlie close behind. Their jaws dropped.

Wesley darted over, his face twisted at the sight of the blood on Drayden's sleeves. "Dude, you okay?"

"Yeah, it's not me. It's Professor Worth. Hurry."

The three boys knelt around the professor, who was drifting in and out of consciousness, his gunshot wound oozing bright red blood. Drayden removed his sweater, biting down on his lower lip from the pain, and pressed it against the grisly hole.

"Holy shkat," Charlie said. "I can't believe Eugene shot him. And you too. I really can't believe you killed Eugene."

"Thank God for my bulletproof vest. I'll tell you all about it, but there's no time now." Drayden wiped his bloody hands on his pants. "Wes, you need to go get Dad. Bring him back here." Being a doctor, he'd know what to do.

Wesley scrambled to his feet. "Yeah, man. Hang tight, I'll be right back."

"Wait!" Drayden shouted. "Did you find the Aeru vaccine?"

He turned around. "No, Charlie did though." He hustled out the door.

Drayden's eyes widened. "You got it?" he asked Charlie.

"Not exactly. I found the room, on the ninth floor. But...it looked fishy, like a trap. It was all lit up, a big empty room, a glass-covered fridge or freezer against the far wall filled with vials of stuff. Keypad outside the door. No way I was moseying in there without running it by you."

Drayden's cheeks flushed with nervous heat. Not only did they need the Aeru vaccine, they now also required medication for Professor Worth. He knew antibiotics were long obsolete. Regardless, he suspected the Bureau had been experimenting with alternatives, or had even created new antibiotics, as Kim had alluded. Whatever they possessed, he *had* to acquire, in addition to pain medication for the professor.

Professor Worth groaned and shook violently, mumbling something unintelligible.

Drayden snagged Charlie's hand and pushed it against the bloody sweater. "Hold this here. Keep the pressure on it. I'm gonna fetch those meds."

Charlie cringed. "Careful, bro. I'm telling you, it looked like a trap."

"If I'm not back in fifteen minutes, something happened. Send someone up to nine."

"Got it."

"Trmphre," Professor Worth muttered.

Drayden dropped his ear to the professor's face. "What did you say? Professor, I didn't understand."

He opened and closed his mouth. "Trip...tripwires."

"Got it. Thank you. I'll watch out for them." Drayden dashed into the lobby outside and made his way up the darkened staircase. Each heavy breath inflamed the stabbing pain in his ribs. Legs burning, he arrived on the ninth floor.

Another generic, unused office sat behind a glass door, except halfway down the interior corridor, bright light emanated from a room on the right. The windows on this floor had been blacked out, presumably to enshroud the luminous section from the outside world.

Although Drayden had to exercise caution, he couldn't dawdle, with only a narrow window to help Professor Worth. He jogged down the hallway, slowing near the yellowish-white light, which was particularly dazzling in the otherwise dim office.

The bare room was precisely as Charlie had described. Through a double-wide open doorway, a faux-tiled floor stretched thirty feet by thirty feet, containing only a freezer built into the back wall. Its glass door, bordered by stainless steel, exposed dozens of vials and test tubes.

Drayden noted the electronic keypad outside the door, plus random circular holes in the left wall. Charlie was right. The keypad alone indicated you needed to enter a code to safely enter the room or unlock the freezer. The whole thing reeked of a trap, just begging for a fool to saunter up to the freezer and help himself.

Recalling a challenge in the Initiation that was triggered by movement, Drayden removed his hat and tossed it into the center of the room.

A blaze of gunfire erupted inside before it even hit the floor.

Drayden fell backward, covering his ears.

Machine guns from the holes on the left wall pounded deafening rapid-fire shots through the room for a good five seconds. A smoky haze filled the space in the aftermath.

Drayden's heart was racing. "Holy shkat," he mumbled as he rose to his feet. How in the hell could he evade those guns? They were likely on a motion detector, since they were activated while his hat was midair. What if he located the motion detector and snuck around it? Or flattened himself against that left wall, somehow maneuvering around those machine gun holes?

Those were preposterous and suicidal ideas. He examined the keypad and debated guessing the code or shooting it out. This was like an Initiation challenge, right down to his need to solve it quickly. In the subway tunnels, he'd always had Catrice's help. He wished she were here.

No. You can do it yourself.

He pictured Professor Worth. What advice would he give Drayden?

Believe.

He'd defeated the Bureau. How? By cutting off the source of their power—the drugs in the Meadow. Without them, they were powerless. Powerless...powerless...

The power.

These booby traps depended on the room having power! If he could shut off the electricity, he might deactivate them.

Drayden scoured the ninth floor until he found one locked door that didn't ostensibly lead to an office. He stood back and fired his gun three times, destroying the lock.

The room resembled a narrow closet, featuring cables, switches, insulation, and some fans.

While this industrial setup was far more complex than the circuit box in his old Dorm apartment, he located the box without a hitch. A series of switches formed two columns with a larger switch at the top, which was clearly the main power. He flipped it and returned to the freezer room.

The lights were off now, thankfully, though the freezer remained illuminated, casting an eerie white glow throughout the darkened room. Perhaps it was hooked up to a generator, which would make sense considering the valuable contents. The million-dollar question was—were any remaining traps coupled to the generator?

Drayden searched his pockets, and rubbed his hands along his body, trying to dig up something to toss into the room. Remembering his backpack, he removed his Palace Guardian shirt and balled it up. Holding his breath, he hurled it inside.

The shirt sailed through the shadowy room, uncoiling, and fell uneventfully to the floor.

He pumped his fist, but this was taking way too long. Professor Worth was dying downstairs. He had to go for it. As soon as he took a step inside, he stopped, recalling the professor's warning.

Tripwires. They could be operated mechanically rather than electronically.

Drayden groaned. He thought about crawling, praying he'd spot any wires before barreling through them, until another idea popped into his head. After hastily removing one of his shoelaces, he extended his arm, letting the lace dangle in front of him, the end of it just scraping the floor. He inched forward, sweat dripping down his cheeks and dampening his back.

A quarter of the way into the room, it was smooth sailing, causing him to second-guess his overabundance of caution. He might have been wasting precious time. A few feet later, the shoelace curved backwards, having brushed over something invisible.

Drayden froze. Wobbling, he knelt.

An extremely fine wire shimmered, hovering inches above the floor.

Breathe.

Thinking he should mark it to avoid triggering it on the way back, he retrieved his Guardian shirt off the floor and positioned the cuff of the sleeve directly beneath the tripwire. Stepping way over it, he continued the nerve-racking march toward the freezer, now only ten feet away.

Five feet to go, he stopped, leaning forward to drag the shoelace the rest of the way.

No more tripwires.

He eyeballed the freezer while he wound up the lace and placed it in his pocket. Would he be lucky and find it unlocked? Maybe the Bureau was magnanimous enough to reward you with the medicine if you made it this far. There was only one way to know.

Drayden wiped the sweat off his forehead and stepped up to the freezer.

The floor gave out.

No!

He dropped straight down, through a trapdoor of some sort, instinctively thrusting his arms out wide. They slammed into the floor as he fell, allowing him to snag the edges of the hole with his fingertips at the last second. He was dangling, his legs swinging.

"Help!" he shrieked, knowing nobody would hear his plea.

Drayden was apparently hanging over a pitch-black room on the eighth floor, which was sufficiently illuminated from the freezer light to discern the horror below.

Cruel-looking spikes jutted up on the ground beneath him.

His heart already pounding, he started hyperventilating. He couldn't adjust his weakening grip without the risk of falling. Either he would lift himself to safety using only his fingertips or get impaled and die.

Drayden squeezed his rapidly fatiguing fingers and pulled with every ounce of muscle he had, willing himself upward. Curling his abs made him cry out in agony. Slowly, he rose up. Over and over he told himself not to let go, imploring mind over body, despite the latter begging to quit.

Once his chin breached the floor, he propelled his arms out, relieving the excruciating weight on his fingertips. He gulped, still far from safe. His eyes filling with tears, he engaged his stomach muscles to help prop up on his elbows. From there, he managed to swing one leg from the hole and wriggle to safety. He lay flat on the floor, his ribcage throbbing.

Having partially recovered, he stood before the freezer, the last step of this godawful challenge. He tugged on the door, which, unsurprisingly, was locked. After tinkering with it for a minute, Drayden's frustration grew, thinking about Professor Worth's suffering. He smashed the glass with the butt of his pistol, cracking it several times.

White gas billowed from the walls and ceiling.

Oh shkat.

Drayden took a deep breath and held it. He rummaged through the vials, which were carefully labeled and numbered. Finally, a break.

He was sifting for ones filled with bluish-green liquid—the distinctive coloring of *Pseudomonas Aeruginosa*. Finding many, he threw a handful in his backpack, after which he hunted for antibiotics and painkillers.

His chest was growing heavier by the second. The ever-increasing gas cloud limited the visibility in the room and burned his eyes, making them tear and blurring his vision. A beeping noise blared behind him. *Beep beep beep...*

A steel gate was slowly lowering from the top of the doorway, soon to be blocking his way out.

Really?

Professor Worth needed some kind of antibiotic, but Drayden was almost out of breath. Thanks to his father, he knew antibiotics often ended in "illin," like penicillin. One vial read "ventrocillin," so he swiped it. He snuck a cursory look back.

The gate was halfway down.

Drayden frantically rifled through for painkillers, knowing he had a second left, at most. He knocked vials out of the way, shattering them on the floor.

Morphine! Barely able to see through his watery eyes, he threw a couple of vials in the bag and sprinted, first leaping over the trap door in the floor and then over the tripwire, nearly losing his untied shoe in the process.

I'm not going to make it.

His eyes felt like they were melting, and he needed to take a breath immediately.

Mere feet away, Drayden dove headfirst at the bottom of the doorway.

Pain exploded in his midsection. With millimeters to spare, he slid beneath the gate.

It closed on his foot, trapping it.

Oh God!

The gate was an unstoppable force, slowly crushing his shoe.

He yanked and yanked, using his hands to jerk his leg. Fortunately not constricted by laces, his foot slid out of the shoe just before the titanic steel gate flattened it into a pancake.

Drayden rocketed to his feet. Seeing stars, unable to hold it any longer, he inhaled, sucking in a chest full of poison gas.

It lit his lungs on fire, inducing a violent coughing fit to reject the toxic substance.

He forced himself to stumble down the hall where he collapsed to his knees, shaking and hacking until he vomited. He rubbed his eyes, which only mashed in the poison further.

On his hands and knees, he crawled until he reached the front door of the office, little more than a glossy blur in his field of vision. He shoved it open and crumpled in the lobby, resting his face on the cool tile.

God, he hated challenges.

CHAPTER 31

Drayden must have looked pretty wretched, because Charlie, Wesley, and his father gawked at him when he limped into the fourth-floor office on one shoe.

Dad clutched him by the shoulders. "Are you all right? Drayden, you look terrible."

"Yeah...I'm...it's too long a story. The room with the meds was booby trapped. I got 'em." He cracked his backpack. "I have the Aeru vaccine, but Professor Worth needs pain meds and some type of antibiotic. I found this thing called ventrocillin, thinking it sounded like penicillin. I also got morphine. Unfortunately, I don't have a syringe."

His father took the backpack and inspected the vial of ventrocillin. "Not familiar with this. Must be something the Bureau developed. Not sure what the dosage would be. Either way, we have to take the professor to a hospital. He needs morphine right away, plus he needs surgery. I can do it, but not here."

Drayden appealed to Wesley and Charlie. "Can you guys carry him? Take him to the hospital that treated us after the Initiation."

"Yes, Beekman Street," Dad said. "That's where I've been working the past few weeks."

Although still alive, Professor Worth was unconscious. Drayden was absolutely wracked with guilt. The professor had already saved his life multiple times, but in this case, he'd sacrificed himself to do it. Drayden *had* to save him. Nevertheless, he'd done all he could personally do. Now it was up to his father. Historically, Dad was a losing bet.

Drayden stood, holding his ribs, while the boys carried Professor Worth out of the room. "Dad, I'll come meet you guys at the hospital. I should head to the safehouse and update everybody. I'm sure they're freaking out. Plus, I need to swing by my apartment and grab a new pair of shoes."

"Be careful, son. It's not safe."

"I will be."

After ditching his remaining shoe, Drayden walked in socks to their apartment building at 75 Wall Street, taking back roads to approach it from the unpopulated southern part of the zone.

The streets were silent and all but deserted, save for the occasional Palace Guardian running amok. He guessed the residents were sheltered in their homes, in shock over the unexpected assault on their zone. As Drayden neared his building, the broadcast siren blared.

He stopped in his tracks. A broadcast? He wondered if Holst would yet again be reassuring everyone that New America was fine. Nothing to see here.

Inside his apartment, Drayden painstakingly changed into his own clothes and fresh sneakers. His body felt broken, and his lungs ached. Glancing around the pad, bereft of personal effects, he pondered if he should take anything in case he never returned. The only items with sentimental value were the drawings Catrice had gifted to him, like the one in which she'd sketched a heart atop the spire of the Empire State Building. He rolled up his favorites, stuffed them in his pockets, and left.

Before going to the safehouse, he needed to find a video screen for the broadcast, and recalled one in Battery Park. Weaving through the empty streets, he entered the northern region of the park, mindful of the nearby Palace Guardian training facilities. God knew he didn't want to bump into Captain Lindrick's crew.

Eugene.

The image of his dead body, left to rot in an abandoned building, kept flashing through Drayden's mind. Some things you couldn't unsee.

Many Palace Guardians were gathered around the screen, looking weary and despondent. A few were hugging.

Drayden hunkered down far away, shielded by a tree, anxiously awaiting the broadcast. From his angle, the late afternoon sun cast a blinding glare on the screen.

A steady beeping ensued and the screen burst to life, revealing the solemn face of Robert Zane. Dark, puffy bags underlined his eyes, while his wild hair poofed out like Albert Einstein's.

Drayden's heart fluttered. *Could it be?*

"Citizens of New America. My name is Robert Zane. Most of you don't know me. I'm a former senior member of the Bureau. Today, I am your acting leader, until we can hold elections. It is the dawn of a new day."

Drayden's jaw dropped.

The Palace Guardians watched in silence, showing little reaction to the shocking news.

"For too long," Zane continued, "the residents of our land have been kept in the dark, lied to, and shortchanged. That ends today. The Bureau is being dissolved. The walls inside the city will be torn down. New America will be reinvented in a way that's beneficial to all its residents, not just a few at the top.

"Despite the persistence of Aeru, the world outside our walls is flourishing. I know this is counter to everything you've always been told. New America has many trading partners, allowing us to import the goods we cannot manufacture or grow. It is true that our primary commodity is narcotics, as some of you have heard, and we want to see that change. Over time, we will adapt."

Drayden looked around, noticing the audio from this broadcast was being aired on some kind of PA system, reverberating throughout the streets. Even in the safehouse, his friends might hear it.

"Starting immediately, food deliveries will resume and the water restriction is lifted. No one is forbidden from any zone. Nobody is required to stay either. You are free to leave the city, but be aware that you will not be allowed back in until we can develop reentry procedures to prevent the introduction of Aeru. There has been great loss of life today; a day that will be remembered for generations. Whichever side you were fighting for, you can be proud that you fought valiantly. Now we are all on the same side. From this moment forward, any murder—combat or otherwise—will be considered a crime and you will face consequences for it."

Was this real? Drayden couldn't believe his ears. Everything he had fought for was coming true. He'd only played a small part, but *they'd won.*

The video cut away to flaunt a forlorn Eli Holst, Harris von Brooks, and several other men in handcuffs under the watch of heavily armed Palace Guardians.

"Eli Holst, several of his top deputies, and many senior Guardians and scientists have been arrested and are in custody now. Senior Dorm leaders who were secretly working with the Bureau have been apprehended as well."

Lily Haddad!

Drayden looked up to the heavens. She wouldn't get away with her treachery—or the murder of his mother—after all.

Zane reappeared on screen. "They will face a trial, charged with crimes against humanity, and will have to take responsibility for deceiving the people of this city for decades. I'll be frank. This is the beginning of a long process of rebirth, reform, and reinvention. We will be drafting a new constitution to govern our land. I would ask each and every one of you to resume your daily job responsibilities right away. Over time, we will see to it that you can change jobs, receive promotions, and hopefully find joy and fulfillment in your daily lives. It will take time, and I ask you for your patience."

It was everything Drayden had ever dreamed. In his lifetime, he never believed he'd see this day.

"Because we are recreating our very existence, and reestablishing something much more similar to what existed in the former United States of America, we will be changing the name of our city. We called ourselves New America at the beginning when we believed we were the only ones left in the world. We are not. In fact, we are but one of many cities thriving in America. As such, our name will rightfully return to New York. When we can get the proper measures in place, we will hold elections so you will be represented by the people whom you wish to lead us. I am but a temporary custodian."

Robert Zane wiped his forehead with a handkerchief. "I will be broadcasting later today, and every day for the foreseeable future. The Guardians will continue enforcing the laws of our land. Today's gruesome battle notwithstanding, they are now one police force. Palace Guardians and regular Guardians will be working side by side. Anyone caught violating or undermining this arrangement will be swiftly expelled from the city. Our path to redemption will not likely be smooth. But it will be fair and equitable. Your voices will be heard. As Abraham Lincoln said in the Gettysburg Address, this is now a government of the people, by the people, for the people. Be well and welcome to the first day in a new world."

Drayden burst into tears. The news was so wonderful, so momentous, he couldn't handle it. The city would be a mess for years to come, and would certainly face a lot of bumps on its road to reinvention, but the authoritarians were finished. The darkness had been lifted. For the first time in a generation, freedom ruled the day and equality had a fighting chance.

CHAPTER 32

Drayden slouched beside Sidney and Nora in the frenzied waiting room at the Beekman Street Hospital. Mortally wounded Guardians were being wheeled through the door by the minute, overwhelming a tiny medical staff ill-prepared for a war.

Kim Craig was pacing with her hands in her pockets. Charlie had Wesley enthralled with harrowing stories from the expedition, while his parents were roaming around somewhere. Catrice and Sidney's grandparents were speaking quietly.

The only one not there was Drayden's father, who was personally operating on Professor Worth. According to Wesley, Dad would have preferred another doctor do it because it'd been so long since he'd performed surgery, but the trauma surgeons were inundated, and the backlog of patients awaiting emergency surgery was endless. The professor would have died waiting.

Drayden could count on one hand the number of times in his life he was proud of his father. This was one of them. Since the Confluence, he'd been a "former" doctor and current lab tech, so Drayden had never witnessed him using the vast medical skills he possessed. It was equal parts impressive and mystifying, like a life-long electrician suddenly picking up a violin and playing Tchaikovsky.

The others had heard the broadcast from Robert Zane over the PA, and the only thing standing in the way of a full-on celebration was Professor Worth's condition. Nevertheless, upon Drayden's arrival at the safehouse, there had been no shortage of hugging and high-fiving. Kim had genuinely seemed as surprised as anyone that the insurrection had succeeded.

Drayden could only imagine the raucous parties in the Dorms right now. The Palace, on the other hand, where the residents had just forfeited their elite status, was somber and chaotic. Everyone was still digesting the news. On the journey to the hospital, Drayden had perceived the palpable tension between the Palace Guardians and regular Guardians. That relationship would not be healed overnight.

Wearing scrubs, Drayden's father emerged through a set of swinging double doors. The teens and Kim rushed to meet him.

He rubbed his eyes. "He's stable."

Kim expelled a long breath and rested her hands on her knees.

"He's not out of the woods yet, but the surgery was a success. He's recovering now."

"Can we see him?" Drayden asked.

His father quickly checked both ways. "He's not awake, but yes," he said quietly. "Follow me."

He led them through a corridor lined with Guardians on stretchers, many gravely injured and moaning.

"Watch out!" A collection of doctors and nurses flew by, pushing a soldier missing an arm and one eye.

They entered a dim, microscopic room without any windows. Professor Worth was asleep in a bed, hooked up to numerous monitors and an IV.

Kim kissed his forehead. "How long will he have to be here?"

"Technically, he should be here a while," said Drayden's father. "He's got a long recovery ahead. It's possible he'll never regain the full functionality he had before. But I know he has a boat to catch. I'll be honest. It's risky. Someone would have to take him, obviously."

"I'll do it," Drayden blurted. He owed it to Professor Worth. He was responsible for bringing him here, and needed to get him home, as promised. Plus, the professor had saved his life too many times to count.

Dad furrowed his brow. "It's a one-way trip, Drayden. It could be years before anyone is allowed to reenter New Amer—New York."

He was well aware of that. In reality, his work was done here. Drayden had helped topple the Bureau and held every person responsible who'd had a hand in his mother's exile. It was time for the next chapter, and if that had to be outside New America, then so be it.

"You're not doing this alone," Wesley said. "We'll come with you. Right, Dad?"

He nodded. "Yes. This family deserves a fresh start. I'm not losing you again, son."

Drayden was so relieved. It was indeed a second chance for them. He swallowed hard and looked into the eyes of his friends.

Charlie shifted uncomfortably on his feet. "I know this is when I usually say you're not going without me, but...I...I think I'm gonna stay here. Because of the new government, I can become a Guardian. It's what I've wanted to do forever. Before now, there was no way. You know?"

Drayden hugged him. "Of course I know. You'll make an amazing Guardian." He was genuinely thrilled for Charlie. His best friend had come a long way from the insecure kid who'd begged Drayden never to leave him. But he loved Charlie too, and he struggled to hide his disappointment about splitting up.

"I'm coming with you," Sidney said, practically glowing. "I am *done* with this place. I'll get my whole family to come along. We can start over in Massachusetts, maybe in Boston after a while?"

Drayden embraced her. "Thank you," he whispered in her ear. She'd always been there for him, and always would be.

Catrice's eyes were teary and downcast. "I think I'm going to stay. We brought the exiles in and there's nobody to take care of them. No one will go near them. We're vaccinated, so I can. They're victims who need help, and I really want to help them. Without someone to advocate for them, I wouldn't be surprised if they were cast back out."

Drayden felt tears welling up. He'd been close with Catrice in a way he'd never been with anyone before. She was his first girl-friend. For years, he'd dreamed about marrying her. And now, despite all the drama, the ups and downs, the waffling between her and Sidney—it was over. They would say goodbye, likely forever. He kissed her on the cheek and held her, the two of them unable to restrain their emotions. They cried together, one last time.

He eventually pulled back. "I love you guys," he said to Catrice and Charlie. "I mean it."

Charlie punched him on the arm. "Right back at you, bro. C'mon, we're gonna see each other again. It might not work out for us here, and if it doesn't, we'll find a way to get to Massachusetts."

"You're always welcome," Drayden said. "I don't care if it's twenty years. I'd love for you to join us."

He gestured toward Professor Worth. "Are you coming, Kim?"

"I can't. Not yet. I'm so grateful to have reunited with him, but this is where I'm needed for the time being. I'm going to be part of this rebuilding process and will have a senior role in the new government. I can't walk away." She stroked her uncle's hand, her touch gentle on his skin. "Once things are settled, though, I would like to move out there to be with him. Thank you for taking care of him."

"He saved my life," Drayden said. "Took a bullet for me. I owe him everything."

Sidney spent a moment with both Charlie and Catrice, hugging and saying goodbye. Drayden was thankful that the girls had grown to understand each other, and become real friends, before going their separate ways.

Drayden's father cleared his throat. "Anyone coming or thinking of coming to Massachusetts needs the Aeru vaccine, which my clever son found. If someone can gather the remaining family members from the lobby, I can administer the vaccine to everyone right here in this room. Even for those of you staying, you should get yourself protected. Hopefully someday soon the city will have enough of this vaccine to immunize everybody."

After that, it was a whirlwind and a race against time to get to the dock in Brooklyn to catch Bud's boat. They hijacked a wheelchair for Professor Worth, who was groggy but conscious. Having briefly stopped overnight by their apartments to collect their belongings and food for the journey, they set off on foot for Mr. Kale's place. They needed to pick up Sidney's parents, vaccinate them, snag Professor Worth's suitcase, and say goodbye to Mr. Kale.

On their way out of the Palace, Drayden had dropped off an anonymous letter to Captain Lindrick at the former Bureau head-quarters, telling him where he could find his son Eugene's body, saying only that he had died heroically.

The farewell to Mr. Kale was an emotional one as well, and Drayden knew it was the last time he'd ever see his mentor.

At the crack of dawn, Drayden and his family, Sidney and her family, and Professor Worth ventured out to the Fifty-Ninth Street Bridge, which took them to Queens, and then Brooklyn. The long trek was routine at this point for Drayden and Sidney, but not so much for everyone else. Through no shortage of complaining, mostly from Sidney's parents, and a few tantrums from Nora, they arrived at the dock in Brooklyn. The one who truly deserved to grumble was Professor Worth, yet he made not a peep. Drayden admired him more every day.

Only then did Drayden worry about Bud taking this small village of people on his boat when he'd agreed to take Professor Worth alone. Bud not showing up at all was also a possibility, in which case they would be locked out of New America with nowhere to go.

Thankfully he did, and, given Professor Worth's condition—plus a couple of bucks from the professor's wallet—they were on their way to Massachusetts and the start of their new lives.

With the Statue of Liberty towering behind them, once again a symbol of freedom and opportunity, Drayden finally understood the significance of their victory over the Bureau. The people always held the power in their hands. They just didn't know it.

Amidst the smell of salty air, and a gentle breeze in their faces, he and Sidney stood alone at the bow. They savored the moment, and the realization that they had their own fresh start together. Holding each other close, they kissed. For the first time ever, Drayden was excited about the future.

THE END

ACKNOWLEDGMENTS

Seeing this series come to an end is both gratifying and bitter-sweet. Along the way, I developed a deep connection to the characters and world of New America. I hope you did too. My greatest thanks are reserved for you, the reader, for embarking on this journey with Drayden, Sidney, Catrice, and Charlie, and for allowing me to tell their story.

A heartfelt thank you goes out to everyone at Permuted Press, Post Hill Press, and Simon & Schuster. Anthony Ziccardi, Michael Wilson, Devon Brown, and Maddie Sturgeon, among many others, made this series possible. Much gratitude to my editors Deborah Halverson, Maya Rock, and Felicia Sullivan, for challenging me to make *The Insurrection* the best it could be. Credit for the beautiful cover goes to artist Ryan Truso and photographer Greg Berg.

Thank you to good friends Jason McCarthy, Kim Spacek, Suri Kasirer, and Bruce Teitelbaum for their generous help and kindness.

To all the bloggers, bookstagrammers, journalists, librarians, booksellers, radio hosts, teachers, school administrators, and friends who helped spread the word about *The Initiation* series, please know how much I appreciate your support.

Finally, to my wife Michelle, daughter Lily, and Mom and Dad—Susan and Suresh Babu—I'm eternally grateful for your steadfast belief in me. I could never have done it without you. I love you all.